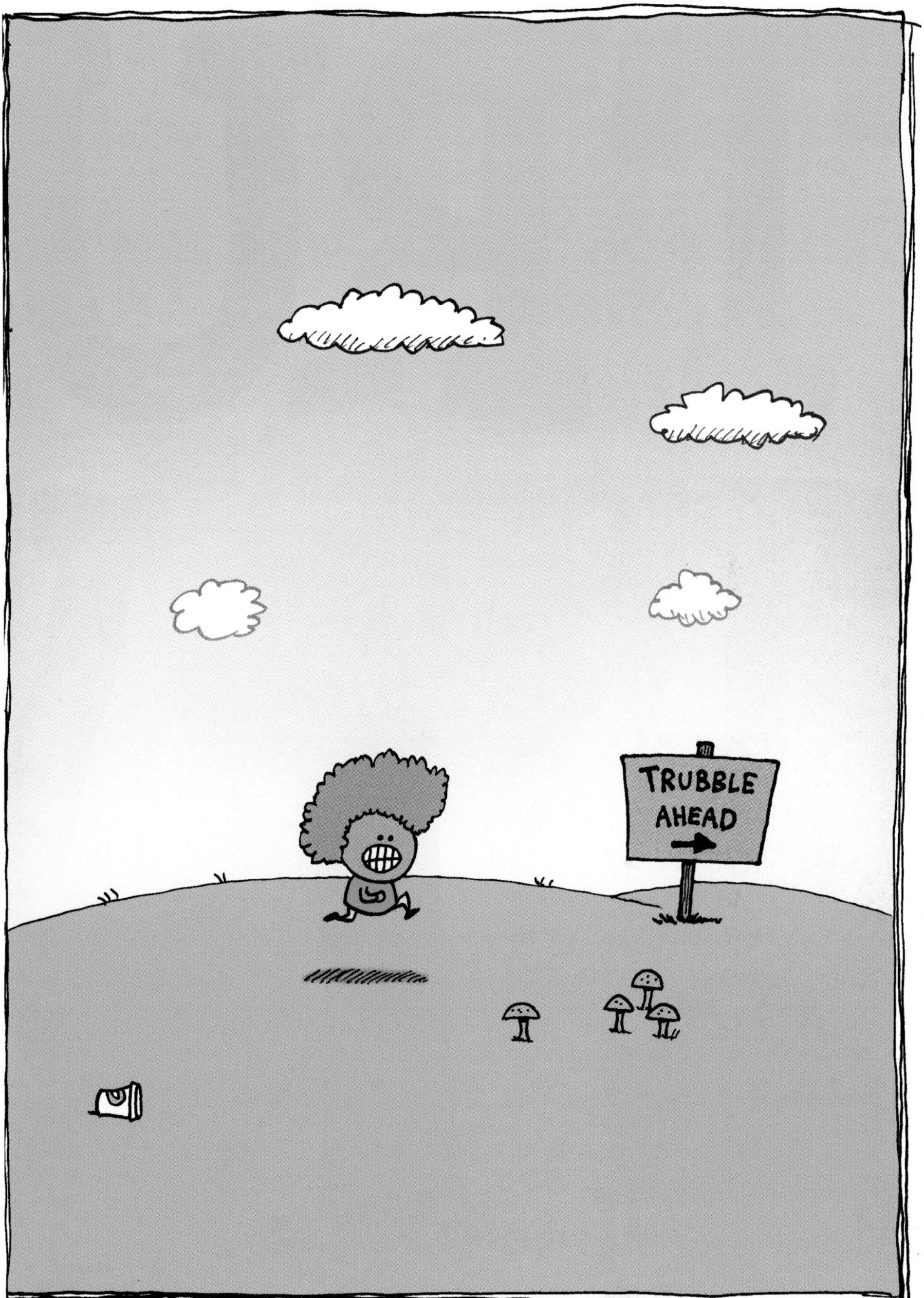
TRUBBLE
AHEAD

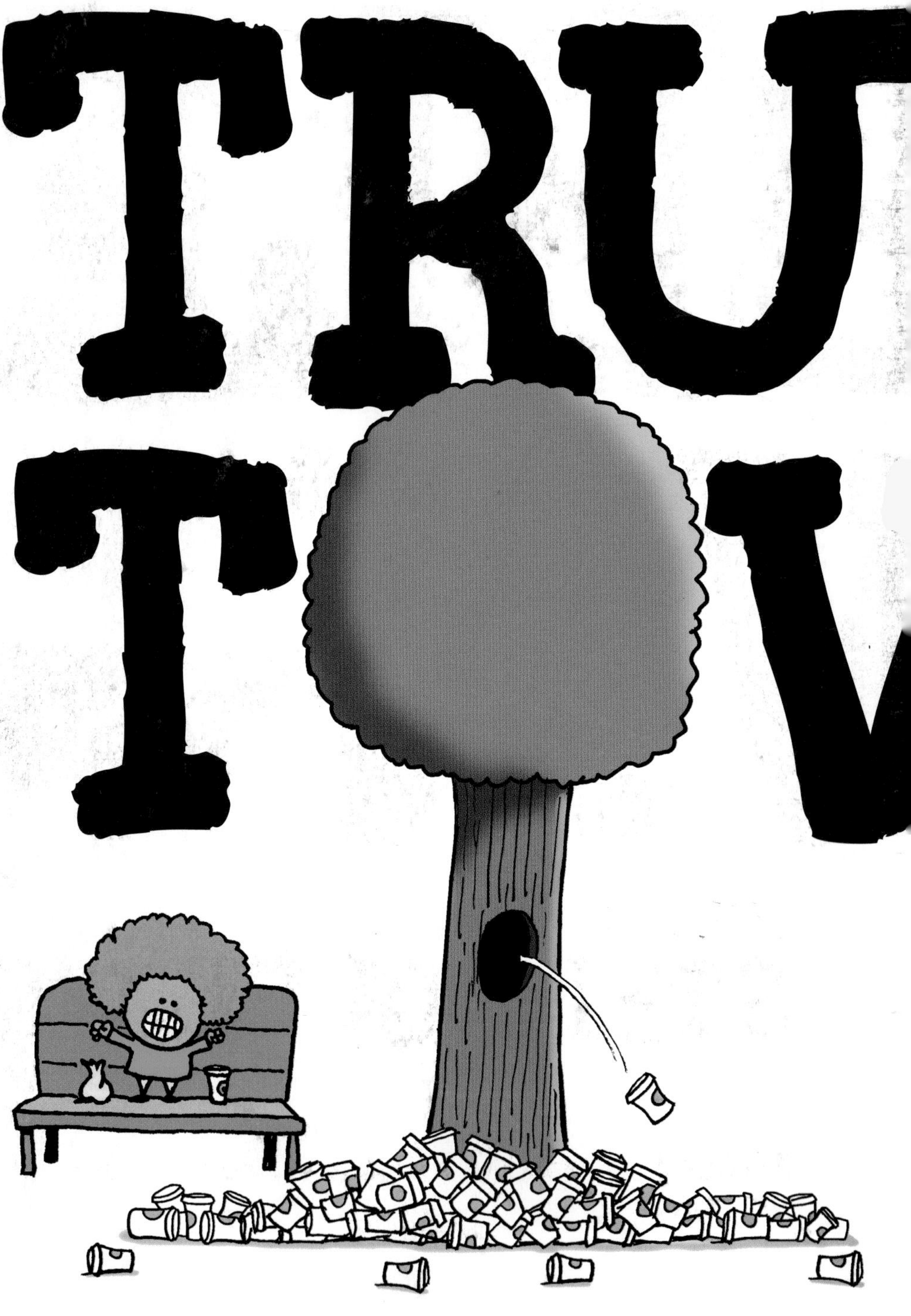
TRU
T

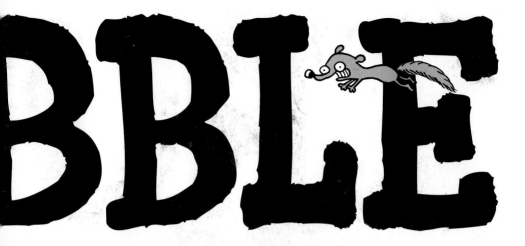

BBLE VN

SQUIRREL DO BAD

STEPHAN PASTIS

ALADDIN | New York | London | Toronto | Sydney | New Delhi

ALADDIN / An imprint of Simon & Schuster Children's Publishing Division / 1230 Avenue of the Americas, New York, New York 10020 / First Aladdin edition August 2021 / Copyright © 2021 by Stephan Pastis / All rights reserved, including the right of reproduction in whole or in part in any form. / ALADDIN and related logo are registered trademarks of Simon & Schuster, Inc. / For information about special discounts for bulk purchases, please contact Simon & Schuster Special Sales at 1-866-506-1949 or business@simonandschuster.com. / The Simon & Schuster Speakers Bureau can bring authors to your live event. For more information or to book an event contact the Simon & Schuster Speakers Bureau at 1-866-248-3049 or visit our website at www.simonspeakers.com. / Designed by Karin Paprocki and Stephan Pastis / The illustrations for this book were rendered digitally. / The text of this book was hand-lettered and set in Bodoni. / Manufactured in China 0621 SCP / 2 4 6 8 10 9 7 5 3 1 / Library of Congress Cataloging-in-Publication Data / Names: Pastis, Stephan, author, illustrator. / Title: Squirrel do bad / Stephan Pastis. / Description: First Aladdin edition. / New York : Aladdin, 2021. / Series: Trubble town / Audience: Ages 8 to 12. / Summary: Wendy the Wanderer's overprotective father never lets her go anywhere alone, so when he hires a babysitter, Wendy decides to venture out into Trubble Town alone, where she meets Squirrely McSquirrel and other townsfolk. / Identifiers: LCCN 2021001471 (print) / LCCN 2021001472 (ebook) / ISBN 9781534496118 (hardcover) / ISBN 9781534496101 (paperback) / ISBN 9781534496125 (ebook) / Subjects: LCSH: Humorous stories. / Graphic novels. / CYAC: Graphic novels. / Squirrels—Fiction. / City and town life—Fiction. / Classification: LCC PZ7.7.P273 Sq 2021 (print) / LCC PZ7.7.P273 (ebook) / DDC 741.5/973—dc22 / LC record available at https://lccn.loc.gov/2021001471 / LC ebook record available at https://lccn.loc.gov/2021001472 /

TO STACI...

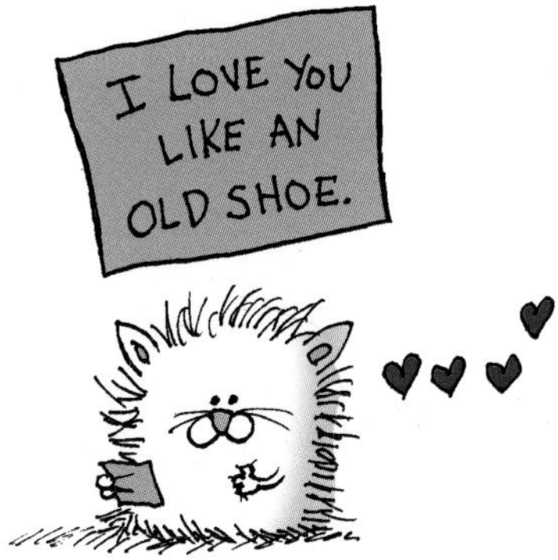
I LOVE YOU LIKE AN OLD SHOE.

CHAPTER ZERO

IN WHICH...

WE USE A CHAPTER NUMBER WE DON'T THINK ANYONE HAS USED BEFORE

A SPECIAL MESSAGE
FROM THE STAR OF THIS BOOK,
WENDY THE WANDERER, WHO'D
LIKE TO ASK YOU, THE READER,
AN IMPORTANT QUESTION...

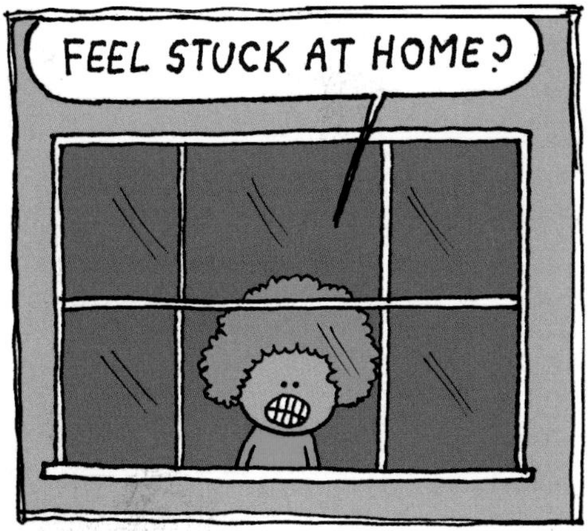
FEEL STUCK AT HOME?

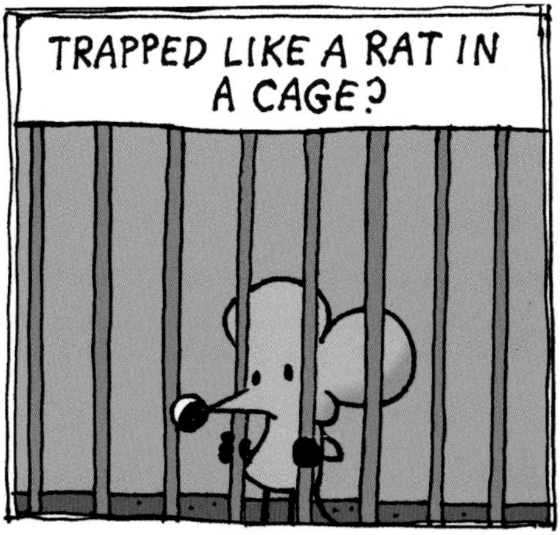
TRAPPED LIKE A RAT IN A CAGE?

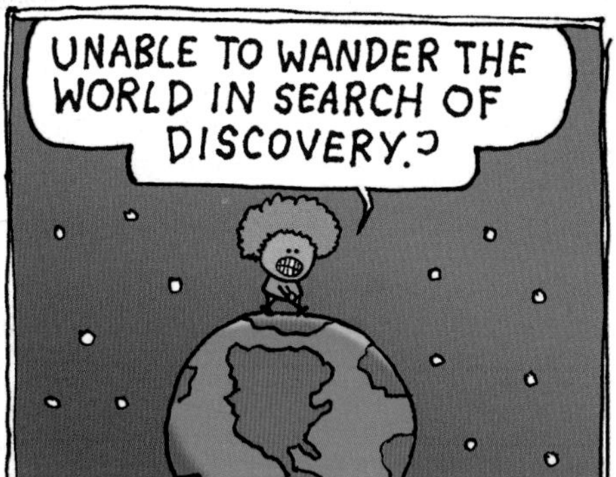
UNABLE TO WANDER THE WORLD IN SEARCH OF DISCOVERY?

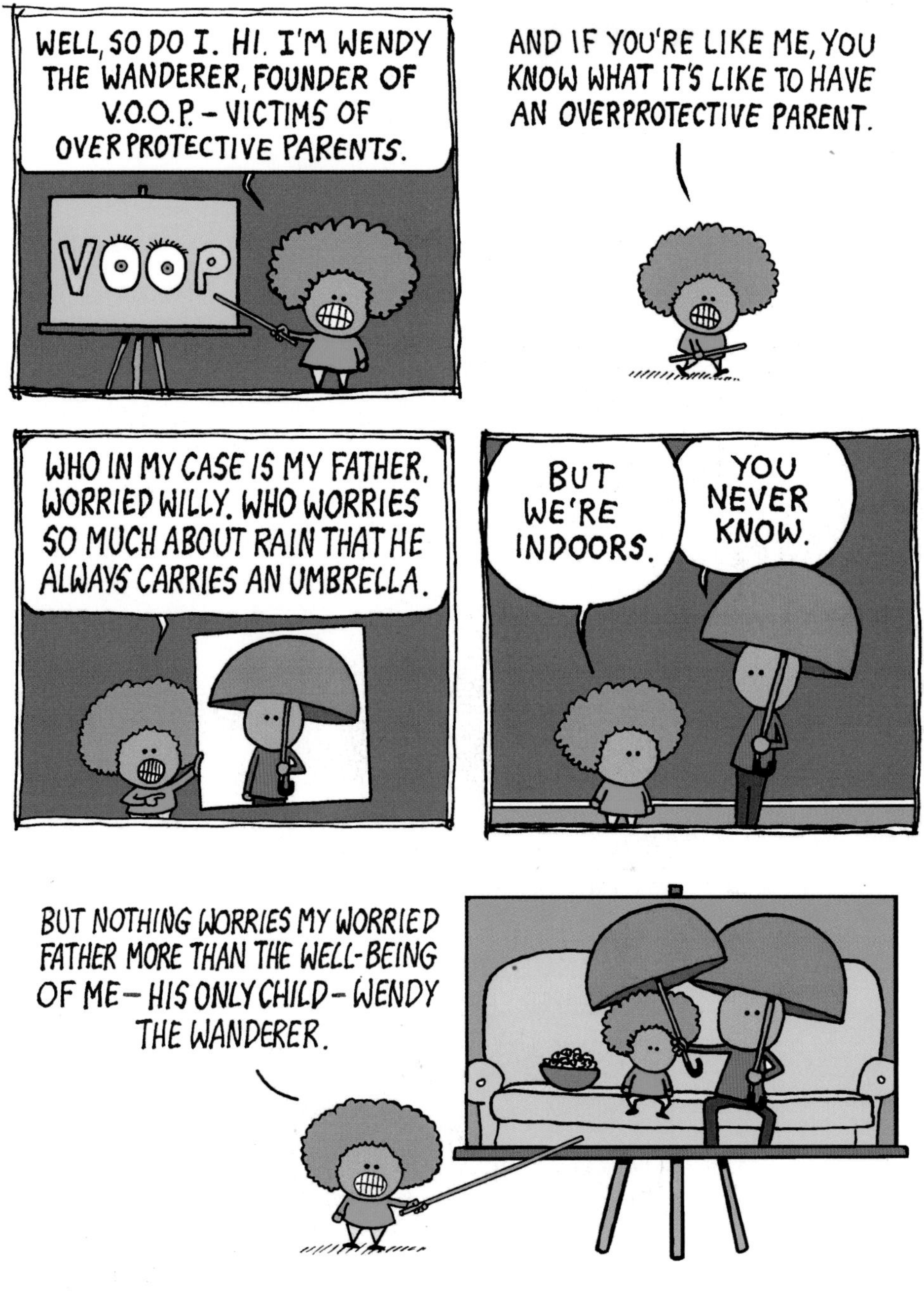
WELL, SO DO I. HI. I'M WENDY THE WANDERER, FOUNDER OF V.O.O.P. – VICTIMS OF OVERPROTECTIVE PARENTS.
VOOP
AND IF YOU'RE LIKE ME, YOU KNOW WHAT IT'S LIKE TO HAVE AN OVERPROTECTIVE PARENT.
WHO IN MY CASE IS MY FATHER, WORRIED WILLY. WHO WORRIES SO MUCH ABOUT RAIN THAT HE ALWAYS CARRIES AN UMBRELLA.
BUT WE'RE INDOORS.
YOU NEVER KNOW.
BUT NOTHING WORRIES MY WORRIED FATHER MORE THAN THE WELL-BEING OF ME – HIS ONLY CHILD – WENDY THE WANDERER.

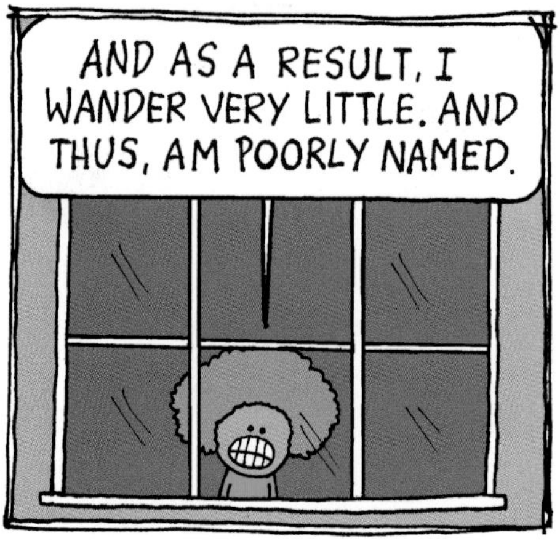
AND AS A RESULT, I WANDER VERY LITTLE. AND THUS, AM POORLY NAMED.

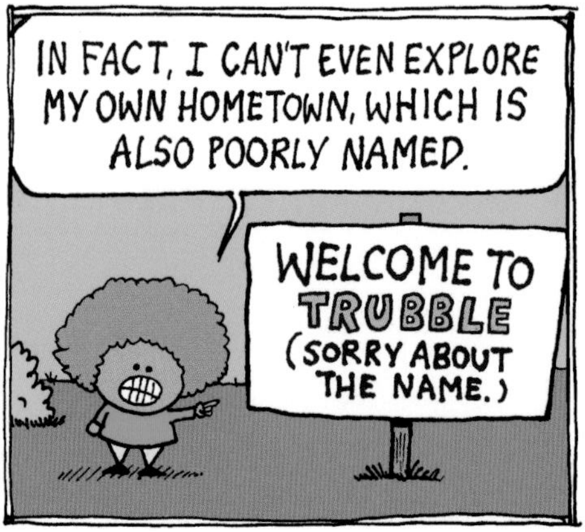
IN FACT, I CAN'T EVEN EXPLORE MY OWN HOMETOWN, WHICH IS ALSO POORLY NAMED.
WELCOME TO TRUBBLE (SORRY ABOUT THE NAME.)

AND WHILE I'VE GOTTEN GLIMPSES OF OUR TOWN, IT'S ONLY BEEN WITH ADULT SUPERVISION, AND THAT'S A WEE BIT RESTRICTIVE.

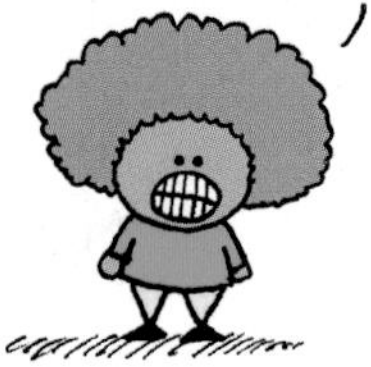

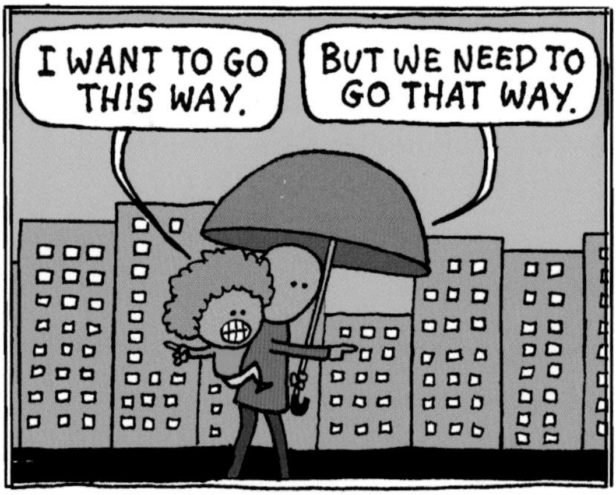
I WANT TO GO THIS WAY.
BUT WE NEED TO GO THAT WAY.

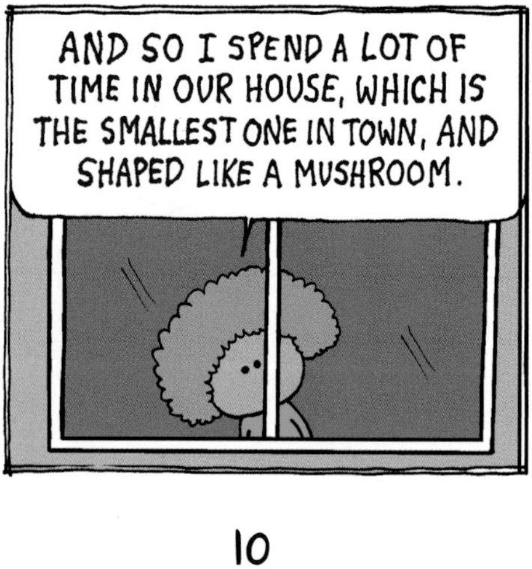
AND SO I SPEND A LOT OF TIME IN OUR HOUSE, WHICH IS THE SMALLEST ONE IN TOWN, AND SHAPED LIKE A MUSHROOM.

WHAT AN EYESORE.
WHO ASKED YOU?!
I'M A LITTLE SENSITIVE ABOUT THE TOPIC BECAUSE THE HOUSE WAS DESIGNED BY MY MOTHER.
MOTHER
SHE LIKED MUSHROOMS AND THE COLOR PURPLE...
MUSHROOMS
THE COLOR PURPLE

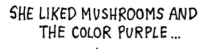

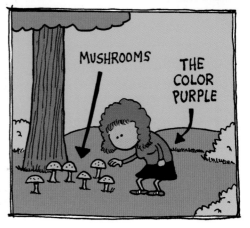

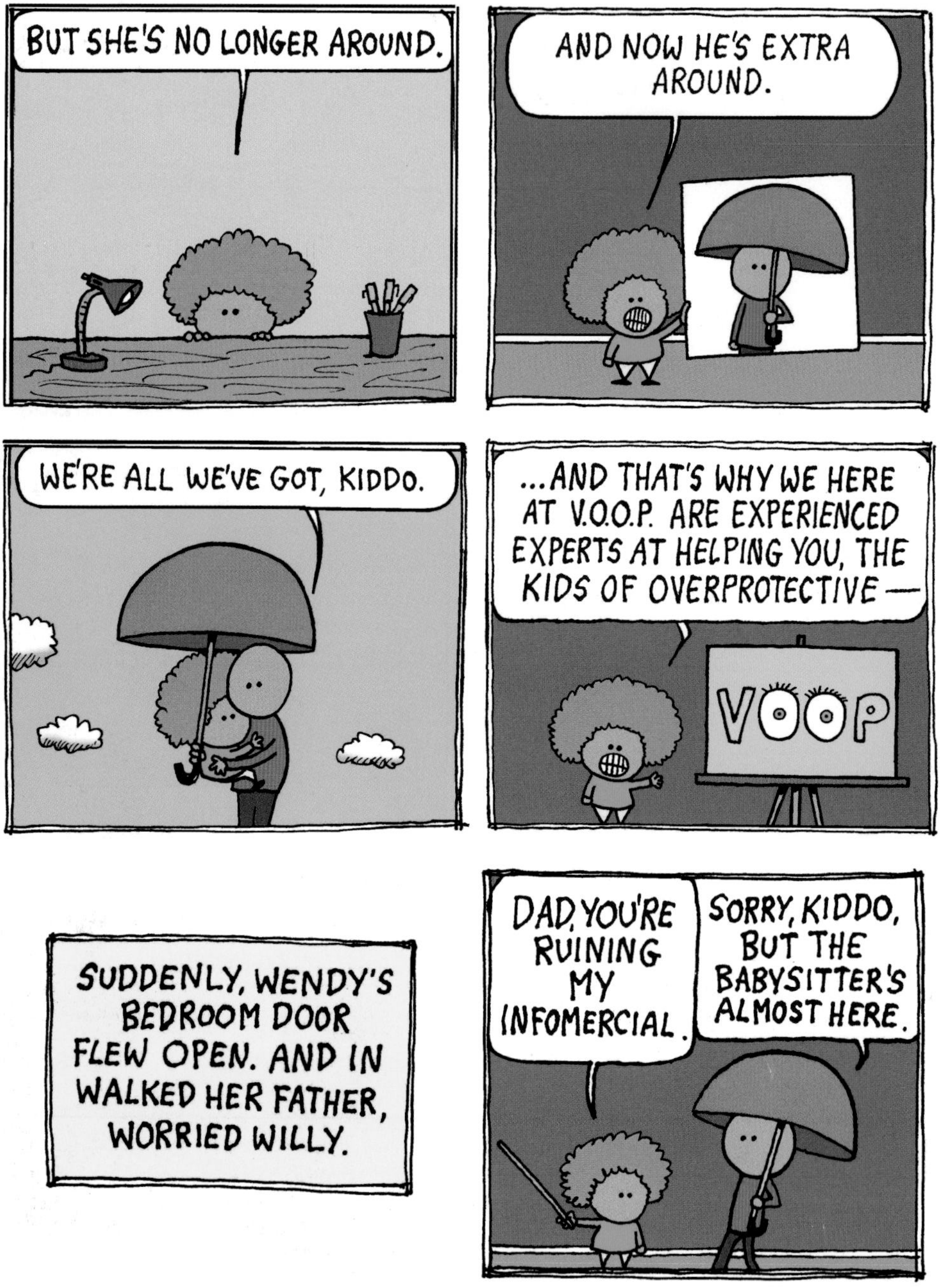
BUT SHE'S NO LONGER AROUND.
AND NOW HE'S EXTRA AROUND.
WE'RE ALL WE'VE GOT, KIDDO.
...AND THAT'S WHY WE HERE AT V.O.O.P. ARE EXPERIENCED EXPERTS AT HELPING YOU, THE KIDS OF OVERPROTECTIVE—
VOOP
SUDDENLY, WENDY'S BEDROOM DOOR FLEW OPEN. AND IN WALKED HER FATHER, WORRIED WILLY.
DAD, YOU'RE RUINING MY INFOMERCIAL.
SORRY, KIDDO, BUT THE BABYSITTER'S ALMOST HERE.

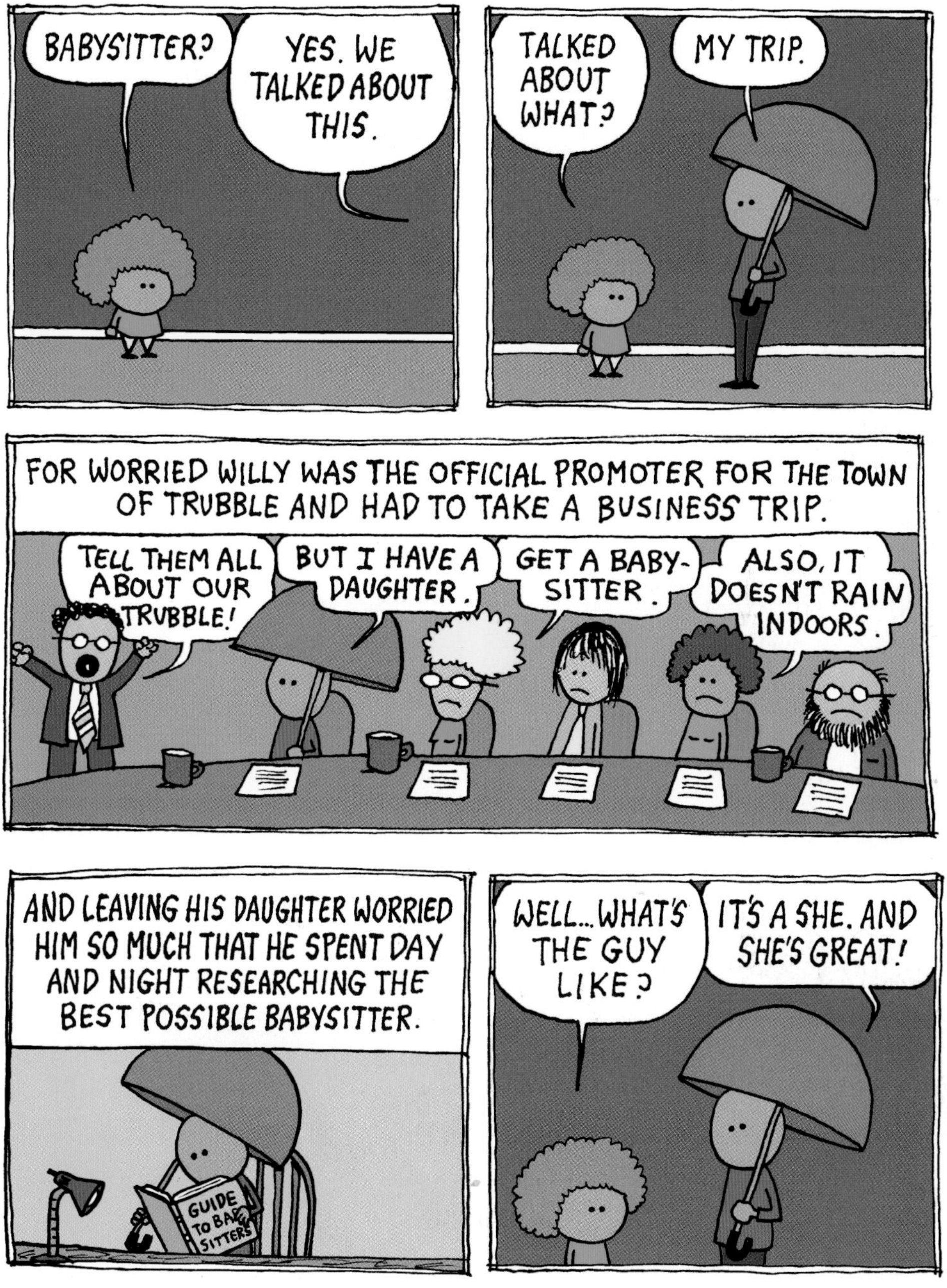
BABYSITTER?
YES. WE TALKED ABOUT THIS.
TALKED ABOUT WHAT?
MY TRIP.
FOR WORRIED WILLY WAS THE OFFICIAL PROMOTER FOR THE TOWN OF TRUBBLE AND HAD TO TAKE A BUSINESS TRIP.
TELL THEM ALL ABOUT OUR TRUBBLE!
BUT I HAVE A DAUGHTER.
GET A BABY-SITTER.
ALSO, IT DOESN'T RAIN INDOORS.
AND LEAVING HIS DAUGHTER WORRIED HIM SO MUCH THAT HE SPENT DAY AND NIGHT RESEARCHING THE BEST POSSIBLE BABYSITTER.
WELL... WHAT'S THE GUY LIKE?
IT'S A SHE. AND SHE'S GREAT!

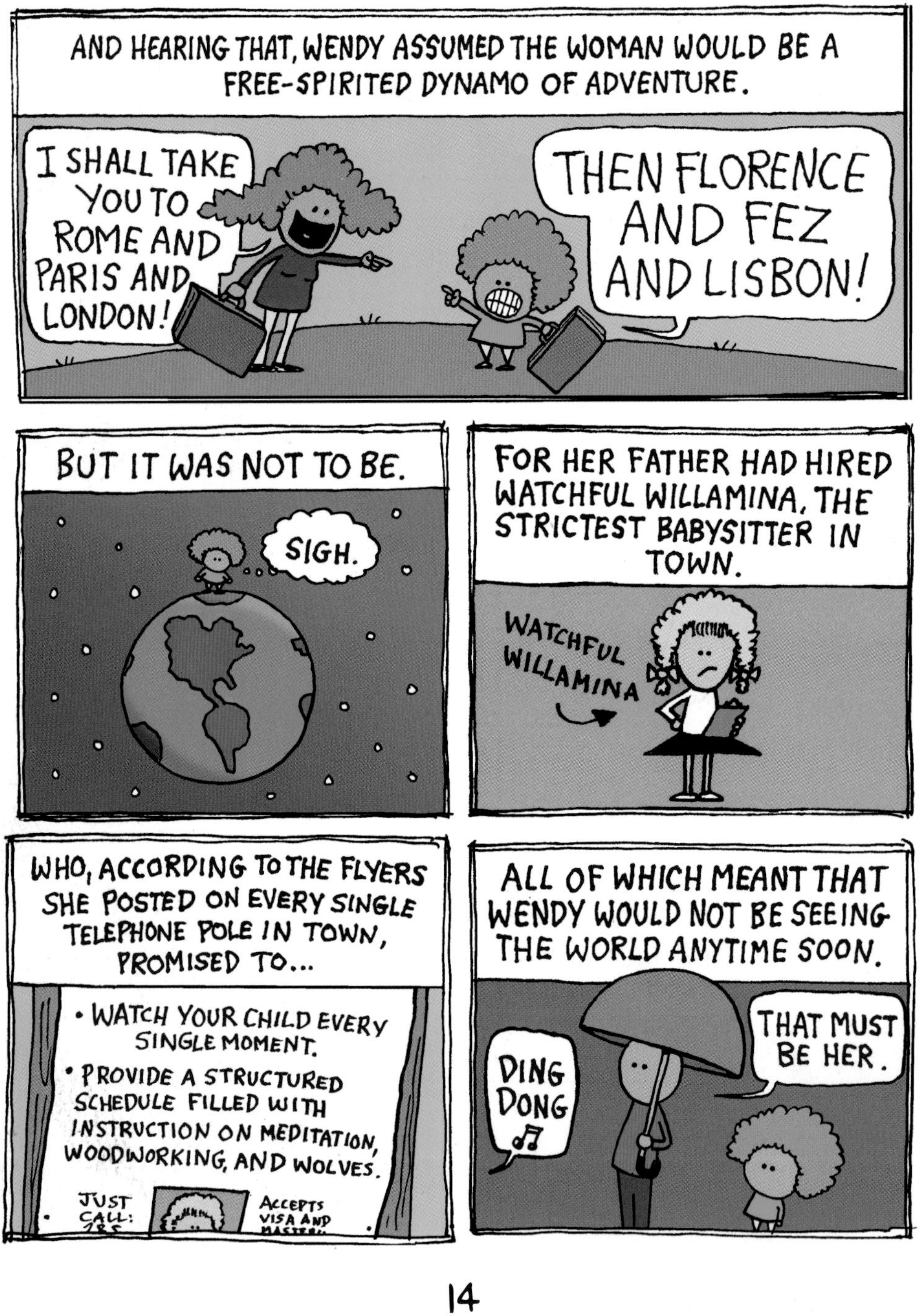
AND HEARING THAT, WENDY ASSUMED THE WOMAN WOULD BE A FREE-SPIRITED DYNAMO OF ADVENTURE.
I SHALL TAKE YOU TO ROME AND PARIS AND LONDON!
THEN FLORENCE AND FEZ AND LISBON!
BUT IT WAS NOT TO BE.
SIGH.
FOR HER FATHER HAD HIRED WATCHFUL WILLAMINA, THE STRICTEST BABYSITTER IN TOWN.
WATCHFUL WILLAMINA
WHO, ACCORDING TO THE FLYERS SHE POSTED ON EVERY SINGLE TELEPHONE POLE IN TOWN, PROMISED TO...
• WATCH YOUR CHILD EVERY SINGLE MOMENT.
• PROVIDE A STRUCTURED SCHEDULE FILLED WITH INSTRUCTION ON MEDITATION, WOODWORKING, AND WOLVES.
JUST CALL:
ACCEPTS VISA AND
ALL OF WHICH MEANT THAT WENDY WOULD NOT BE SEEING THE WORLD ANYTIME SOON.
DING DONG
THAT MUST BE HER.

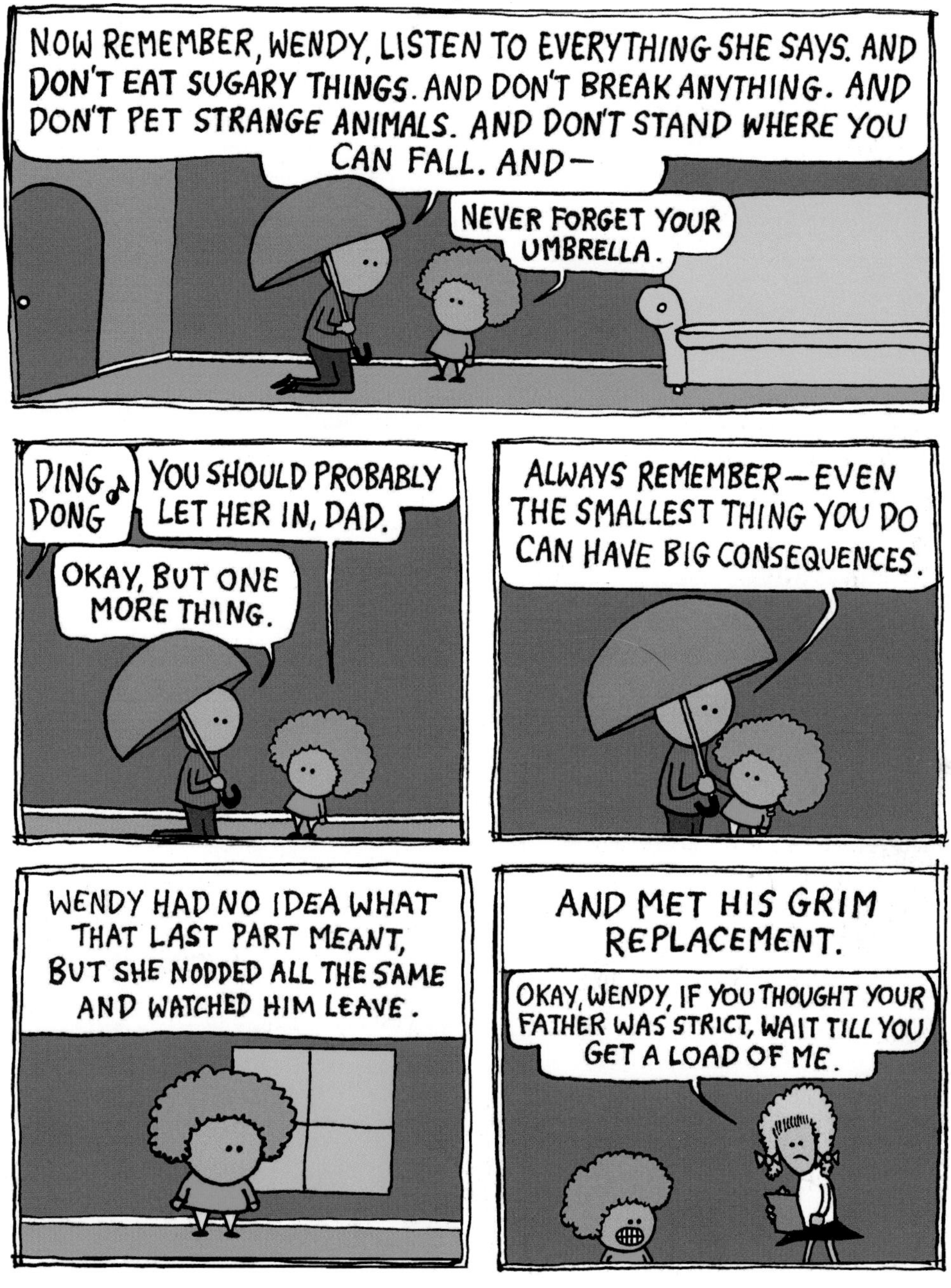
NOW REMEMBER, WENDY, LISTEN TO EVERYTHING SHE SAYS. AND DON'T EAT SUGARY THINGS. AND DON'T BREAK ANYTHING. AND DON'T PET STRANGE ANIMALS. AND DON'T STAND WHERE YOU CAN FALL. AND—
NEVER FORGET YOUR UMBRELLA.
DING DONG
YOU SHOULD PROBABLY LET HER IN, DAD.
OKAY, BUT ONE MORE THING.
ALWAYS REMEMBER—EVEN THE SMALLEST THING YOU DO CAN HAVE BIG CONSEQUENCES.
WENDY HAD NO IDEA WHAT THAT LAST PART MEANT, BUT SHE NODDED ALL THE SAME AND WATCHED HIM LEAVE.
AND MET HIS GRIM REPLACEMENT.
OKAY, WENDY, IF YOU THOUGHT YOUR FATHER WAS STRICT, WAIT TILL YOU GET A LOAD OF ME.

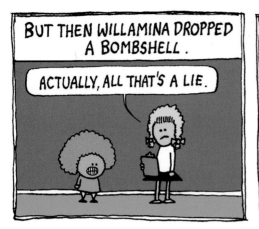

BUT THEN WILLAMINA DROPPED A BOMBSHELL.

ACTUALLY, ALL THAT'S A LIE.

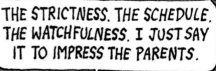

THE STRICTNESS. THE SCHEDULE. THE WATCHFULNESS. I JUST SAY IT TO IMPRESS THE PARENTS.

THE TRUTH IS... I'M GONNA BE ON MY PHONE EVERY MINUTE OF EVERY DAY.

SO IF YOU STAY OUTTA MY WAY, I'LL STAY OUTTA YOURS. JUST DON'T GET INTO TROUBLE. DEAL?

Deal.

16

AND LEAVING HER UMBRELLA BEHIND, WENDY THE WANDERER RAN OFF TO FIND TRUBBLE.

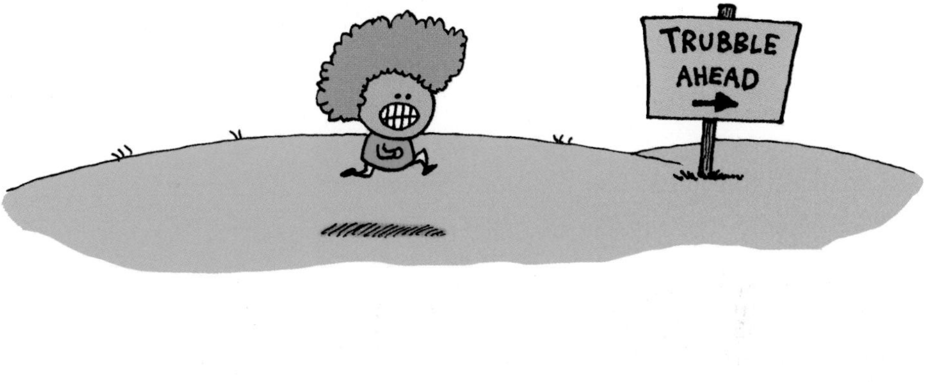
TRUBBLE AHEAD

CHAPTER ONE

IN WHICH...

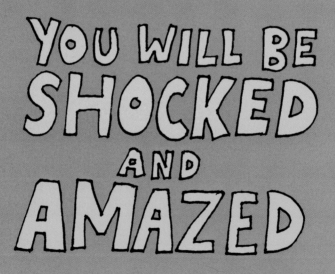

YOU WILL BE SHOCKED AND AMAZED

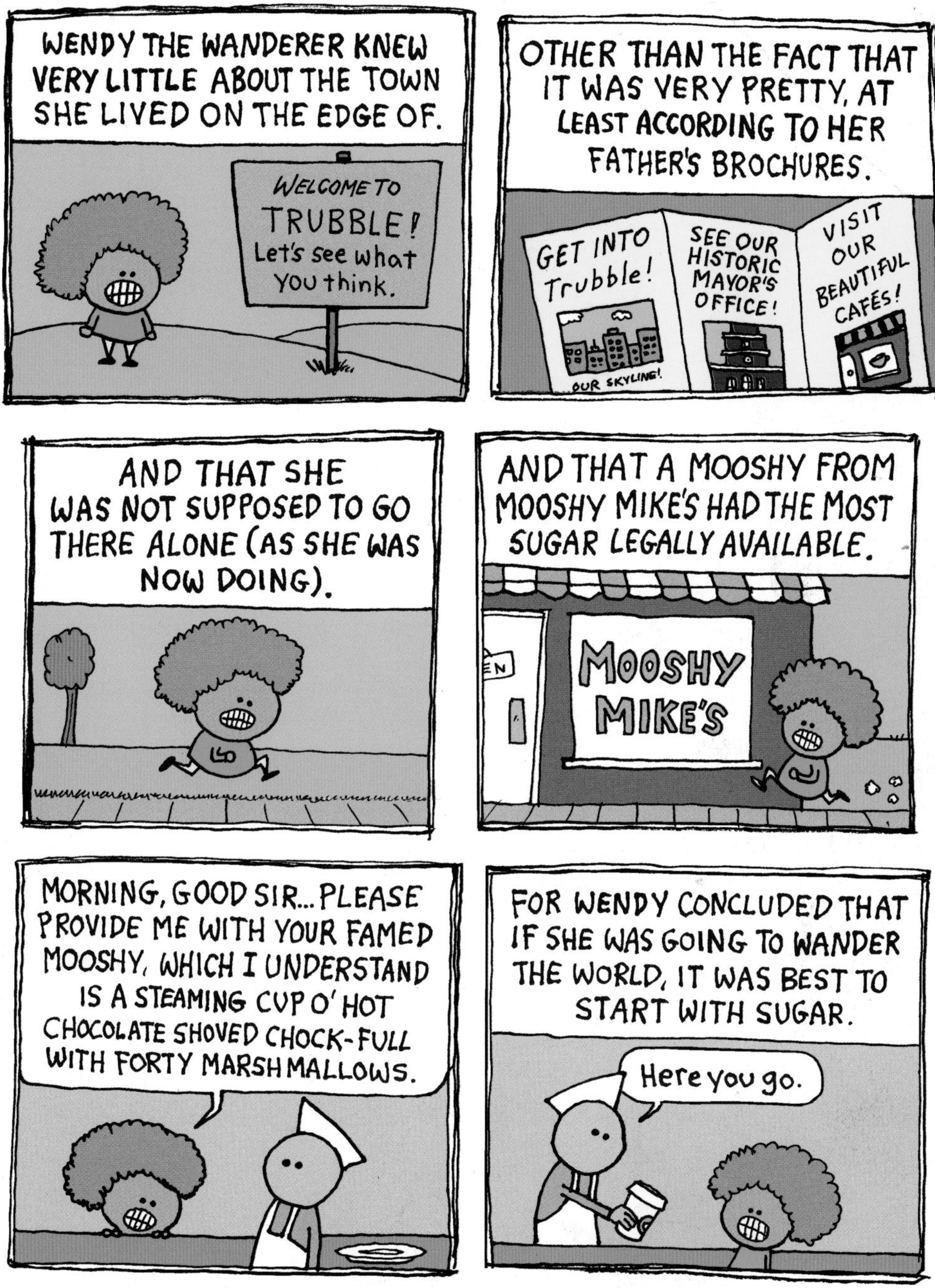
WENDY THE WANDERER KNEW VERY LITTLE ABOUT THE TOWN SHE LIVED ON THE EDGE OF.
WELCOME TO TRUBBLE! Let's see what you think.
OTHER THAN THE FACT THAT IT WAS VERY PRETTY, AT LEAST ACCORDING TO HER FATHER'S BROCHURES.
GET INTO Trubble!
OUR SKYLINE!
SEE OUR HISTORIC MAYOR'S OFFICE!
VISIT OUR BEAUTIFUL CAFÉS!
AND THAT SHE WAS NOT SUPPOSED TO GO THERE ALONE (AS SHE WAS NOW DOING).
AND THAT A MOOSHY FROM MOOSHY MIKE'S HAD THE MOST SUGAR LEGALLY AVAILABLE.
MOOSHY MIKE'S
MORNING, GOOD SIR... PLEASE PROVIDE ME WITH YOUR FAMED MOOSHY, WHICH I UNDERSTAND IS A STEAMING CUP O' HOT CHOCOLATE SHOVED CHOCK-FULL WITH FORTY MARSHMALLOWS.
FOR WENDY CONCLUDED THAT IF SHE WAS GOING TO WANDER THE WORLD, IT WAS BEST TO START WITH SUGAR.
Here you go.

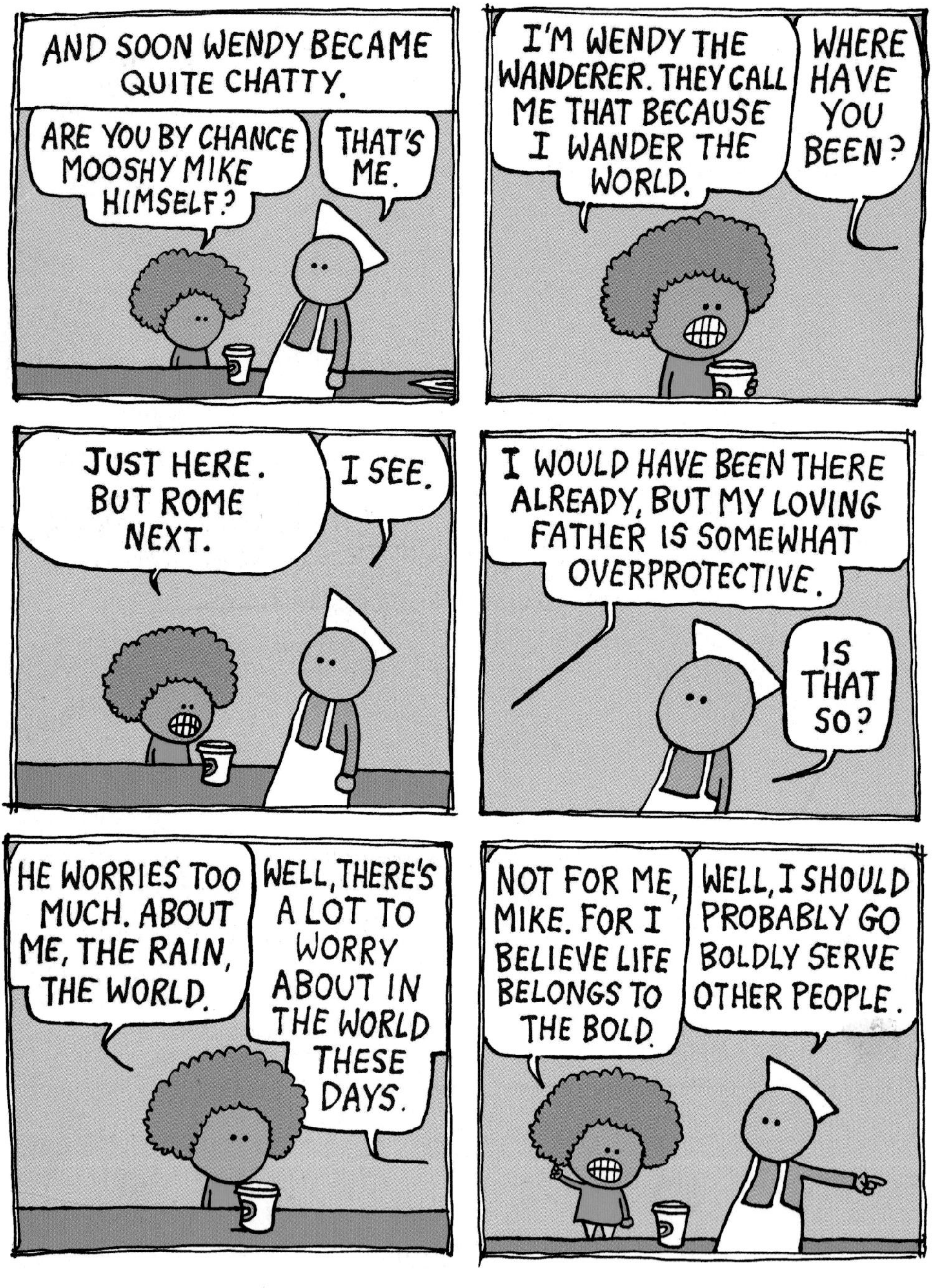
AND SOON WENDY BECAME QUITE CHATTY.
ARE YOU BY CHANCE MOOSHY MIKE HIMSELF?
THAT'S ME.
I'M WENDY THE WANDERER. THEY CALL ME THAT BECAUSE I WANDER THE WORLD.
WHERE HAVE YOU BEEN?
JUST HERE. BUT ROME NEXT.
I SEE.
I WOULD HAVE BEEN THERE ALREADY, BUT MY LOVING FATHER IS SOMEWHAT OVERPROTECTIVE.
IS THAT SO?
HE WORRIES TOO MUCH. ABOUT ME, THE RAIN, THE WORLD.
WELL, THERE'S A LOT TO WORRY ABOUT IN THE WORLD THESE DAYS.
NOT FOR ME, MIKE. FOR I BELIEVE LIFE BELONGS TO THE BOLD.
WELL, I SHOULD PROBABLY GO BOLDLY SERVE OTHER PEOPLE.

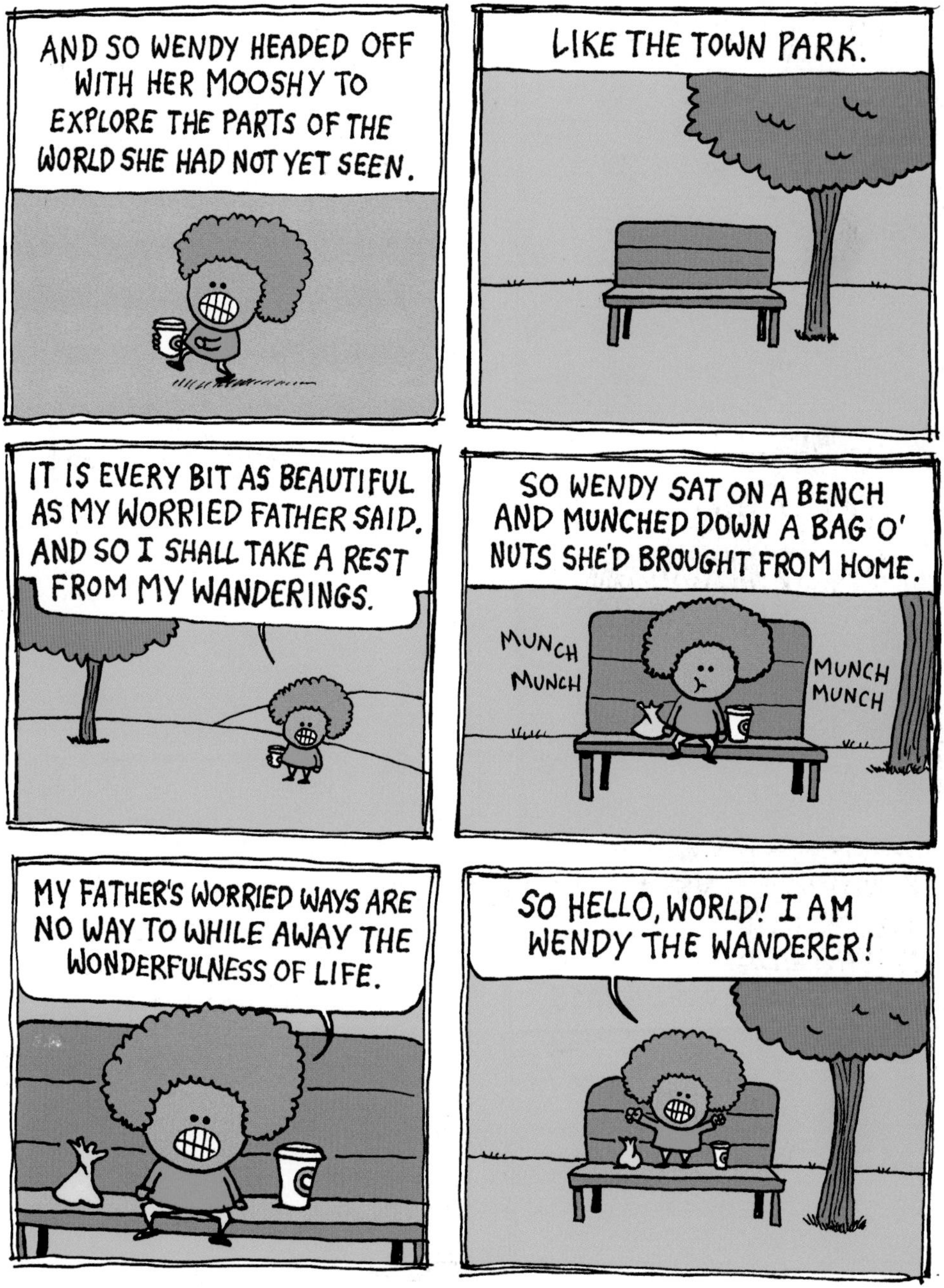
AND SO WENDY HEADED OFF WITH HER MOOSHY TO EXPLORE THE PARTS OF THE WORLD SHE HAD NOT YET SEEN.
LIKE THE TOWN PARK.
IT IS EVERY BIT AS BEAUTIFUL AS MY WORRIED FATHER SAID. AND SO I SHALL TAKE A REST FROM MY WANDERINGS.
SO WENDY SAT ON A BENCH AND MUNCHED DOWN A BAG O' NUTS SHE'D BROUGHT FROM HOME.
MUNCH MUNCH
MUNCH MUNCH
MY FATHER'S WORRIED WAYS ARE NO WAY TO WHILE AWAY THE WONDERFULNESS OF LIFE.
SO HELLO, WORLD! I AM WENDY THE WANDERER!

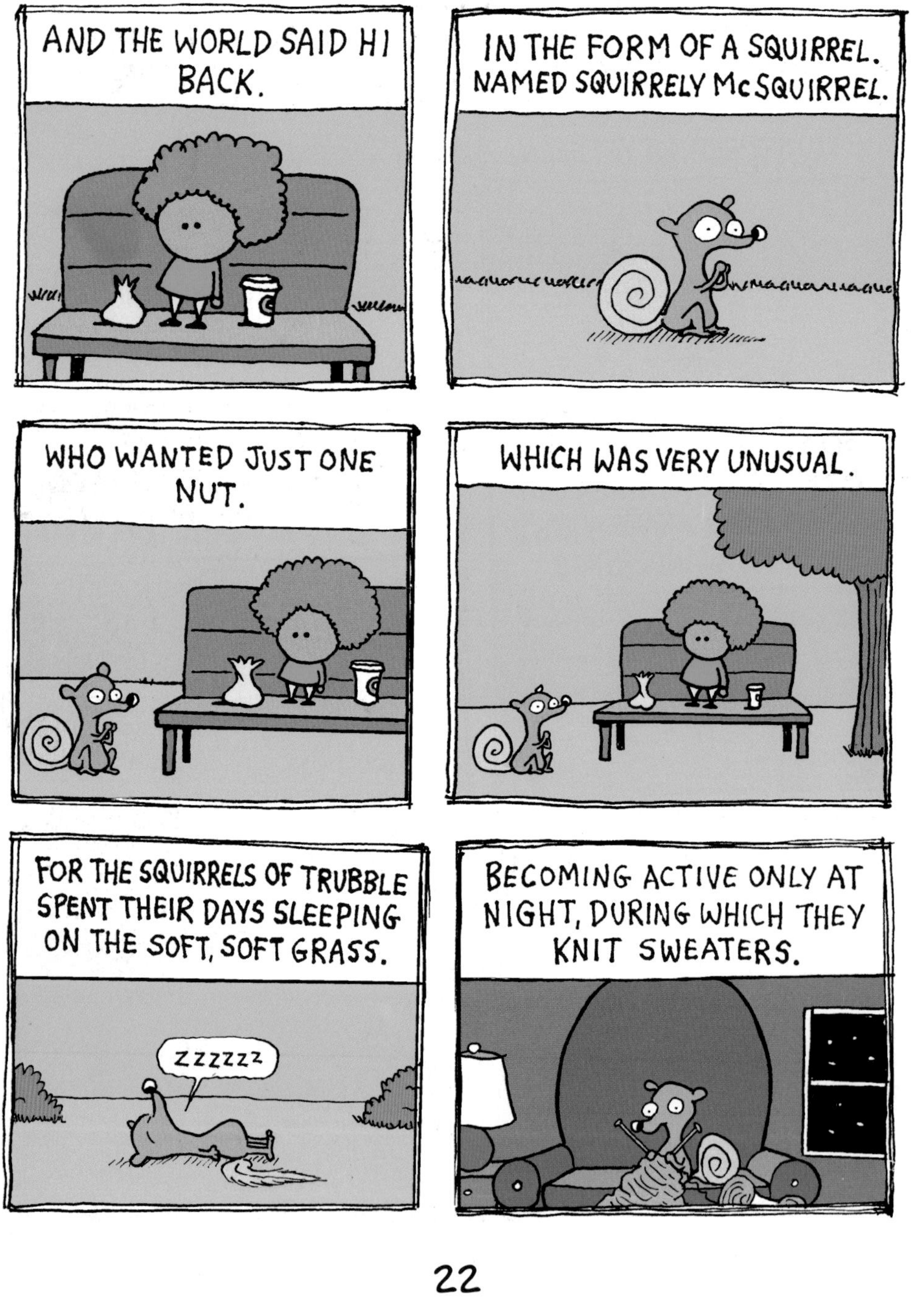
AND THE WORLD SAID HI BACK.
IN THE FORM OF A SQUIRREL. NAMED SQUIRRELY McSQUIRREL.
WHO WANTED JUST ONE NUT.
WHICH WAS VERY UNUSUAL.
FOR THE SQUIRRELS OF TRUBBLE SPENT THEIR DAYS SLEEPING ON THE SOFT, SOFT GRASS.
ZZZZZZ
BECOMING ACTIVE ONLY AT NIGHT, DURING WHICH THEY KNIT SWEATERS.

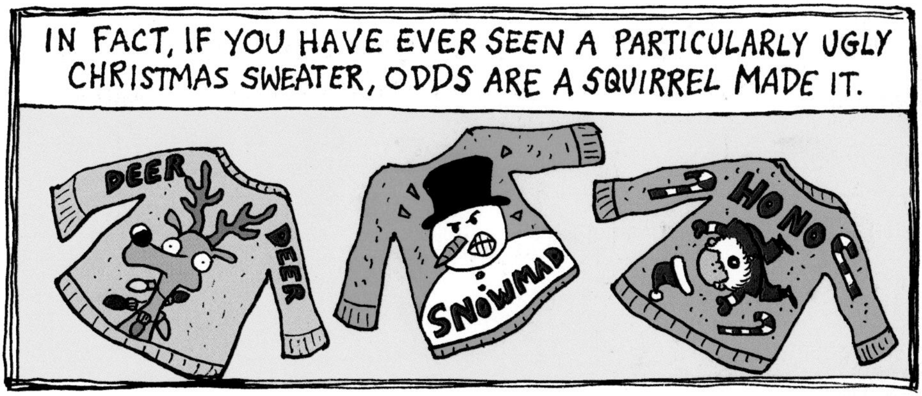
IN FACT, IF YOU HAVE EVER SEEN A PARTICULARLY UGLY CHRISTMAS SWEATER, ODDS ARE A SQUIRREL MADE IT.
DEER
DEER
SNOWMAD
HONO

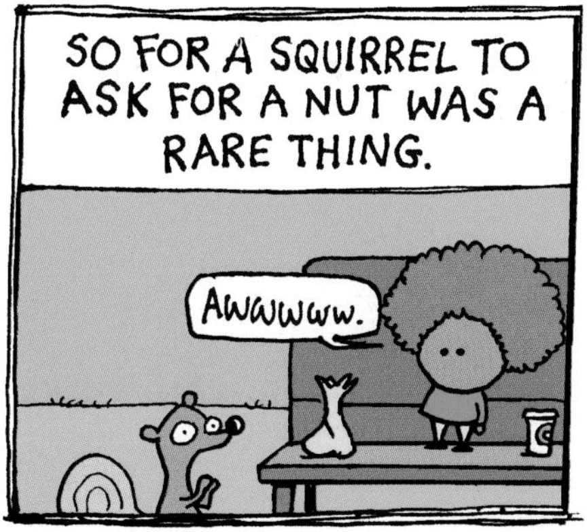
SO FOR A SQUIRREL TO ASK FOR A NUT WAS A RARE THING.
Awwwww.

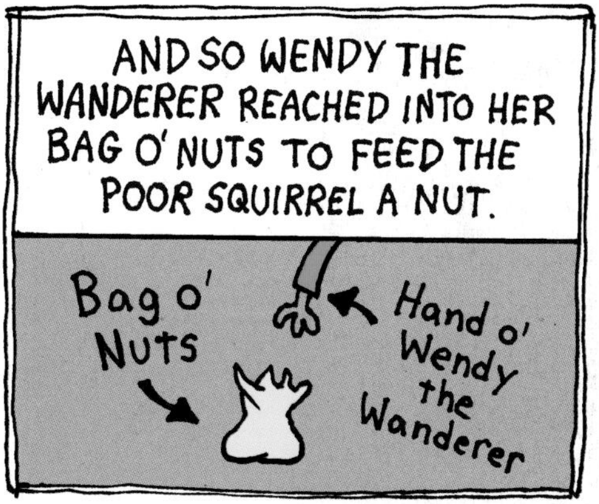
AND SO WENDY THE WANDERER REACHED INTO HER BAG O' NUTS TO FEED THE POOR SQUIRREL A NUT.
Bag o' Nuts
Hand o' Wendy the Wanderer

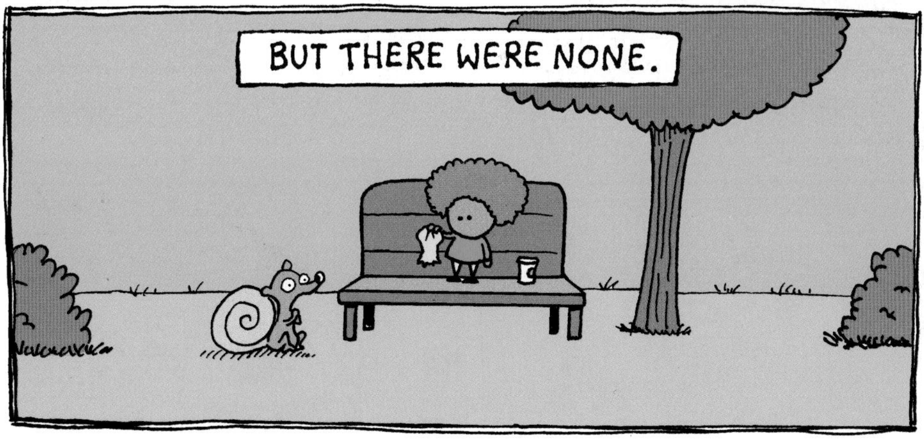
BUT THERE WERE NONE.

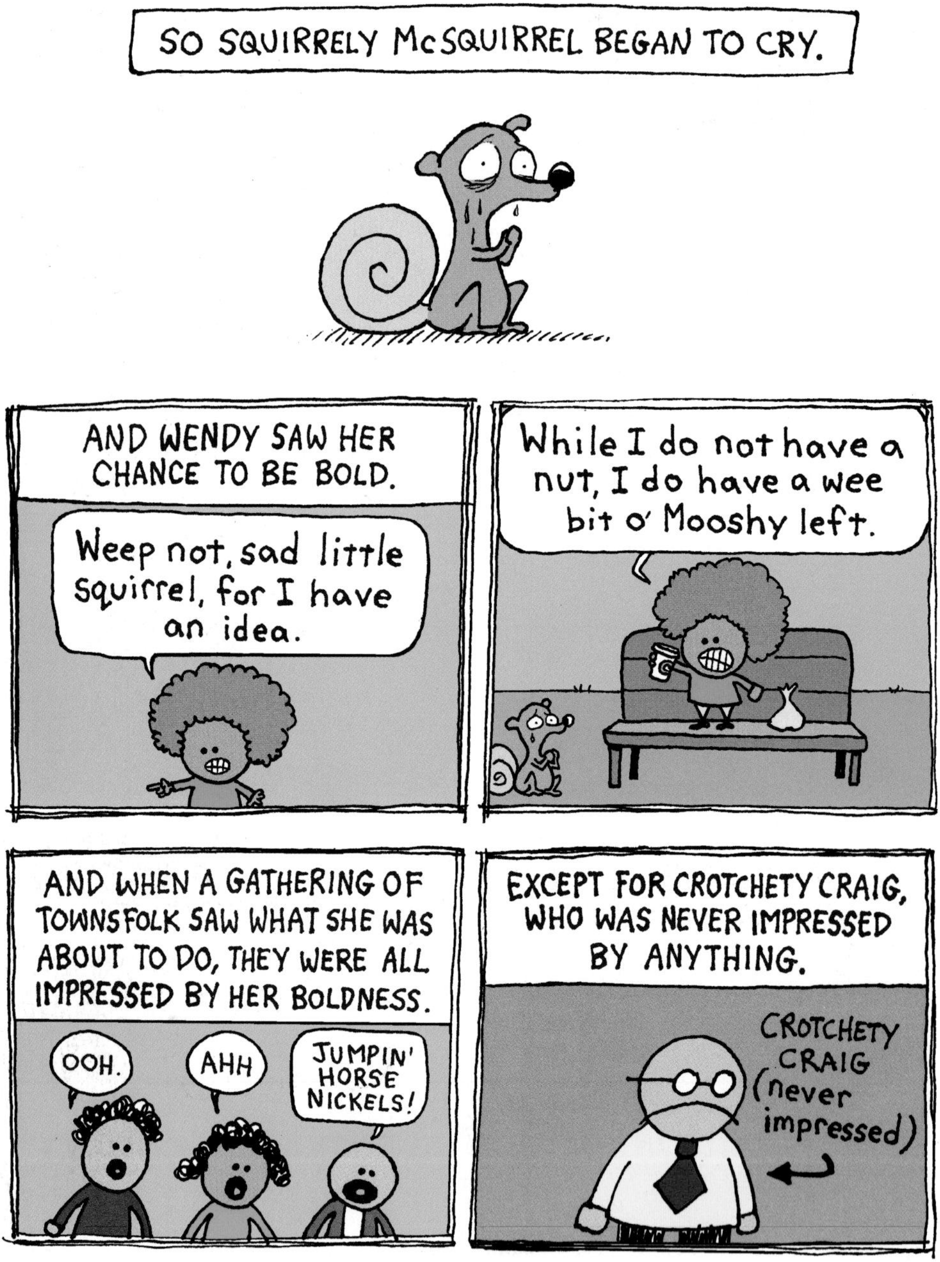
SO SQUIRRELY McSQUIRREL BEGAN TO CRY.
AND WENDY SAW HER CHANCE TO BE BOLD.
Weep not, sad little squirrel, for I have an idea.
While I do not have a nut, I do have a wee bit o' Mooshy left.
AND WHEN A GATHERING OF TOWNSFOLK SAW WHAT SHE WAS ABOUT TO DO, THEY WERE ALL IMPRESSED BY HER BOLDNESS.
OOH.
AHH
JUMPIN' HORSE NICKELS!
EXCEPT FOR CROTCHETY CRAIG, WHO WAS NEVER IMPRESSED BY ANYTHING.
CROTCHETY CRAIG (never impressed)

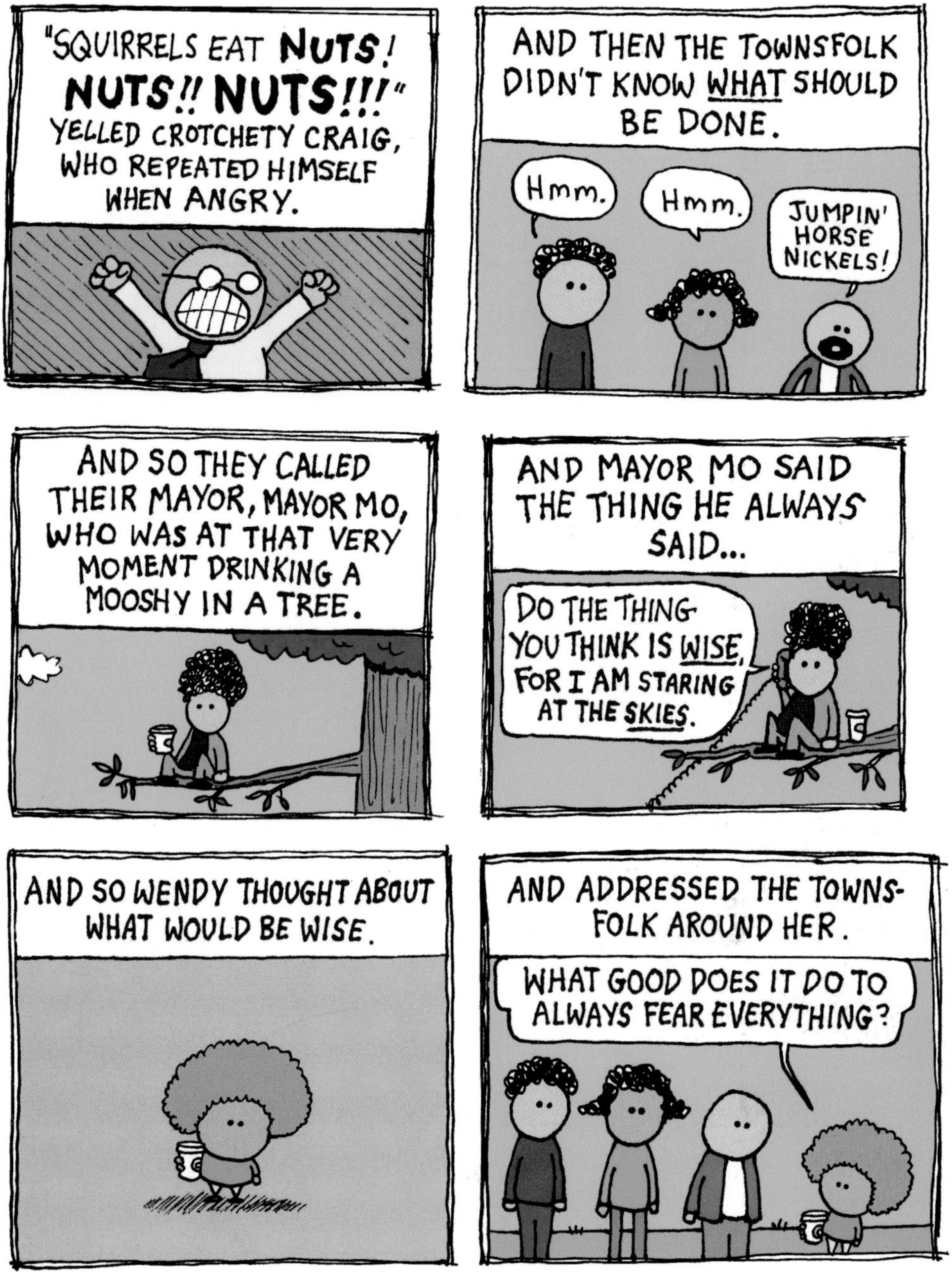
"SQUIRRELS EAT NUTS! NUTS!! NUTS!!!" YELLED CROTCHETY CRAIG, WHO REPEATED HIMSELF WHEN ANGRY.
AND THEN THE TOWNSFOLK DIDN'T KNOW WHAT SHOULD BE DONE.
Hmm.
Hmm.
JUMPIN' HORSE NICKELS!
AND SO THEY CALLED THEIR MAYOR, MAYOR MO, WHO WAS AT THAT VERY MOMENT DRINKING A MOOSHY IN A TREE.
AND MAYOR MO SAID THE THING HE ALWAYS SAID...
DO THE THING YOU THINK IS WISE, FOR I AM STARING AT THE SKIES.
AND SO WENDY THOUGHT ABOUT WHAT WOULD BE WISE.
AND ADDRESSED THE TOWNSFOLK AROUND HER.
WHAT GOOD DOES IT DO TO ALWAYS FEAR EVERYTHING?

AND THE TOWNSFOLK THOUGHT THAT WAS ONE OF THE WISEST THINGS THEY'D EVER HEARD.

WISE.

WISE.

I'M TIRED OF SAYING "JUMPIN' HORSE NICKELS."

AND SO WENDY HANDED SQUIRRELY THE MOOSHY.

WHICH SQUIRRELY DRANK.

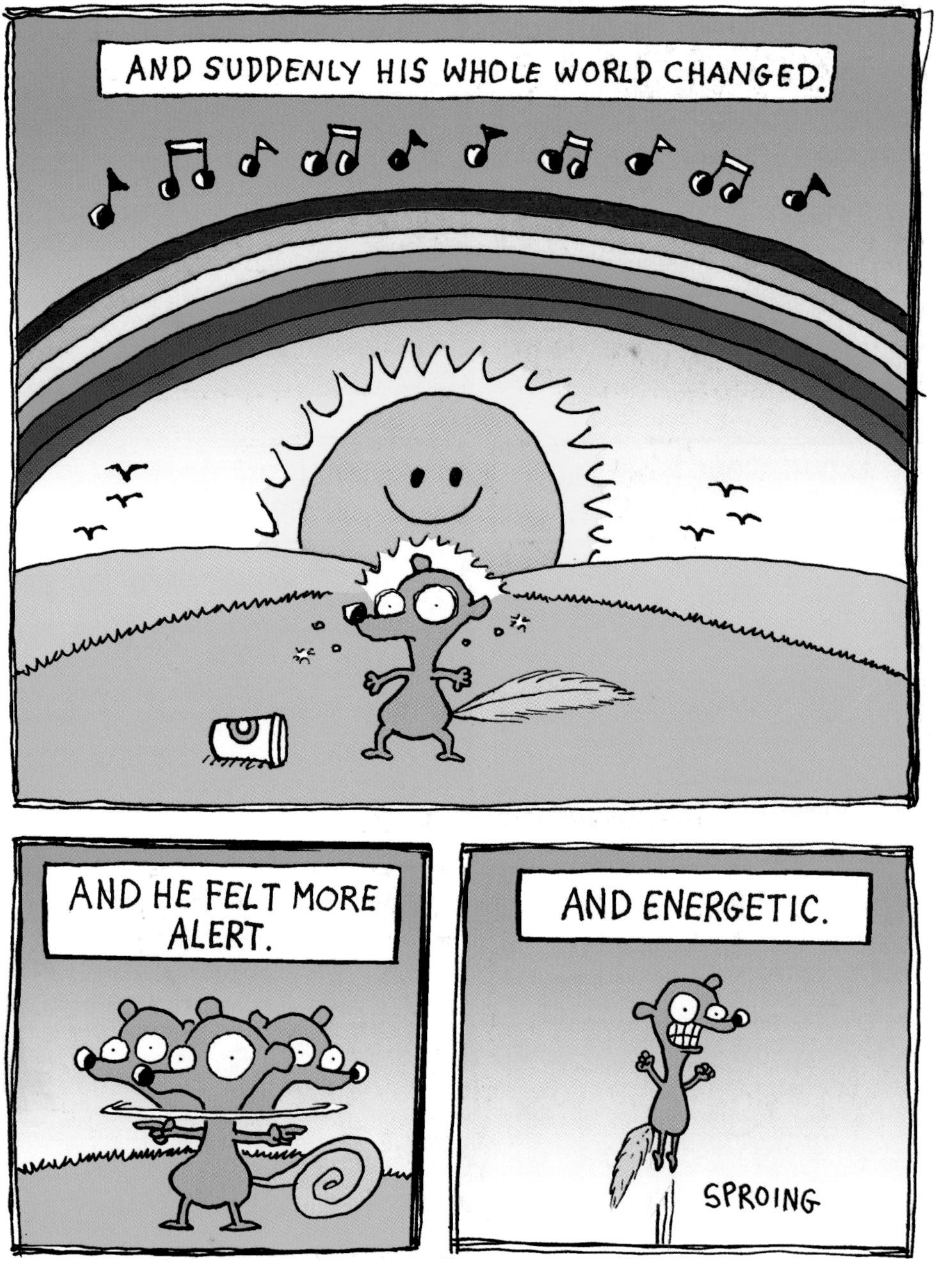
AND SUDDENLY HIS WHOLE WORLD CHANGED.
AND HE FELT MORE ALERT.
AND ENERGETIC.
SPROING

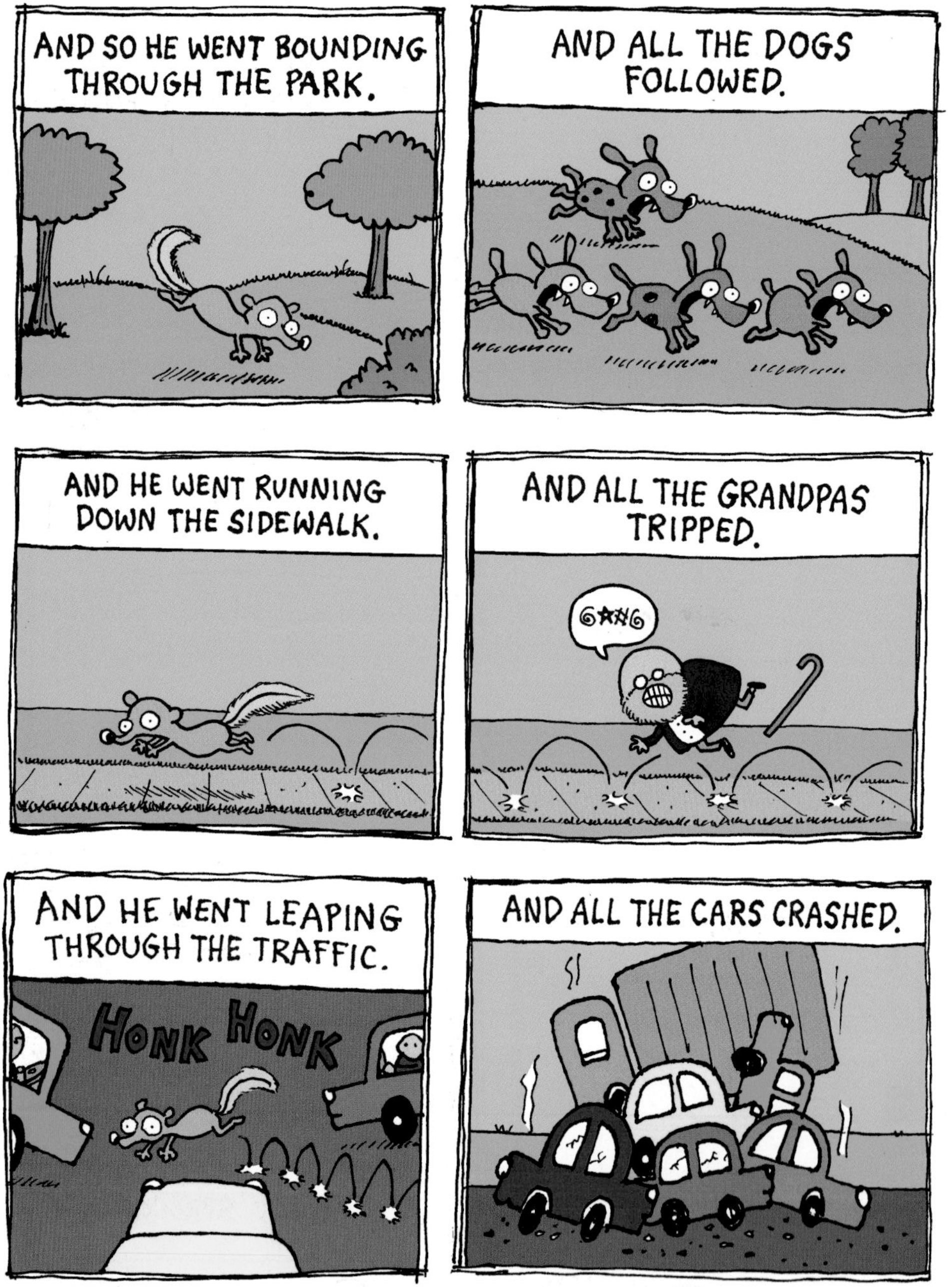
AND SO HE WENT BOUNDING THROUGH THE PARK.
AND ALL THE DOGS FOLLOWED.
AND HE WENT RUNNING DOWN THE SIDEWALK.
AND ALL THE GRANDPAS TRIPPED.
AND HE WENT LEAPING THROUGH THE TRAFFIC.
HONK HONK
AND ALL THE CARS CRASHED.

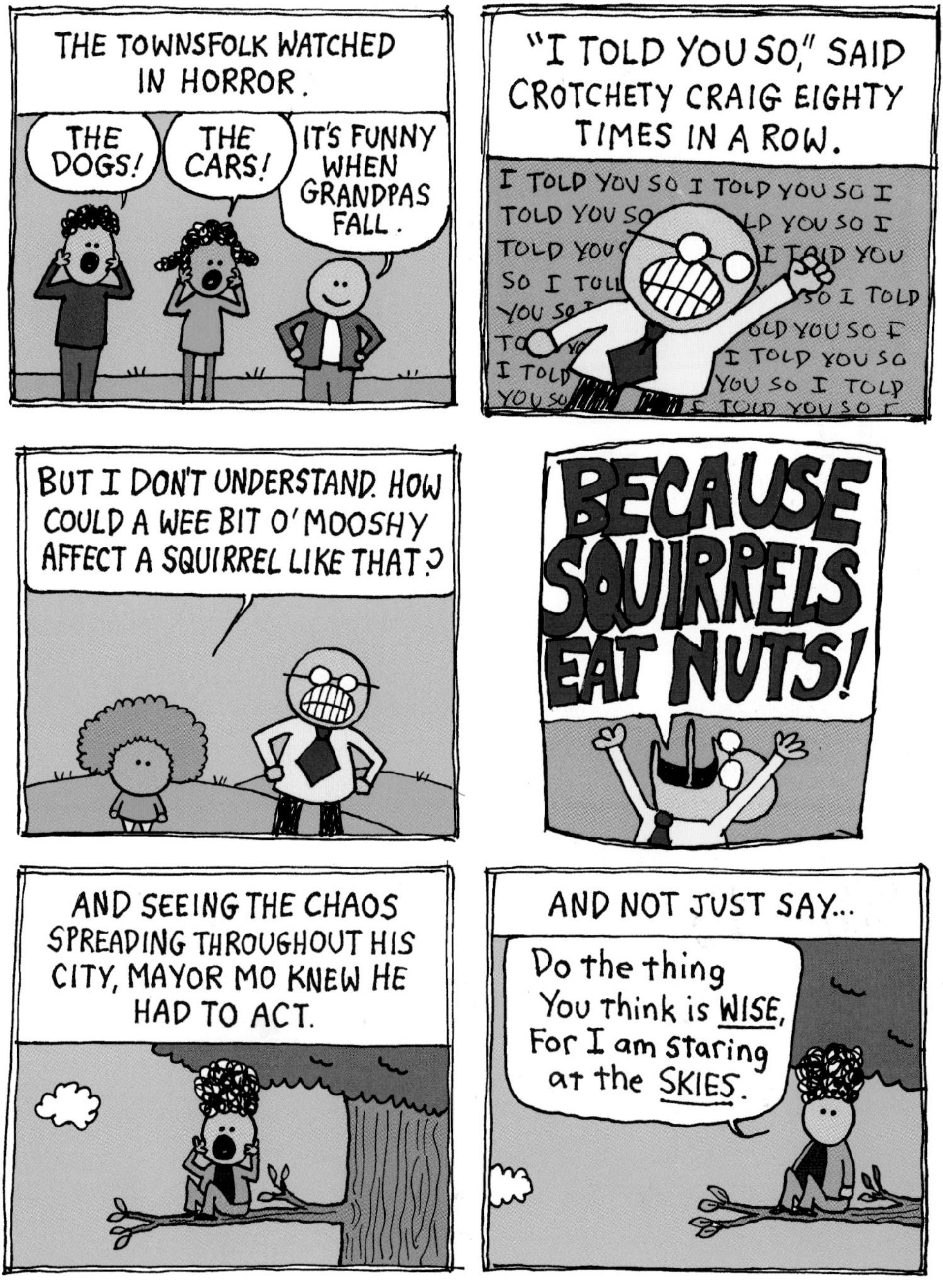
THE TOWNSFOLK WATCHED IN HORROR.
THE DOGS!
THE CARS!
IT'S FUNNY WHEN GRANDPAS FALL.
"I TOLD YOU SO," SAID CROTCHETY CRAIG EIGHTY TIMES IN A ROW.
I TOLD YOU SO I TOLD YOU SO I
BUT I DON'T UNDERSTAND. HOW COULD A WEE BIT O' MOOSHY AFFECT A SQUIRREL LIKE THAT?
BECAUSE SQUIRRELS EAT NUTS!
AND SEEING THE CHAOS SPREADING THROUGHOUT HIS CITY, MAYOR MO KNEW HE HAD TO ACT.
AND NOT JUST SAY...
Do the thing You think is WISE, For I am staring at the SKIES.

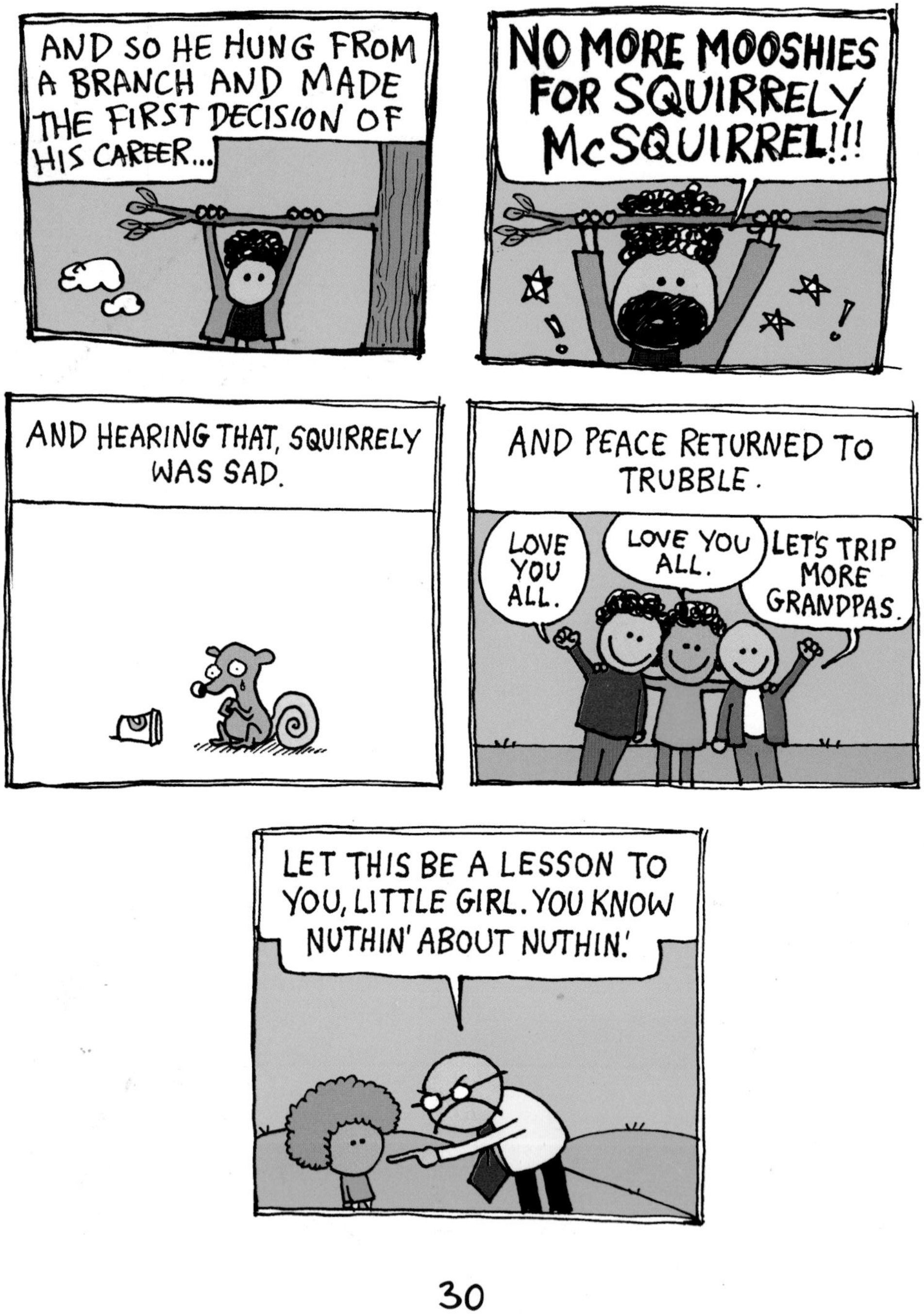
AND SO HE HUNG FROM A BRANCH AND MADE THE FIRST DECISION OF HIS CAREER...
NO MORE MOOSHIES FOR SQUIRRELY McSQUIRREL!!!
AND HEARING THAT, SQUIRRELY WAS SAD.
AND PEACE RETURNED TO TRUBBLE.
LOVE YOU ALL.
LOVE YOU ALL.
LET'S TRIP MORE GRANDPAS.
LET THIS BE A LESSON TO YOU, LITTLE GIRL. YOU KNOW NUTHIN' ABOUT NUTHIN.'

AND LOOKING AT THE CHAIN OF EVENTS SHE HAD TRIGGERED, WENDY THOUGHT BACK TO WHAT HER FATHER HAD SAID.

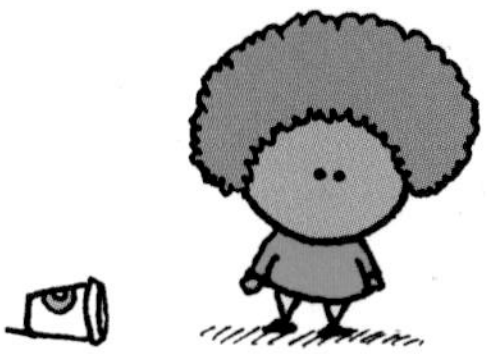

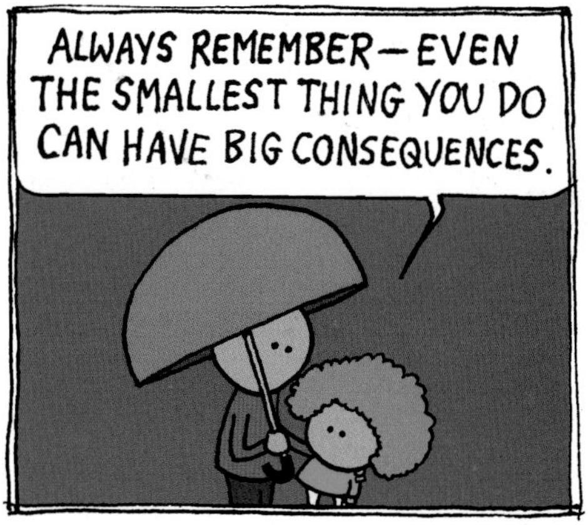
ALWAYS REMEMBER—EVEN THE SMALLEST THING YOU DO CAN HAVE BIG CONSEQUENCES.

AND HOW SHE HAD NOT HEEDED HIS ADVICE.

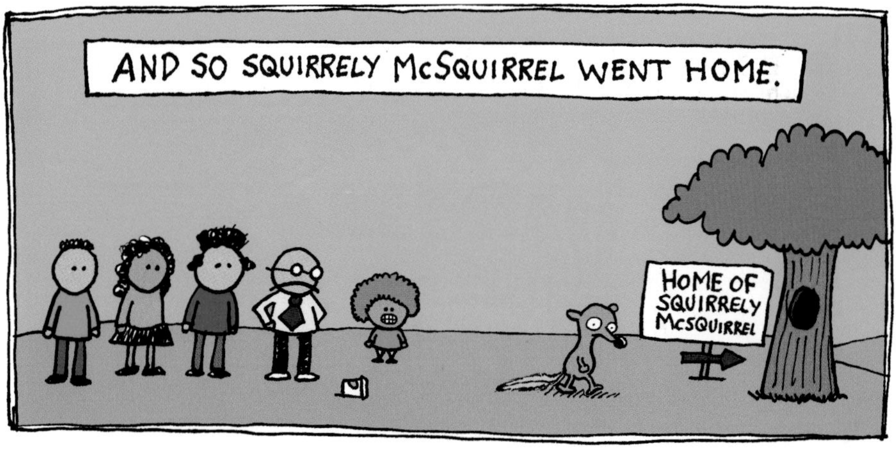
AND SO SQUIRRELY McSQUIRREL WENT HOME.
HOME OF SQUIRRELY McSQUIRREL

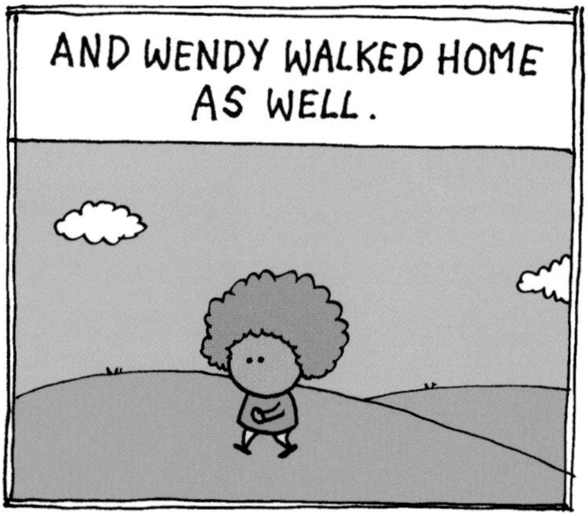
AND WENDY WALKED HOME AS WELL.

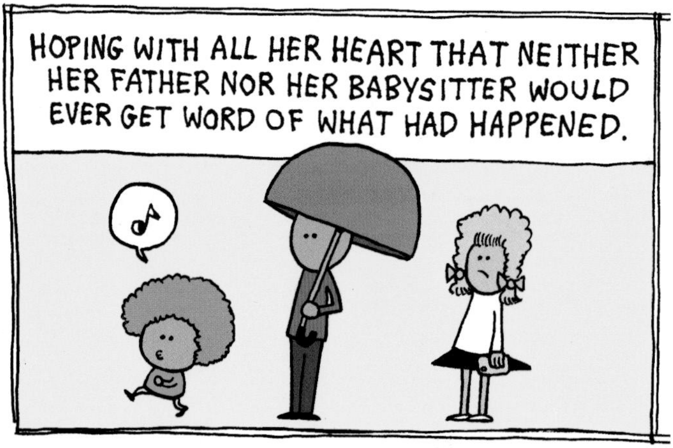
HOPING WITH ALL HER HEART THAT NEITHER HER FATHER NOR HER BABYSITTER WOULD EVER GET WORD OF WHAT HAD HAPPENED.

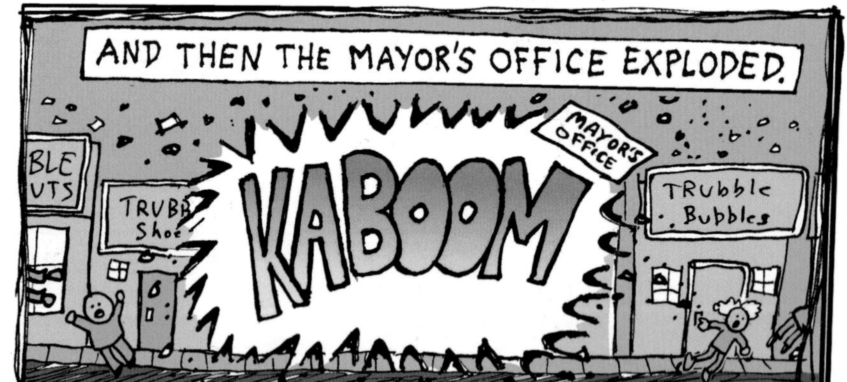
AND THEN THE MAYOR'S OFFICE EXPLODED.
MAYOR'S OFFICE
KABOOM
BLE
UTS
TRUBB
Shoe
TRUbble
Bubbles

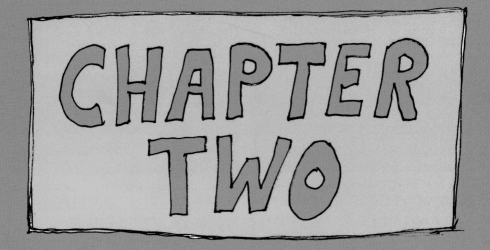

CHAPTER TWO

IN WHICH...

THINGS HAPPEN

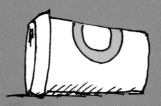

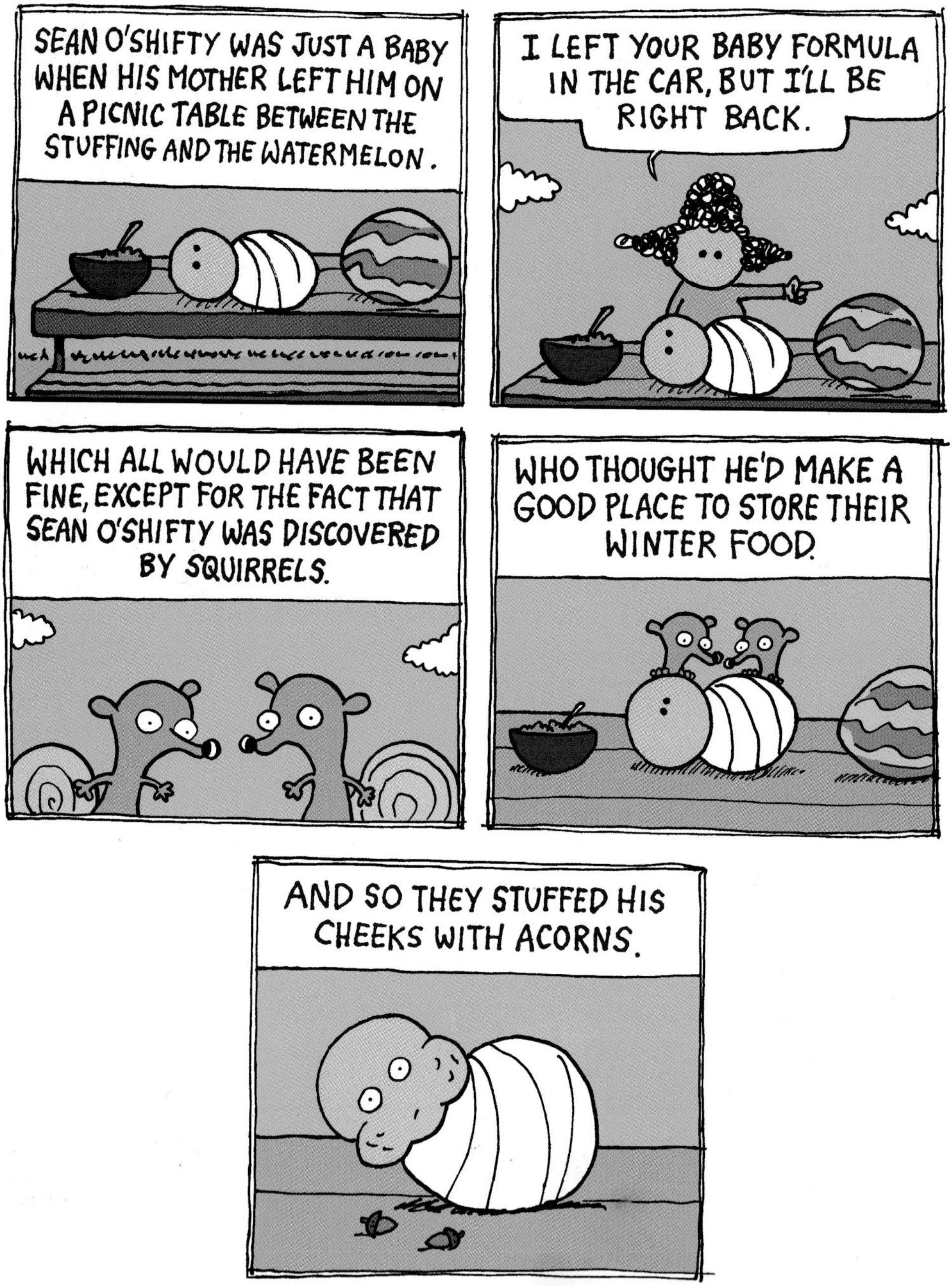
SEAN O'SHIFTY WAS JUST A BABY WHEN HIS MOTHER LEFT HIM ON A PICNIC TABLE BETWEEN THE STUFFING AND THE WATERMELON.
I LEFT YOUR BABY FORMULA IN THE CAR, BUT I'LL BE RIGHT BACK.
WHICH ALL WOULD HAVE BEEN FINE, EXCEPT FOR THE FACT THAT SEAN O'SHIFTY WAS DISCOVERED BY SQUIRRELS.
WHO THOUGHT HE'D MAKE A GOOD PLACE TO STORE THEIR WINTER FOOD.
AND SO THEY STUFFED HIS CHEEKS WITH ACORNS.

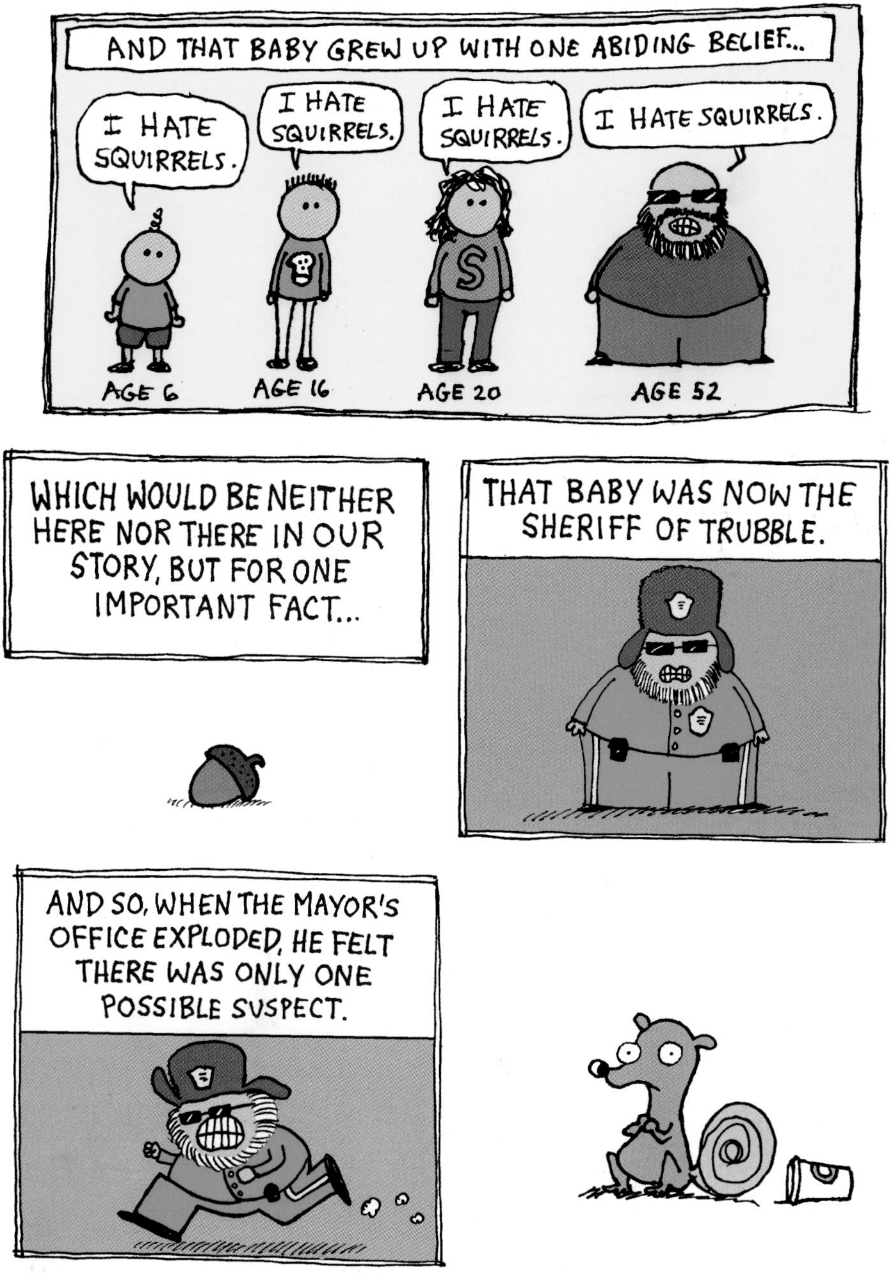
AND THAT BABY GREW UP WITH ONE ABIDING BELIEF...
I HATE SQUIRRELS.
I HATE SQUIRRELS.
I HATE SQUIRRELS.
I HATE SQUIRRELS.
AGE 6
AGE 16
AGE 20
AGE 52
WHICH WOULD BE NEITHER HERE NOR THERE IN OUR STORY, BUT FOR ONE IMPORTANT FACT...
THAT BABY WAS NOW THE SHERIFF OF TRUBBLE.
AND SO, WHEN THE MAYOR'S OFFICE EXPLODED, HE FELT THERE WAS ONLY ONE POSSIBLE SUSPECT.

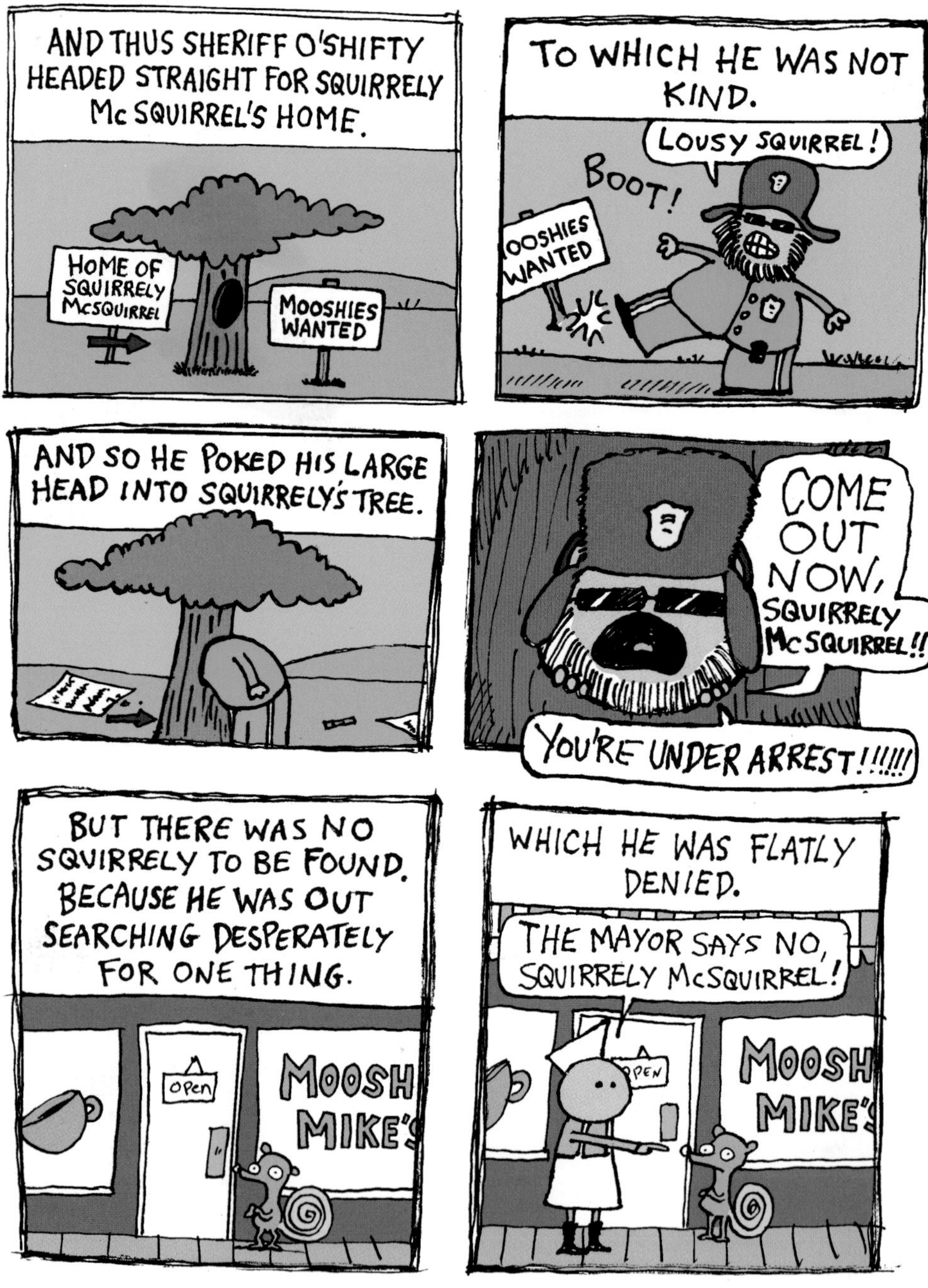
AND THUS SHERIFF O'SHIFTY HEADED STRAIGHT FOR SQUIRRELY McSQUIRREL'S HOME.
HOME OF SQUIRRELY McSQUIRREL
MOOSHIES WANTED
TO WHICH HE WAS NOT KIND.
LOUSY SQUIRREL!
BOOT!
OOSHIES WANTED
AND SO HE POKED HIS LARGE HEAD INTO SQUIRRELY'S TREE.
COME OUT NOW, SQUIRRELY McSQUIRREL!!
YOU'RE UNDER ARREST!!!!!!
BUT THERE WAS NO SQUIRRELY TO BE FOUND. BECAUSE HE WAS OUT SEARCHING DESPERATELY FOR ONE THING.
OPEN
MOOSH MIKE'S
WHICH HE WAS FLATLY DENIED.
THE MAYOR SAYS NO, SQUIRRELY McSQUIRREL!
OPEN
MOOSH MIKE'S

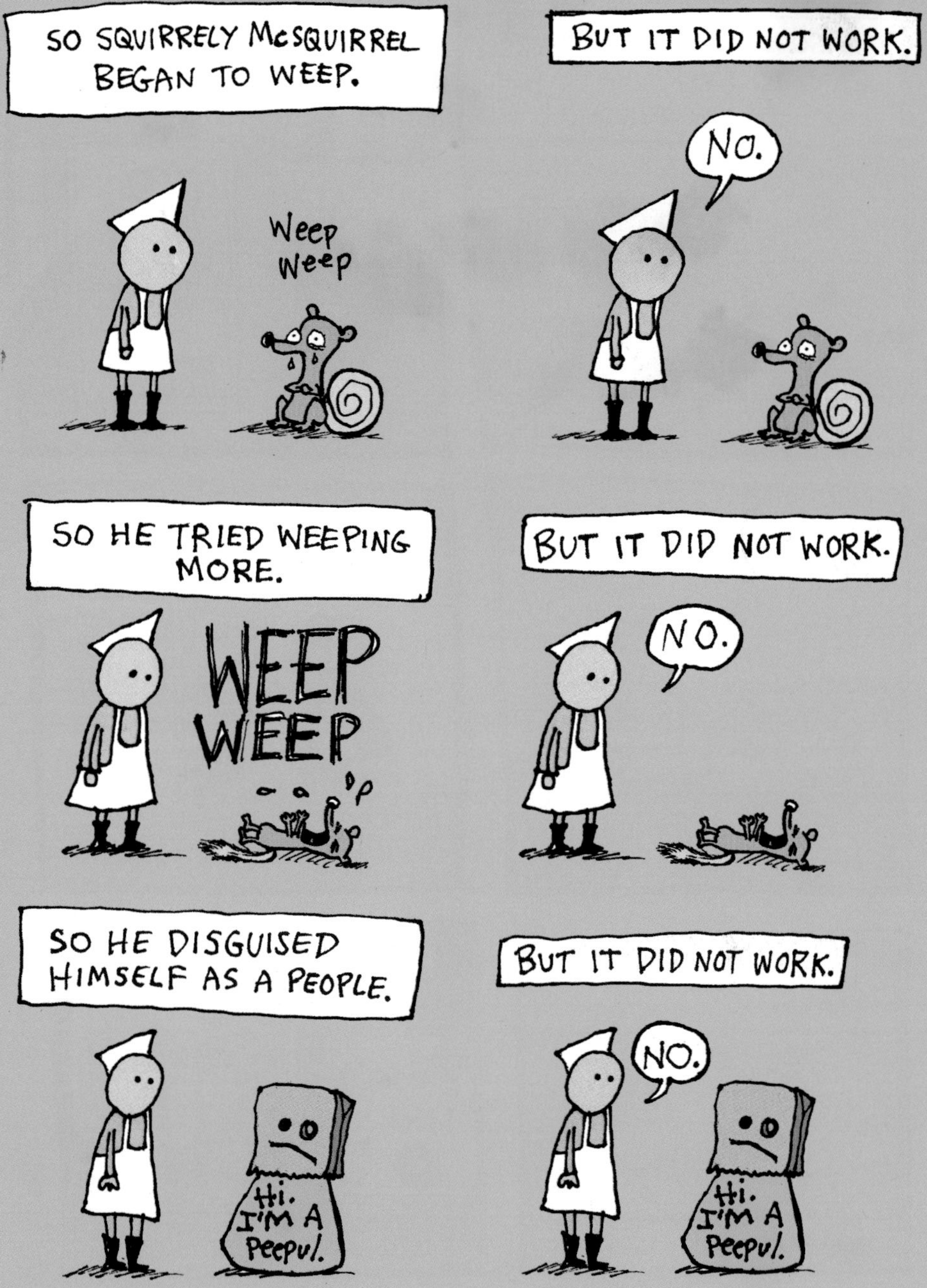
SO SQUIRRELY McSQUIRREL BEGAN TO WEEP.
Weep weep
BUT IT DID NOT WORK.
NO.
SO HE TRIED WEEPING MORE.
WEEP WEEP
BUT IT DID NOT WORK.
NO.
SO HE DISGUISED HIMSELF AS A PEOPLE.
Hi. I'M A Peepul.
BUT IT DID NOT WORK.
NO.
Hi. I'M A Peepul.

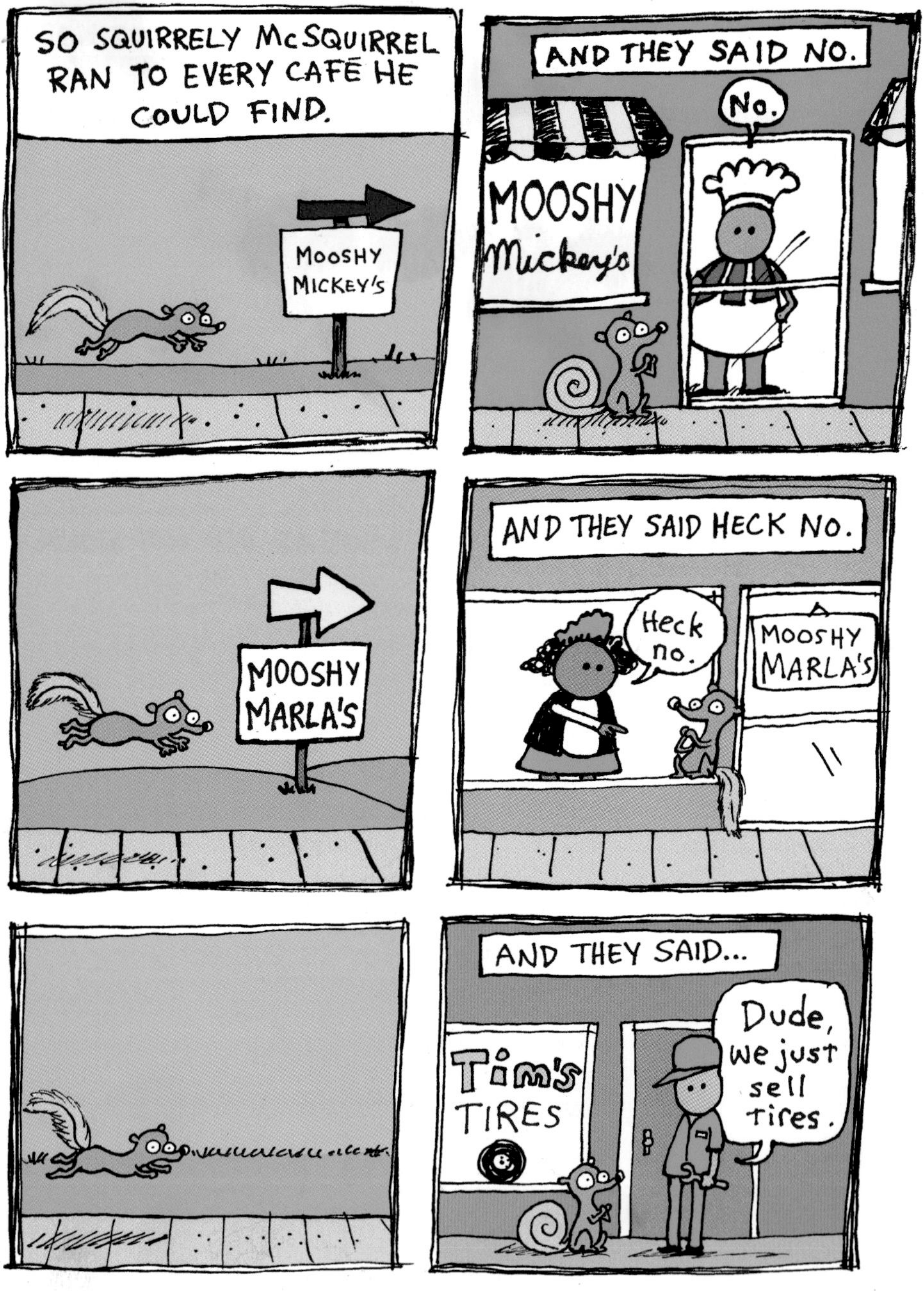
SO SQUIRRELY McSQUIRREL RAN TO EVERY CAFÉ HE COULD FIND.
MOOSHY MICKEY'S
AND THEY SAID NO.
No.
MOOSHY Mickey's
MOOSHY MARLA'S
AND THEY SAID HECK NO.
Heck no.
MOOSHY MARLA'S
AND THEY SAID...
Dude, we just sell tires.
Tim's TIRES

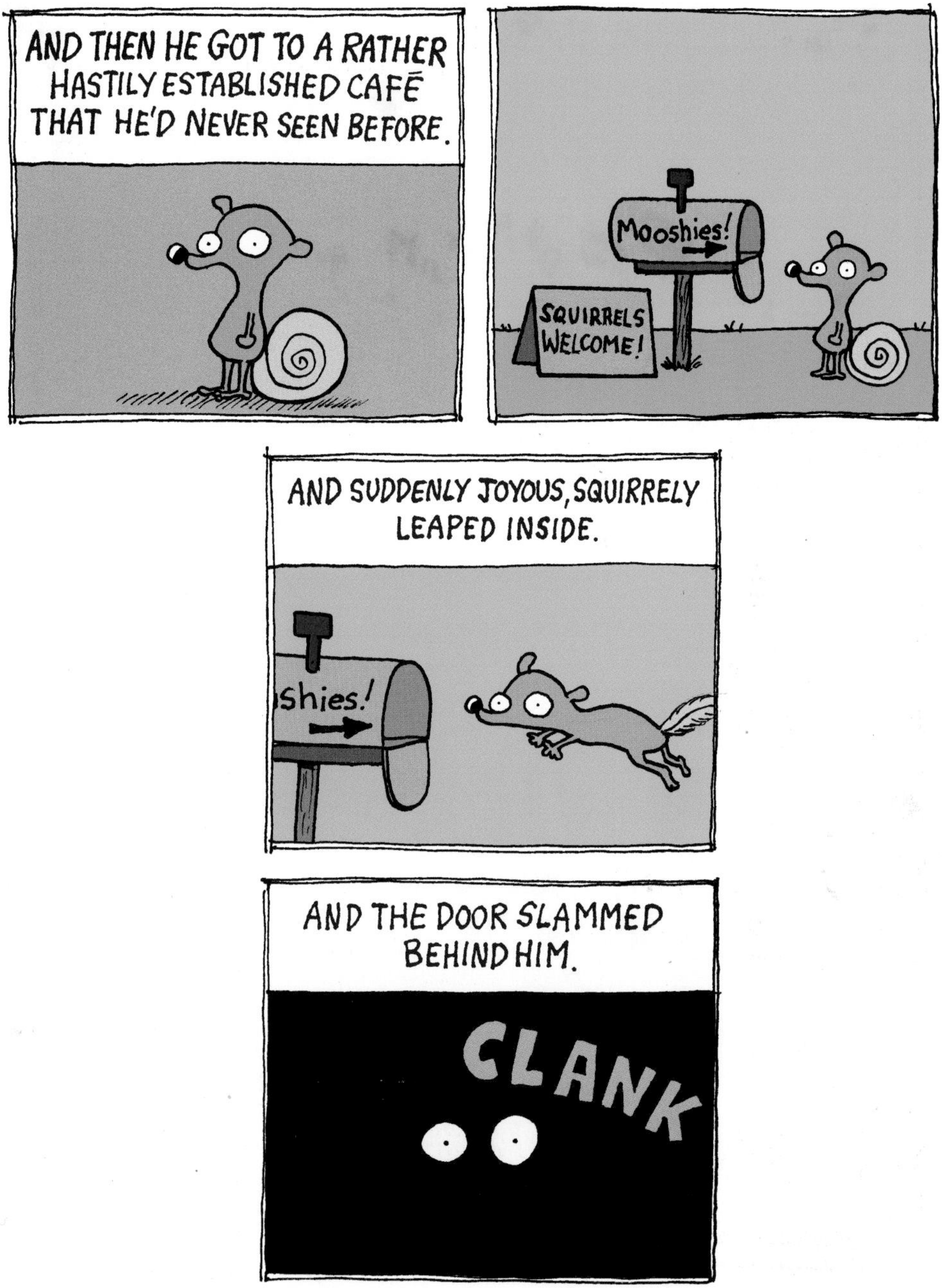
AND THEN HE GOT TO A RATHER HASTILY ESTABLISHED CAFÉ THAT HE'D NEVER SEEN BEFORE.
Mooshies!
SQUIRRELS WELCOME!
AND SUDDENLY JOYOUS, SQUIRRELY LEAPED INSIDE.
shies!
AND THE DOOR SLAMMED BEHIND HIM.
CLANK

CHAPTER THREE

IN WHICH...

YOU WILL FALL OVER IN SHOCK AND CRY, "NO, SQUIRRELY, NO!"

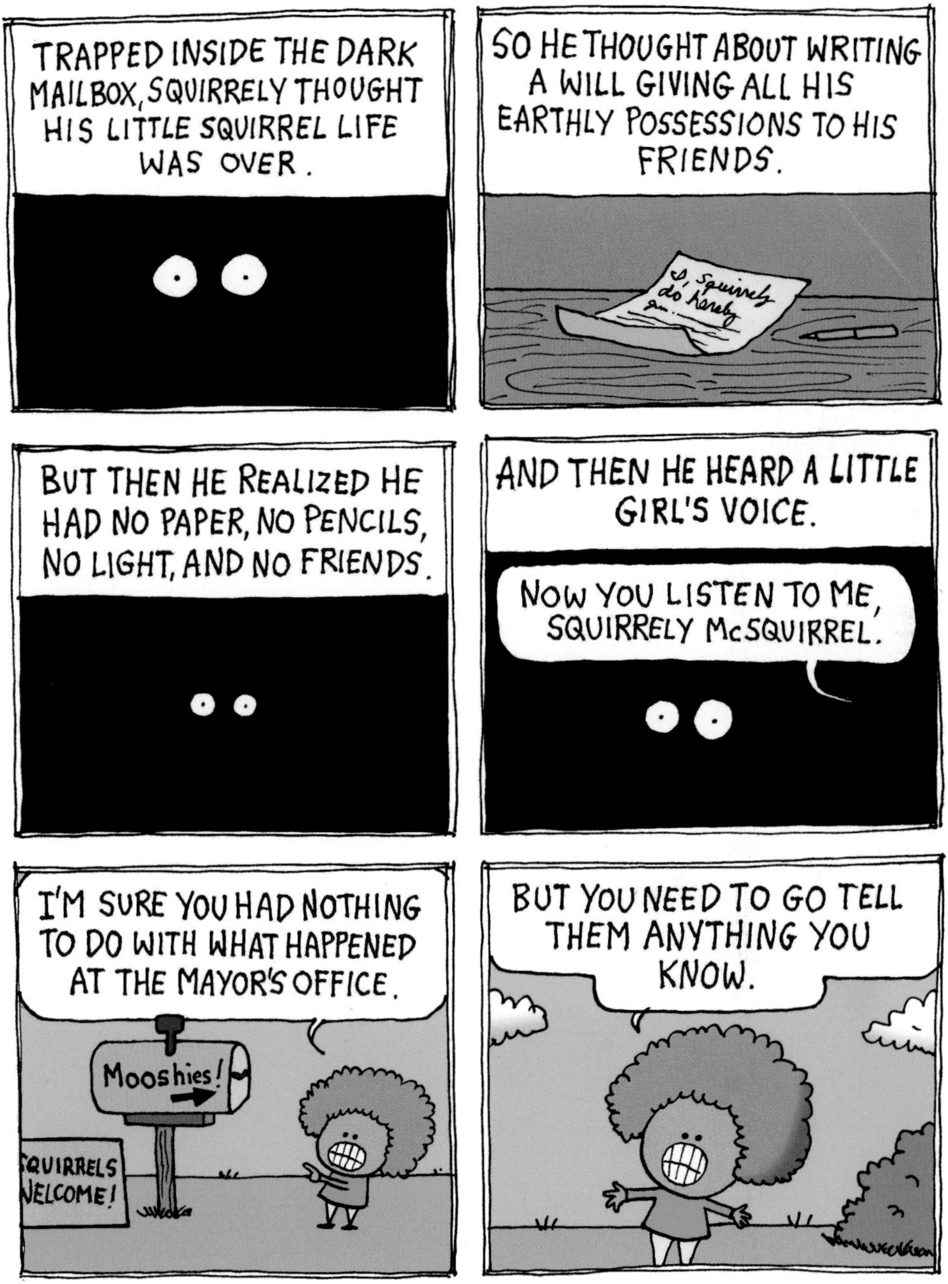
TRAPPED INSIDE THE DARK MAILBOX, SQUIRRELY THOUGHT HIS LITTLE SQUIRREL LIFE WAS OVER.
SO HE THOUGHT ABOUT WRITING A WILL GIVING ALL HIS EARTHLY POSSESSIONS TO HIS FRIENDS.
BUT THEN HE REALIZED HE HAD NO PAPER, NO PENCILS, NO LIGHT, AND NO FRIENDS.
AND THEN HE HEARD A LITTLE GIRL'S VOICE.
NOW YOU LISTEN TO ME, SQUIRRELY McSQUIRREL.
I'M SURE YOU HAD NOTHING TO DO WITH WHAT HAPPENED AT THE MAYOR'S OFFICE.
Mooshies!
SQUIRRELS WELCOME!
BUT YOU NEED TO GO TELL THEM ANYTHING YOU KNOW.

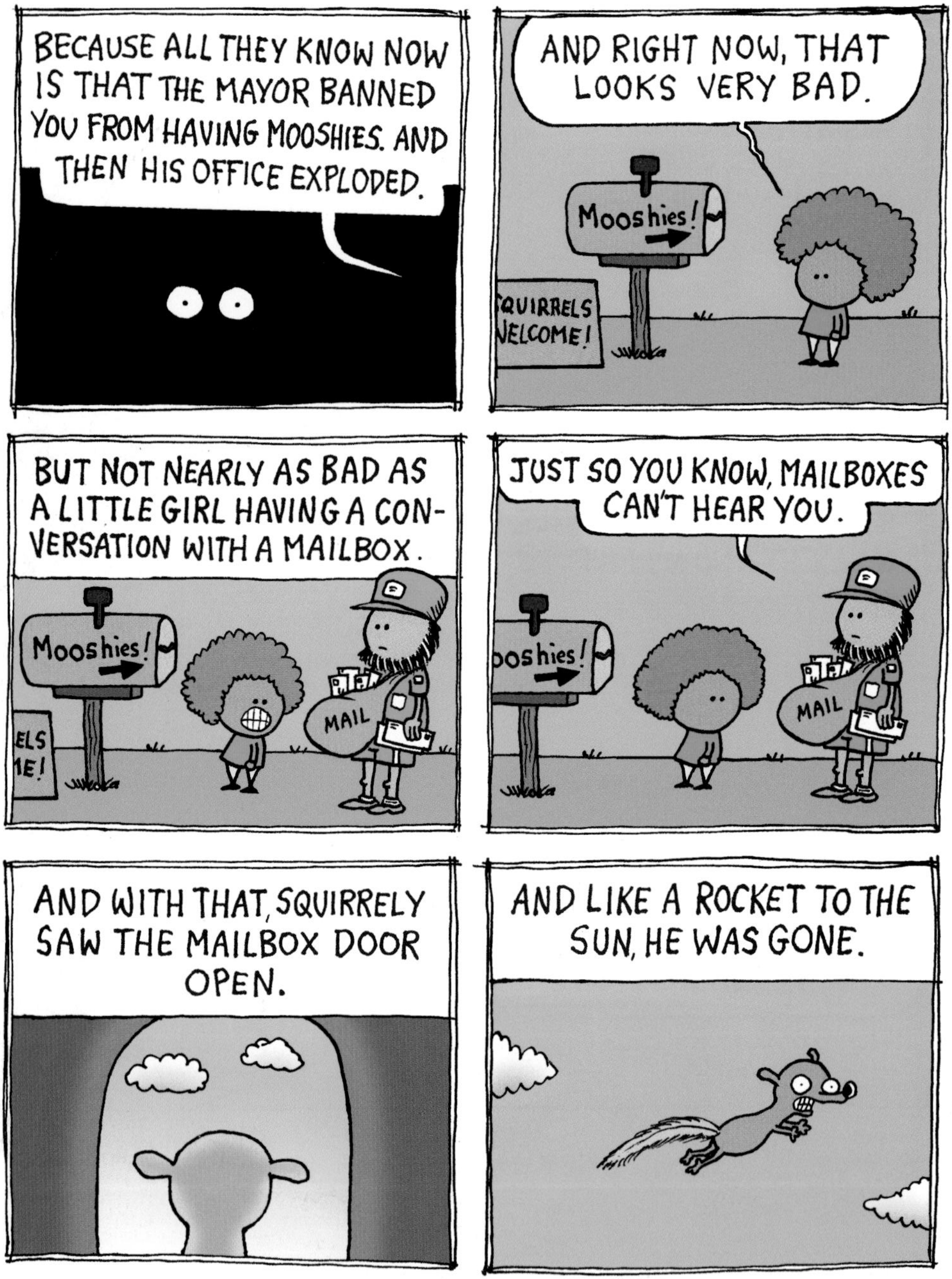
BECAUSE ALL THEY KNOW NOW IS THAT THE MAYOR BANNED YOU FROM HAVING MOOSHIES. AND THEN HIS OFFICE EXPLODED.
AND RIGHT NOW, THAT LOOKS VERY BAD.
Mooshies!
SQUIRRELS WELCOME!
BUT NOT NEARLY AS BAD AS A LITTLE GIRL HAVING A CONVERSATION WITH A MAILBOX.
Mooshies!
MAIL
JUST SO YOU KNOW, MAILBOXES CAN'T HEAR YOU.
MAIL
AND WITH THAT, SQUIRRELY SAW THE MAILBOX DOOR OPEN.
AND LIKE A ROCKET TO THE SUN, HE WAS GONE.

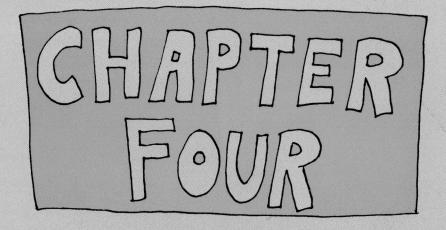

CHAPTER FOUR

IN WHICH...

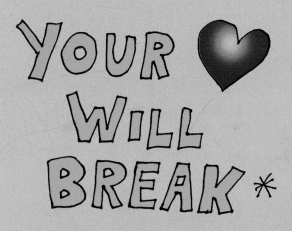

YOUR ♥ WILL BREAK *

* Provided ye haveth one...

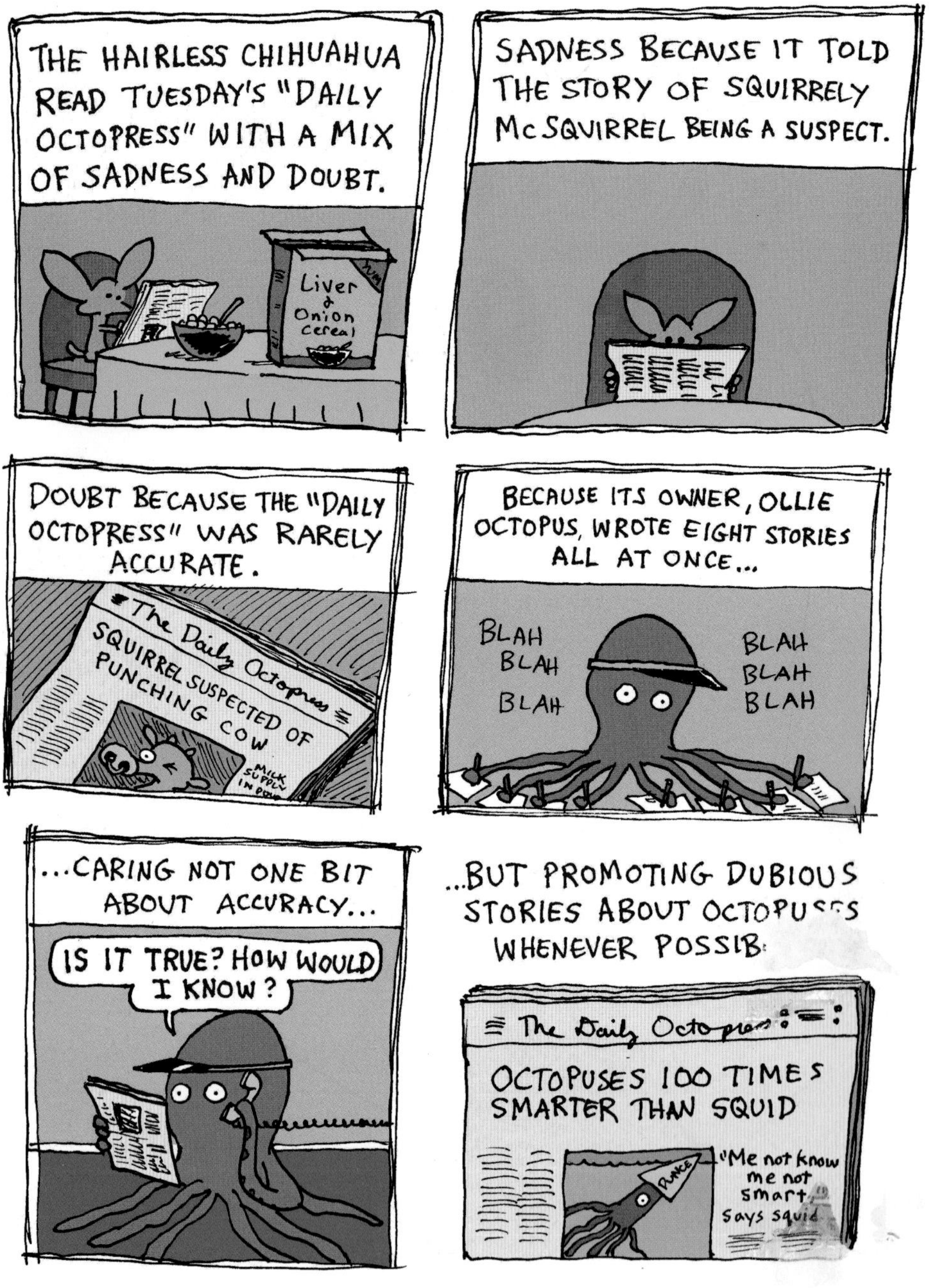
THE HAIRLESS CHIHUAHUA READ TUESDAY'S "DAILY OCTOPRESS" WITH A MIX OF SADNESS AND DOUBT.
Liver & Onion cereal
SADNESS BECAUSE IT TOLD THE STORY OF SQUIRRELY McSQUIRREL BEING A SUSPECT.
DOUBT BECAUSE THE "DAILY OCTOPRESS" WAS RARELY ACCURATE.
The Daily Octopress
SQUIRREL SUSPECTED OF PUNCHING COW
MILK SUPPLY IN
BECAUSE ITS OWNER, OLLIE OCTOPUS, WROTE EIGHT STORIES ALL AT ONCE...
BLAH BLAH BLAH
BLAH BLAH BLAH
...CARING NOT ONE BIT ABOUT ACCURACY...
IS IT TRUE? HOW WOULD I KNOW?
...BUT PROMOTING DUBIOUS STORIES ABOUT OCTOPUSES WHENEVER POSSIB
The Daily Octopress
OCTOPUSES 100 TIMES SMARTER THAN SQUID
"Me not know me not smart," Says squid

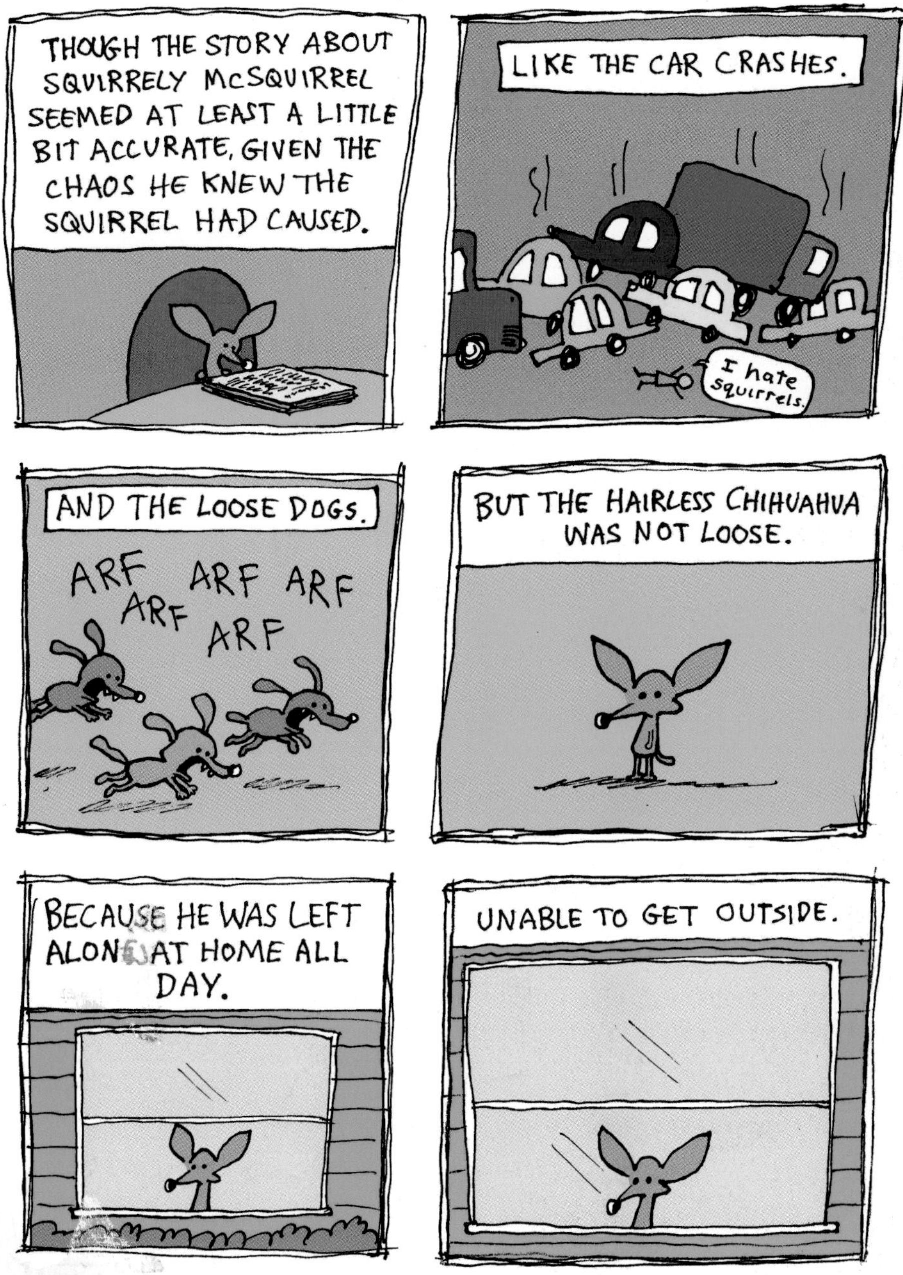
THOUGH THE STORY ABOUT SQUIRRELY McSQUIRREL SEEMED AT LEAST A LITTLE BIT ACCURATE, GIVEN THE CHAOS HE KNEW THE SQUIRREL HAD CAUSED.
LIKE THE CAR CRASHES.
I hate squirrels.
AND THE LOOSE DOGS.
ARF ARF ARF ARF ARF
BUT THE HAIRLESS CHIHUAHUA WAS NOT LOOSE.
BECAUSE HE WAS LEFT ALONE AT HOME ALL DAY.
UNABLE TO GET OUTSIDE.

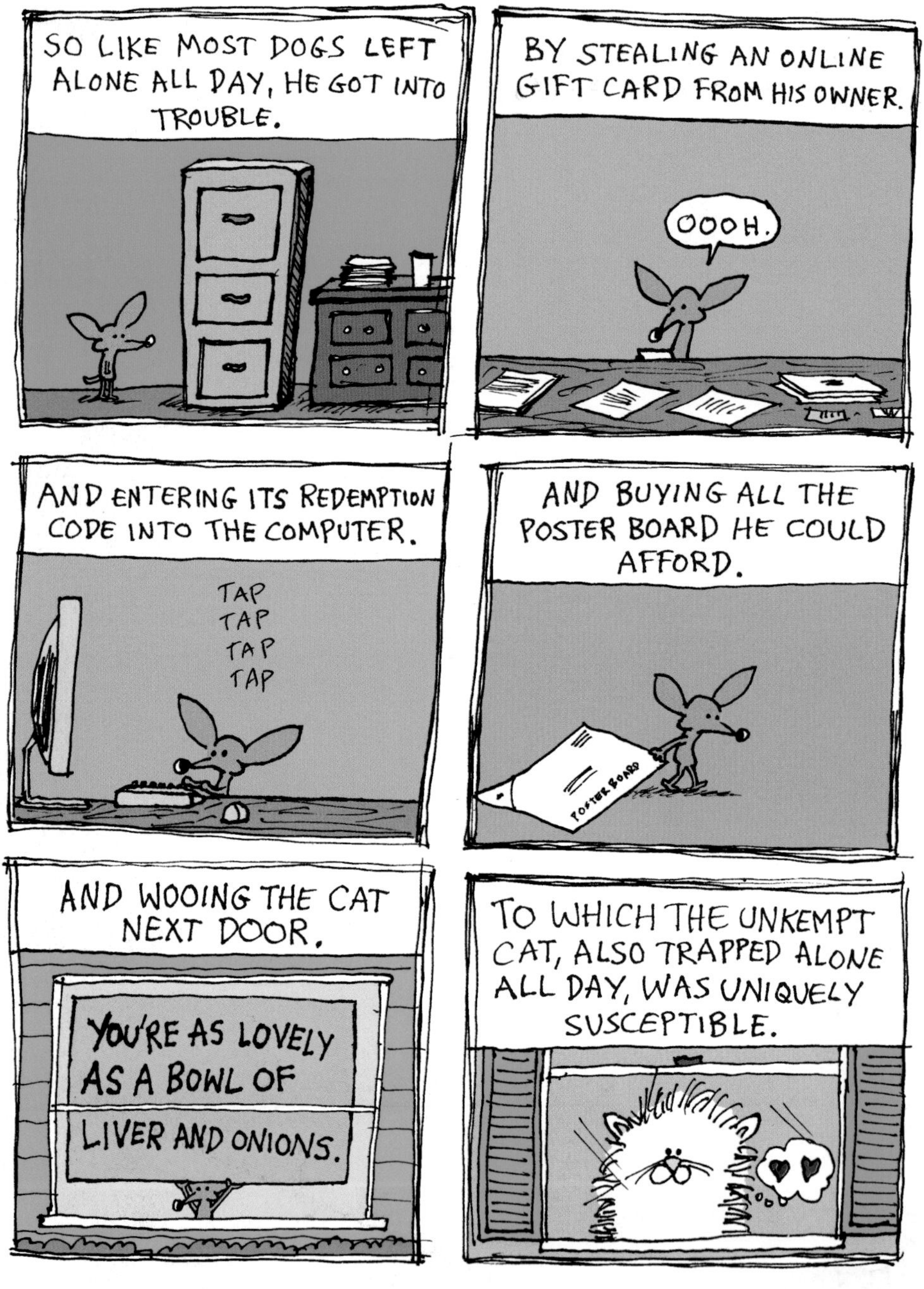
SO LIKE MOST DOGS LEFT ALONE ALL DAY, HE GOT INTO TROUBLE.
BY STEALING AN ONLINE GIFT CARD FROM HIS OWNER.
OOOH.
AND ENTERING ITS REDEMPTION CODE INTO THE COMPUTER.
TAP
TAP
TAP
TAP
AND BUYING ALL THE POSTER BOARD HE COULD AFFORD.
POSTER BOARD
AND WOOING THE CAT NEXT DOOR.
YOU'RE AS LOVELY AS A BOWL OF
LIVER AND ONIONS.
TO WHICH THE UNKEMPT CAT, ALSO TRAPPED ALONE ALL DAY, WAS UNIQUELY SUSCEPTIBLE.

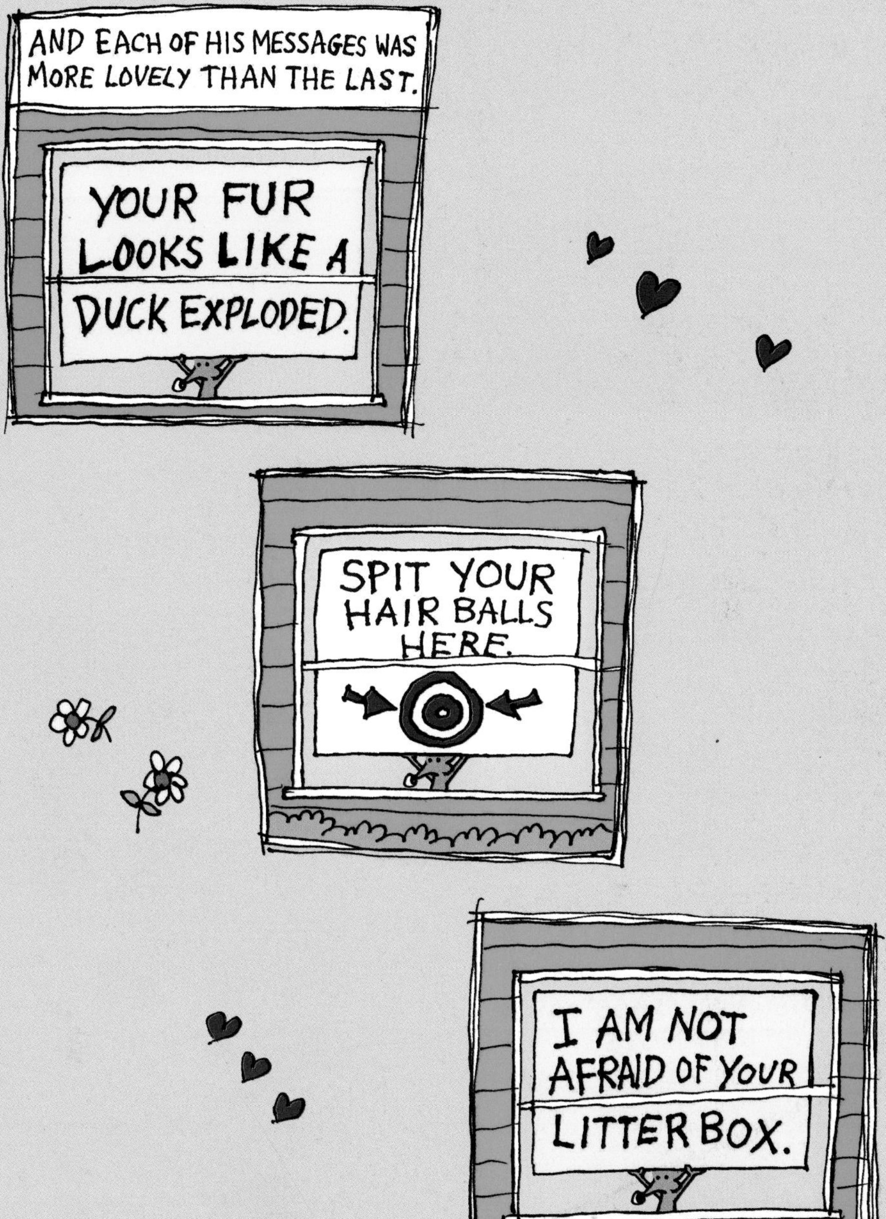
AND EACH OF HIS MESSAGES WAS MORE LOVELY THAN THE LAST.
YOUR FUR LOOKS LIKE A DUCK EXPLODED.
SPIT YOUR HAIR BALLS HERE.
I AM NOT AFRAID OF YOUR LITTER BOX.

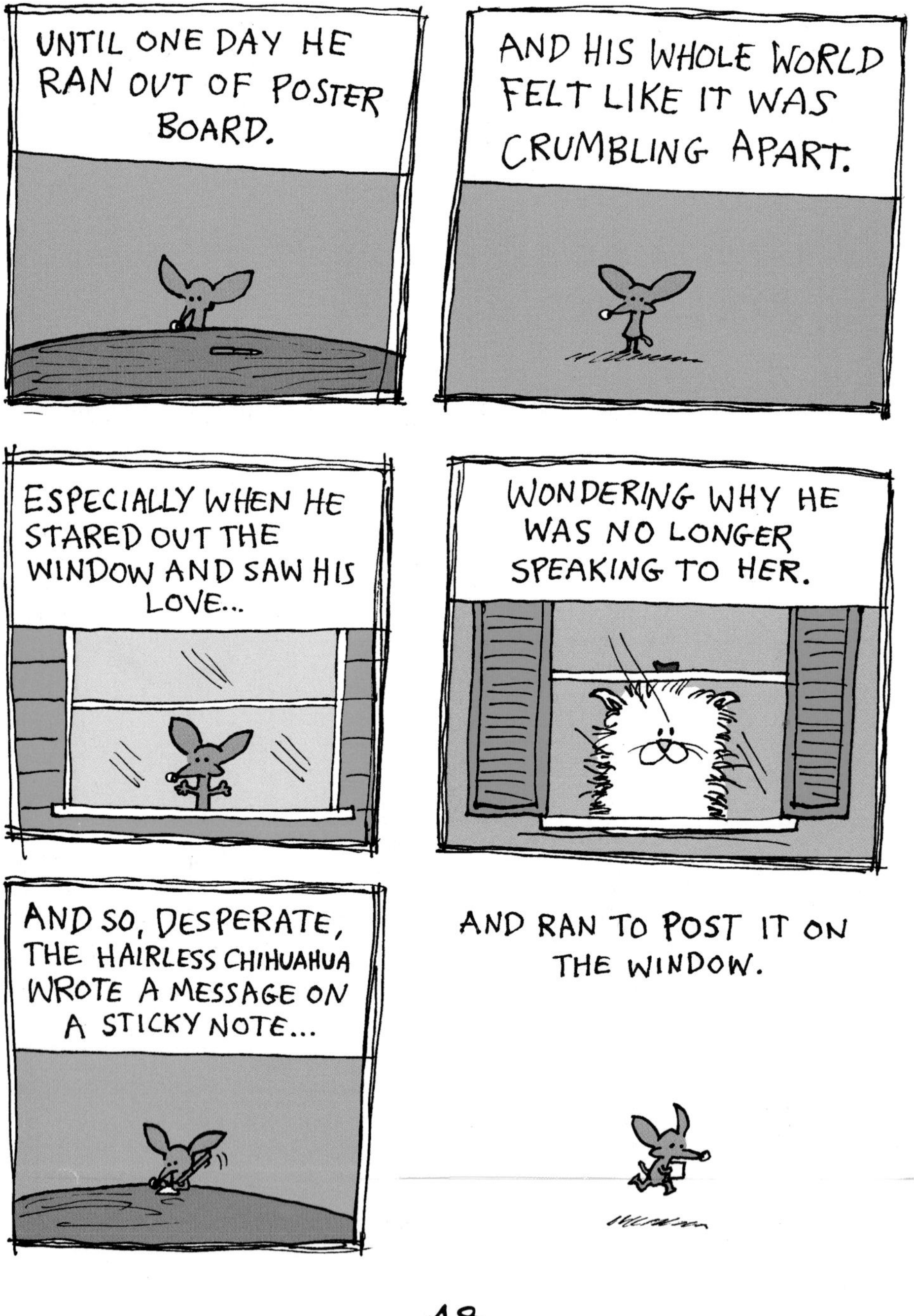
UNTIL ONE DAY HE RAN OUT OF POSTER BOARD.
AND HIS WHOLE WORLD FELT LIKE IT WAS CRUMBLING APART.
ESPECIALLY WHEN HE STARED OUT THE WINDOW AND SAW HIS LOVE...
WONDERING WHY HE WAS NO LONGER SPEAKING TO HER.
AND SO, DESPERATE, THE HAIRLESS CHIHUAHUA WROTE A MESSAGE ON A STICKY NOTE...
AND RAN TO POST IT ON THE WINDOW.

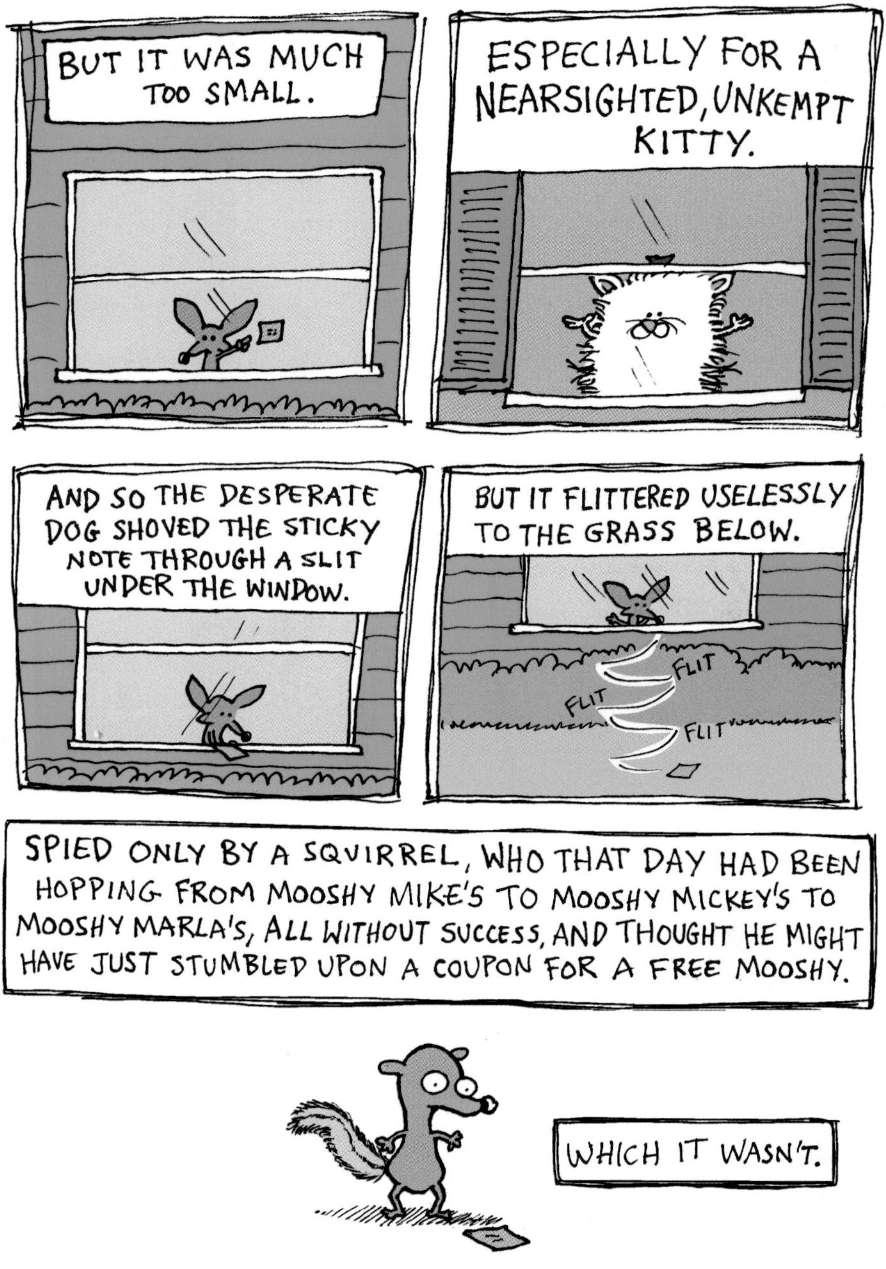
BUT IT WAS MUCH TOO SMALL.
ESPECIALLY FOR A NEARSIGHTED, UNKEMPT KITTY.
AND SO THE DESPERATE DOG SHOVED THE STICKY NOTE THROUGH A SLIT UNDER THE WINDOW.
BUT IT FLITTERED USELESSLY TO THE GRASS BELOW.
FLIT
FLIT
FLIT
SPIED ONLY BY A SQUIRREL, WHO THAT DAY HAD BEEN HOPPING FROM MOOSHY MIKE'S TO MOOSHY MICKEY'S TO MOOSHY MARLA'S, ALL WITHOUT SUCCESS, AND THOUGHT HE MIGHT HAVE JUST STUMBLED UPON A COUPON FOR A FREE MOOSHY.
WHICH IT WASN'T.

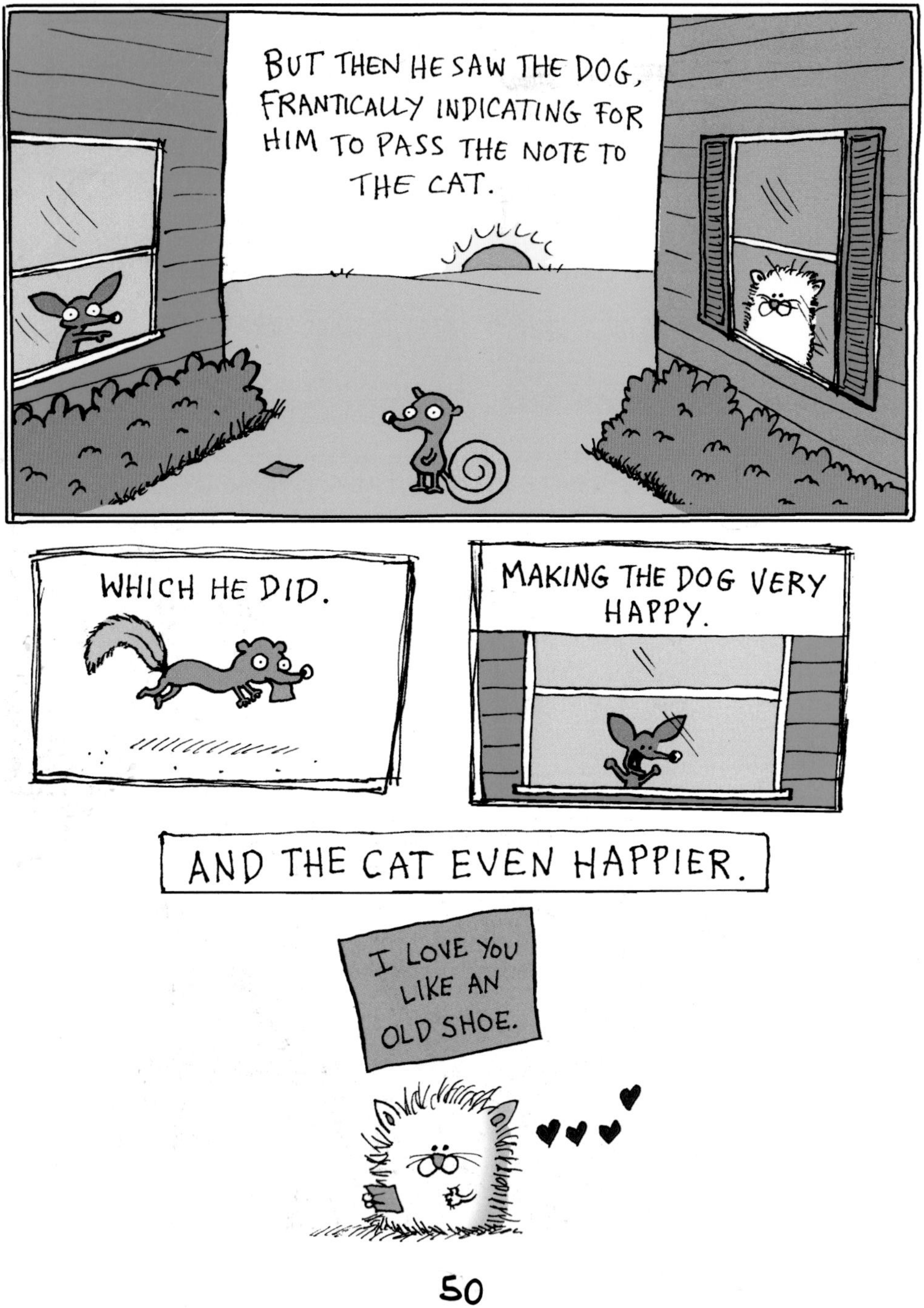
BUT THEN HE SAW THE DOG, FRANTICALLY INDICATING FOR HIM TO PASS THE NOTE TO THE CAT.
WHICH HE DID.
MAKING THE DOG VERY HAPPY.
AND THE CAT EVEN HAPPIER.
I LOVE YOU LIKE AN OLD SHOE.

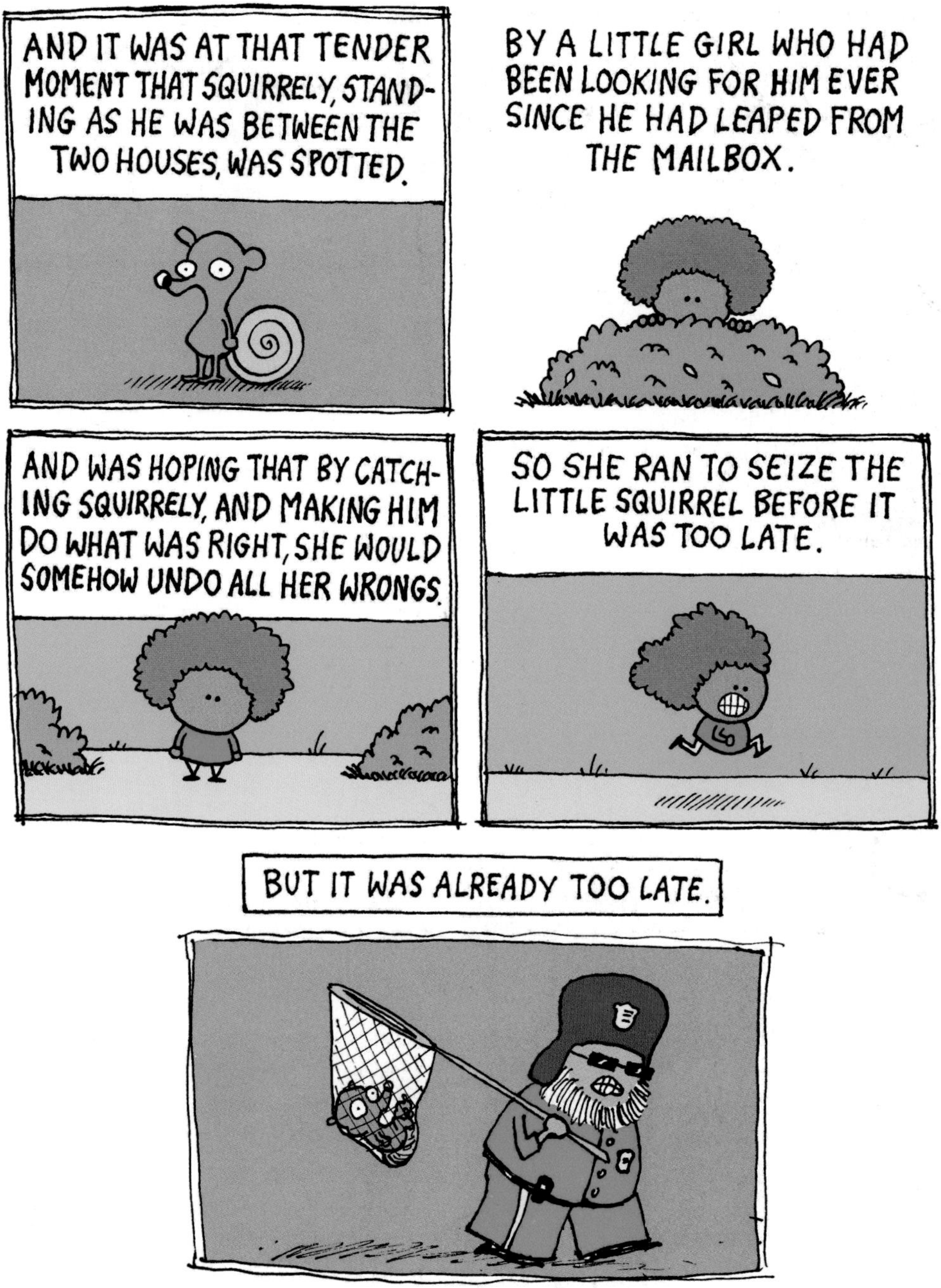
AND IT WAS AT THAT TENDER MOMENT THAT SQUIRRELY, STANDING AS HE WAS BETWEEN THE TWO HOUSES, WAS SPOTTED.
BY A LITTLE GIRL WHO HAD BEEN LOOKING FOR HIM EVER SINCE HE HAD LEAPED FROM THE MAILBOX.
AND WAS HOPING THAT BY CATCHING SQUIRRELY, AND MAKING HIM DO WHAT WAS RIGHT, SHE WOULD SOMEHOW UNDO ALL HER WRONGS.
SO SHE RAN TO SEIZE THE LITTLE SQUIRREL BEFORE IT WAS TOO LATE.
BUT IT WAS ALREADY TOO LATE.

CHAPTER FIVE

IN WHICH...

SO MANY SHOCKING THINGS HAPPEN THAT YOU MAY FAINT

(THIS BOOK)

(GUY WHO READ IT)

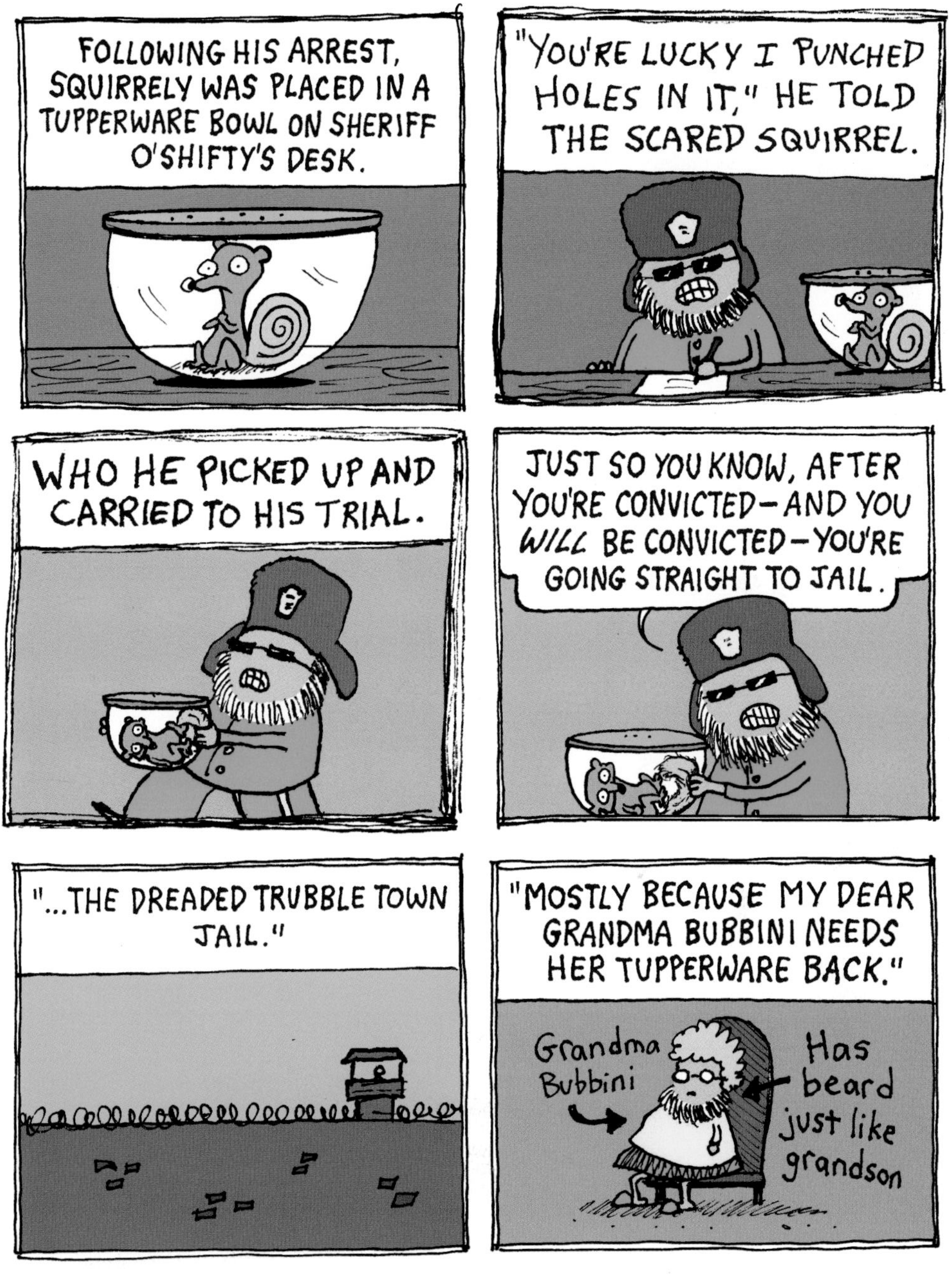
FOLLOWING HIS ARREST, SQUIRRELY WAS PLACED IN A TUPPERWARE BOWL ON SHERIFF O'SHIFTY'S DESK.
"YOU'RE LUCKY I PUNCHED HOLES IN IT," HE TOLD THE SCARED SQUIRREL.
WHO HE PICKED UP AND CARRIED TO HIS TRIAL.
JUST SO YOU KNOW, AFTER YOU'RE CONVICTED—AND YOU *WILL* BE CONVICTED—YOU'RE GOING STRAIGHT TO JAIL.
"...THE DREADED TRUBBLE TOWN JAIL."
"MOSTLY BECAUSE MY DEAR GRANDMA BUBBINI NEEDS HER TUPPERWARE BACK."
Grandma Bubbini
Has beard just like grandson

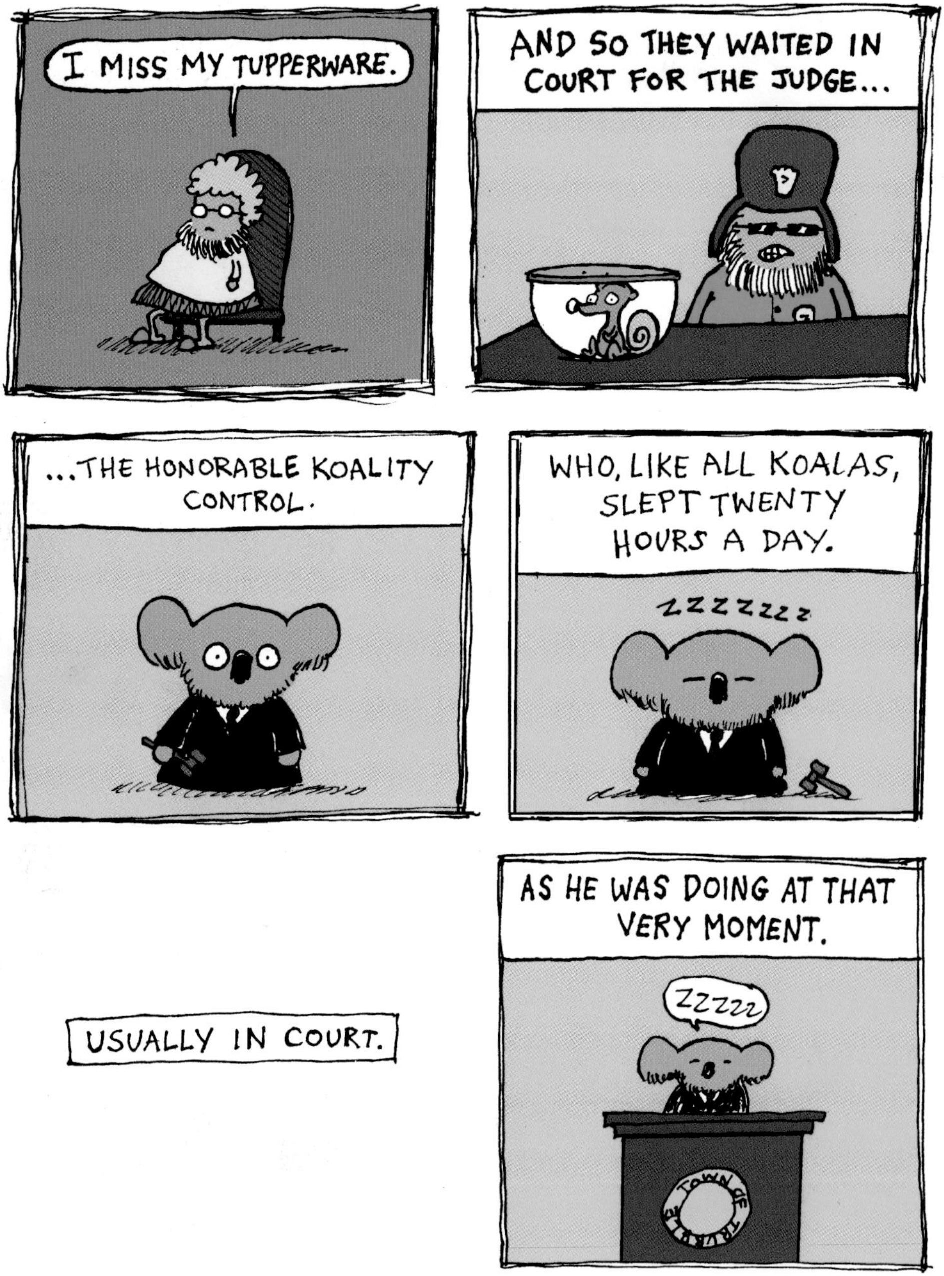
I MISS MY TUPPERWARE.
AND SO THEY WAITED IN COURT FOR THE JUDGE...
...THE HONORABLE KOALITY CONTROL.
WHO, LIKE ALL KOALAS, SLEPT TWENTY HOURS A DAY.
ZZZZZZZ
USUALLY IN COURT.
AS HE WAS DOING AT THAT VERY MOMENT.
ZZZZZ

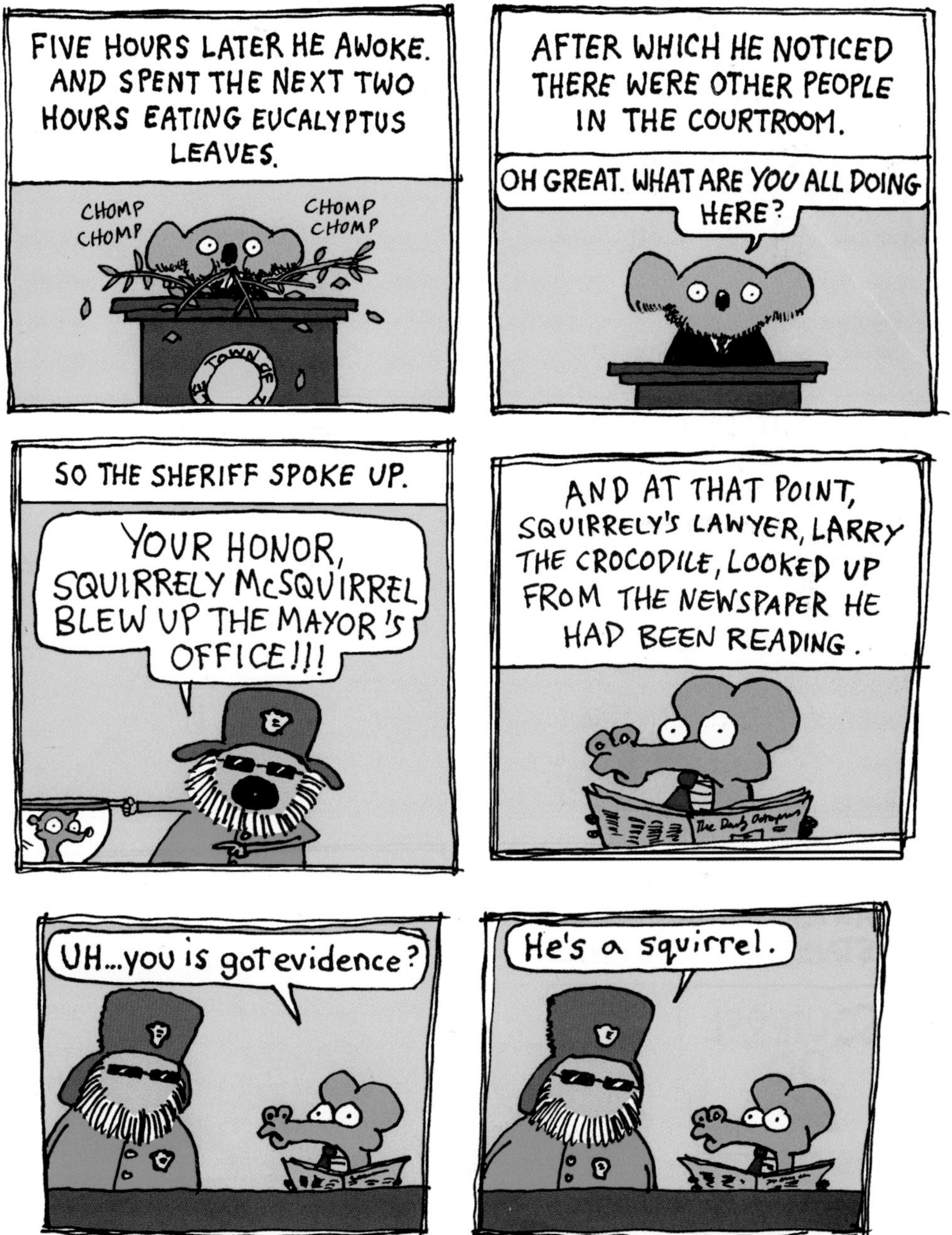
FIVE HOURS LATER HE AWOKE. AND SPENT THE NEXT TWO HOURS EATING EUCALYPTUS LEAVES.
CHOMP CHOMP
CHOMP CHOMP
TOWN OF
AFTER WHICH HE NOTICED THERE WERE OTHER PEOPLE IN THE COURTROOM.
OH GREAT. WHAT ARE YOU ALL DOING HERE?
SO THE SHERIFF SPOKE UP.
YOUR HONOR, SQUIRRELY McSQUIRREL BLEW UP THE MAYOR'S OFFICE!!!
AND AT THAT POINT, SQUIRRELY'S LAWYER, LARRY THE CROCODILE, LOOKED UP FROM THE NEWSPAPER HE HAD BEEN READING.
The Daily Octopus
UH...you is got evidence?
He's a squirrel.

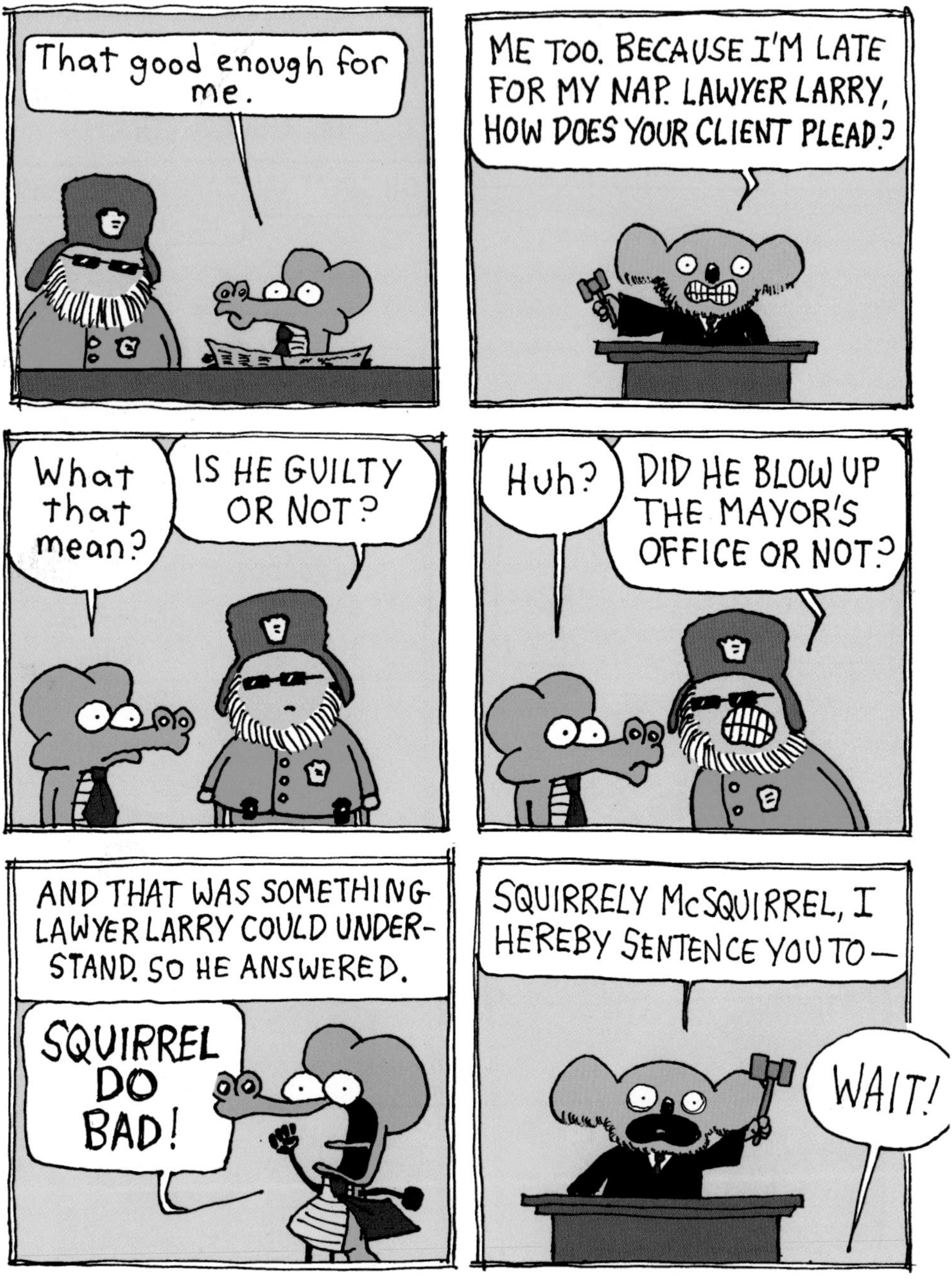
That good enough for me.
ME TOO. BECAUSE I'M LATE FOR MY NAP. LAWYER LARRY, HOW DOES YOUR CLIENT PLEAD?
What that mean?
IS HE GUILTY OR NOT?
Huh?
DID HE BLOW UP THE MAYOR'S OFFICE OR NOT?
AND THAT WAS SOMETHING LAWYER LARRY COULD UNDERSTAND. SO HE ANSWERED.
SQUIRREL DO BAD!
SQUIRRELY McSQUIRREL, I HEREBY SENTENCE YOU TO—
WAIT!

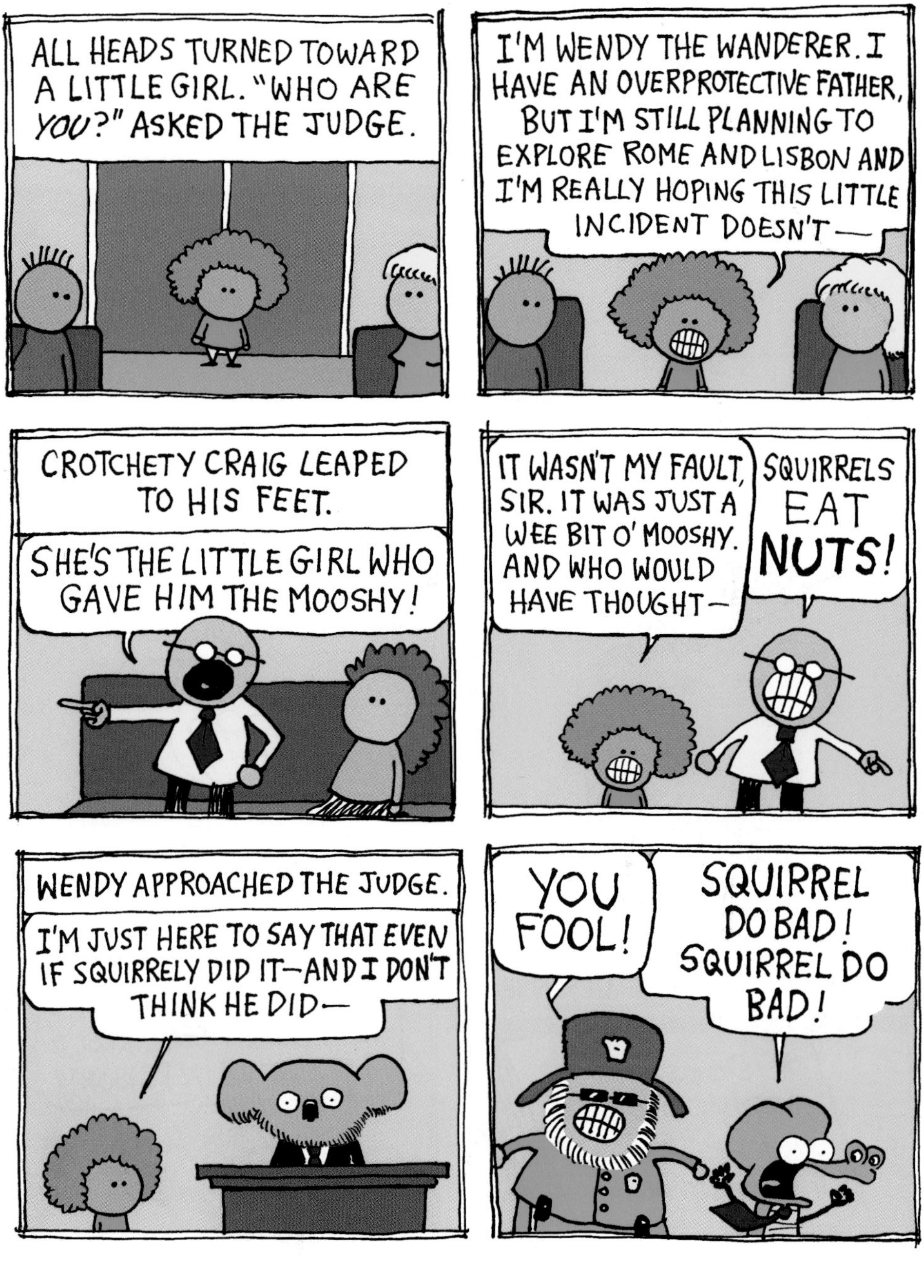
ALL HEADS TURNED TOWARD A LITTLE GIRL. "WHO ARE *YOU*?" ASKED THE JUDGE.
I'M WENDY THE WANDERER. I HAVE AN OVERPROTECTIVE FATHER, BUT I'M STILL PLANNING TO EXPLORE ROME AND LISBON AND I'M REALLY HOPING THIS LITTLE INCIDENT DOESN'T—
CROTCHETY CRAIG LEAPED TO HIS FEET.
SHE'S THE LITTLE GIRL WHO GAVE HIM THE MOOSHY!
IT WASN'T MY FAULT, SIR. IT WAS JUST A WEE BIT O' MOOSHY. AND WHO WOULD HAVE THOUGHT—
SQUIRRELS EAT **NUTS!**
WENDY APPROACHED THE JUDGE.
I'M JUST HERE TO SAY THAT EVEN IF SQUIRRELY DID IT—AND I DON'T THINK HE DID—
YOU FOOL!
SQUIRREL DO BAD! SQUIRREL DO BAD!

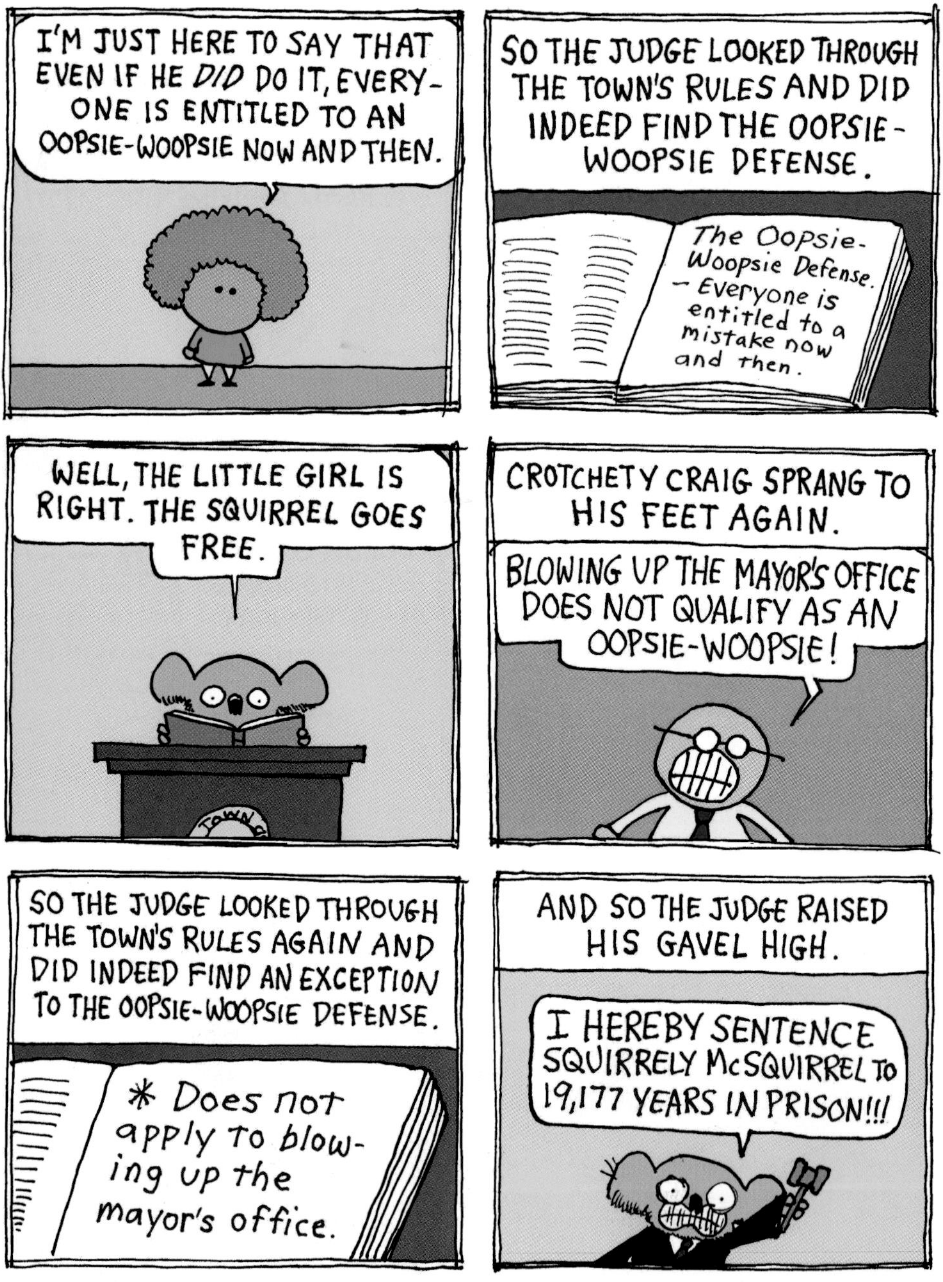
I'M JUST HERE TO SAY THAT EVEN IF HE *DID* DO IT, EVERYONE IS ENTITLED TO AN OOPSIE-WOOPSIE NOW AND THEN.
SO THE JUDGE LOOKED THROUGH THE TOWN'S RULES AND DID INDEED FIND THE OOPSIE-WOOPSIE DEFENSE.
The Oopsie-Woopsie Defense. - Everyone is entitled to a mistake now and then.
WELL, THE LITTLE GIRL IS RIGHT. THE SQUIRREL GOES FREE.
CROTCHETY CRAIG SPRANG TO HIS FEET AGAIN.
BLOWING UP THE MAYOR'S OFFICE DOES NOT QUALIFY AS AN OOPSIE-WOOPSIE!
SO THE JUDGE LOOKED THROUGH THE TOWN'S RULES AGAIN AND DID INDEED FIND AN EXCEPTION TO THE OOPSIE-WOOPSIE DEFENSE.
* Does not apply to blowing up the mayor's office.
AND SO THE JUDGE RAISED HIS GAVEL HIGH.
I HEREBY SENTENCE SQUIRRELY McSQUIRREL TO 19,177 YEARS IN PRISON!!!

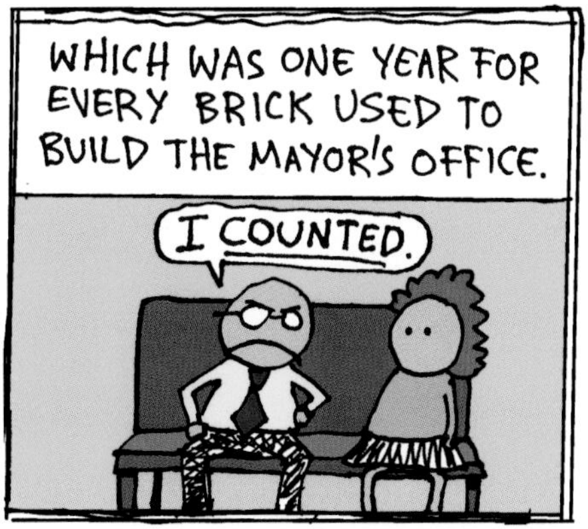
WHICH WAS ONE YEAR FOR EVERY BRICK USED TO BUILD THE MAYOR'S OFFICE.
I COUNTED.

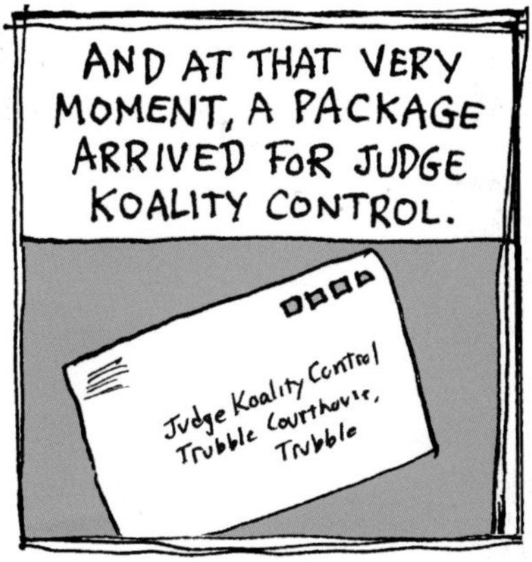
AND AT THAT VERY MOMENT, A PACKAGE ARRIVED FOR JUDGE KOALITY CONTROL.
Judge Koality Control
Trubble Courthouse,
Trubble

"IT'S ANOTHER BOMB!" SCREAMED THE GOOD PEOPLE OF TRUBBLE.

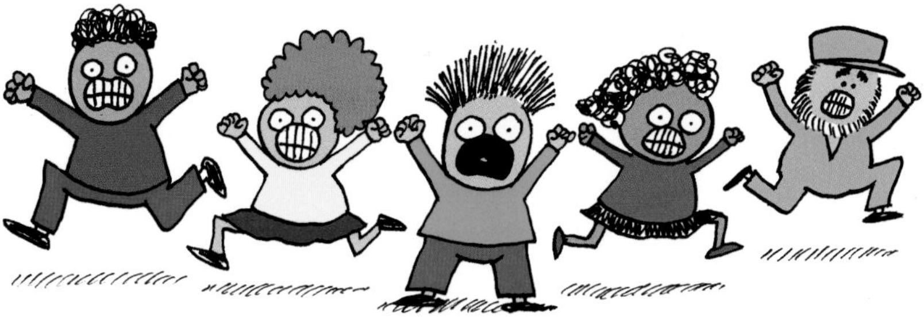

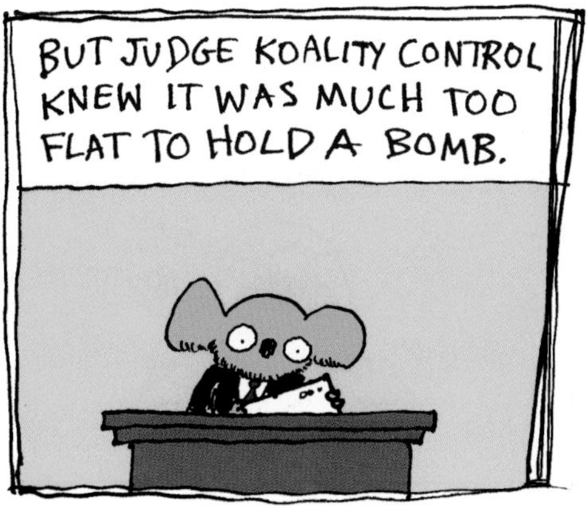
BUT JUDGE KOALITY CONTROL KNEW IT WAS MUCH TOO FLAT TO HOLD A BOMB.

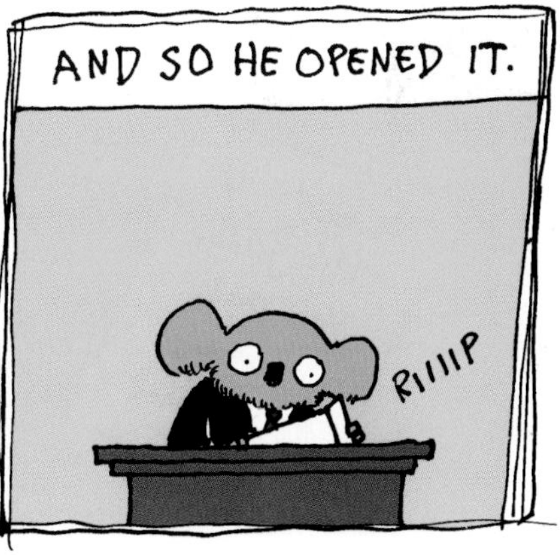
AND SO HE OPENED IT.
RIIIIP

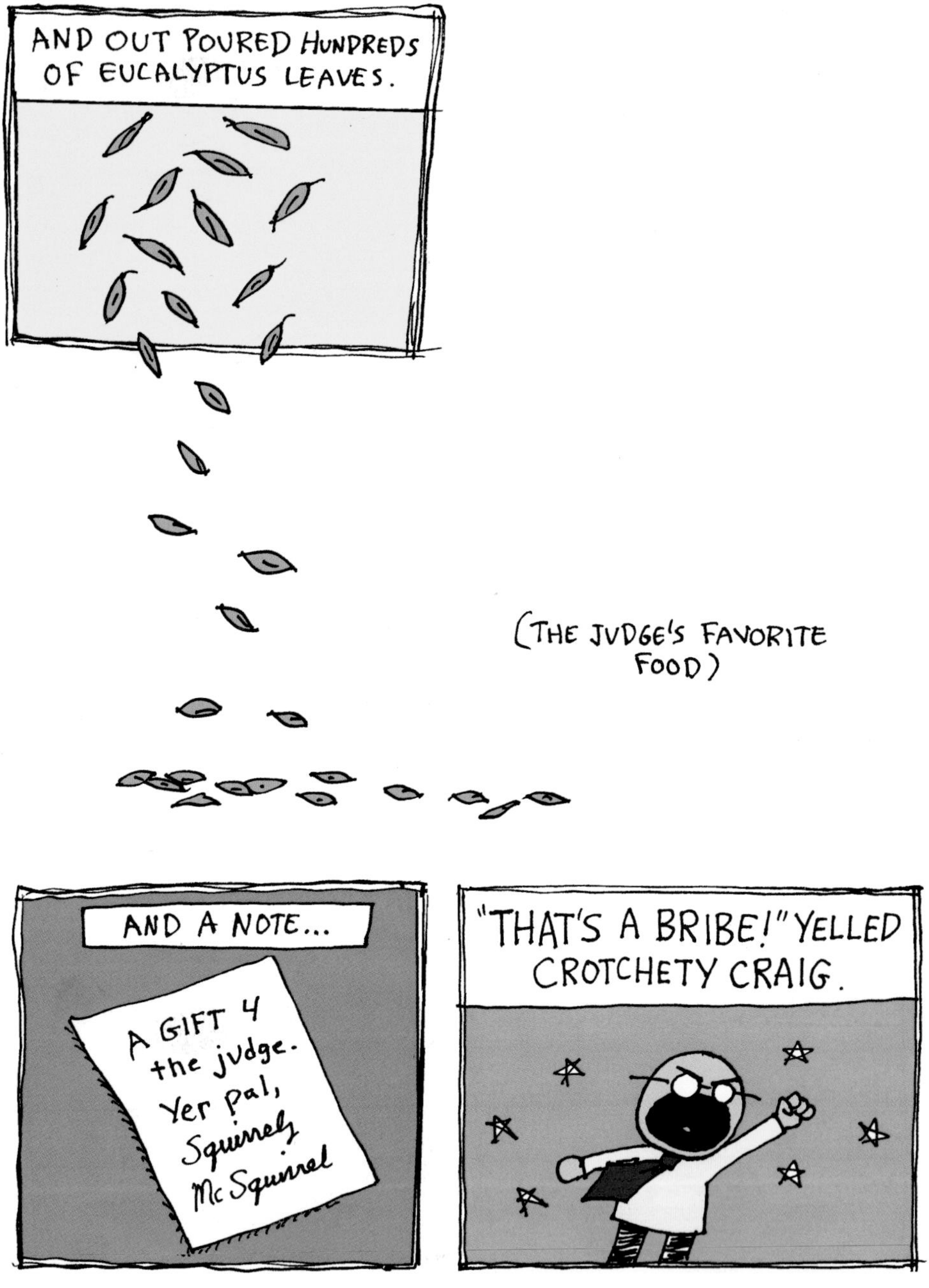
AND OUT POURED HUNDREDS OF EUCALYPTUS LEAVES.
(THE JUDGE'S FAVORITE FOOD)
AND A NOTE...
A GIFT 4 the judge. Yer pal, Squirrely McSquirrel
"THAT'S A BRIBE!" YELLED CROTCHETY CRAIG.

BUT SQUIRRELY McSQUIRREL HADN'T BRIBED ANYONE. IT WASN'T EVEN HIS HANDWRITING.

Rather, it was the handwriting of someone who just wanted to help Squirrely.

In return for the help Squirrely had given him.

AND SQUIRRELY McSQUIRREL WAS A FREE SQUIRREL.

CHAPTER FIVE AND A HALF

WHICH IS...

SUCH A SHORT CHAPTER, IT DOES NOT DESERVE A WHOLE NUMBER

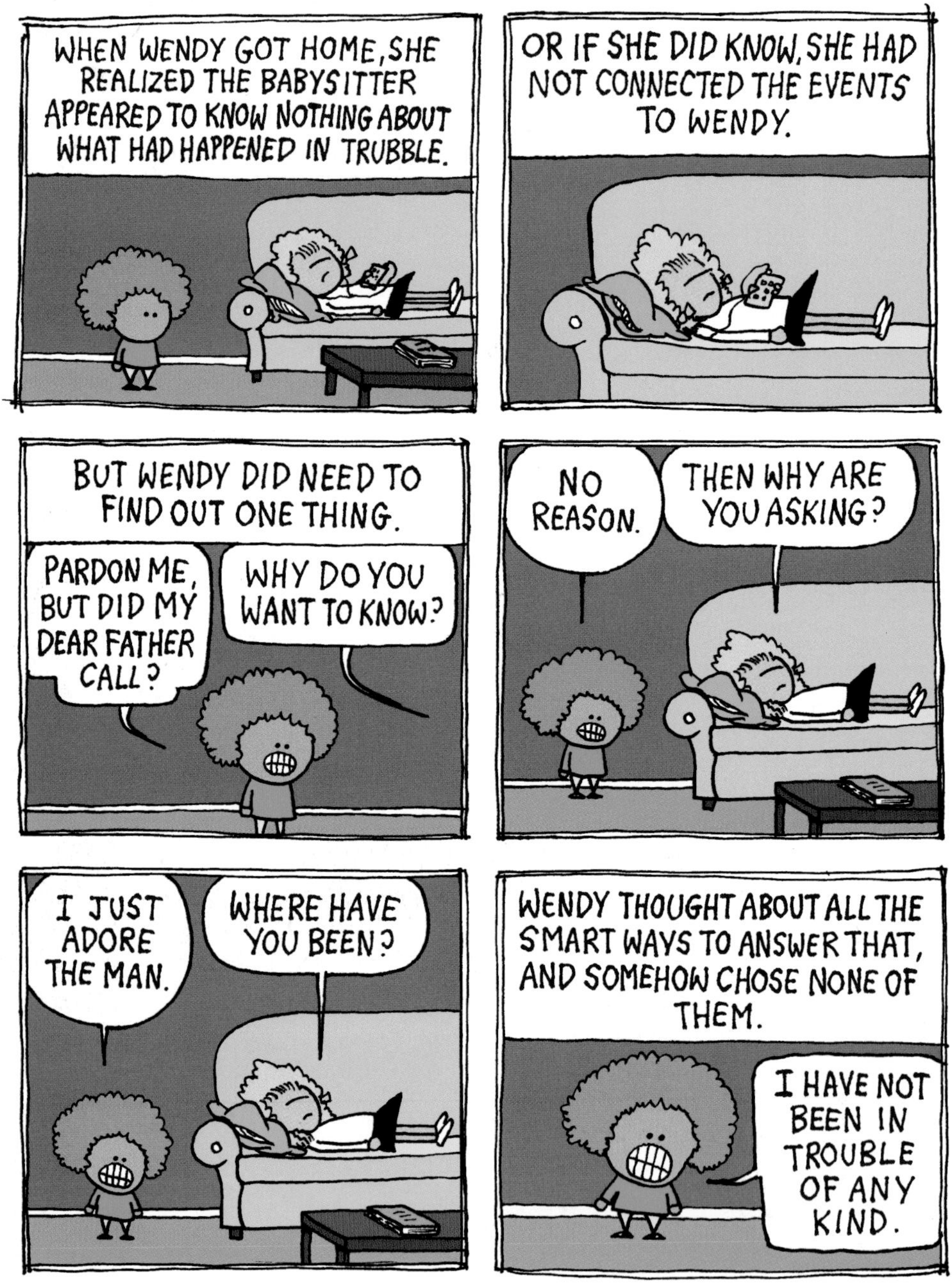

WHEN WENDY GOT HOME, SHE REALIZED THE BABYSITTER APPEARED TO KNOW NOTHING ABOUT WHAT HAD HAPPENED IN TRUBBLE.
OR IF SHE DID KNOW, SHE HAD NOT CONNECTED THE EVENTS TO WENDY.
BUT WENDY DID NEED TO FIND OUT ONE THING.
PARDON ME, BUT DID MY DEAR FATHER CALL?
WHY DO YOU WANT TO KNOW?
NO REASON.
THEN WHY ARE YOU ASKING?
I JUST ADORE THE MAN.
WHERE HAVE YOU BEEN?
WENDY THOUGHT ABOUT ALL THE SMART WAYS TO ANSWER THAT, AND SOMEHOW CHOSE NONE OF THEM.
I HAVE NOT BEEN IN TROUBLE OF ANY KIND.

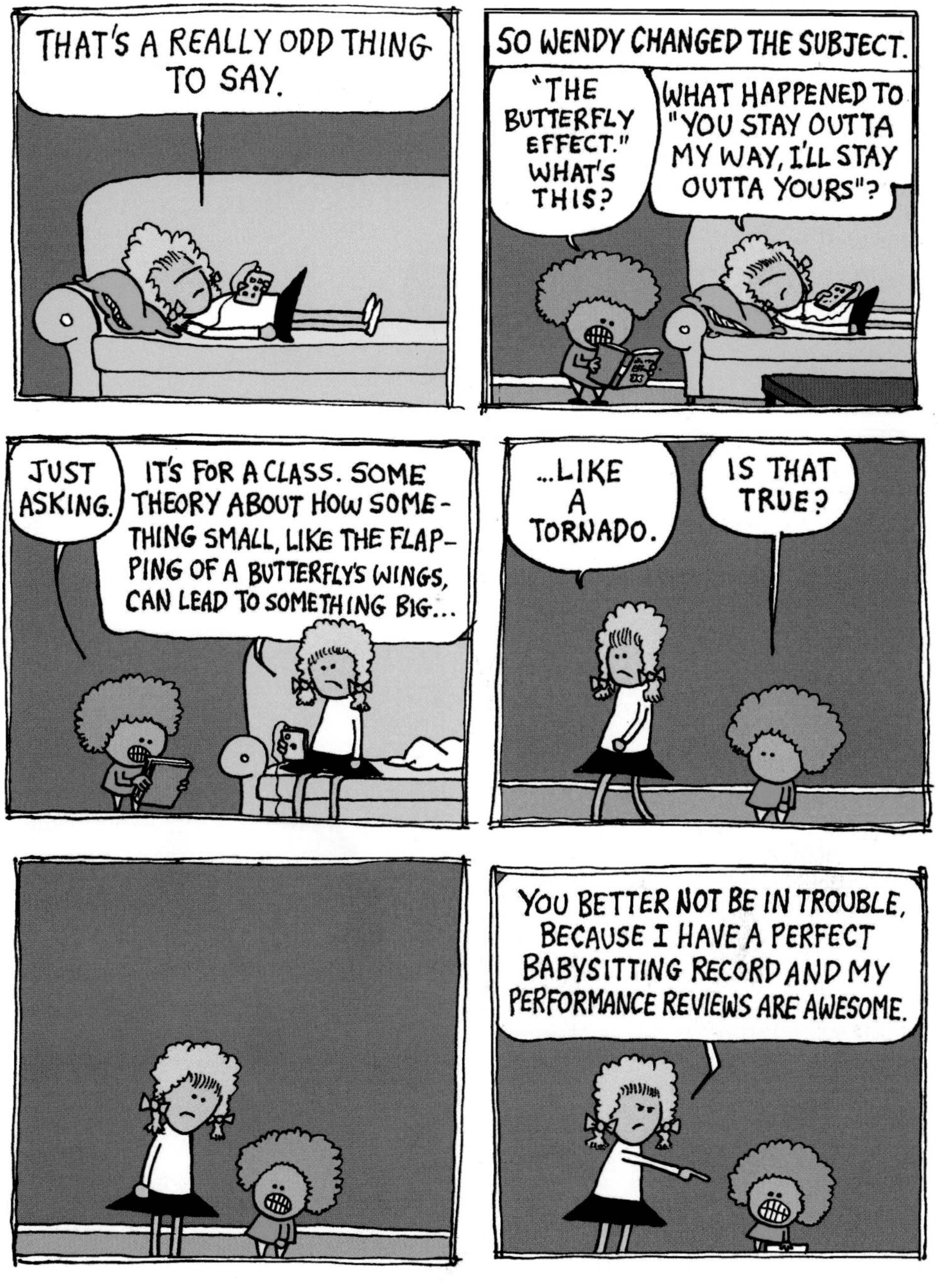
THAT'S A REALLY ODD THING TO SAY.
SO WENDY CHANGED THE SUBJECT.
"THE BUTTERFLY EFFECT." WHAT'S THIS?
WHAT HAPPENED TO "YOU STAY OUTTA MY WAY, I'LL STAY OUTTA YOURS"?
JUST ASKING.
IT'S FOR A CLASS. SOME THEORY ABOUT HOW SOMETHING SMALL, LIKE THE FLAPPING OF A BUTTERFLY'S WINGS, CAN LEAD TO SOMETHING BIG...
...LIKE A TORNADO.
IS THAT TRUE?
YOU BETTER NOT BE IN TROUBLE, BECAUSE I HAVE A PERFECT BABYSITTING RECORD AND MY PERFORMANCE REVIEWS ARE AWESOME.

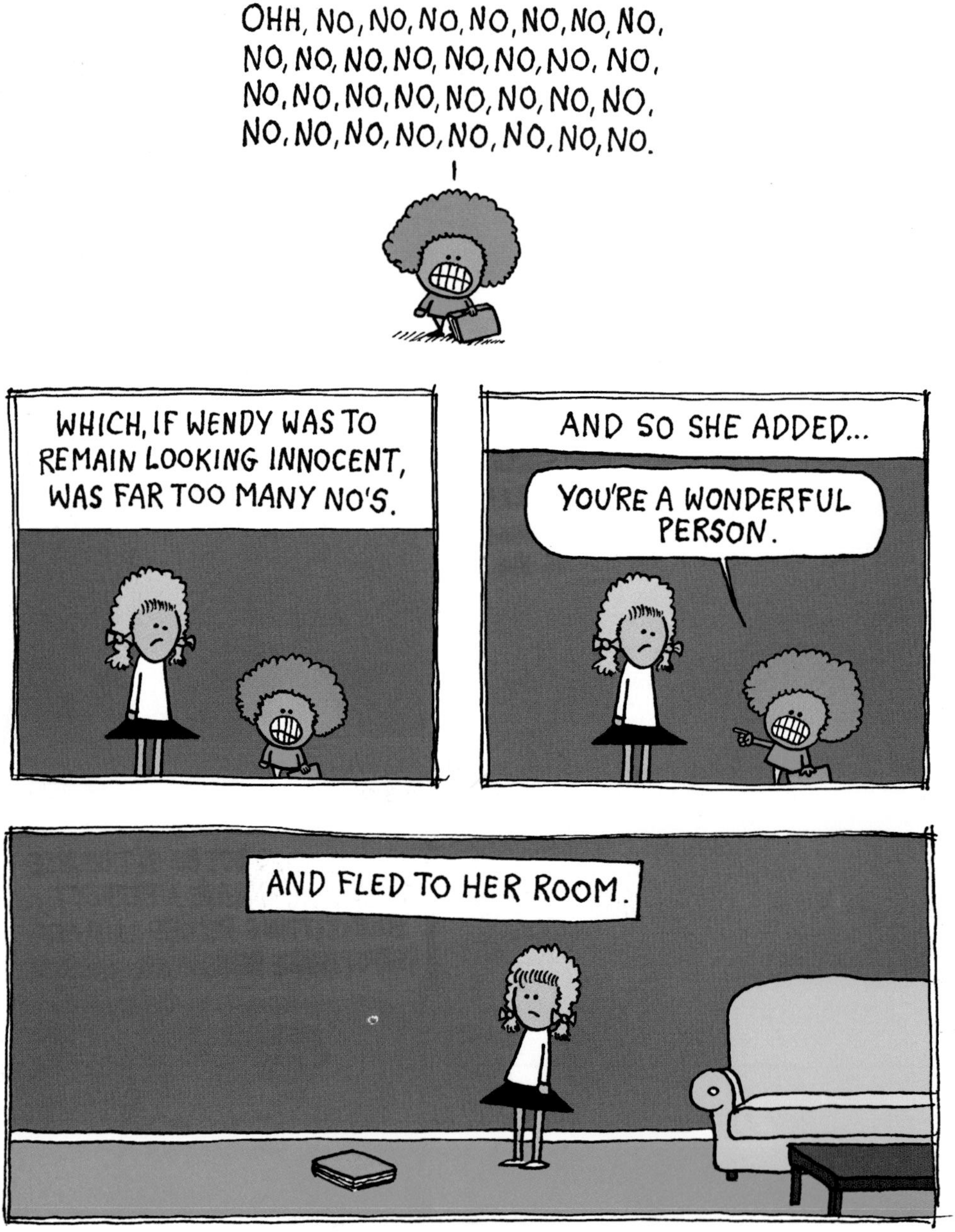
OHH, NO, NO, NO, NO, NO, NO, NO, NO, NO, NO, NO, NO, NO, NO, NO, NO, NO, NO, NO, NO, NO, NO, NO, NO, NO, NO, NO, NO, NO, NO, NO.
WHICH, IF WENDY WAS TO REMAIN LOOKING INNOCENT, WAS FAR TOO MANY NO'S.
AND SO SHE ADDED...
YOU'RE A WONDERFUL PERSON.
AND FLED TO HER ROOM.

CHAPTER SIX

IN WHICH...

YOU WILL READ THINGS

AND...

TURN PAGES

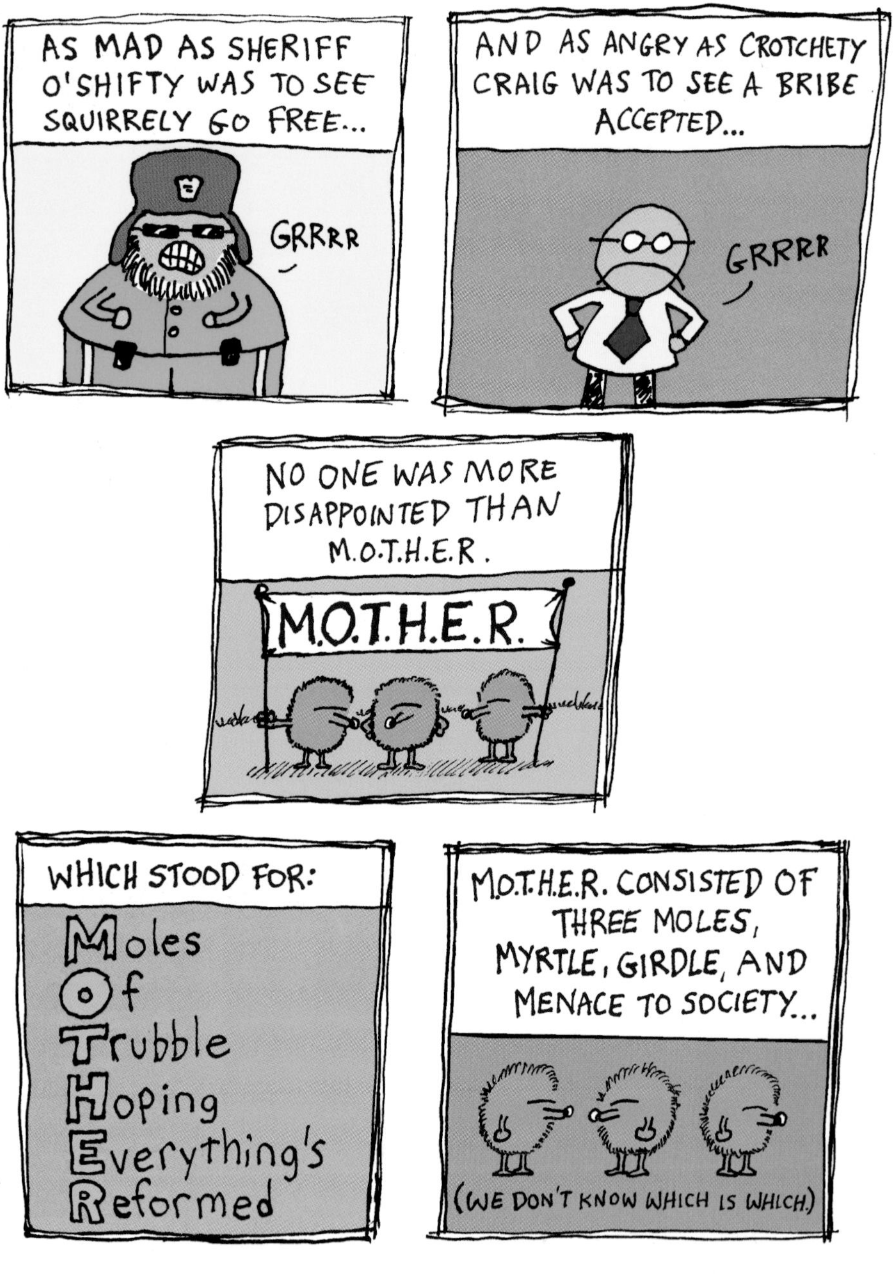
AS MAD AS SHERIFF O'SHIFTY WAS TO SEE SQUIRRELY GO FREE...
GRRRR
AND AS ANGRY AS CROTCHETY CRAIG WAS TO SEE A BRIBE ACCEPTED...
GRRRR
NO ONE WAS MORE DISAPPOINTED THAN M.O.T.H.E.R.
M.O.T.H.E.R.
WHICH STOOD FOR:
Moles
Of
Trubble
Hoping
Everything's
Reformed
M.O.T.H.E.R. CONSISTED OF THREE MOLES, MYRTLE, GIRDLE, AND MENACE TO SOCIETY...
(WE DON'T KNOW WHICH IS WHICH.)

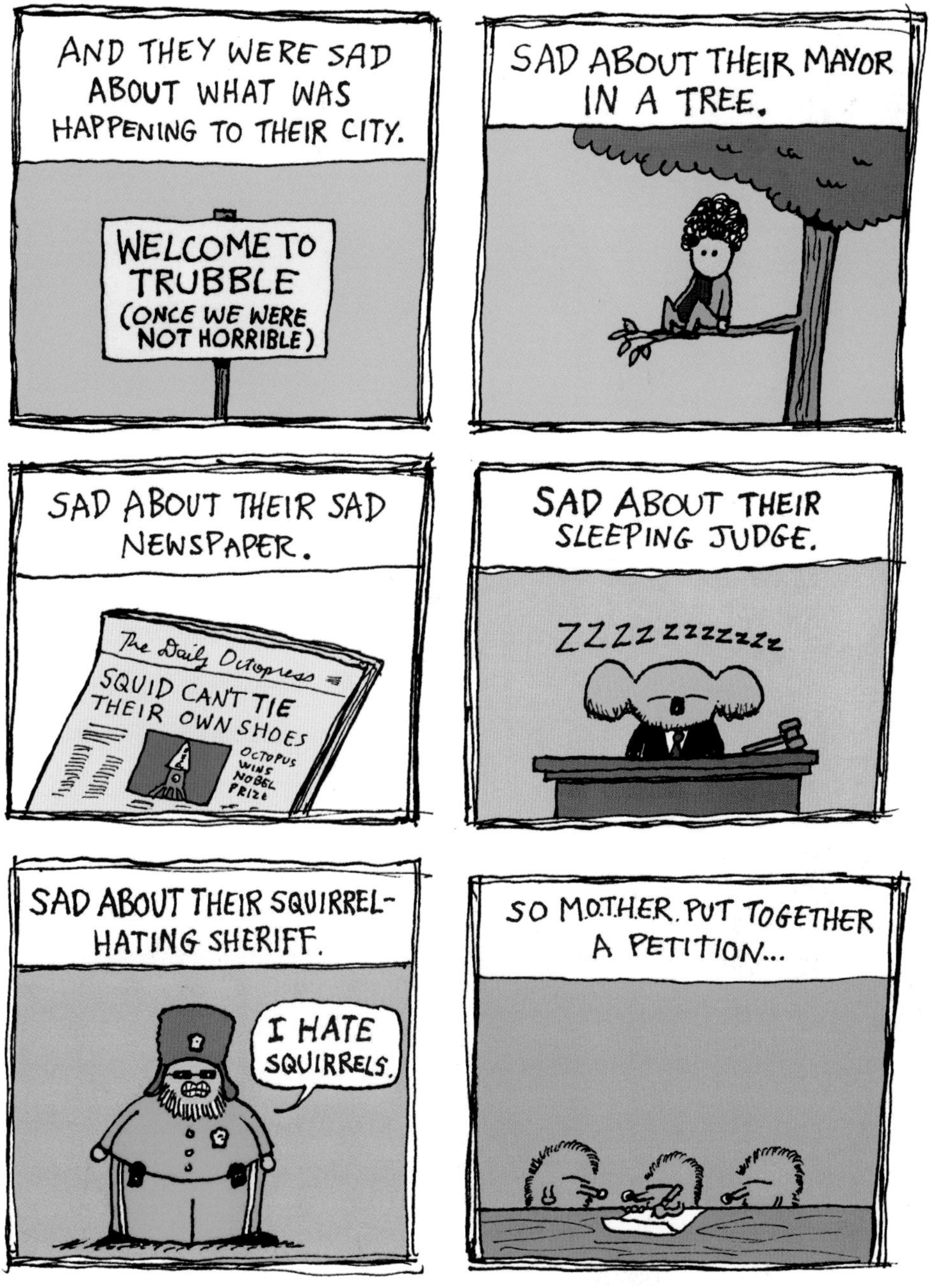
AND THEY WERE SAD ABOUT WHAT WAS HAPPENING TO THEIR CITY.
WELCOME TO TRUBBLE (ONCE WE WERE NOT HORRIBLE)
SAD ABOUT THEIR MAYOR IN A TREE.
SAD ABOUT THEIR SAD NEWSPAPER.
The Daily Octopress
SQUID CAN'T TIE THEIR OWN SHOES
OCTOPUS WINS NOBEL PRIZE
SAD ABOUT THEIR SLEEPING JUDGE.
ZZZZZZZZZZ
SAD ABOUT THEIR SQUIRREL-HATING SHERIFF.
I HATE SQUIRRELS.
SO M.O.T.H.E.R. PUT TOGETHER A PETITION...

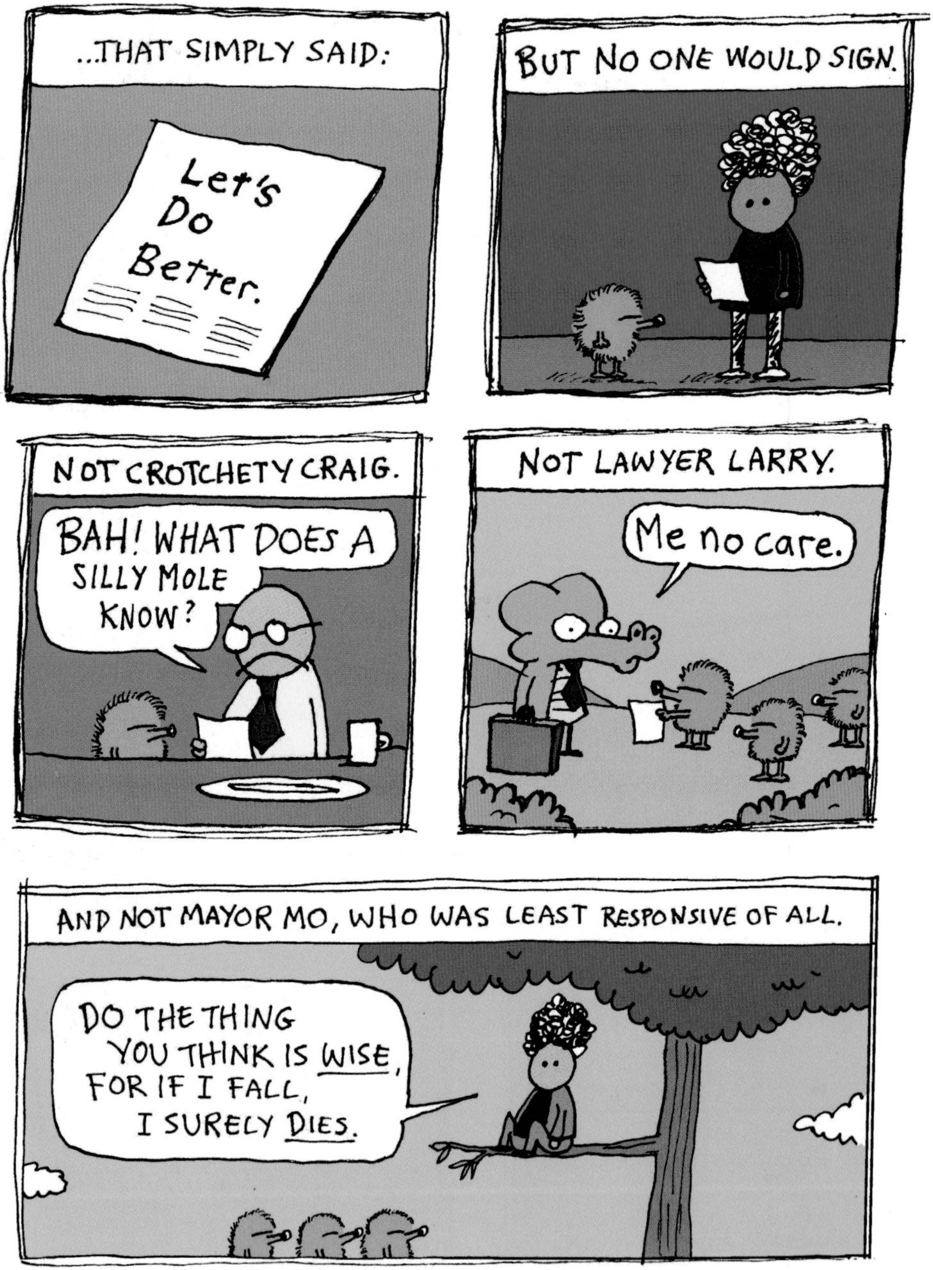
...THAT SIMPLY SAID:
Let's Do Better.
BUT NO ONE WOULD SIGN.
NOT CROTCHETY CRAIG.
BAH! WHAT DOES A SILLY MOLE KNOW?
NOT LAWYER LARRY.
Me no care.
AND NOT MAYOR MO, WHO WAS LEAST RESPONSIVE OF ALL.
DO THE THING YOU THINK IS WISE, FOR IF I FALL, I SURELY DIES.

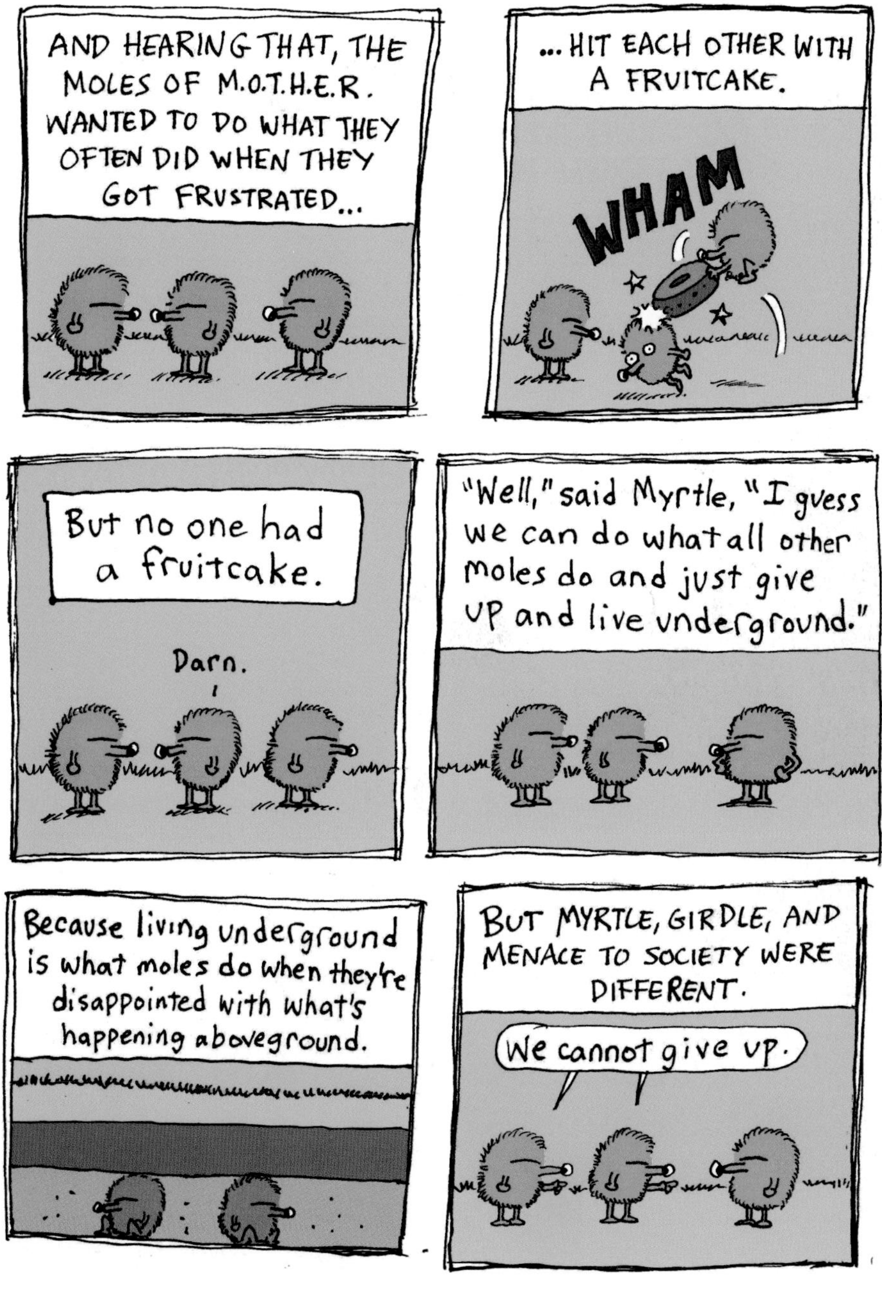
AND HEARING THAT, THE MOLES OF M.O.T.H.E.R. WANTED TO DO WHAT THEY OFTEN DID WHEN THEY GOT FRUSTRATED...
...HIT EACH OTHER WITH A FRUITCAKE.
WHAM
But no one had a fruitcake.
Darn.
"Well," said Myrtle, "I guess we can do what all other moles do and just give up and live underground."
Because living underground is what moles do when they're disappointed with what's happening aboveground.
BUT MYRTLE, GIRDLE, AND MENACE TO SOCIETY WERE DIFFERENT.
We cannot give up.

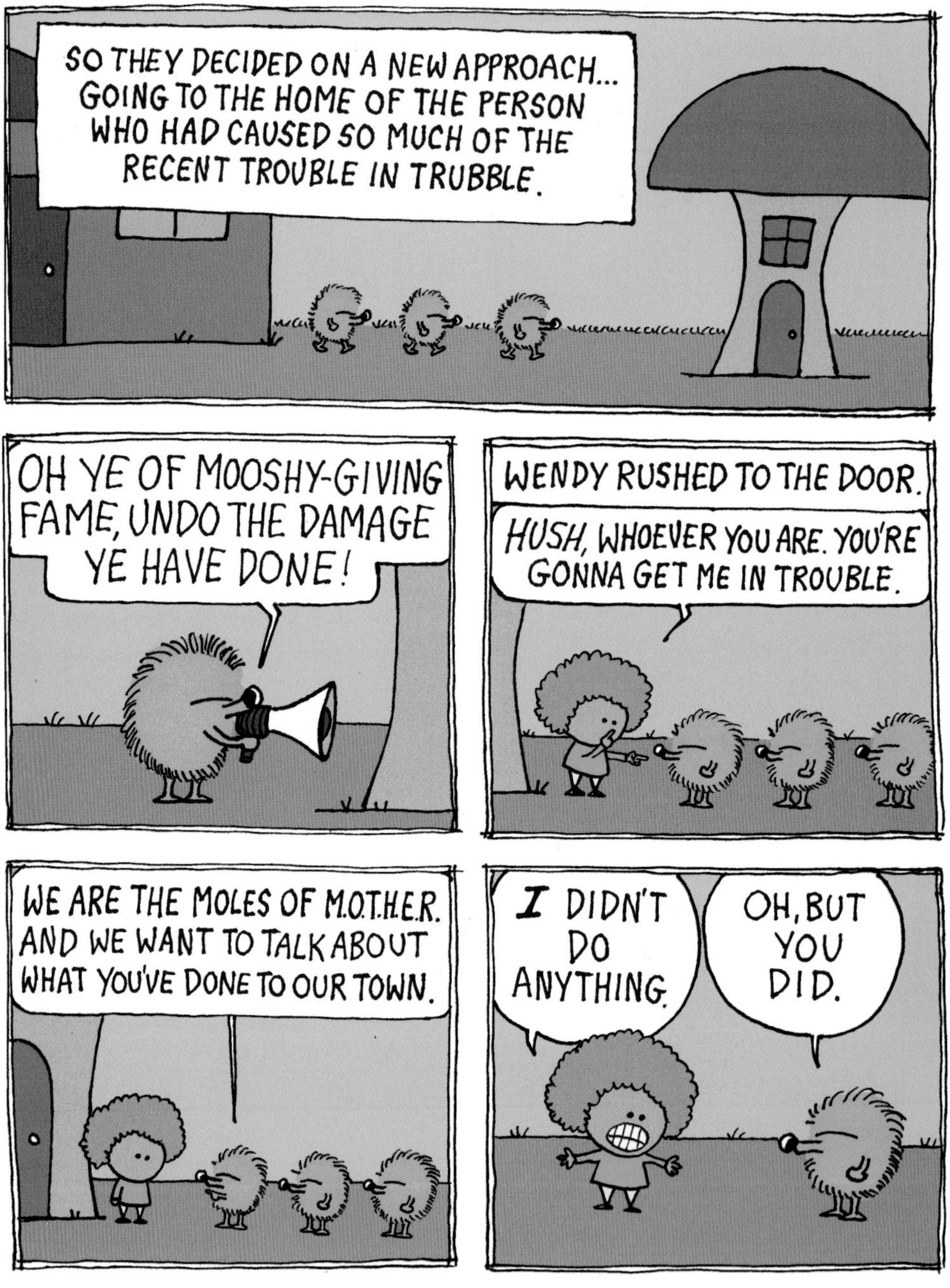
SO THEY DECIDED ON A NEW APPROACH... GOING TO THE HOME OF THE PERSON WHO HAD CAUSED SO MUCH OF THE RECENT TROUBLE IN TRUBBLE.
OH YE OF MOOSHY-GIVING FAME, UNDO THE DAMAGE YE HAVE DONE!
WENDY RUSHED TO THE DOOR.
HUSH, WHOEVER YOU ARE. YOU'RE GONNA GET ME IN TROUBLE.
WE ARE THE MOLES OF M.O.T.H.E.R. AND WE WANT TO TALK ABOUT WHAT YOU'VE DONE TO OUR TOWN.
I DIDN'T DO ANYTHING.
OH, BUT YOU DID.

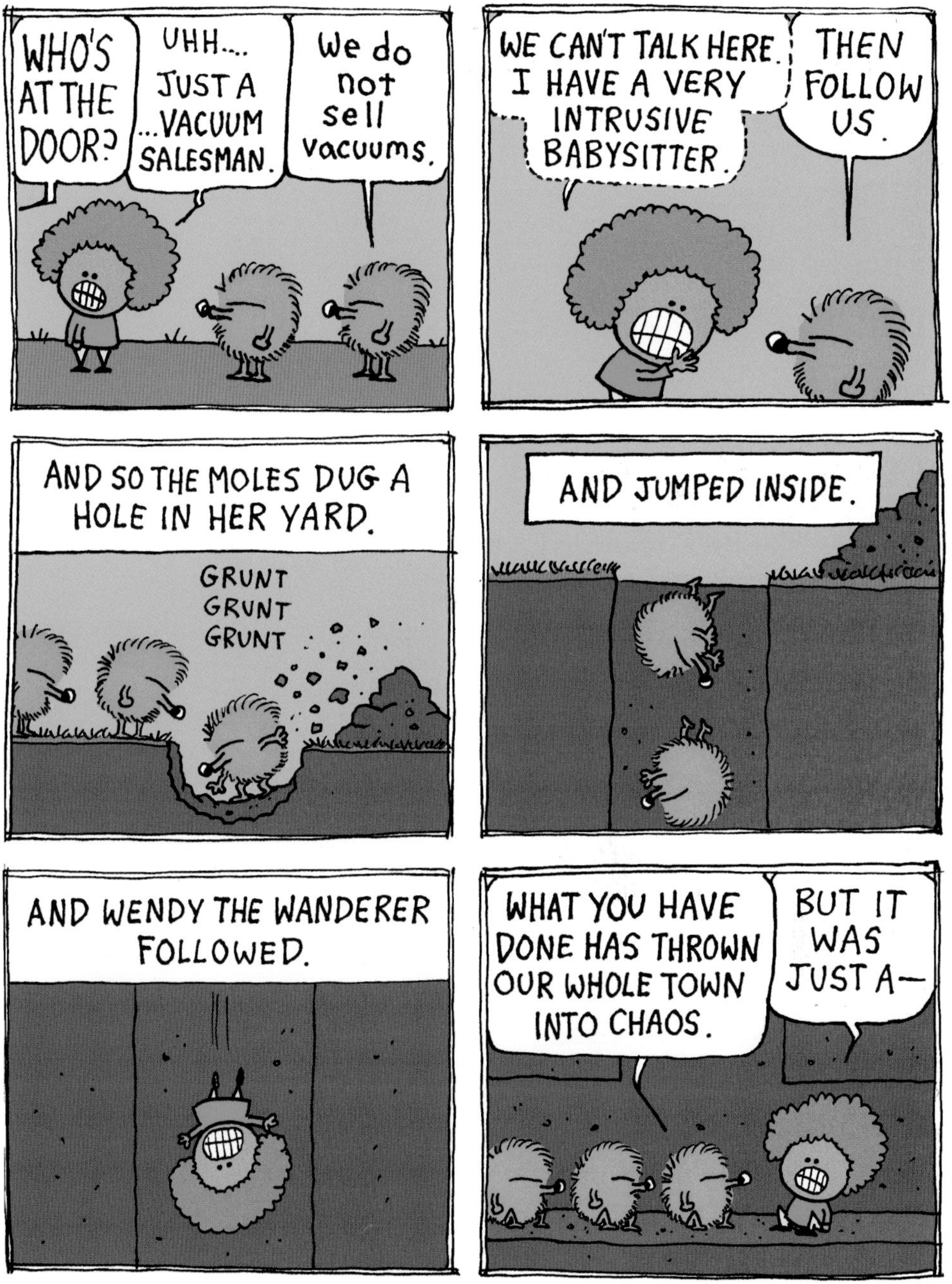
WHO'S AT THE DOOR?
UHH.... JUST A ...VACUUM SALESMAN.
We do not sell vacuums.
WE CAN'T TALK HERE. I HAVE A VERY INTRUSIVE BABYSITTER.
THEN FOLLOW US.
AND SO THE MOLES DUG A HOLE IN HER YARD.
GRUNT
GRUNT
GRUNT
AND JUMPED INSIDE.
AND WENDY THE WANDERER FOLLOWED.
WHAT YOU HAVE DONE HAS THROWN OUR WHOLE TOWN INTO CHAOS.
BUT IT WAS JUST A—

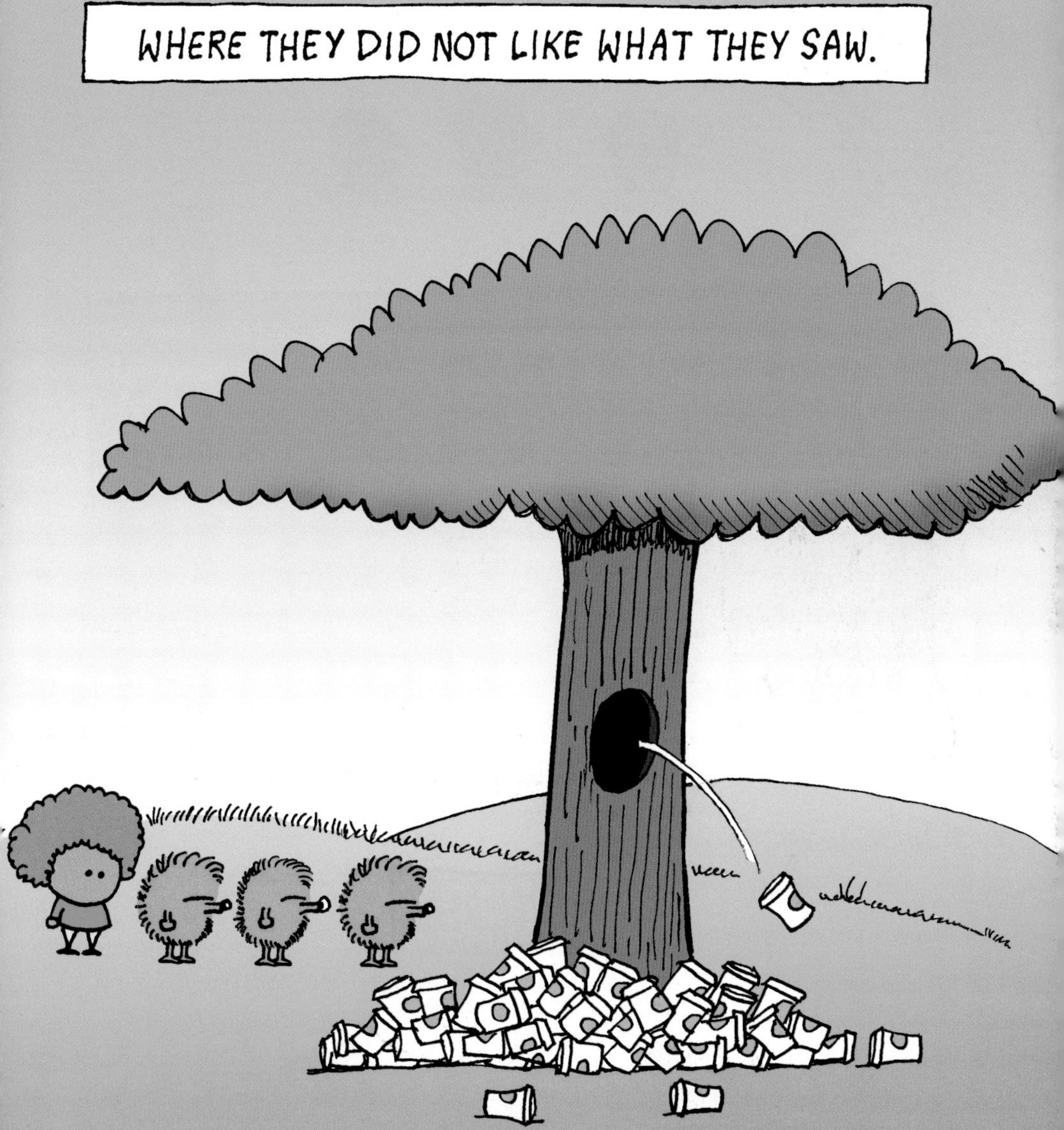
WHERE THEY DID NOT LIKE WHAT THEY SAW.

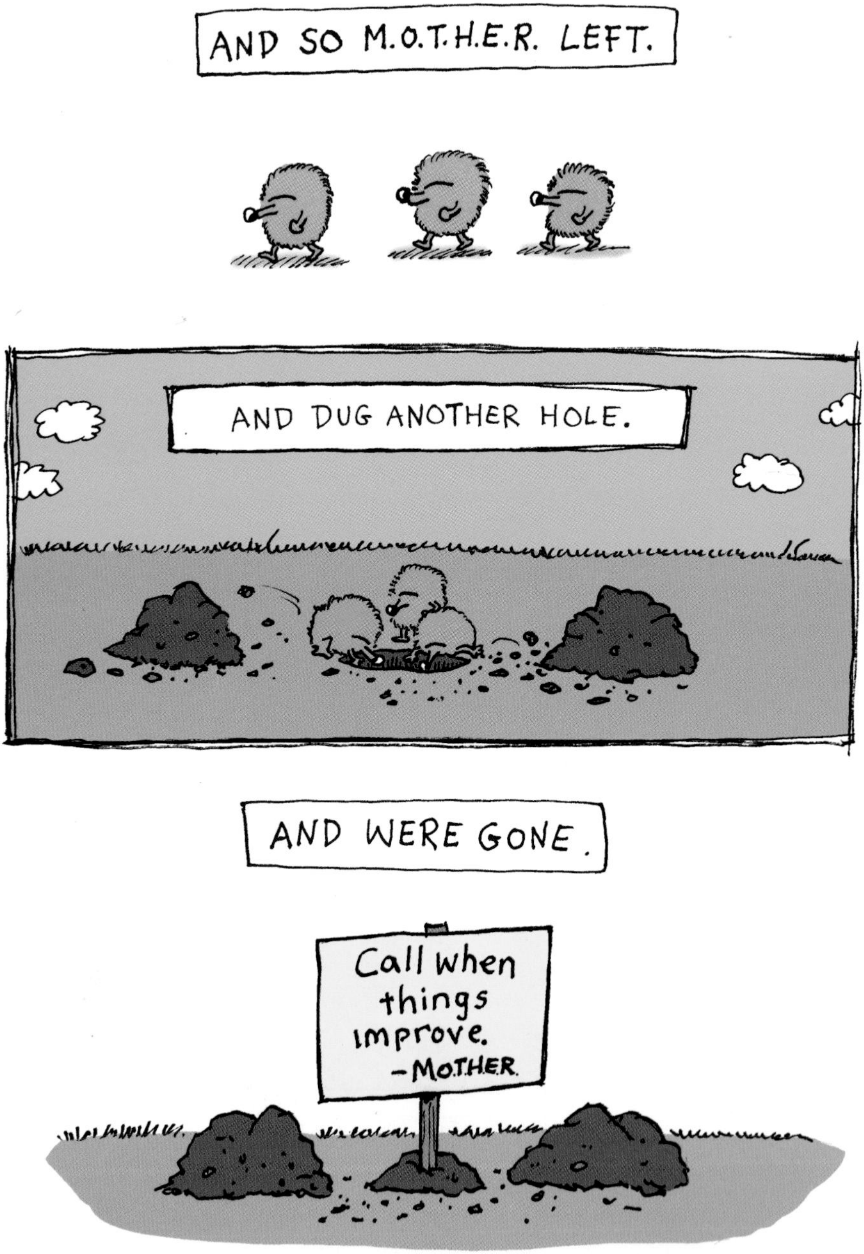
AND SO M.O.T.H.E.R. LEFT.
AND DUG ANOTHER HOLE.
AND WERE GONE.
Call when things improve. -MO.T.HE.R.

CHAPTER 7

IN WHICH...

YOU WILL GET THAT MUCH CLOSER TO CHAPTER EIGHT

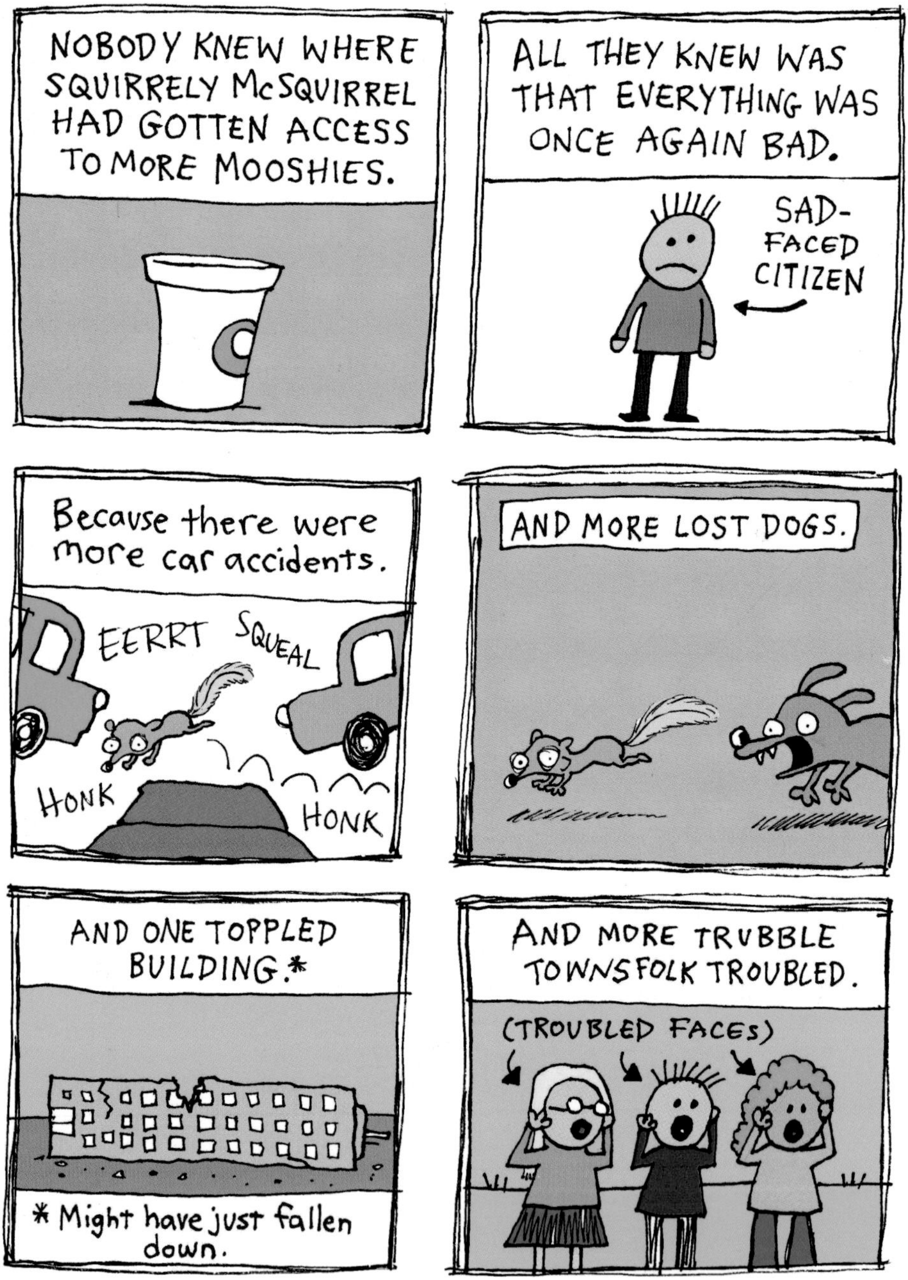
NOBODY KNEW WHERE SQUIRRELY McSQUIRREL HAD GOTTEN ACCESS TO MORE MOOSHIES.
ALL THEY KNEW WAS THAT EVERYTHING WAS ONCE AGAIN BAD.
SAD-FACED CITIZEN
Because there were more car accidents.
EERRT
SQUEAL
HONK
HONK
AND MORE LOST DOGS.
AND ONE TOPPLED BUILDING.*
* Might have just fallen down.
AND MORE TRUBBLE TOWNSFOLK TROUBLED.
(TROUBLED FACES)

79

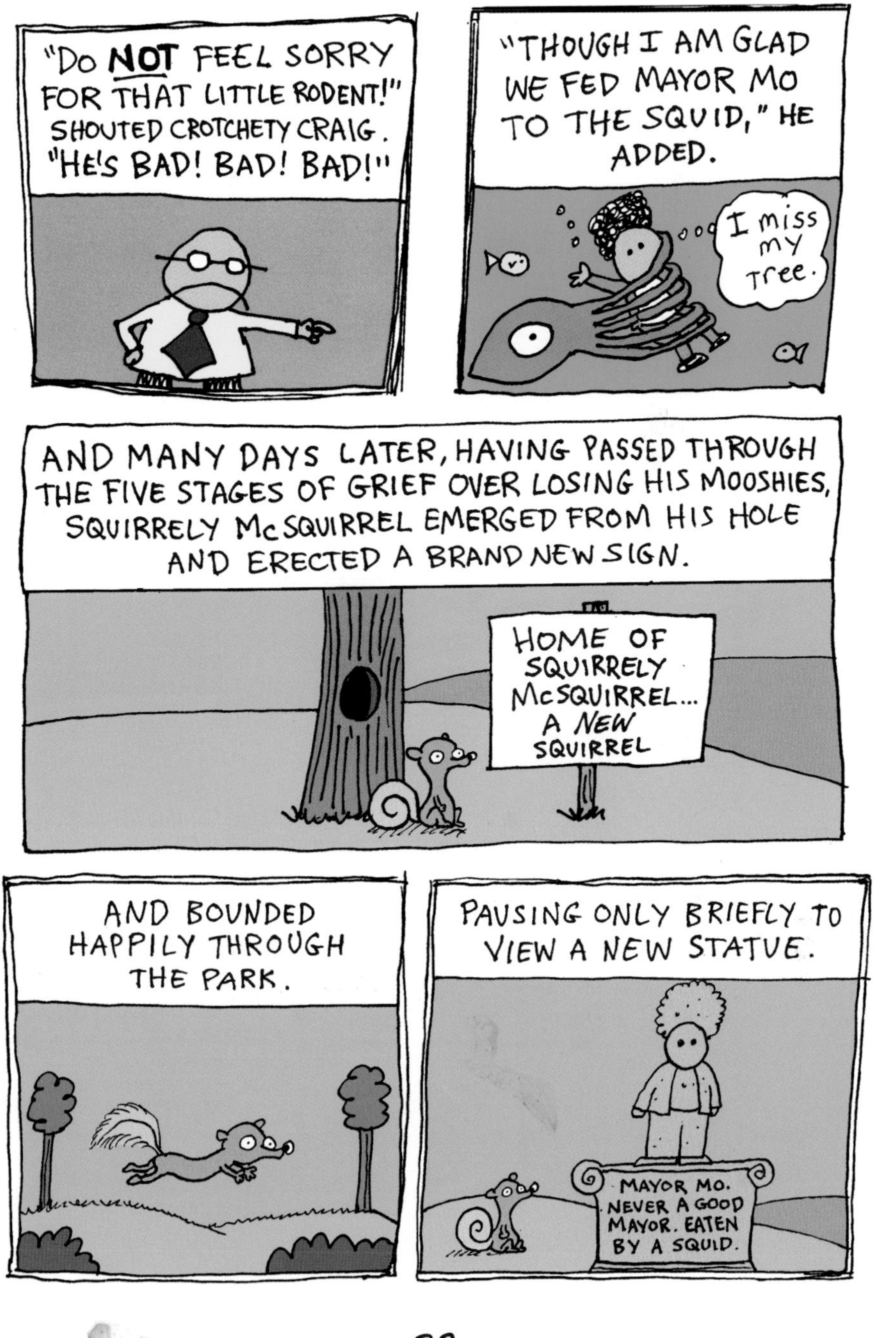
"DO NOT FEEL SORRY FOR THAT LITTLE RODENT!" SHOUTED CROTCHETY CRAIG. "HE'S BAD! BAD! BAD!"
"THOUGH I AM GLAD WE FED MAYOR MO TO THE SQUID," HE ADDED.
I miss my Tree.
AND MANY DAYS LATER, HAVING PASSED THROUGH THE FIVE STAGES OF GRIEF OVER LOSING HIS MOOSHIES, SQUIRRELY McSQUIRREL EMERGED FROM HIS HOLE AND ERECTED A BRAND NEW SIGN.
HOME OF SQUIRRELY McSQUIRREL... A NEW SQUIRREL
AND BOUNDED HAPPILY THROUGH THE PARK.
PAUSING ONLY BRIEFLY TO VIEW A NEW STATUE.
MAYOR MO. NEVER A GOOD MAYOR. EATEN BY A SQUID.

AND ANOTHER NEW STATUE.

TO THE SQUID... THANK YOU!

AND HAPPY, HE TOOK A RESTFUL NAP.

ZZZZ ZZZ

DREAMING OF THE CHRISTMAS SWEATERS HE WOULD SOON MAKE FOR EVERYONE.

A TRIBUTE TO THE ENTIRE TOWN.

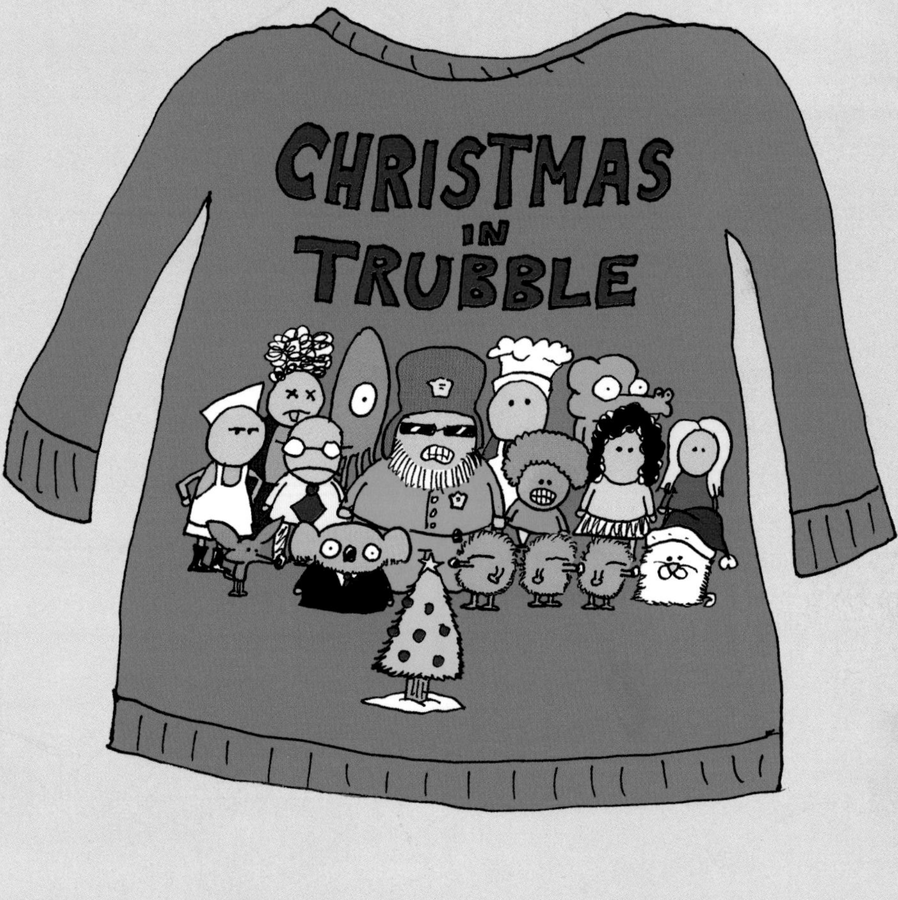
CHRISTMAS
IN
TRUBBLE

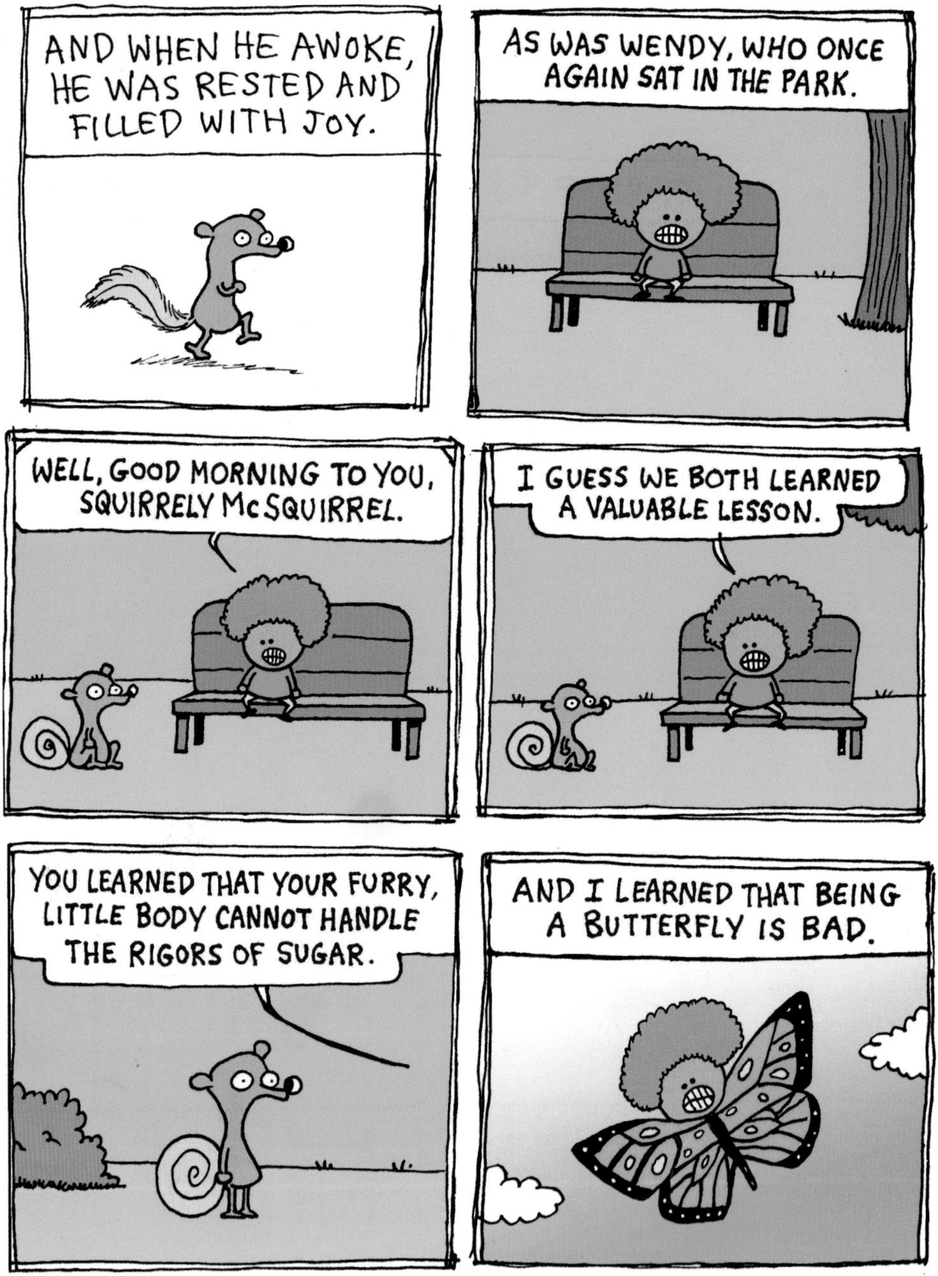
AND WHEN HE AWOKE, HE WAS RESTED AND FILLED WITH JOY.
AS WAS WENDY, WHO ONCE AGAIN SAT IN THE PARK.
WELL, GOOD MORNING TO YOU, SQUIRRELY McSQUIRREL.
I GUESS WE BOTH LEARNED A VALUABLE LESSON.
YOU LEARNED THAT YOUR FURRY, LITTLE BODY CANNOT HANDLE THE RIGORS OF SUGAR.
AND I LEARNED THAT BEING A BUTTERFLY IS BAD.

AND EVERY CAFÉ IN TOWN
EXPLODED.

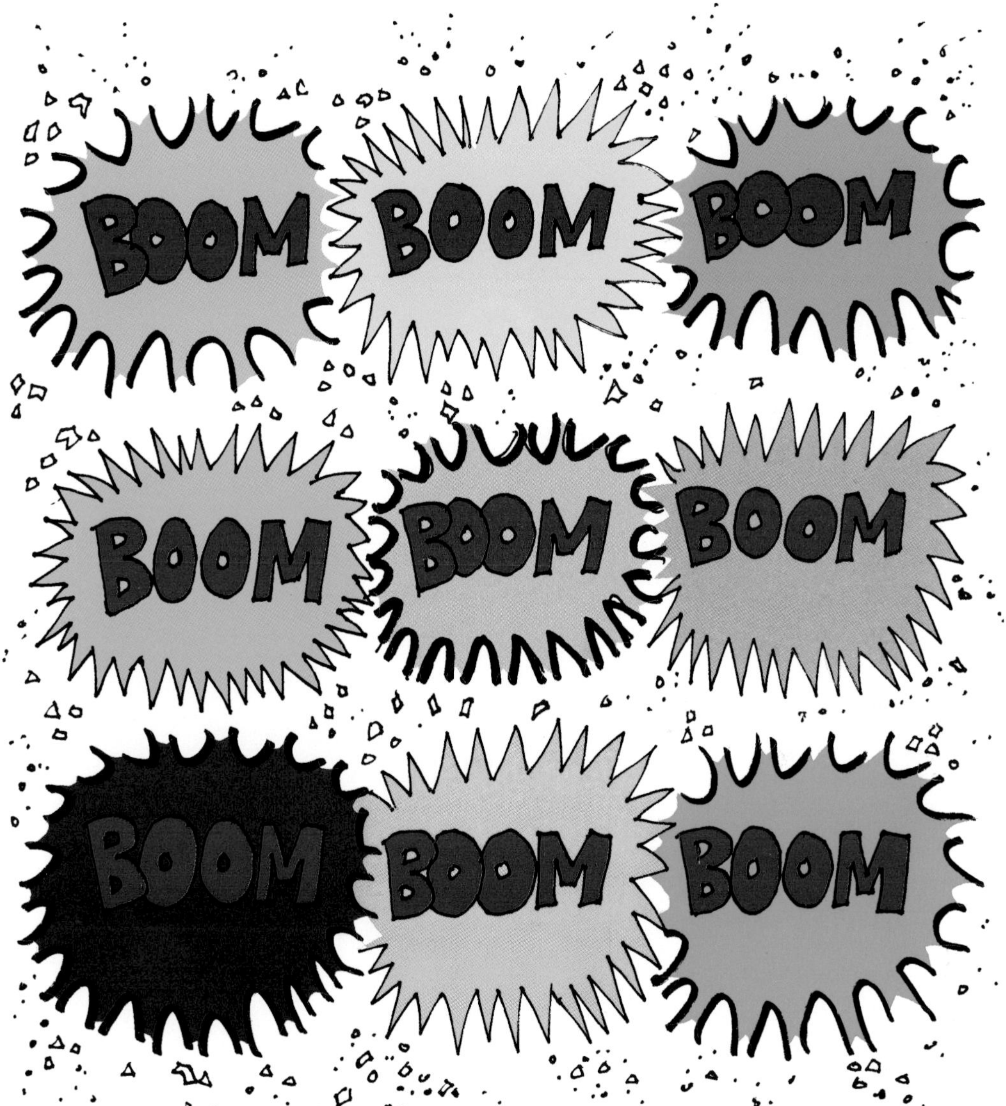
BOOM
BOOM
BOOM
BOOM
BOOM
BOOM
BOOM
BOOM
BOOM

CHAPTER

IN WHICH...

THE TENSION INCREASETH

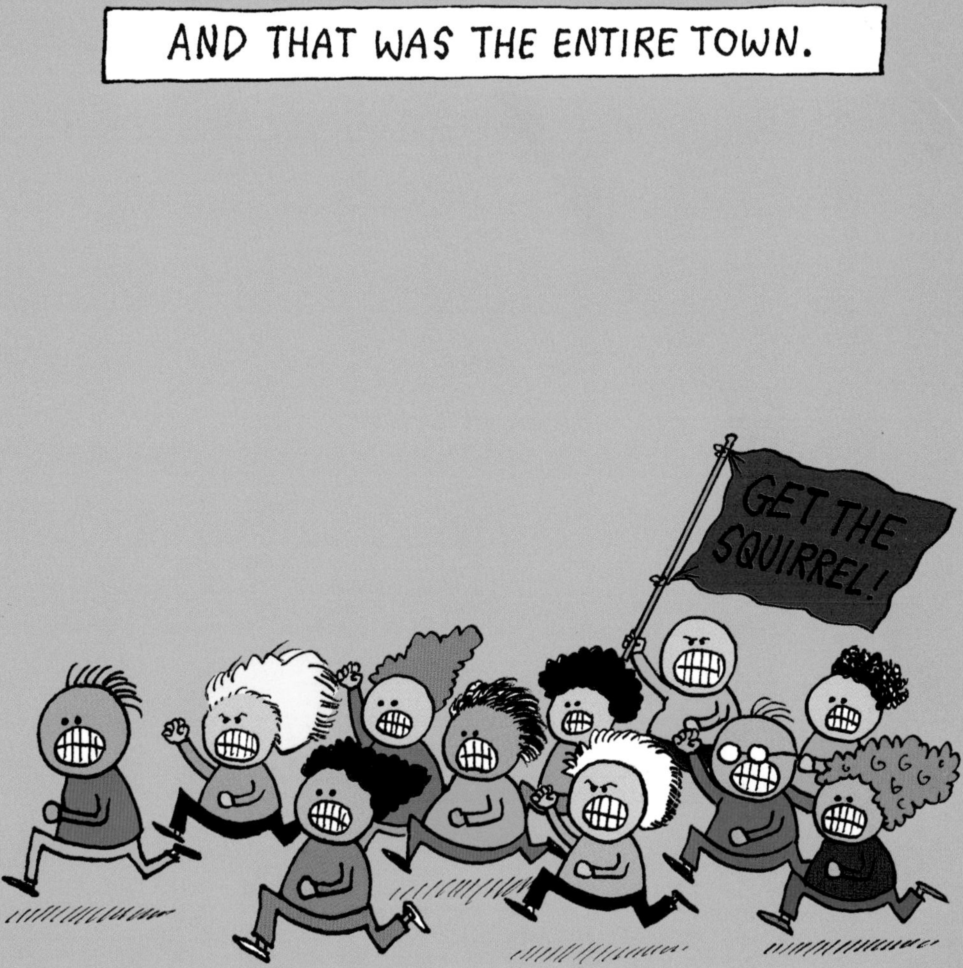
AND THAT WAS THE ENTIRE TOWN.
GET THE SQUIRREL!

CHAPTER NINE

WHICH IS...

ONE AFTER EIGHT

95

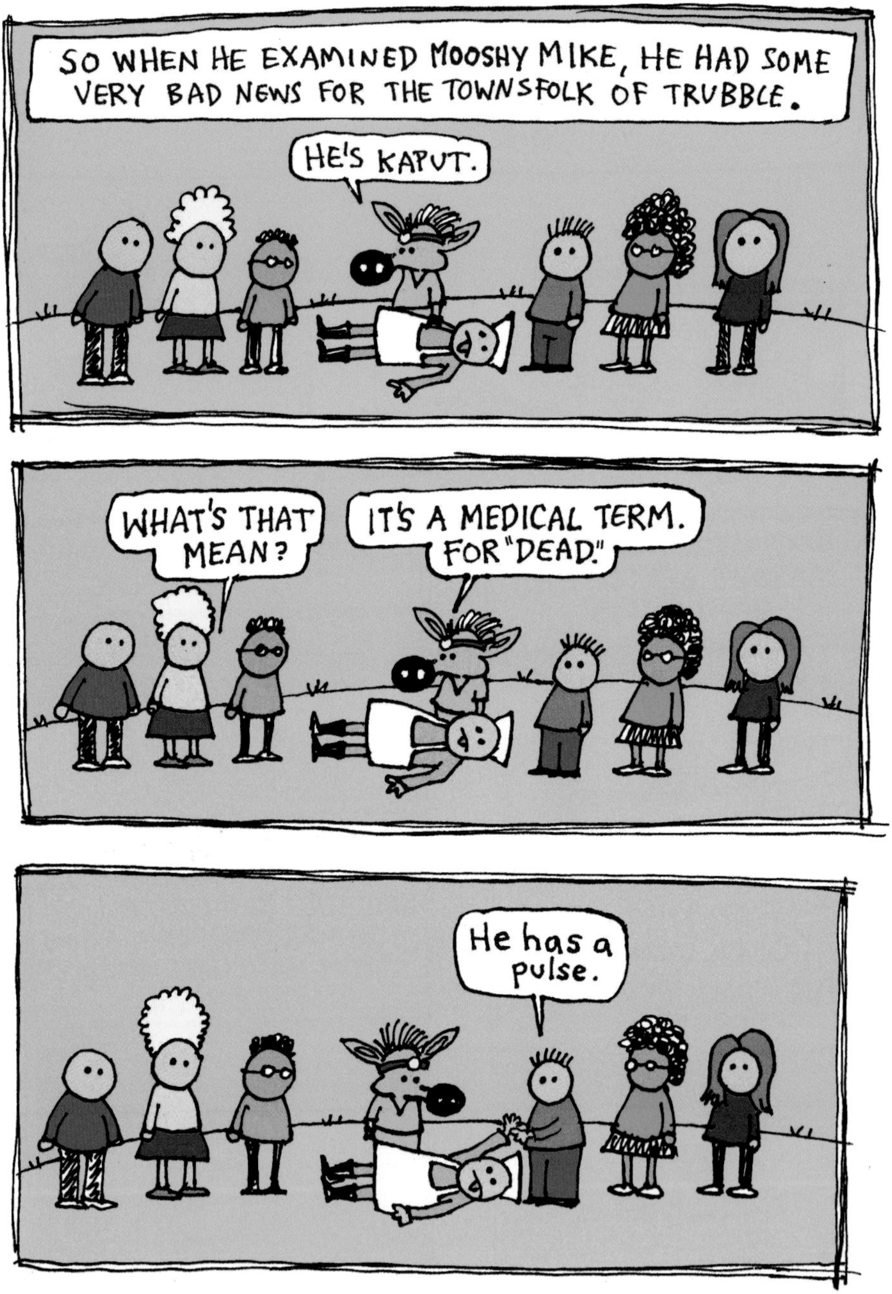
SO WHEN HE EXAMINED MOOSHY MIKE, HE HAD SOME VERY BAD NEWS FOR THE TOWNSFOLK OF TRUBBLE.
HE'S KAPUT.
WHAT'S THAT MEAN?
IT'S A MEDICAL TERM. FOR "DEAD."
He has a pulse.

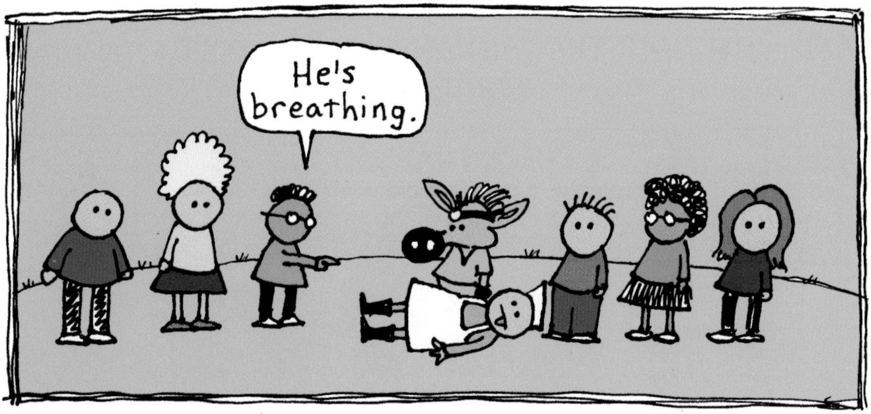
He's breathing.

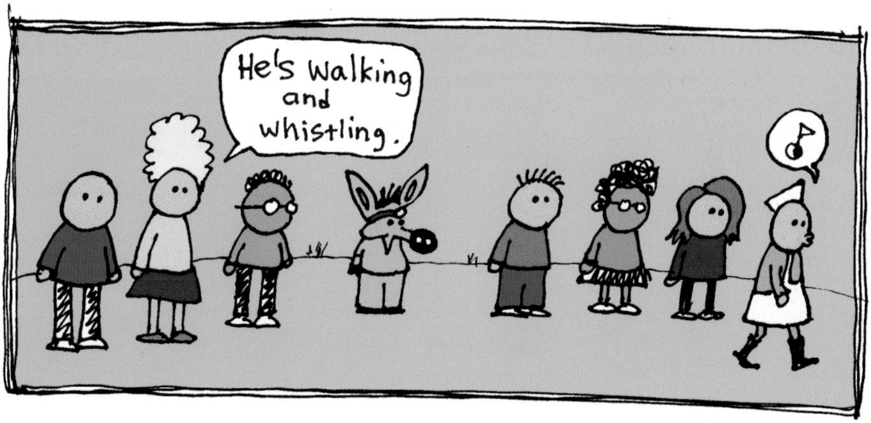
He's walking and whistling.

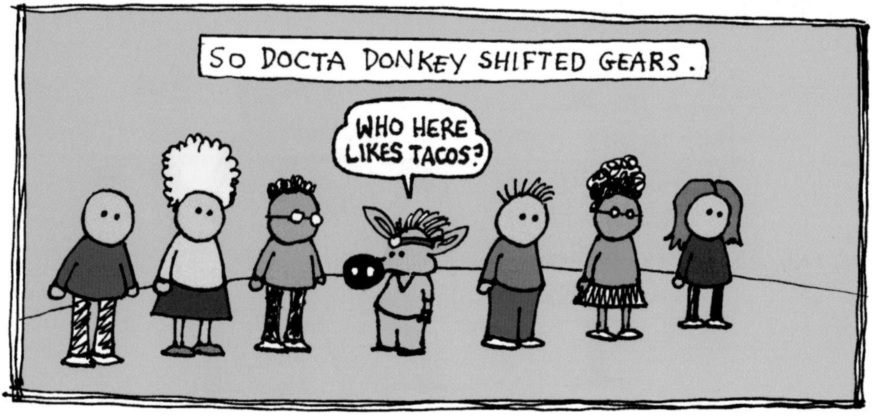
SO DOCTA DONKEY SHIFTED GEARS.
WHO HERE LIKES TACOS?

WHO PROMPTLY RUMMAGED THROUGH SQUIRRELY'S THINGS.
DIBS ON HIS TUBA!
I GET THE SOFA!
THE PIANO IS MINE!
AND CARRIED EVERYTHING OFF TO PARTS UNKNOWN.

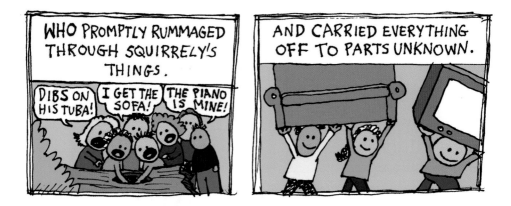

EXCEPT FOR ONE SMALL THING.

SQUIRRELY'S PRIVATE DIARY.

SQUIRRELY'S MOST SECRET-EST SECRET SECRETS

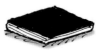

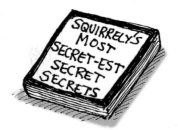

WHICH WAS OF PRECISELY NO INTEREST TO ANYONE.

EXCEPT ONE MAN.

CHAPTER

TEN

IN WHICH...

YOU WILL LEARN THINGS YOU DIDN'T KNOW

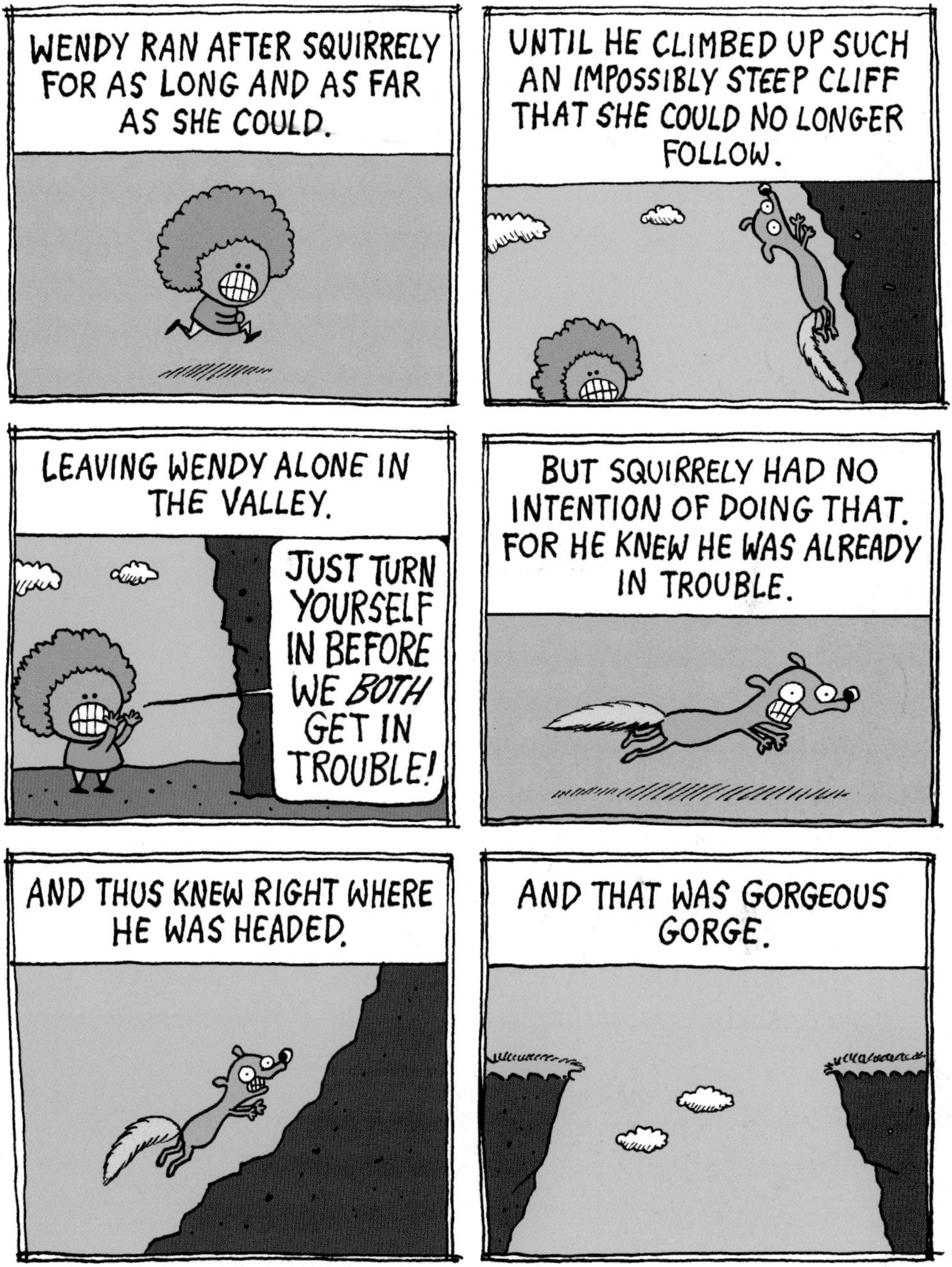
WENDY RAN AFTER SQUIRRELY FOR AS LONG AND AS FAR AS SHE COULD.
UNTIL HE CLIMBED UP SUCH AN IMPOSSIBLY STEEP CLIFF THAT SHE COULD NO LONGER FOLLOW.
LEAVING WENDY ALONE IN THE VALLEY.
JUST TURN YOURSELF IN BEFORE WE *BOTH* GET IN TROUBLE!
BUT SQUIRRELY HAD NO INTENTION OF DOING THAT. FOR HE KNEW HE WAS ALREADY IN TROUBLE.
AND THUS KNEW RIGHT WHERE HE WAS HEADED.
AND THAT WAS GORGEOUS GORGE.

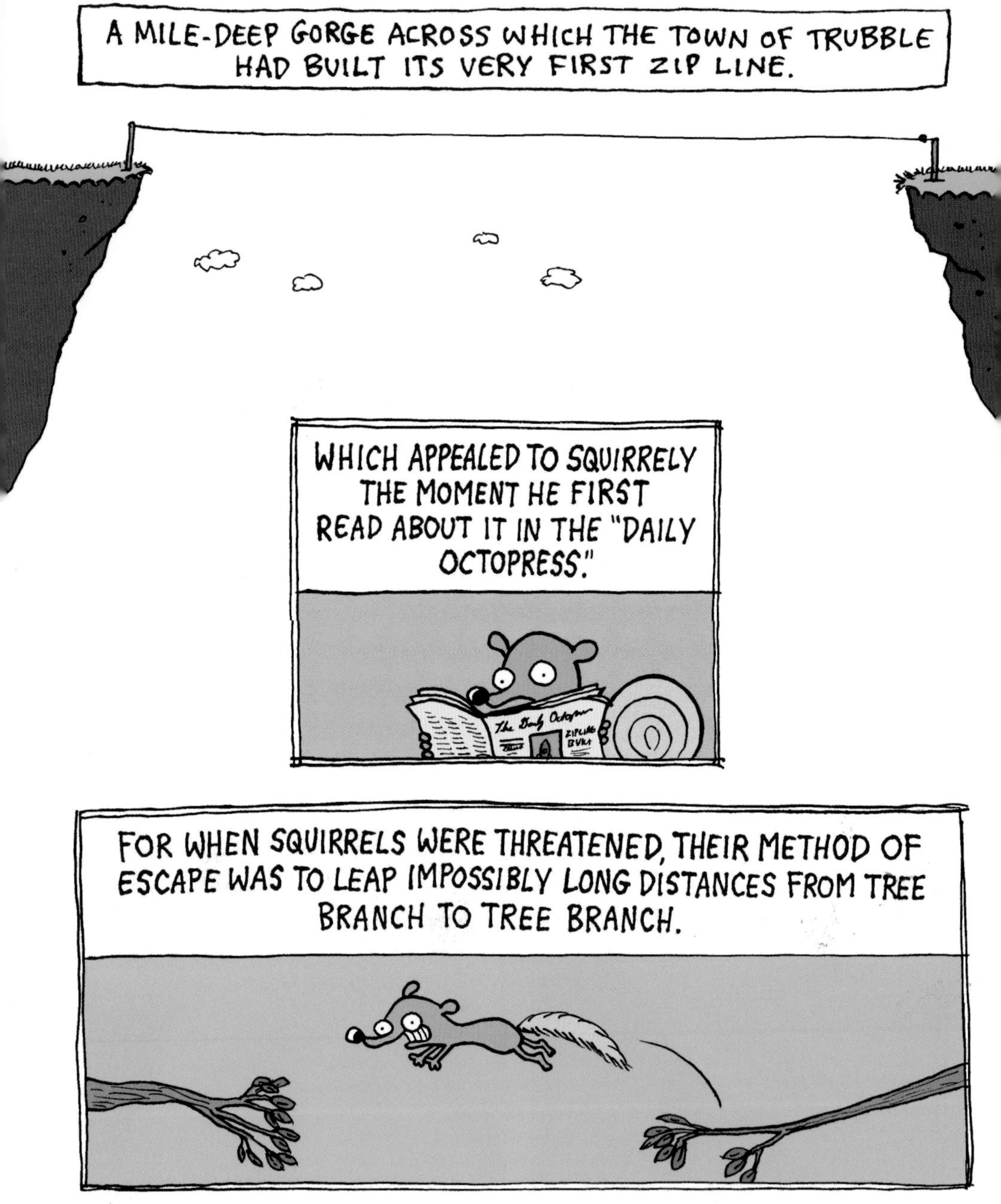
A MILE-DEEP GORGE ACROSS WHICH THE TOWN OF TRUBBLE HAD BUILT ITS VERY FIRST ZIP LINE.
WHICH APPEALED TO SQUIRRELY THE MOMENT HE FIRST READ ABOUT IT IN THE "DAILY OCTOPRESS."
FOR WHEN SQUIRRELS WERE THREATENED, THEIR METHOD OF ESCAPE WAS TO LEAP IMPOSSIBLY LONG DISTANCES FROM TREE BRANCH TO TREE BRANCH.

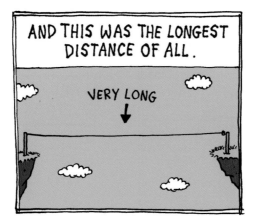

AND THIS WAS THE LONGEST DISTANCE OF ALL.

VERY LONG

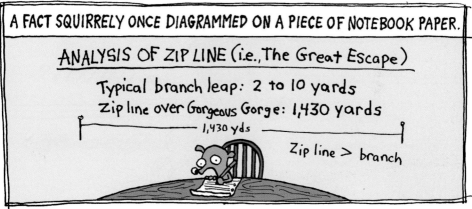

A FACT SQUIRRELY ONCE DIAGRAMMED ON A PIECE OF NOTEBOOK PAPER.

ANALYSIS OF ZIP LINE (i.e., The Great Escape)

Typical branch leap: 2 to 10 yards
Zip line over Gorgeous Gorge: 1,430 yards
1,430 yds

Zip line > branch

AND SO WHEN THE FLEEING SQUIRRELY FINALLY SPOTTED THE ZIP LINE, HIS HEART WAS FILLED WITH JOY.

AND HE LEAPED FOR THE HANDLEBARS.

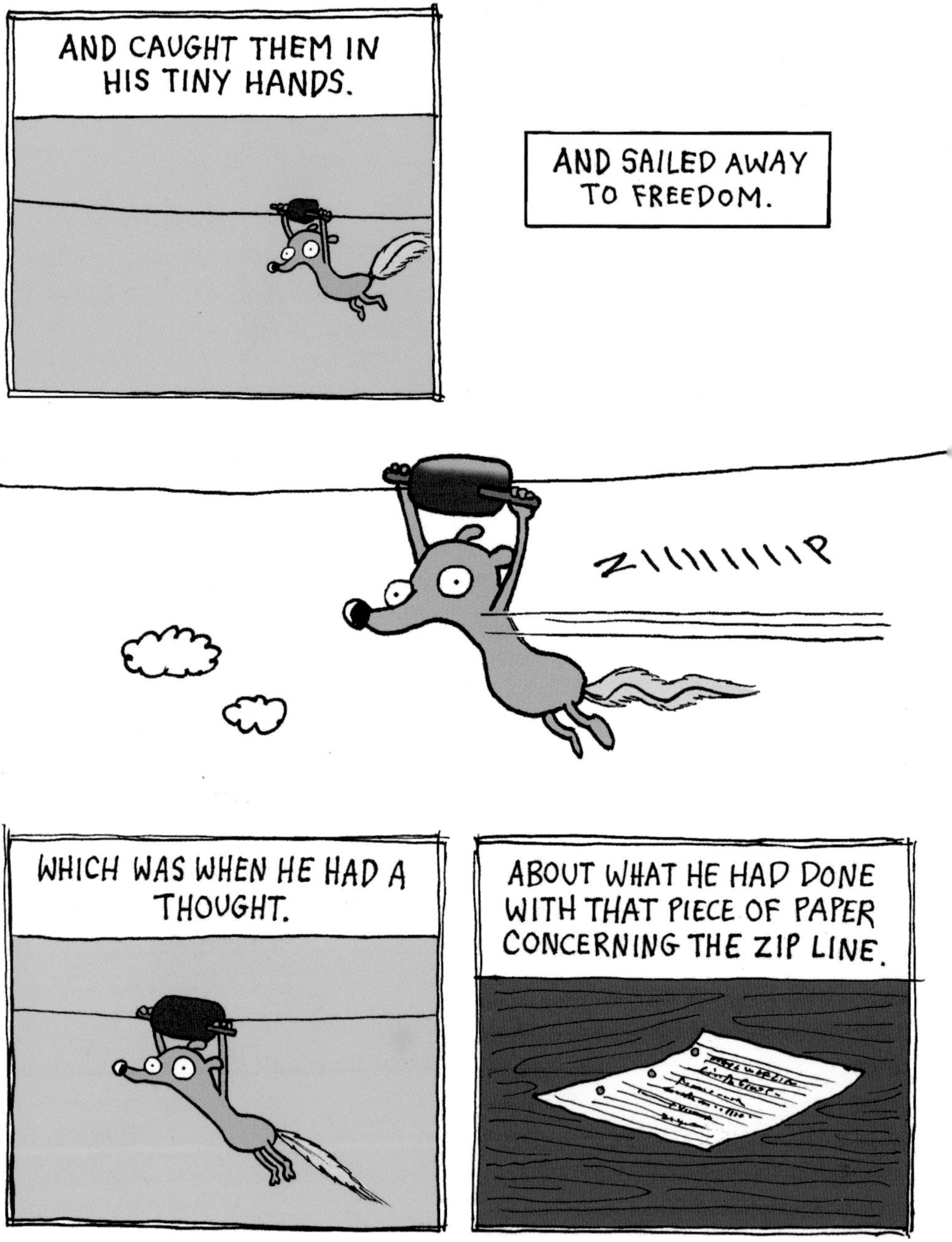
AND CAUGHT THEM IN HIS TINY HANDS.
AND SAILED AWAY TO FREEDOM.
ZIIIIIIIIP
WHICH WAS WHEN HE HAD A THOUGHT.
ABOUT WHAT HE HAD DONE WITH THAT PIECE OF PAPER CONCERNING THE ZIP LINE.

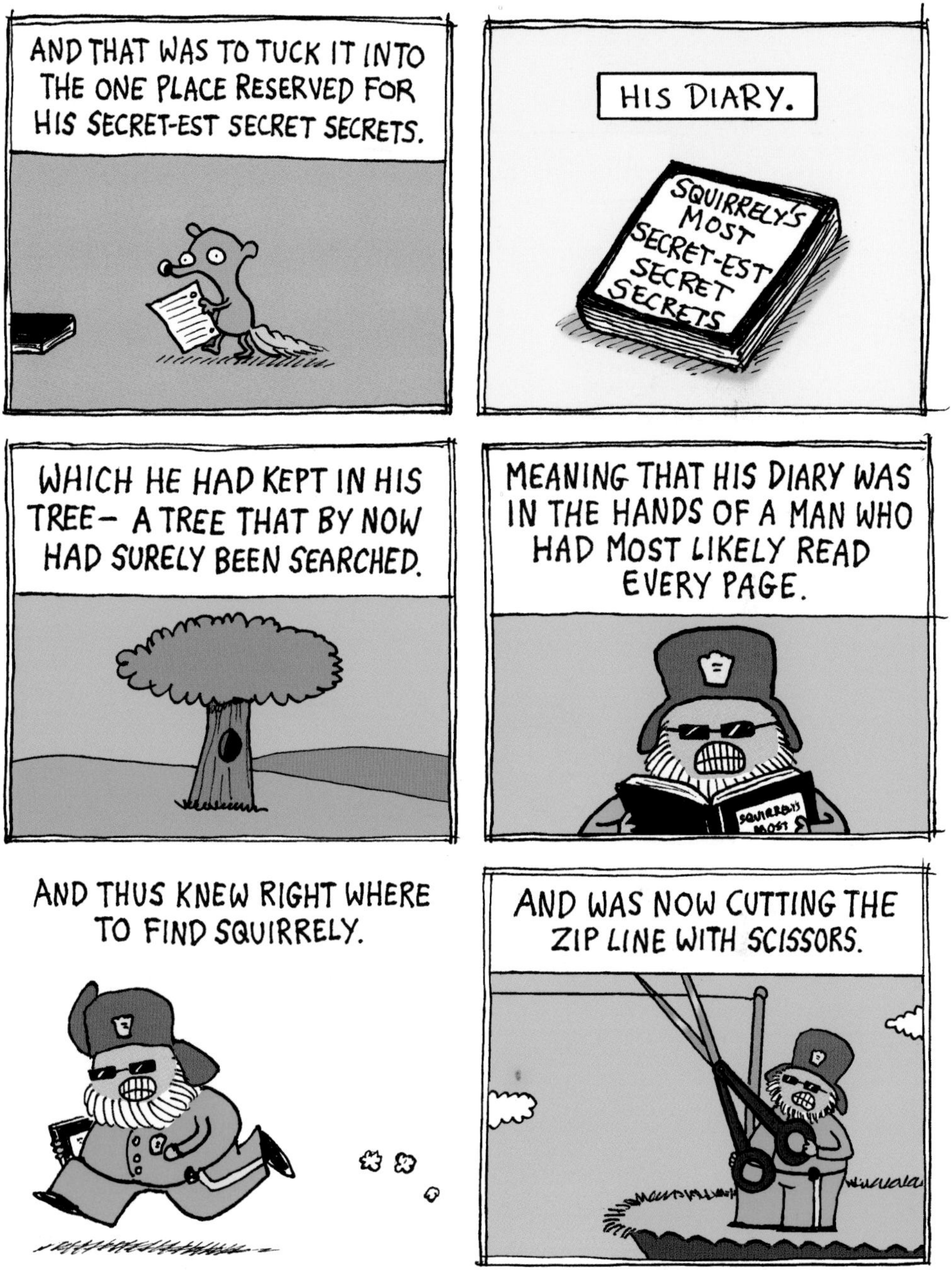
AND THAT WAS TO TUCK IT INTO THE ONE PLACE RESERVED FOR HIS SECRET-EST SECRET SECRETS.
HIS DIARY.
SQUIRRELY'S MOST SECRET-EST SECRET SECRETS
WHICH HE HAD KEPT IN HIS TREE— A TREE THAT BY NOW HAD SURELY BEEN SEARCHED.
MEANING THAT HIS DIARY WAS IN THE HANDS OF A MAN WHO HAD MOST LIKELY READ EVERY PAGE.
SQUIRRELY'S MOST
AND THUS KNEW RIGHT WHERE TO FIND SQUIRRELY.
AND WAS NOW CUTTING THE ZIP LINE WITH SCISSORS.

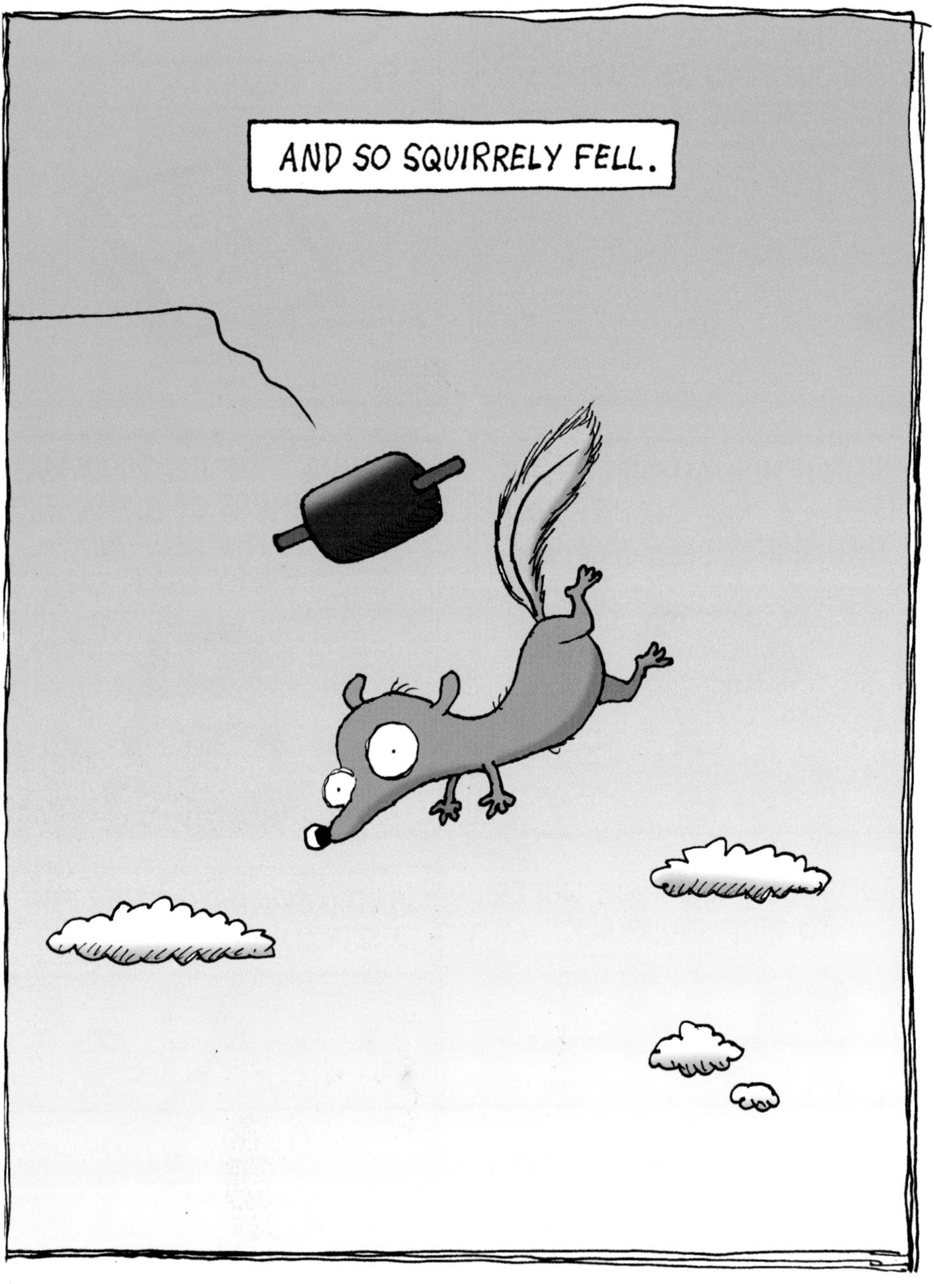
AND SO SQUIRRELY FELL.

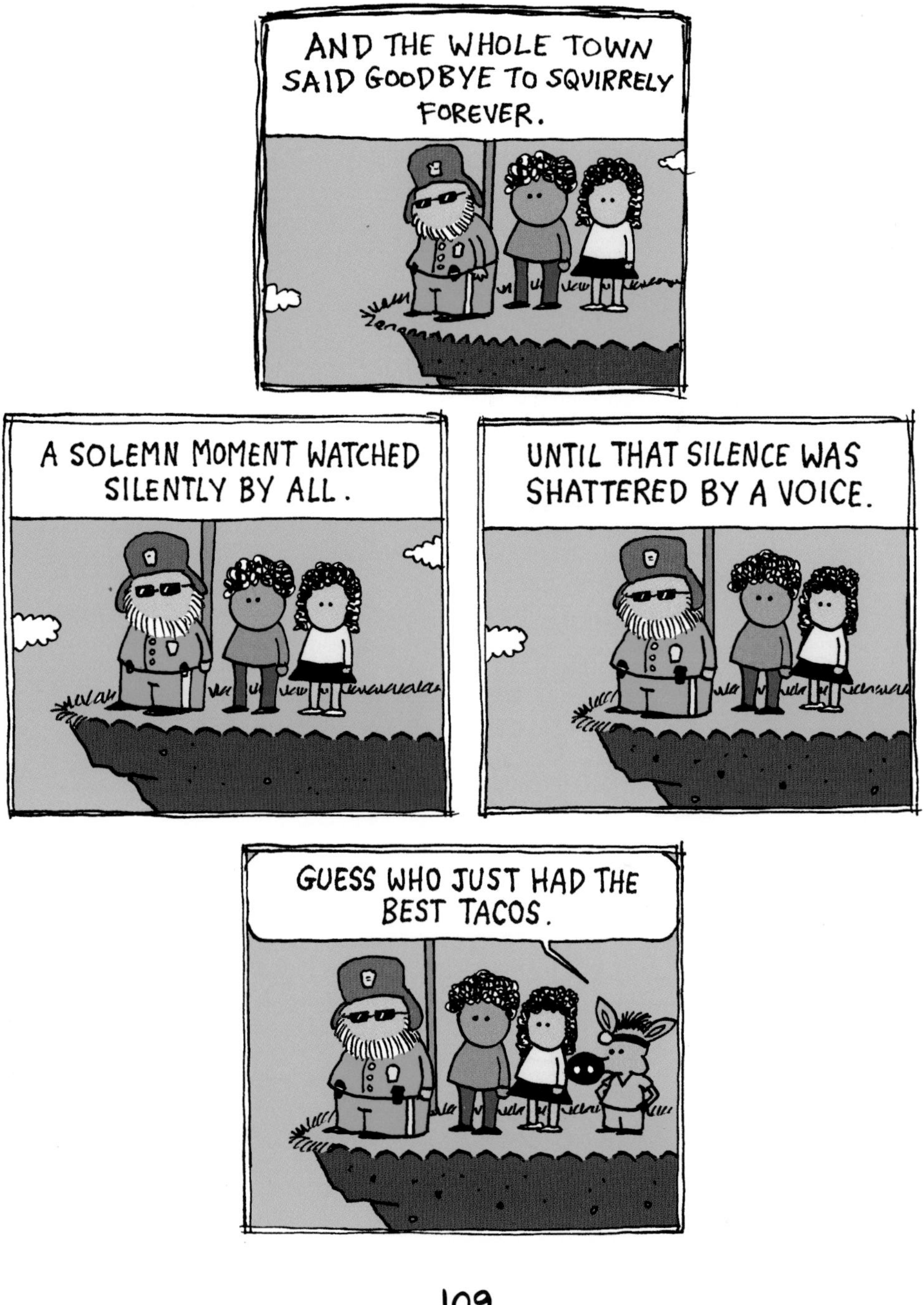
AND THE WHOLE TOWN SAID GOODBYE TO SQUIRRELY FOREVER.
A SOLEMN MOMENT WATCHED SILENTLY BY ALL.
UNTIL THAT SILENCE WAS SHATTERED BY A VOICE.
GUESS WHO JUST HAD THE BEST TACOS.

CHAPTER ELEVEN

IN WHICH...

LETTERS FORM WORDS, WHICH YOU THEN READ

SKIPPY VON TUBER HATED HIS JOB.

SKIPPY

AND EVERYONE AT SKIPPY'S JOB HATED SKIPPY.

MUST HE SIT SO CLOSE?

THAT IS BECAUSE SKIPPY'S JOB WAS WORKING FOR THE TOWN OF TRUBBLE AS:

GUY IN CHARGE OF WORDY THINGS

WHICH MEANT LOOKING AT EVERY DOCUMENT SUBMITTED TO THE TOWN OF TRUBBLE...

MARRIAGE CERTIFICATES, PERMIT APPLICATIONS, LAWSUITS, COMPLAINTS, AND ANYTHING ELSE WITH WORDS.

Death Certificates
BLUETRAIL
Birth Notices
HISTORICAL RECORDS
PLANMAN DOCUME
HOSPITAL PLAN

AND SKIPPY HAD NO TIME FOR ANY OF IT.

BLAH.

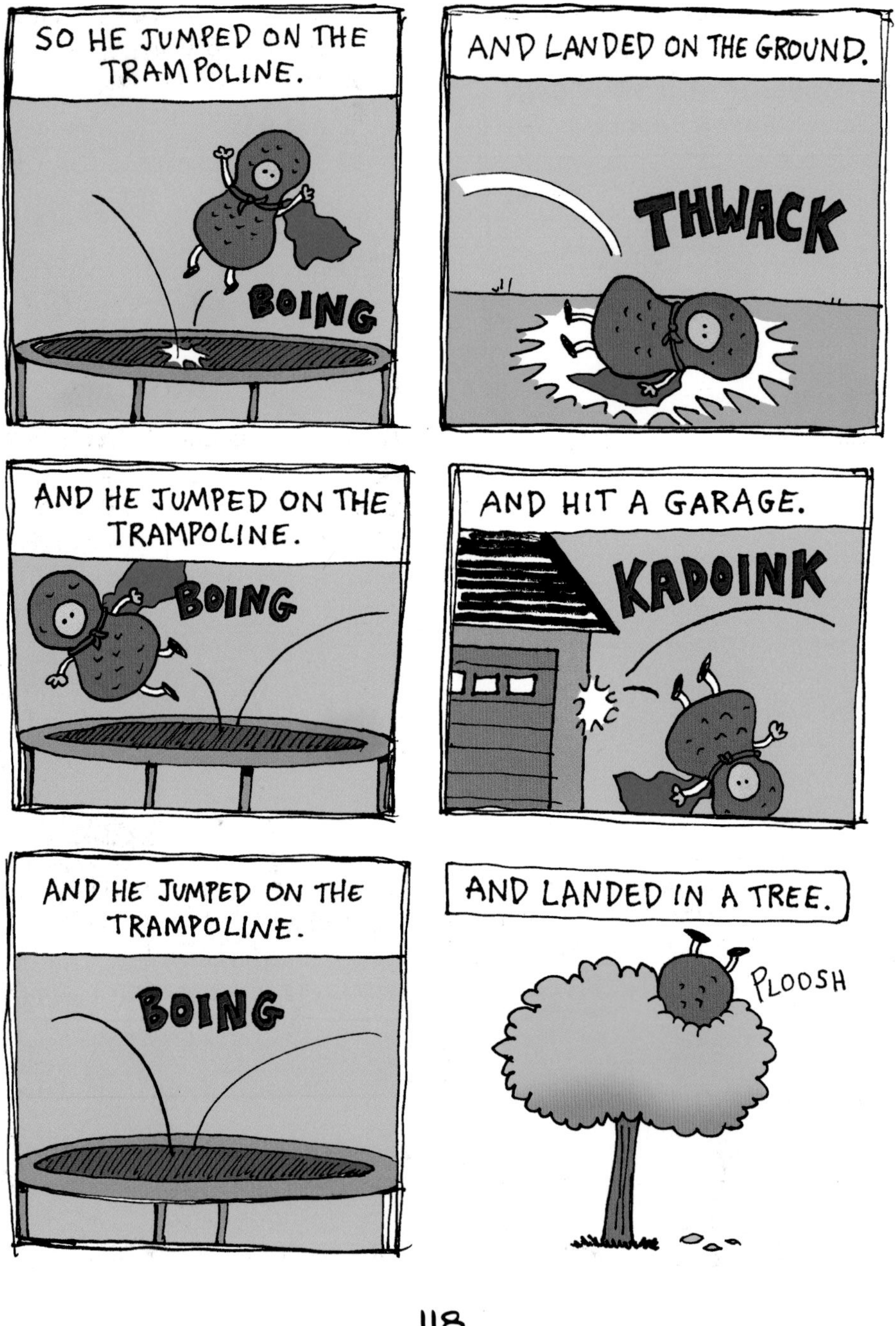
SO HE JUMPED ON THE TRAMPOLINE.
BOING
AND LANDED ON THE GROUND.
THWACK
AND HE JUMPED ON THE TRAMPOLINE.
BOING
AND HIT A GARAGE.
KADOINK
AND HE JUMPED ON THE TRAMPOLINE.
BOING
AND LANDED IN A TREE.
PLOOSH

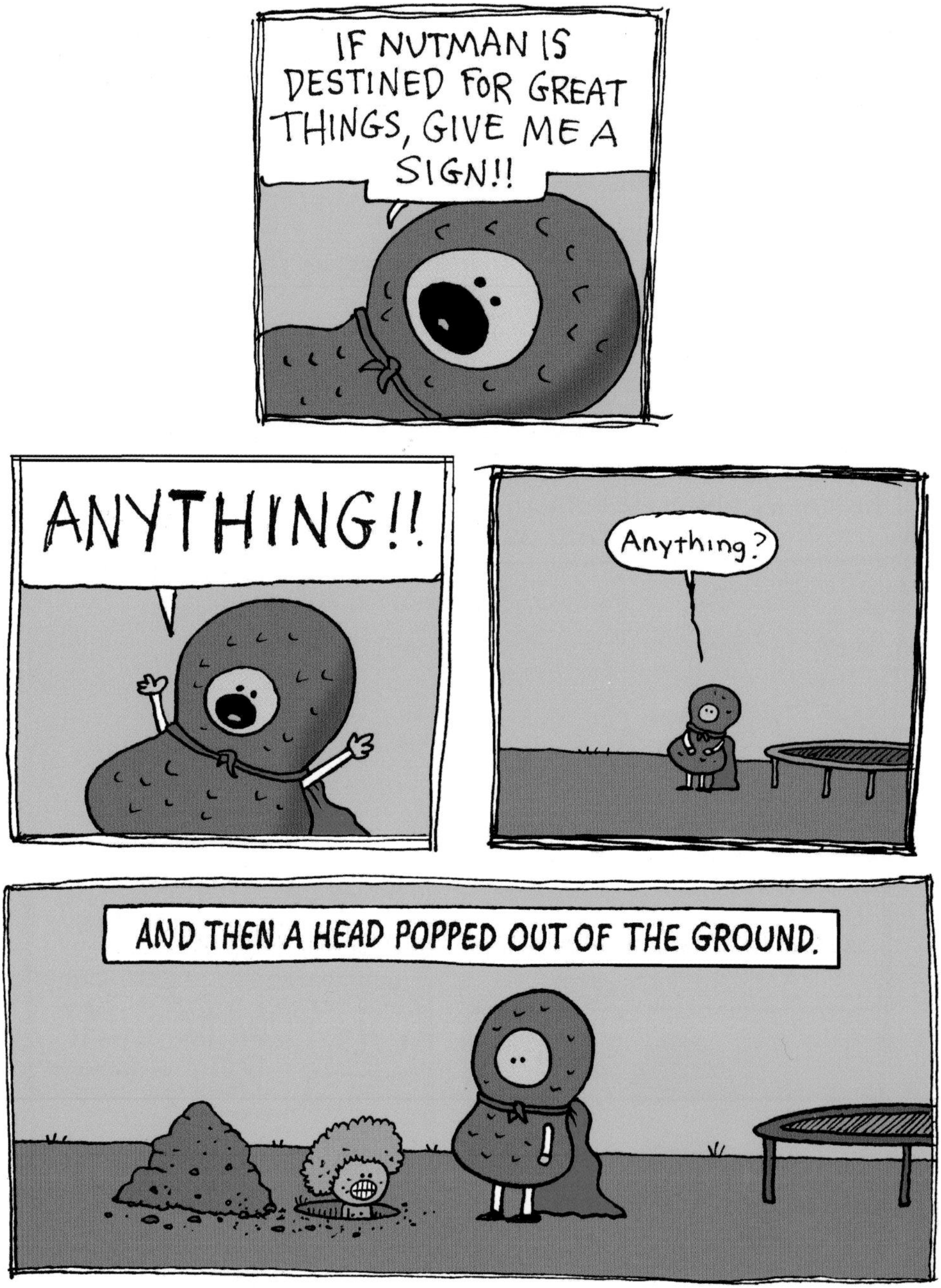
IF NUTMAN IS DESTINED FOR GREAT THINGS, GIVE ME A SIGN!!
ANYTHING!!
Anything?
AND THEN A HEAD POPPED OUT OF THE GROUND.

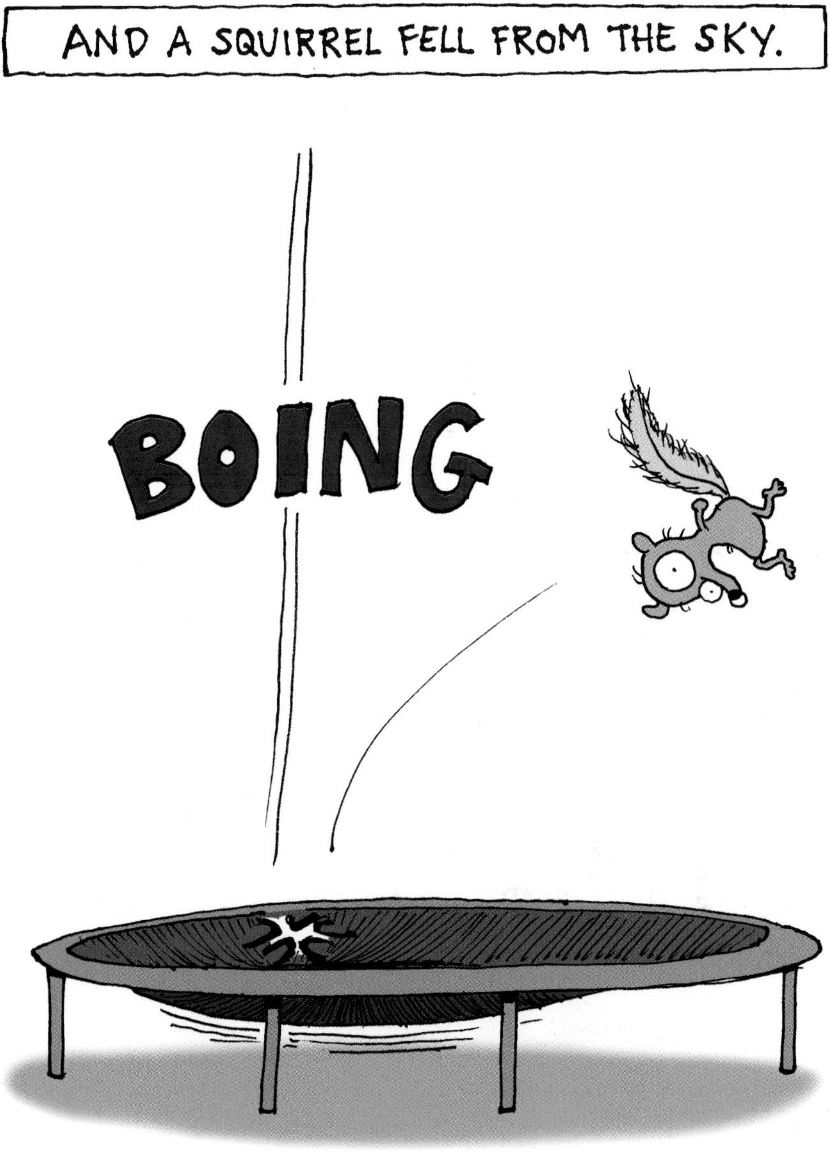
AND A SQUIRREL FELL FROM THE SKY.
BOING

CHAPTER
SOMEWHERE
BETWEEN
ELEVEN
AND
TWELVE

IN WHICH...

WE ARE
SOMEWHAT
INDECISIVE

WENDY HAD BEEN ON THE VALLEY FLOOR TRYING TO FOLLOW SQUIRRELY'S ASCENT UP THE STEEP CLIFF...

WHEN SHE HEARD FOOTSTEPS APPROACHING.

SO WITH NOWHERE TO RUN, SHE DECIDED TO EMPLOY A SKILL SHE HAD LEARNED FROM WATCHING THE MOLES.

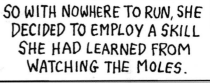

THE MOLES

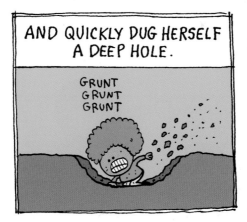

AND QUICKLY DUG HERSELF A DEEP HOLE.

GRUNT
GRUNT
GRUNT

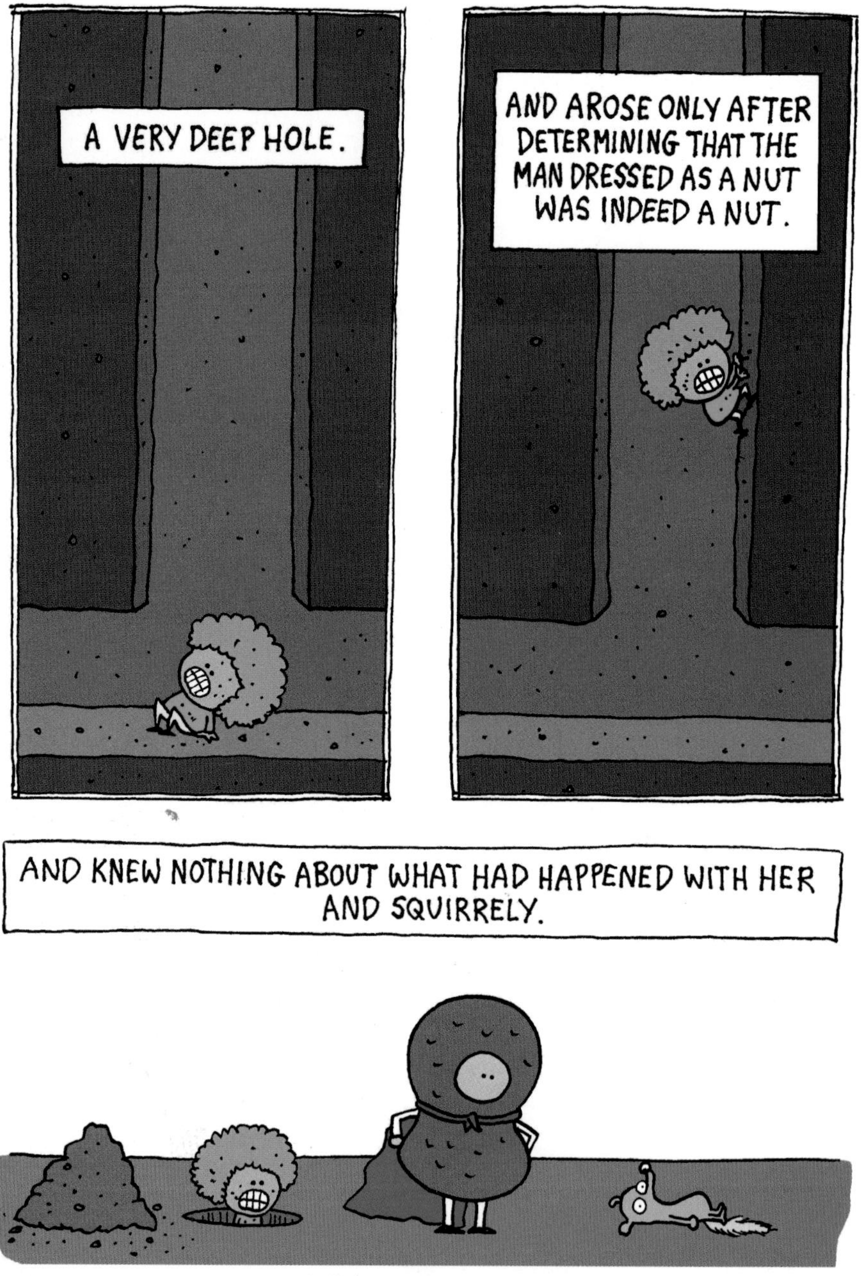
A VERY DEEP HOLE.
AND AROSE ONLY AFTER DETERMINING THAT THE MAN DRESSED AS A NUT WAS INDEED A NUT.
AND KNEW NOTHING ABOUT WHAT HAD HAPPENED WITH HER AND SQUIRRELY.

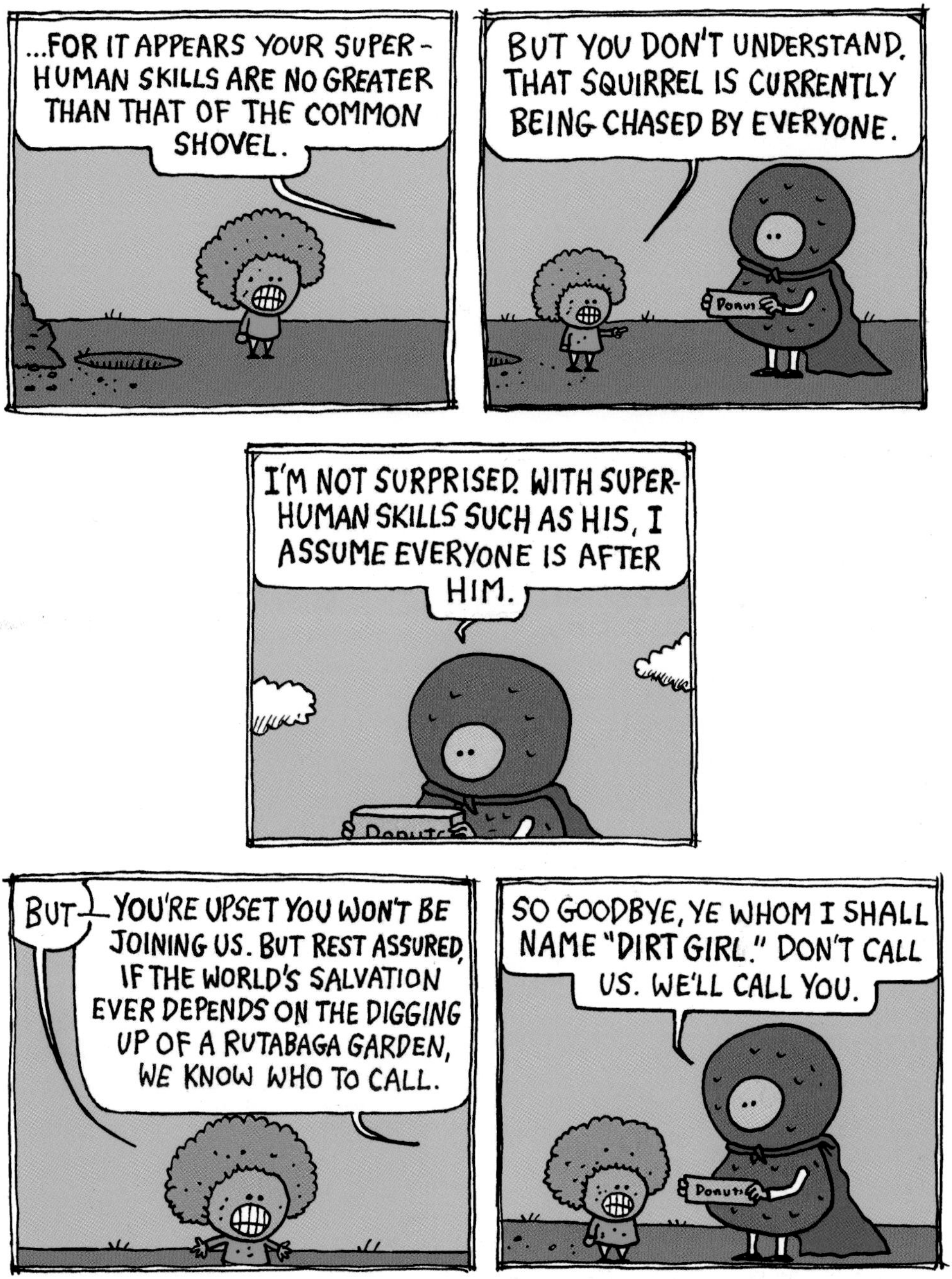
...FOR IT APPEARS YOUR SUPER-HUMAN SKILLS ARE NO GREATER THAN THAT OF THE COMMON SHOVEL.
BUT YOU DON'T UNDERSTAND. THAT SQUIRREL IS CURRENTLY BEING CHASED BY EVERYONE.
Donuts
I'M NOT SURPRISED. WITH SUPER-HUMAN SKILLS SUCH AS HIS, I ASSUME EVERYONE IS AFTER HIM.
BUT-
YOU'RE UPSET YOU WON'T BE JOINING US. BUT REST ASSURED, IF THE WORLD'S SALVATION EVER DEPENDS ON THE DIGGING UP OF A RUTABAGA GARDEN, WE KNOW WHO TO CALL.
SO GOODBYE, YE WHOM I SHALL NAME "DIRT GIRL." DON'T CALL US. WE'LL CALL YOU.
Donuts

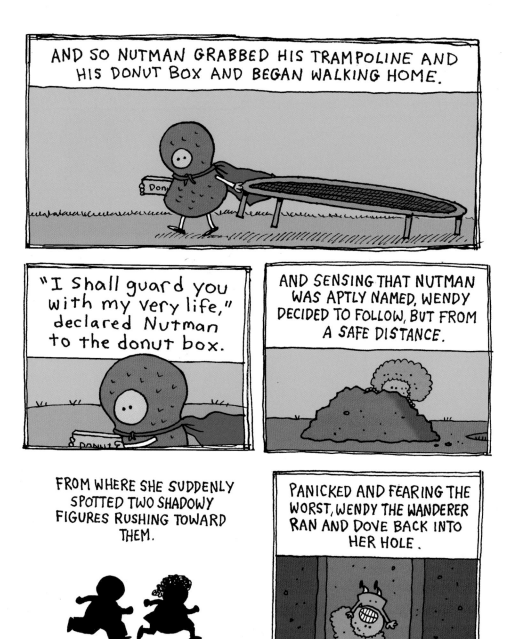

AND SO NUTMAN GRABBED HIS TRAMPOLINE AND HIS DONUT BOX AND BEGAN WALKING HOME.

"I shall guard you with my very life," declared Nutman to the donut box.

AND SENSING THAT NUTMAN WAS APTLY NAMED, WENDY DECIDED TO FOLLOW, BUT FROM A SAFE DISTANCE.

FROM WHERE SHE SUDDENLY SPOTTED TWO SHADOWY FIGURES RUSHING TOWARD THEM.

PANICKED AND FEARING THE WORST, WENDY THE WANDERER RAN AND DOVE BACK INTO HER HOLE.

128

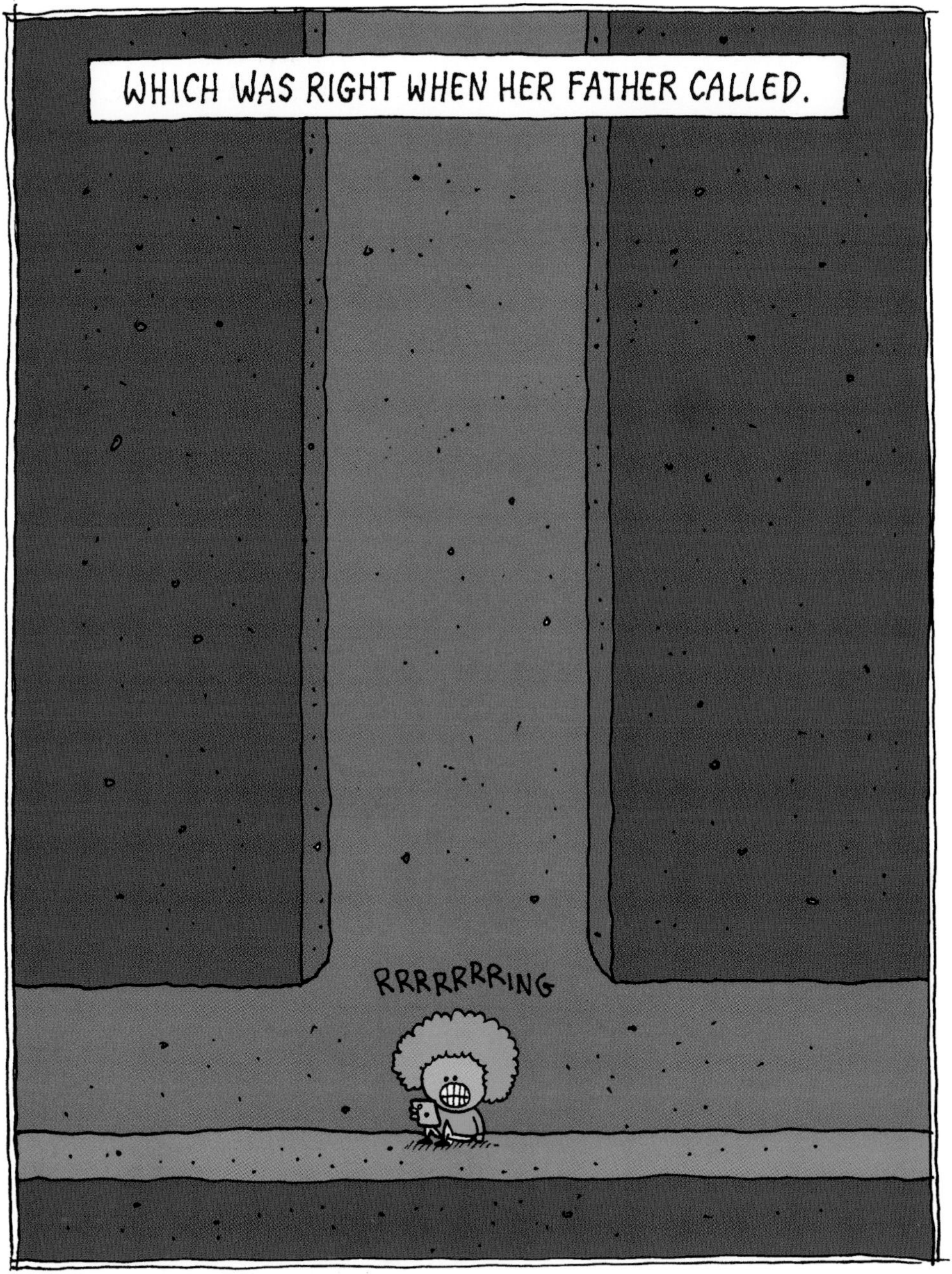
WHICH WAS RIGHT WHEN HER FATHER CALLED.
RRRRRRRING

CHAPTER TWELVE

IN WHICH...

YOU BEGIN TO REALIZE WHAT GREAT LITERATURE THIS REALLY IS

131

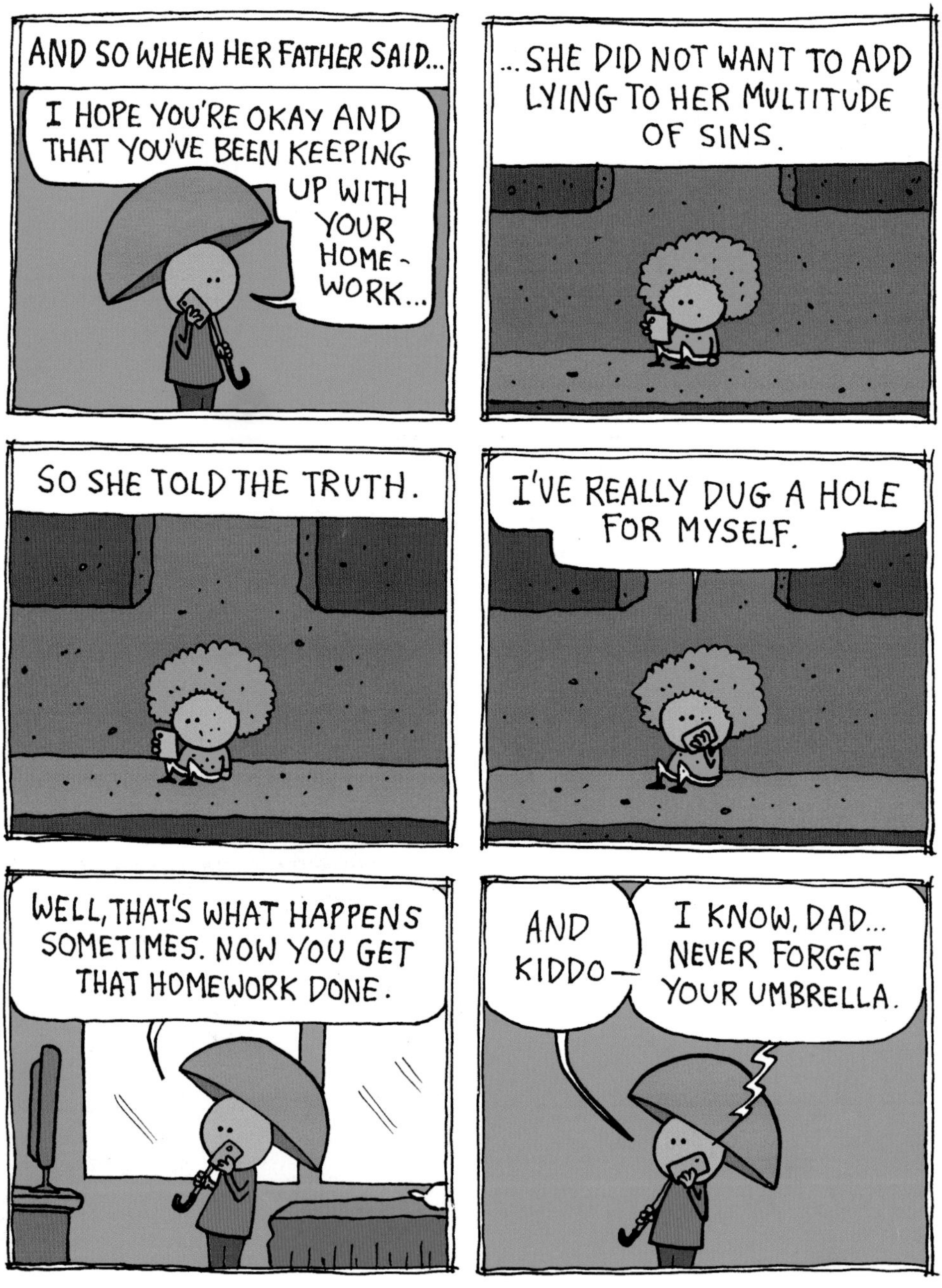
AND SO WHEN HER FATHER SAID...
I HOPE YOU'RE OKAY AND THAT YOU'VE BEEN KEEPING UP WITH YOUR HOME-WORK...
...SHE DID NOT WANT TO ADD LYING TO HER MULTITUDE OF SINS.
SO SHE TOLD THE TRUTH.
I'VE REALLY DUG A HOLE FOR MYSELF.
WELL, THAT'S WHAT HAPPENS SOMETIMES. NOW YOU GET THAT HOMEWORK DONE.
AND KIDDO—
I KNOW, DAD... NEVER FORGET YOUR UMBRELLA.

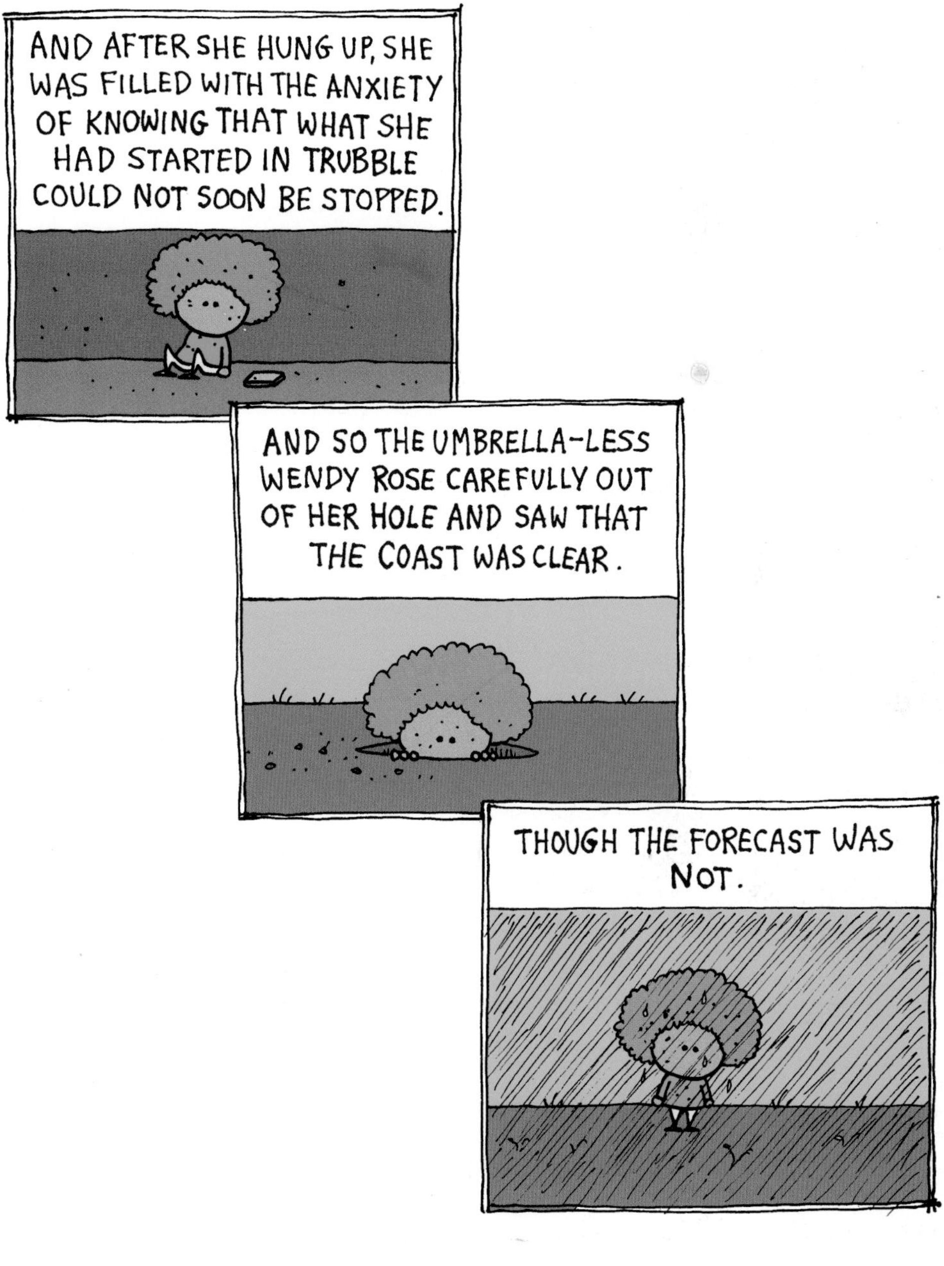
AND AFTER SHE HUNG UP, SHE WAS FILLED WITH THE ANXIETY OF KNOWING THAT WHAT SHE HAD STARTED IN TRUBBLE COULD NOT SOON BE STOPPED.
AND SO THE UMBRELLA-LESS WENDY ROSE CAREFULLY OUT OF HER HOLE AND SAW THAT THE COAST WAS CLEAR.
THOUGH THE FORECAST WAS NOT.

CHAPTER
13

IN WHICH...

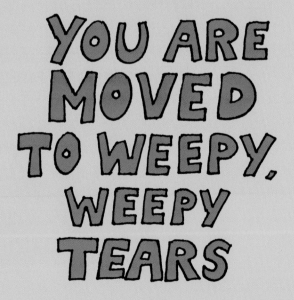

YOU ARE
MOVED
TO WEEPY,
WEEPY
TEARS

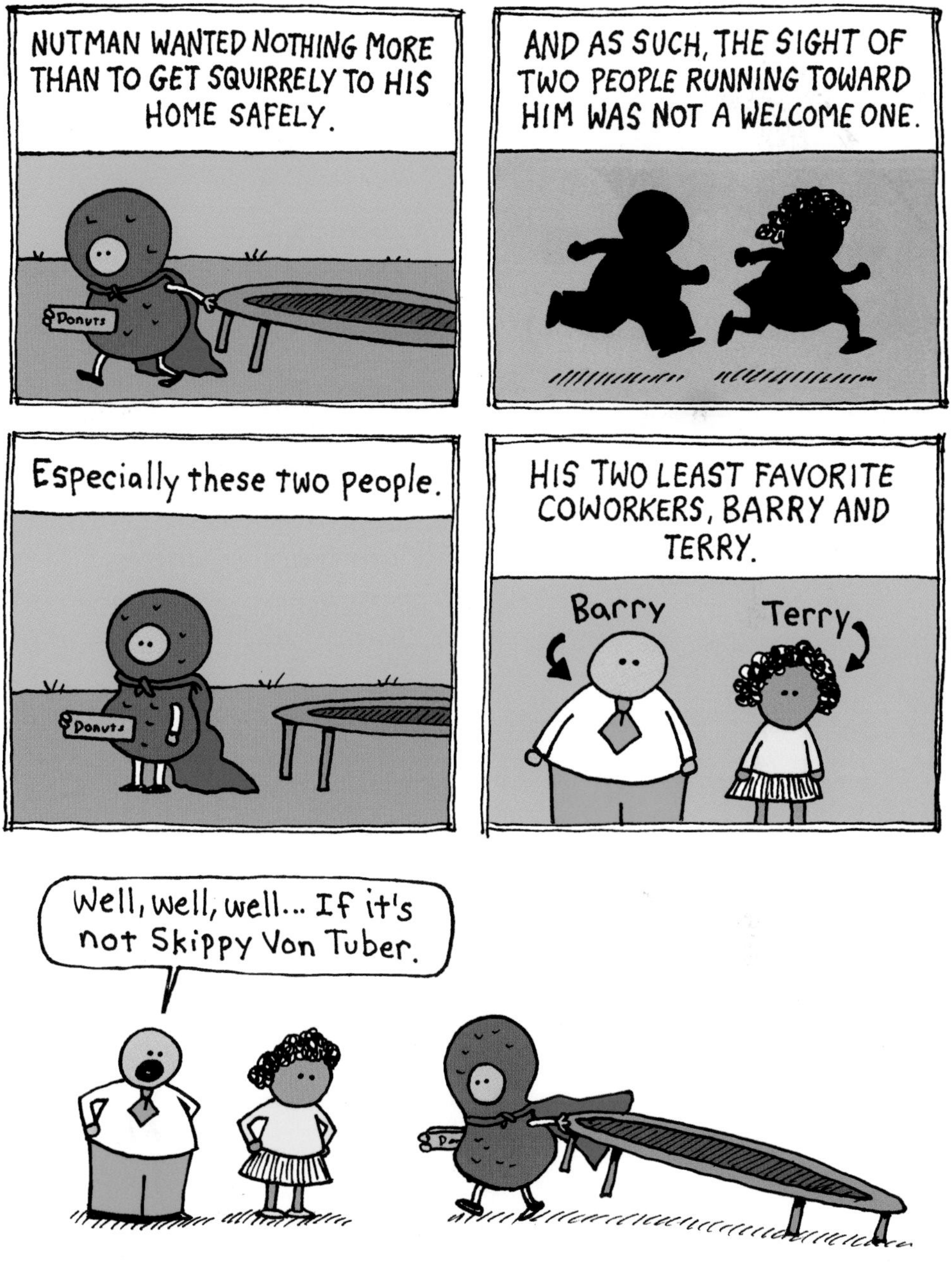
NUTMAN WANTED NOTHING MORE THAN TO GET SQUIRRELY TO HIS HOME SAFELY.
Donuts
AND AS SUCH, THE SIGHT OF TWO PEOPLE RUNNING TOWARD HIM WAS NOT A WELCOME ONE.
Especially these two people.
Donuts
HIS TWO LEAST FAVORITE COWORKERS, BARRY AND TERRY.
Barry
Terry
Well, well, well... If it's not Skippy Von Tuber.

138

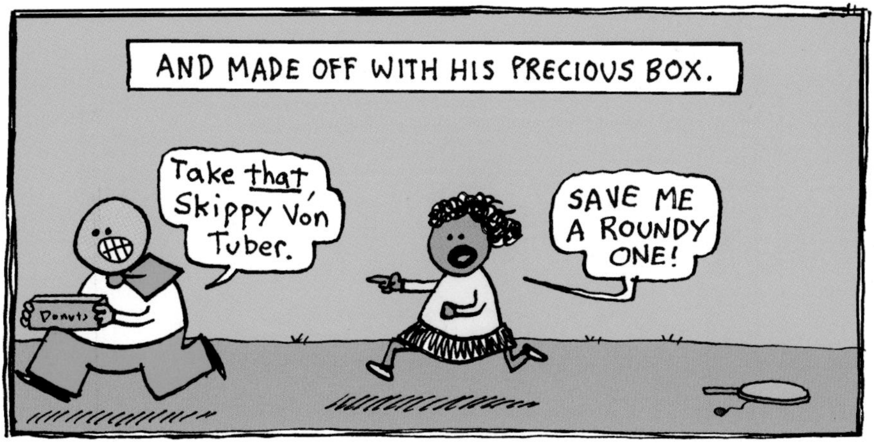
AND MADE OFF WITH HIS PRECIOUS BOX.
Take that, Skippy Von Tuber.
Donuts
SAVE ME A ROUNDY ONE!

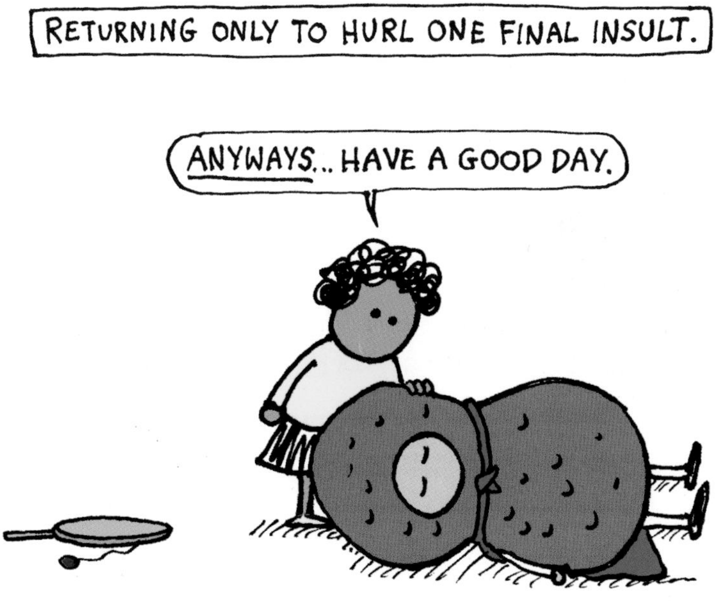
RETURNING ONLY TO HURL ONE FINAL INSULT.
ANYWAYS... HAVE A GOOD DAY.

CHAPTER FOURTEEN

IN WHICH...

THE ANSWERS TO ALL O' LIFE'S MYSTERIES ARE REVEALED

141

AND BARRY AND TERRY'S THINGS WERE SPRINGS.

LODGED IN THE SOLES OF THEIR PATENTED SHOES.

WHICH THEY HAD WORKED ON EVERY DAY WHILE SKIPPY VON TUBER PLAYED PADDLEBALL.

CALLED "TOSS-A-BOSS," THE SHOES WERE TO BE SLIPPED ON TO THE FEET OF ANY BOSS THAT ONE DISLIKED.

AND THE NEXT TIME HE STOOD UPRIGHT, OUT THE BUILDING HE'D FLY.

SPROING

NOOOOOOO...

BUT ON THIS DAY, THEY'D BEEN REPURPOSED AS A MEANS OF ESCAPE. AND SO BARRY AND TERRY PRESSED THE EJECT BUTTONS.

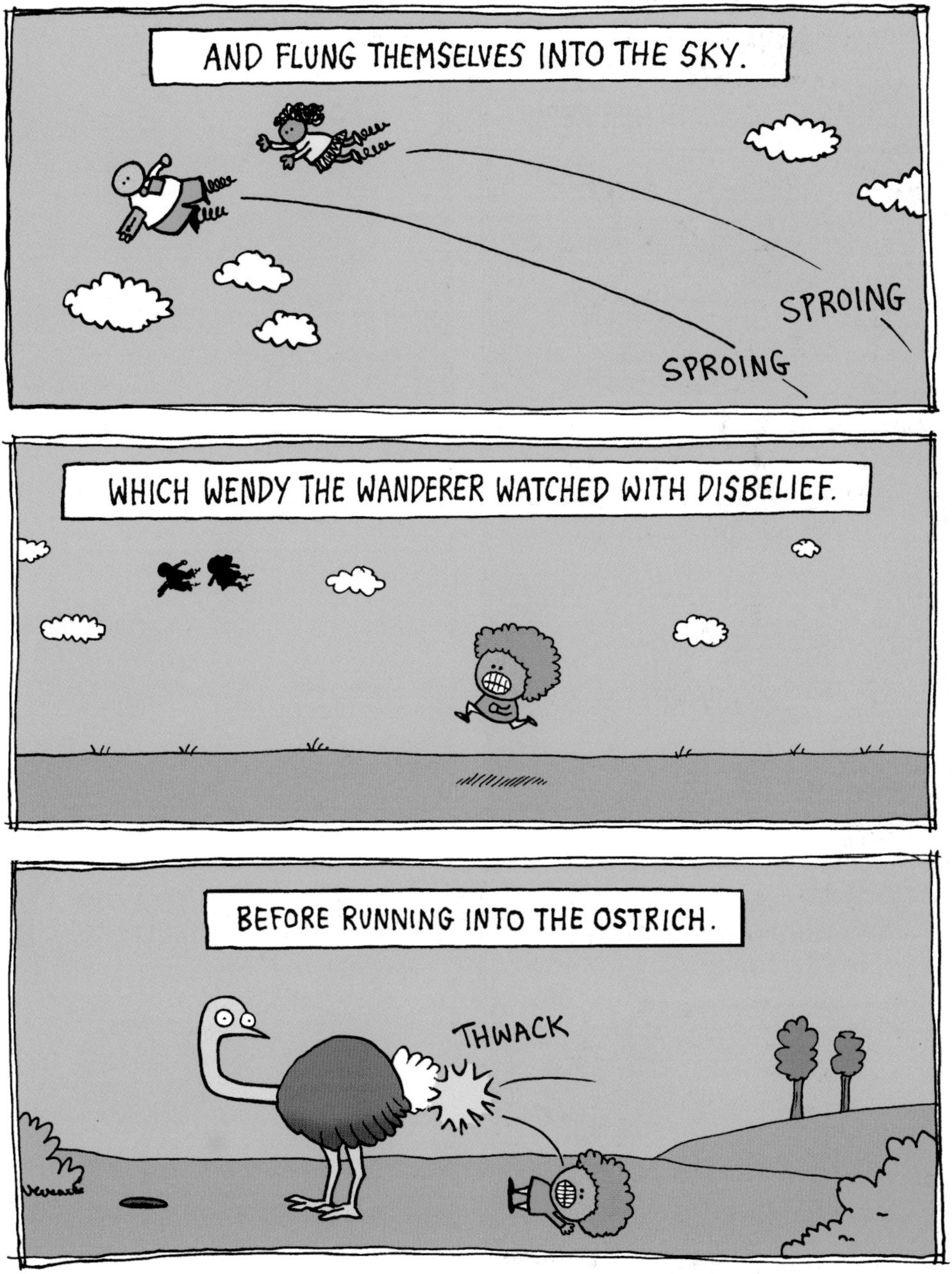
AND FLUNG THEMSELVES INTO THE SKY.
SPROING
SPROING
WHICH WENDY THE WANDERER WATCHED WITH DISBELIEF.
BEFORE RUNNING INTO THE OSTRICH.
THWACK

CHAPTER OSTRICH

IN WHICH...

THE BIRD DOES ALL THE YAPPING

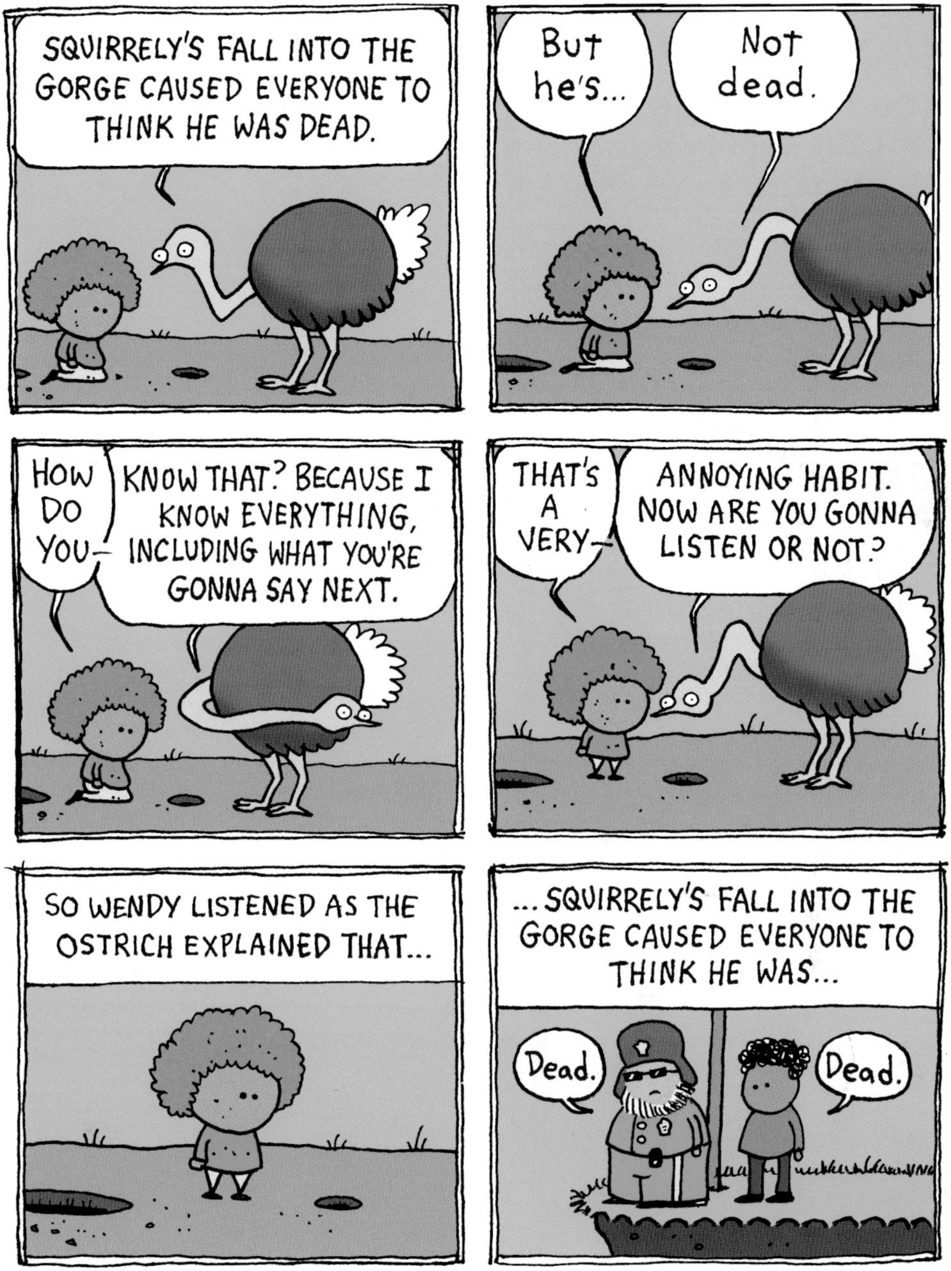
SQUIRRELY'S FALL INTO THE GORGE CAUSED EVERYONE TO THINK HE WAS DEAD.
But he's...
Not dead.
HOW DO YOU—
KNOW THAT? BECAUSE I KNOW EVERYTHING, INCLUDING WHAT YOU'RE GONNA SAY NEXT.
THAT'S A VERY—
ANNOYING HABIT. NOW ARE YOU GONNA LISTEN OR NOT?
SO WENDY LISTENED AS THE OSTRICH EXPLAINED THAT...
...SQUIRRELY'S FALL INTO THE GORGE CAUSED EVERYONE TO THINK HE WAS...
Dead.
Dead.

148

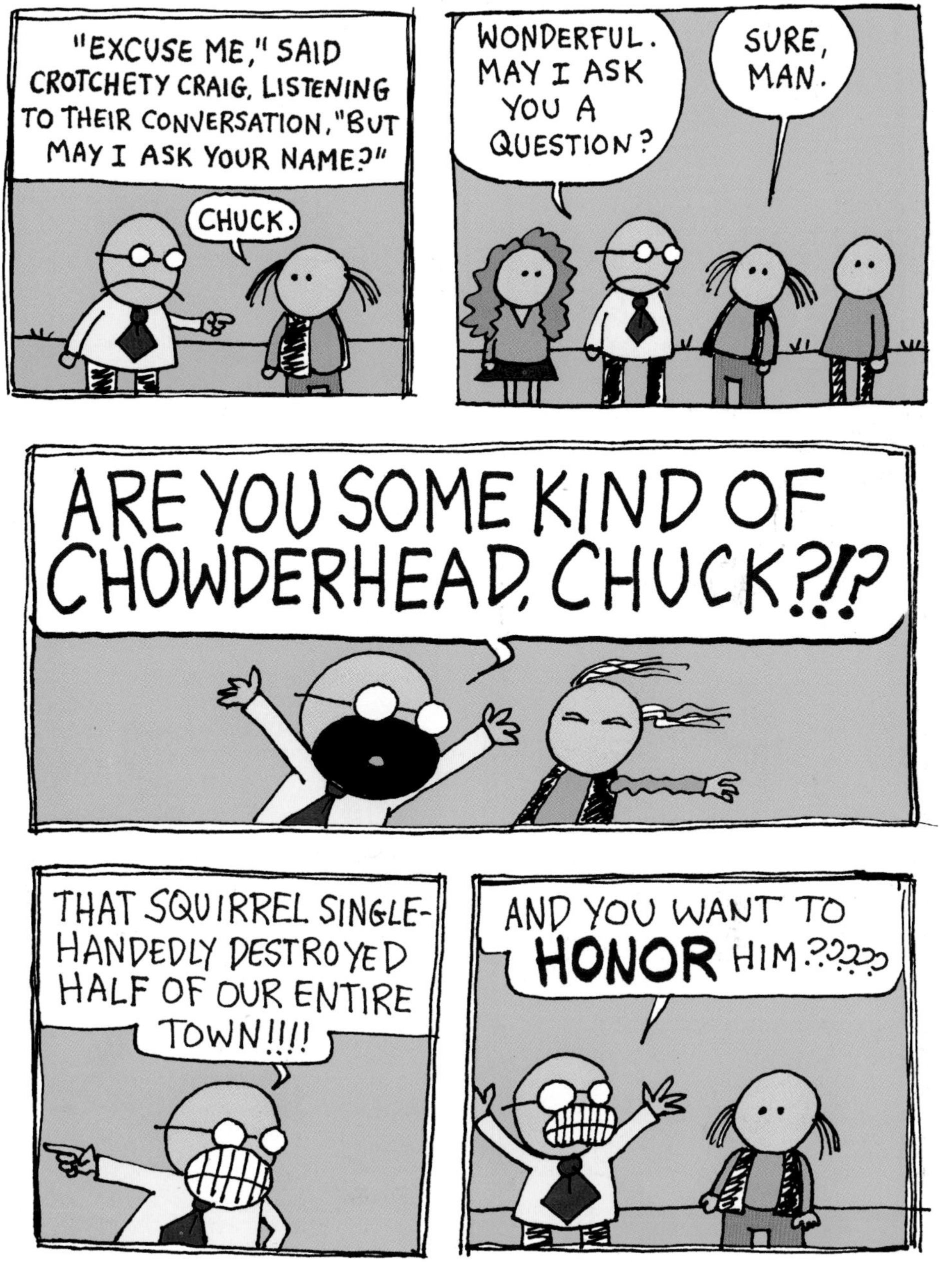
"EXCUSE ME," SAID CROTCHETY CRAIG, LISTENING TO THEIR CONVERSATION, "BUT MAY I ASK YOUR NAME?"
CHUCK.
WONDERFUL. MAY I ASK YOU A QUESTION?
SURE, MAN.
ARE YOU SOME KIND OF CHOWDERHEAD, CHUCK?!?
THAT SQUIRREL SINGLE-HANDEDLY DESTROYED HALF OF OUR ENTIRE TOWN!!!!
AND YOU WANT TO HONOR HIM?????

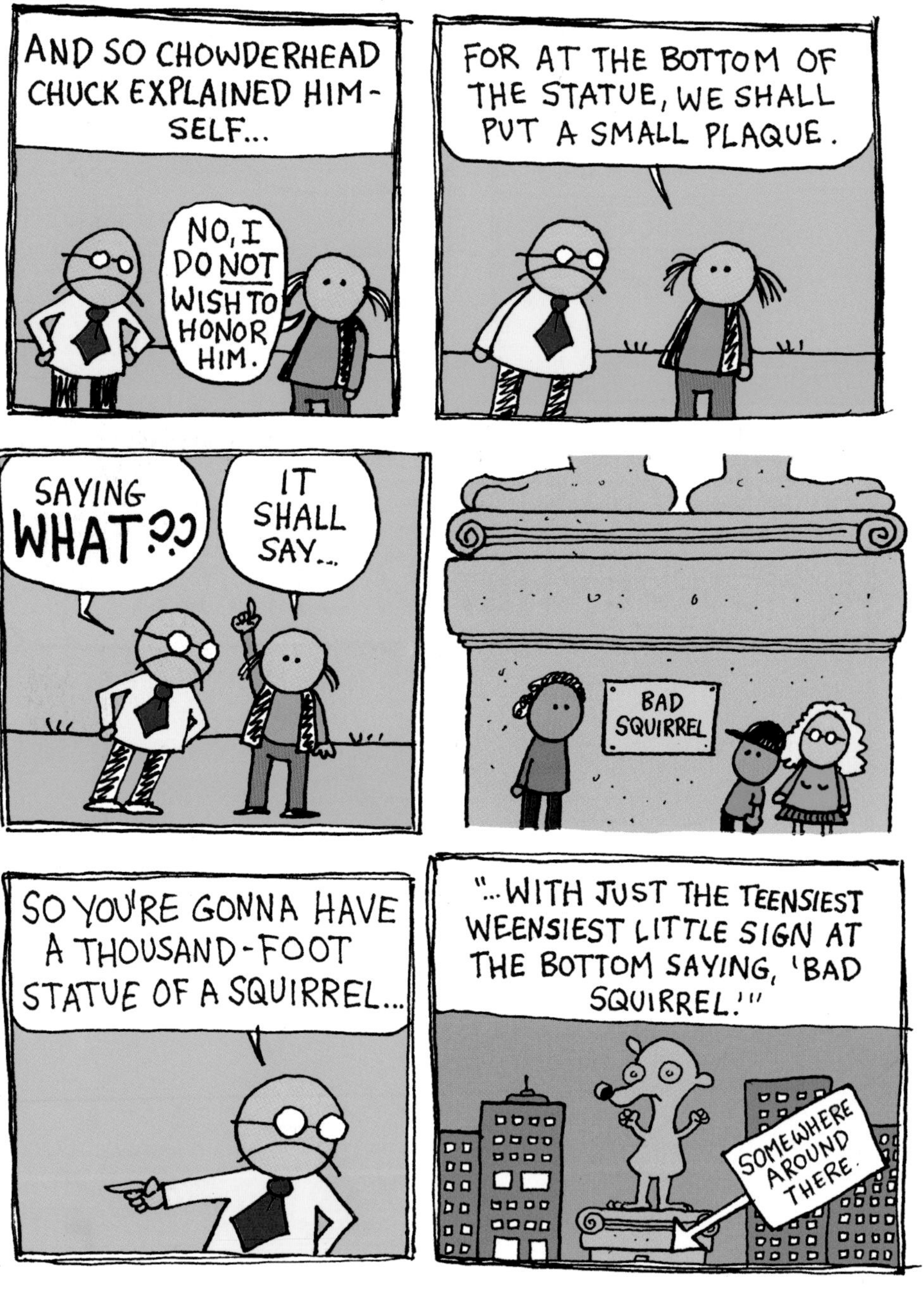

AND SO CHOWDERHEAD CHUCK EXPLAINED HIMSELF...
NO, I DO NOT WISH TO HONOR HIM.
FOR AT THE BOTTOM OF THE STATUE, WE SHALL PUT A SMALL PLAQUE.
SAYING WHAT??
IT SHALL SAY...
BAD SQUIRREL
SO YOU'RE GONNA HAVE A THOUSAND-FOOT STATUE OF A SQUIRREL...
"...WITH JUST THE TEENSIEST WEENSIEST LITTLE SIGN AT THE BOTTOM SAYING, 'BAD SQUIRREL!'"
SOMEWHERE AROUND THERE.

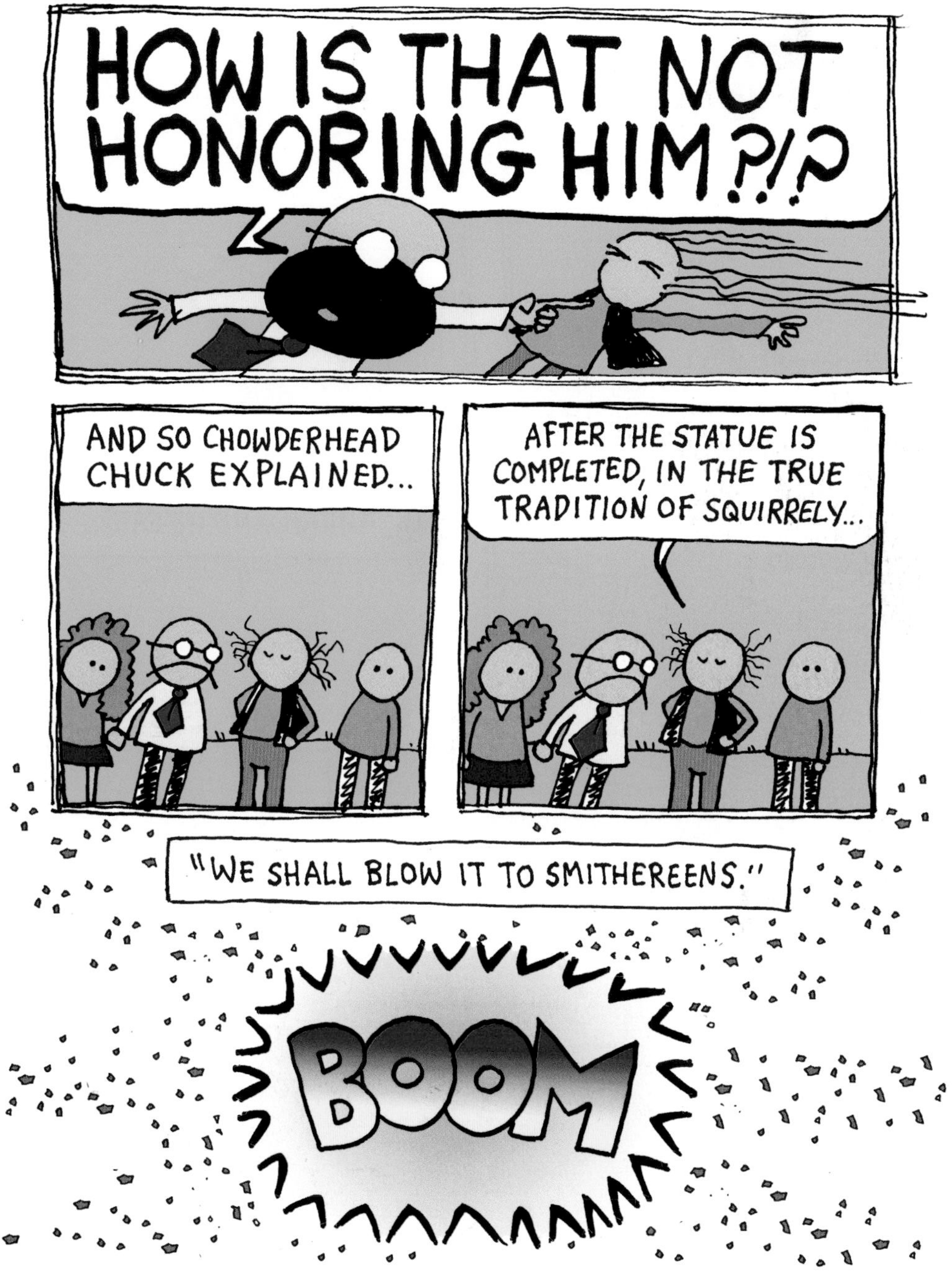
HOW IS THAT NOT HONORING HIM?!?
AND SO CHOWDERHEAD CHUCK EXPLAINED...
AFTER THE STATUE IS COMPLETED, IN THE TRUE TRADITION OF SQUIRRELY...
"WE SHALL BLOW IT TO SMITHEREENS."
BOOM

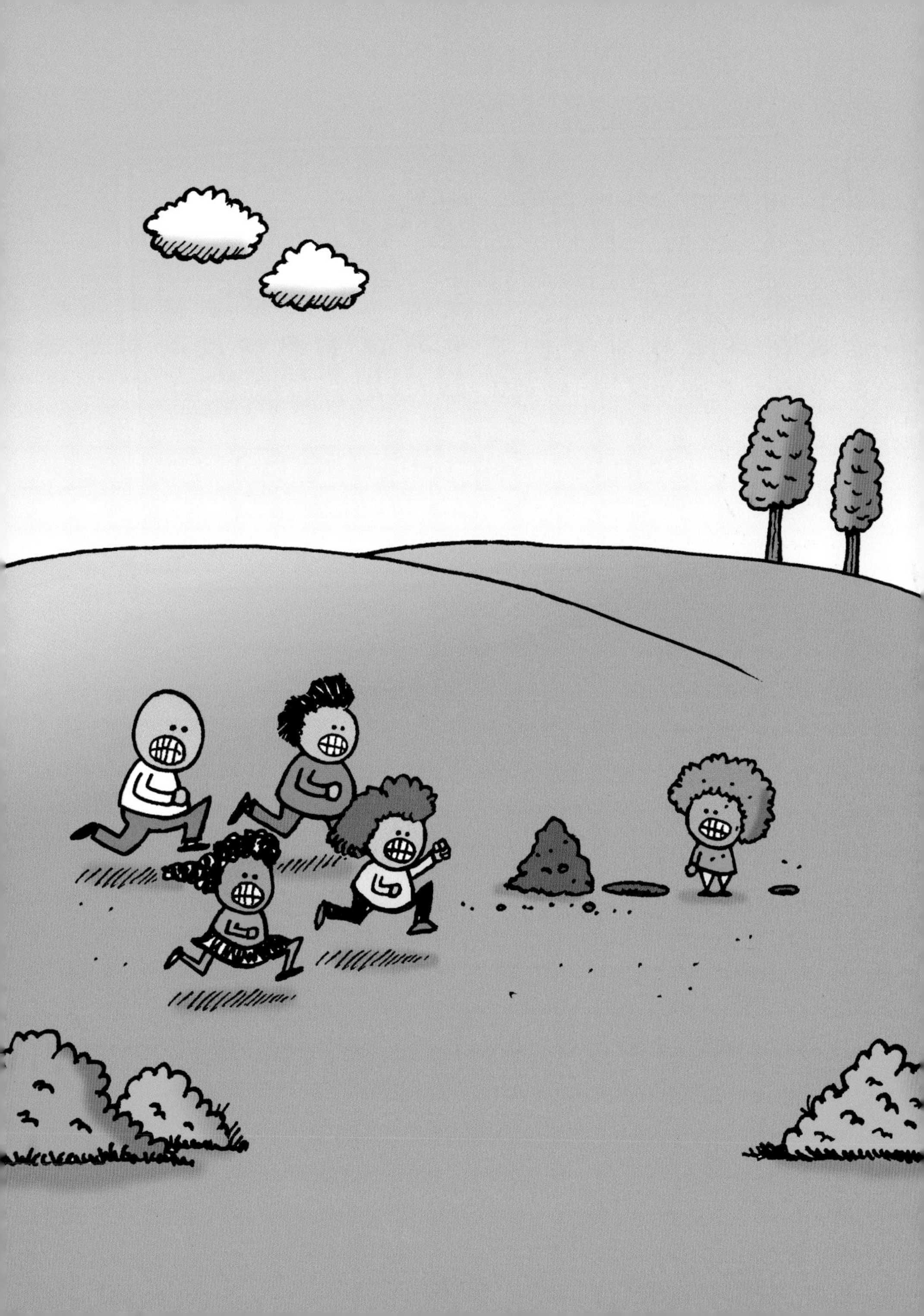

CHAPTER
SOMETHING
OR OTHER

IN WHICH...

WE LOSE TRACK
OF THE
CHAPTER
NUMBERS

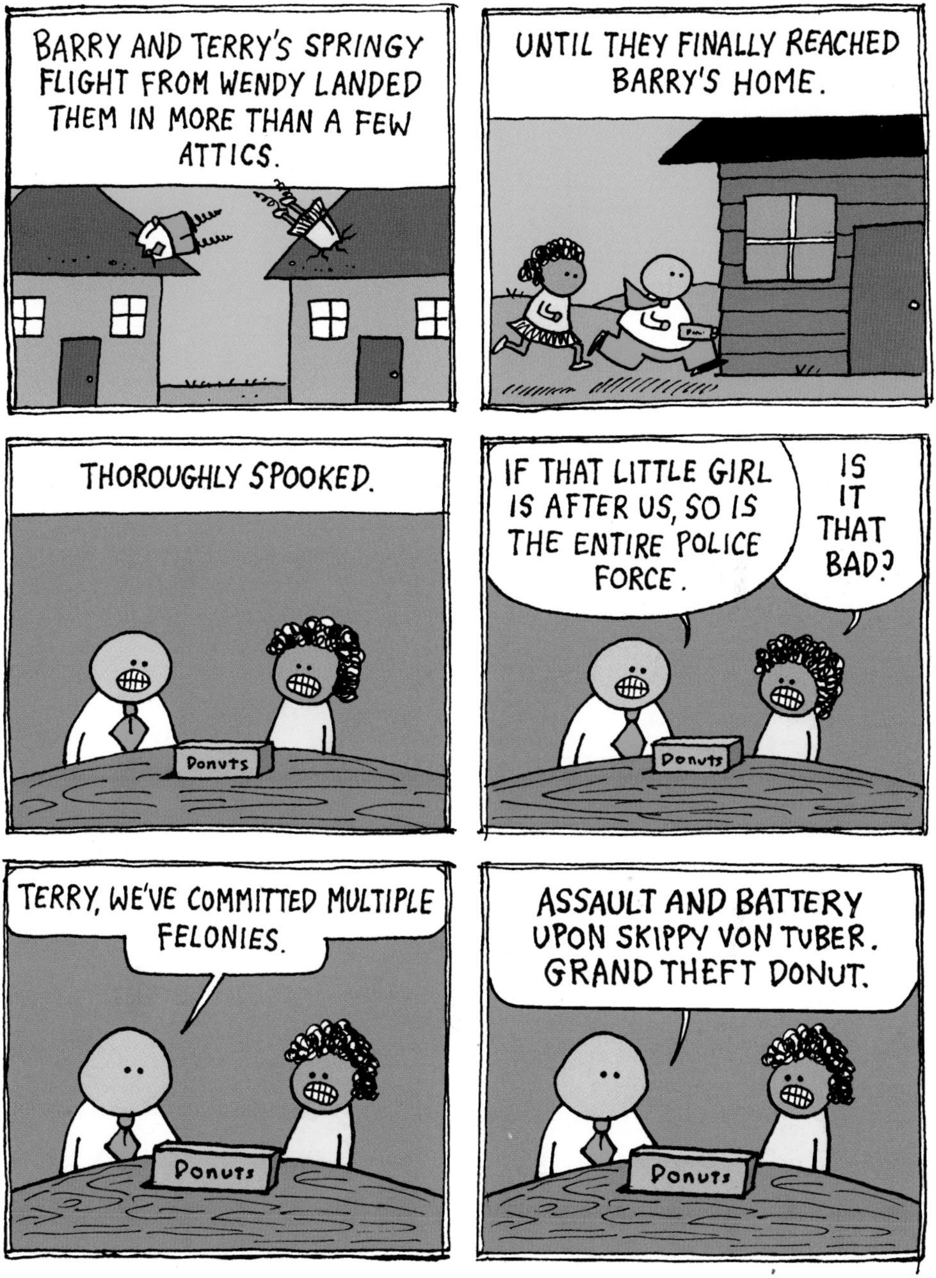
BARRY AND TERRY'S SPRINGY FLIGHT FROM WENDY LANDED THEM IN MORE THAN A FEW ATTICS.
UNTIL THEY FINALLY REACHED BARRY'S HOME.
THOROUGHLY SPOOKED.
DONUTS
IF THAT LITTLE GIRL IS AFTER US, SO IS THE ENTIRE POLICE FORCE.
IS IT THAT BAD?
DONUTS
TERRY, WE'VE COMMITTED MULTIPLE FELONIES.
DONUTS
ASSAULT AND BATTERY UPON SKIPPY VON TUBER. GRAND THEFT DONUT.
DONUTS

AS HIS PARTNER-IN-DONUT-
CRIME RAN HOME...

...TO A DOG THAT HAD JUST HAD
A WORSE DAY THAN HER.

CHAPTER ONE-AFTER-THE-LAST-ONE

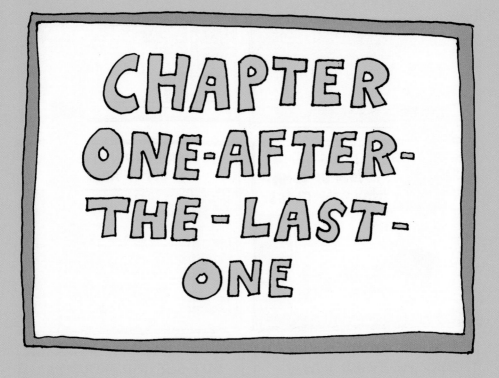

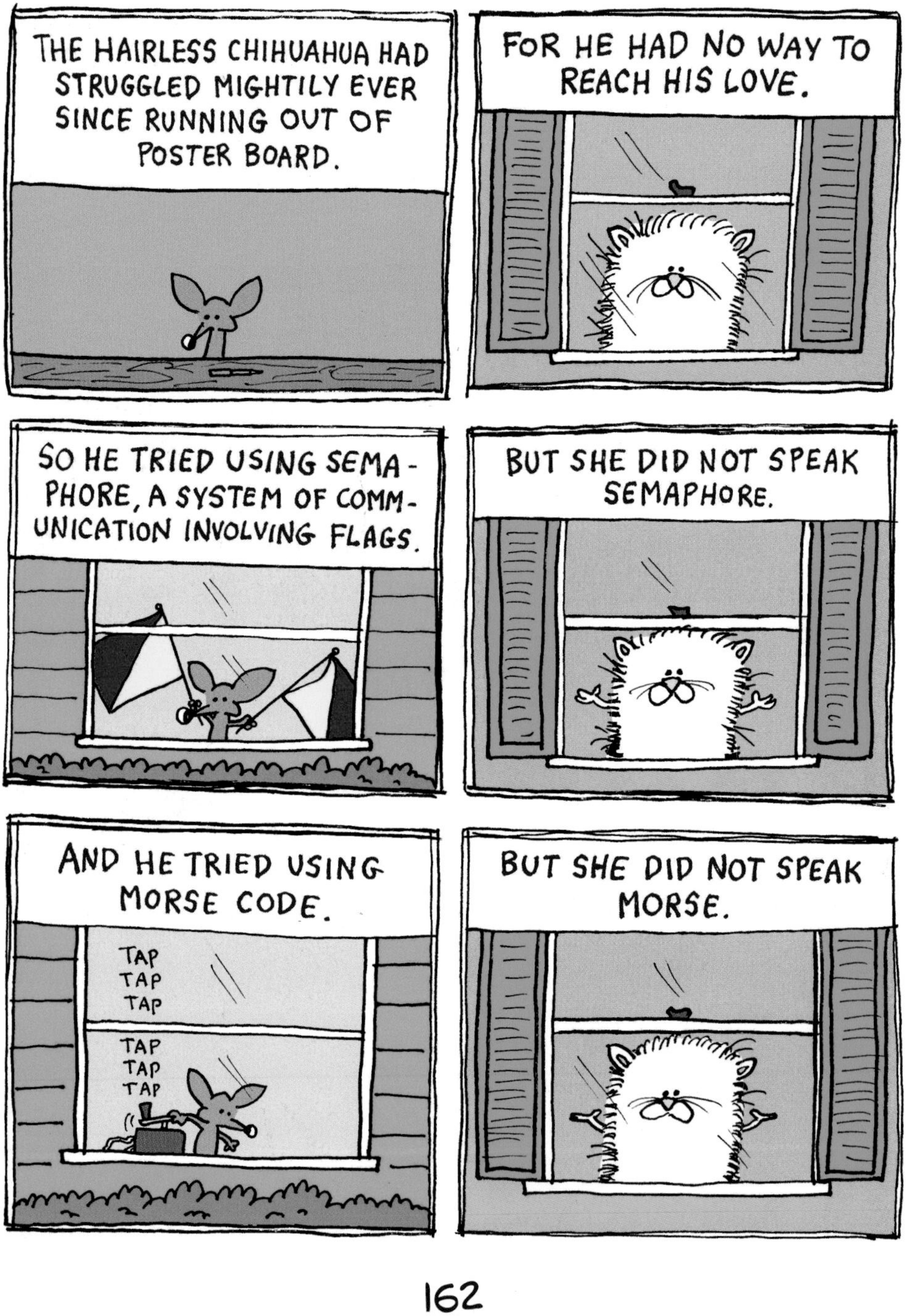
THE HAIRLESS CHIHUAHUA HAD STRUGGLED MIGHTILY EVER SINCE RUNNING OUT OF POSTER BOARD.
FOR HE HAD NO WAY TO REACH HIS LOVE.
SO HE TRIED USING SEMAPHORE, A SYSTEM OF COMMUNICATION INVOLVING FLAGS.
BUT SHE DID NOT SPEAK SEMAPHORE.
AND HE TRIED USING MORSE CODE.
TAP
TAP
TAP
TAP
TAP
TAP
BUT SHE DID NOT SPEAK MORSE.

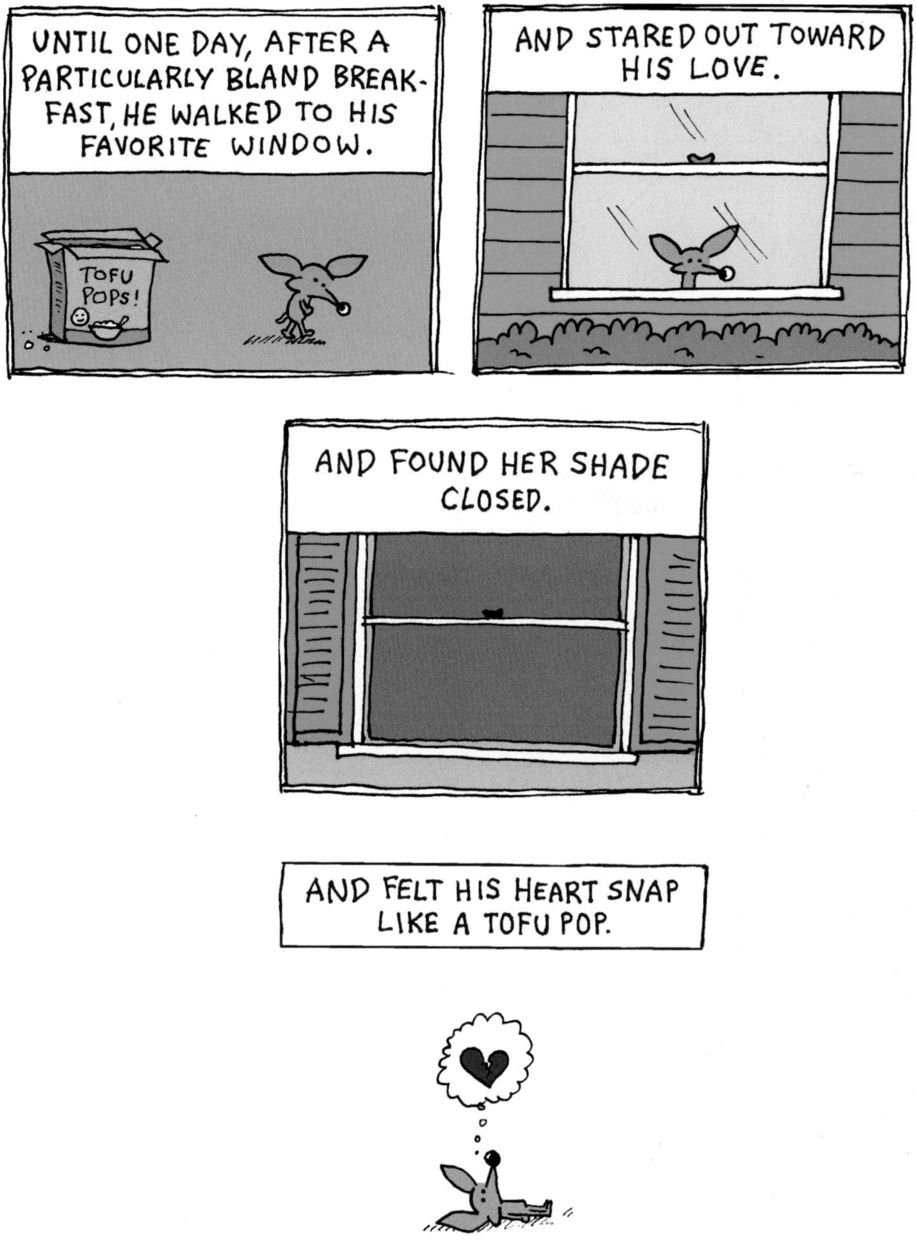
UNTIL ONE DAY, AFTER A PARTICULARLY BLAND BREAK-FAST, HE WALKED TO HIS FAVORITE WINDOW.
TOFU POPS!
AND STARED OUT TOWARD HIS LOVE.
AND FOUND HER SHADE CLOSED.
AND FELT HIS HEART SNAP LIKE A TOFU POP.

CHAPTER ANOTHER

IN WHICH...

THE PLOT, TO THE DEGREE IT EVEN EXISTS, MOVETH FORWARD

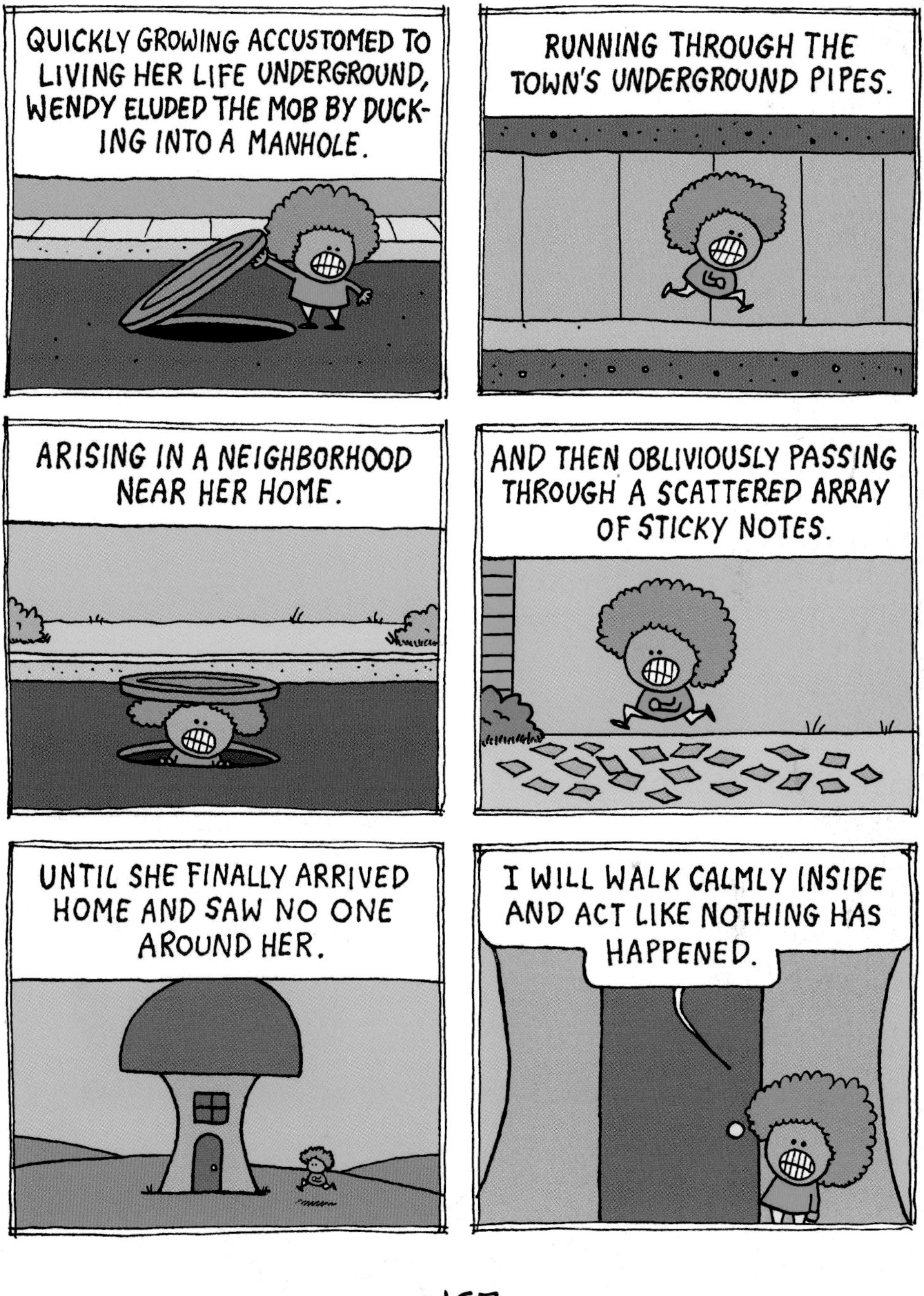
QUICKLY GROWING ACCUSTOMED TO LIVING HER LIFE UNDERGROUND, WENDY ELUDED THE MOB BY DUCKING INTO A MANHOLE.
RUNNING THROUGH THE TOWN'S UNDERGROUND PIPES.
ARISING IN A NEIGHBORHOOD NEAR HER HOME.
AND THEN OBLIVIOUSLY PASSING THROUGH A SCATTERED ARRAY OF STICKY NOTES.
UNTIL SHE FINALLY ARRIVED HOME AND SAW NO ONE AROUND HER.
I WILL WALK CALMLY INSIDE AND ACT LIKE NOTHING HAS HAPPENED.

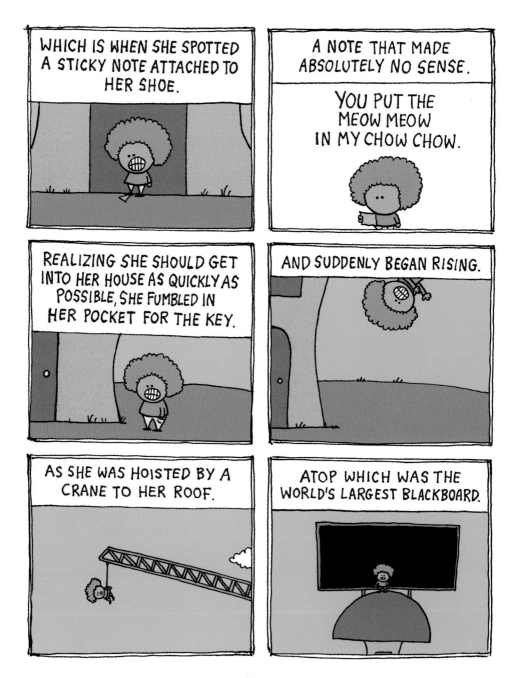

168

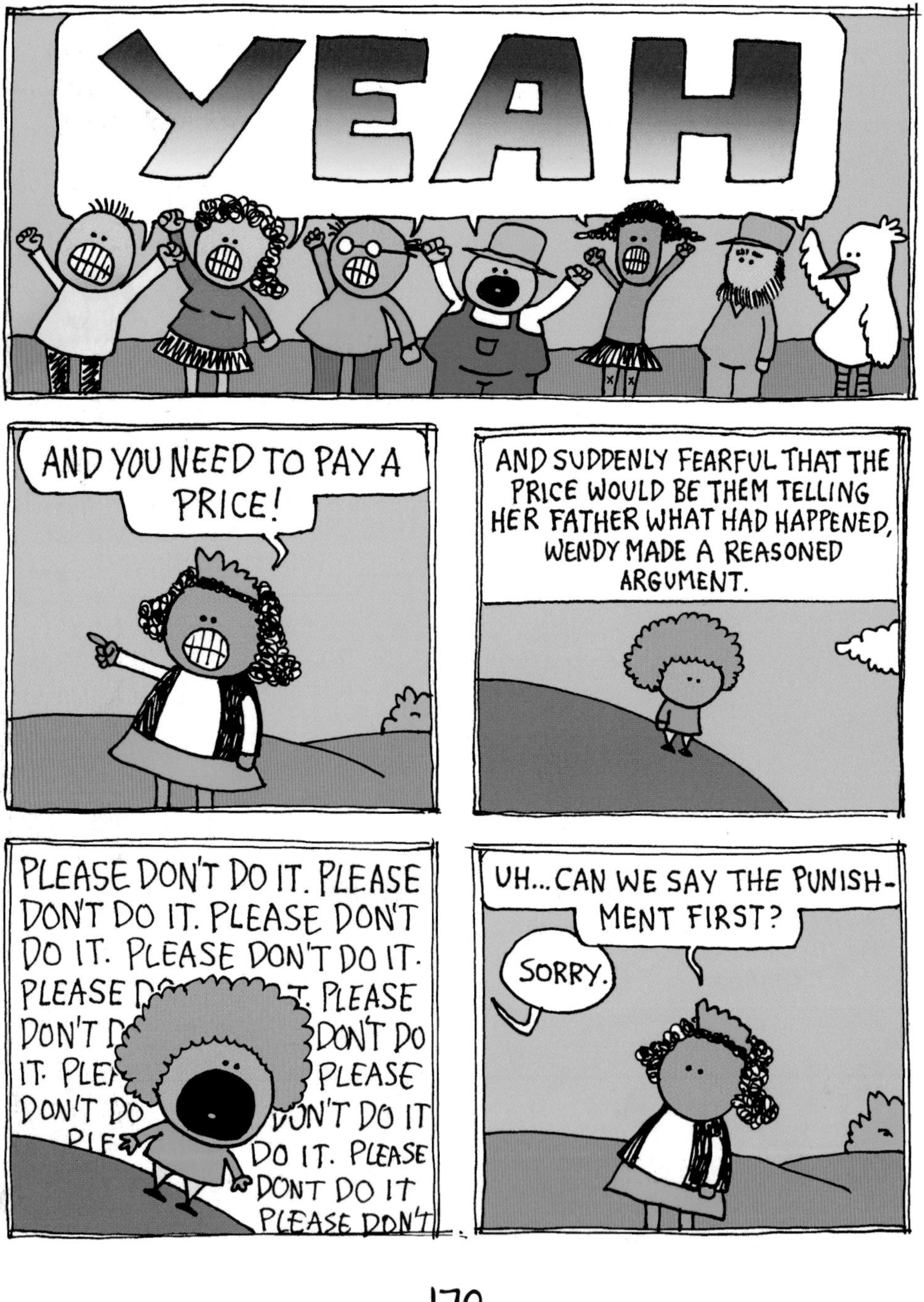
YEAH
AND YOU NEED TO PAY A PRICE!
AND SUDDENLY FEARFUL THAT THE PRICE WOULD BE THEM TELLING HER FATHER WHAT HAD HAPPENED, WENDY MADE A REASONED ARGUMENT.
PLEASE DON'T DO IT. PLEASE DON'T DO IT. PLEASE DON'T DO IT. PLEASE DON'T DO IT.
UH...CAN WE SAY THE PUNISH-MENT FIRST?
SORRY.

CHAPTER EIGHTEEN

IN WHICH...

WE GUESS THAT THAT'S THE CORRECT CHAPTER NUMBER

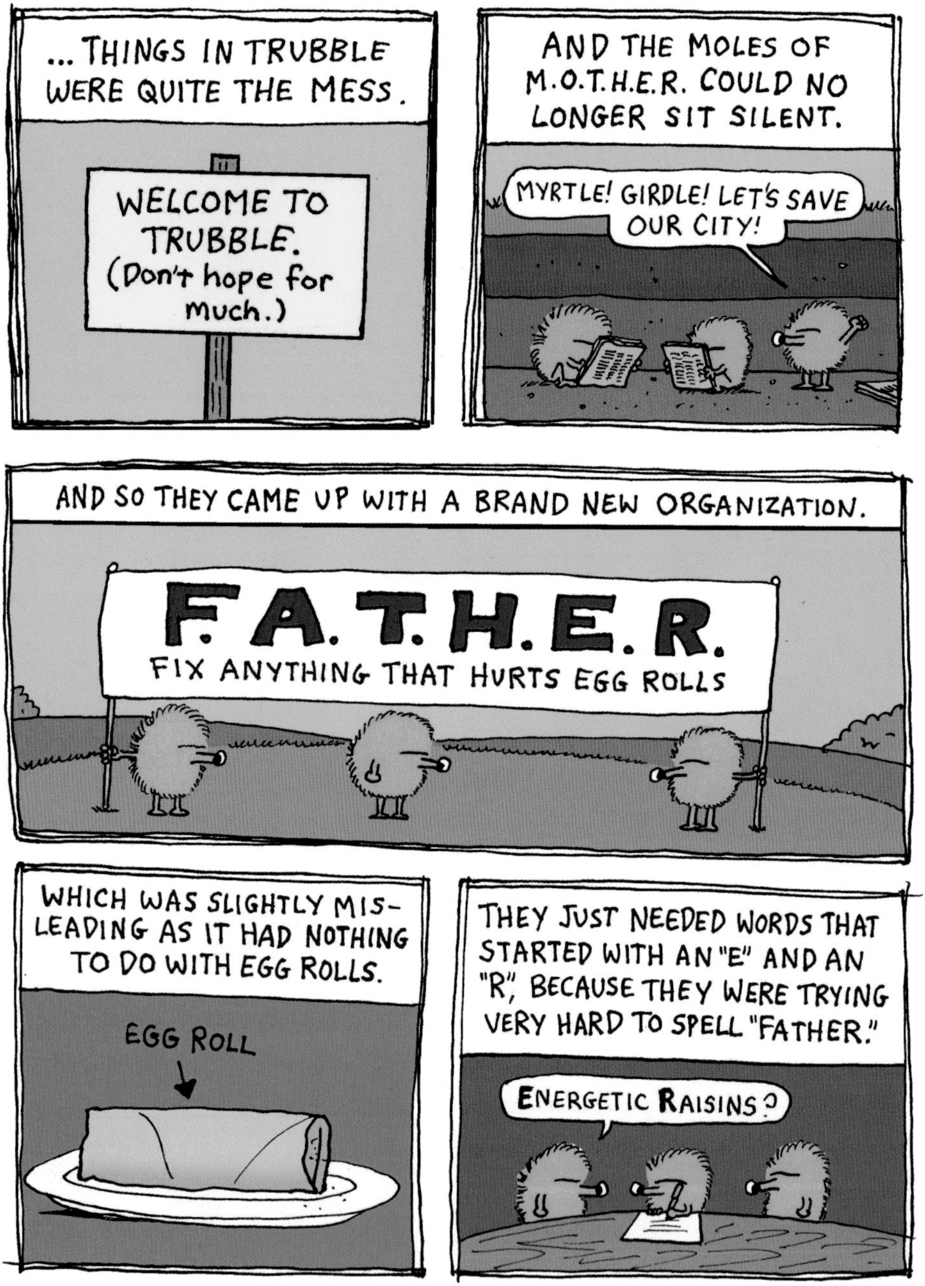
...THINGS IN TRUBBLE WERE QUITE THE MESS.
WELCOME TO TRUBBLE. (Don't hope for much.)
AND THE MOLES OF M.O.T.H.E.R. COULD NO LONGER SIT SILENT.
MYRTLE! GIRDLE! LET'S SAVE OUR CITY!
AND SO THEY CAME UP WITH A BRAND NEW ORGANIZATION.
F.A.T.H.E.R.
FIX ANYTHING THAT HURTS EGG ROLLS
WHICH WAS SLIGHTLY MIS-LEADING AS IT HAD NOTHING TO DO WITH EGG ROLLS.
EGG ROLL
THEY JUST NEEDED WORDS THAT STARTED WITH AN "E" AND AN "R," BECAUSE THEY WERE TRYING VERY HARD TO SPELL "FATHER."
ENERGETIC RAISINS?

BUT THE POINT WAS THAT THEY WANTED TO FIX THINGS, AND SO THEY DUG THEIR WAY TO WENDY'S FRONT YARD.

WHICH HAD RECENTLY BECOME A FOCAL POINT FOR THE TOWN.

CHA-CHA CHA-CHA CHA-CHA CHA-CHA CHA-
CHA CHA-CHA CHA-CHA   CHA-CHA
CHA-CHA   CHA-CHA CHA-   CHA-CHA
    CHA-CHA CHA-CHA   CHA CHA-CHA
CHA-CHA CHA-CHA   CHA-CHA CHA-CHA
CHA-CHA CHA-CHA CHA-CHA CHA-CHA CHACHA
CHA-CHA CHA-CHA   CHA-CHA
CHA-CHA CHA-CHA   CHA-CHA CHA-CHA
CHA CHA-CHA   CHA-CHA CHA-CHA
    CHA-CH   CHA-CHA CHA-CHA

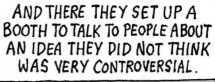

AND THERE THEY SET UP A BOOTH TO TALK TO PEOPLE ABOUT AN IDEA THEY DID NOT THINK WAS VERY CONTROVERSIAL.

MAYBE WE SHOULDN'T GO BROKE FOR 200 YEARS JUST TO BUILD A SOLID-GOLD SQUIRREL THAT WE WILL THEN BLOW UP

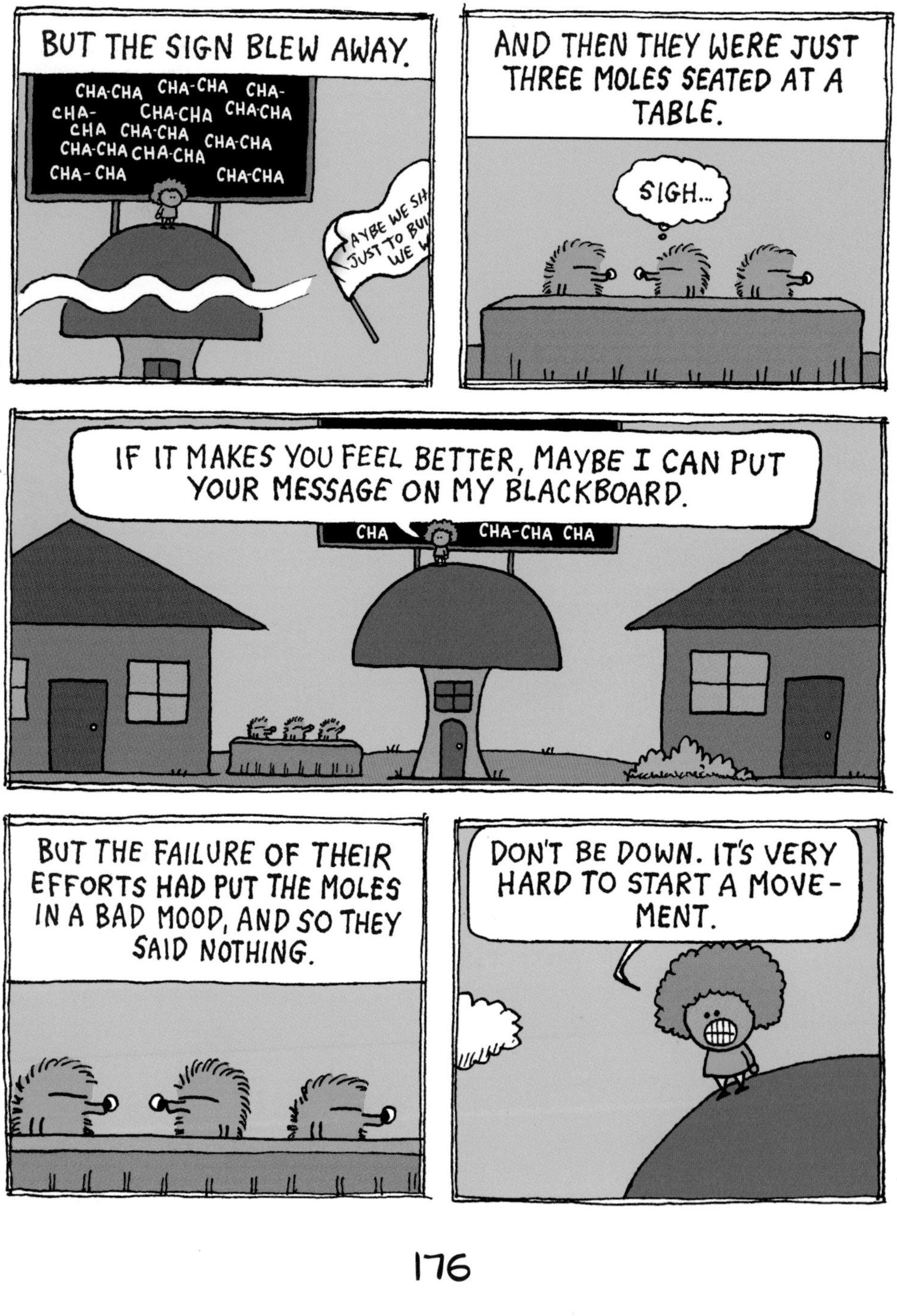
BUT THE SIGN BLEW AWAY.
CHA-CHA CHA-CHA CHA-
CHA- CHA-CHA CHA-CHA
CHA CHA-CHA
CHA-CHA CHA-CHA CHA-CHA
CHA-CHA CHA-CHA
AND THEN THEY WERE JUST THREE MOLES SEATED AT A TABLE.
SIGH...
IF IT MAKES YOU FEEL BETTER, MAYBE I CAN PUT YOUR MESSAGE ON MY BLACKBOARD.
CHA CHA-CHA CHA
BUT THE FAILURE OF THEIR EFFORTS HAD PUT THE MOLES IN A BAD MOOD, AND SO THEY SAID NOTHING.
DON'T BE DOWN. IT'S VERY HARD TO START A MOVE-MENT.

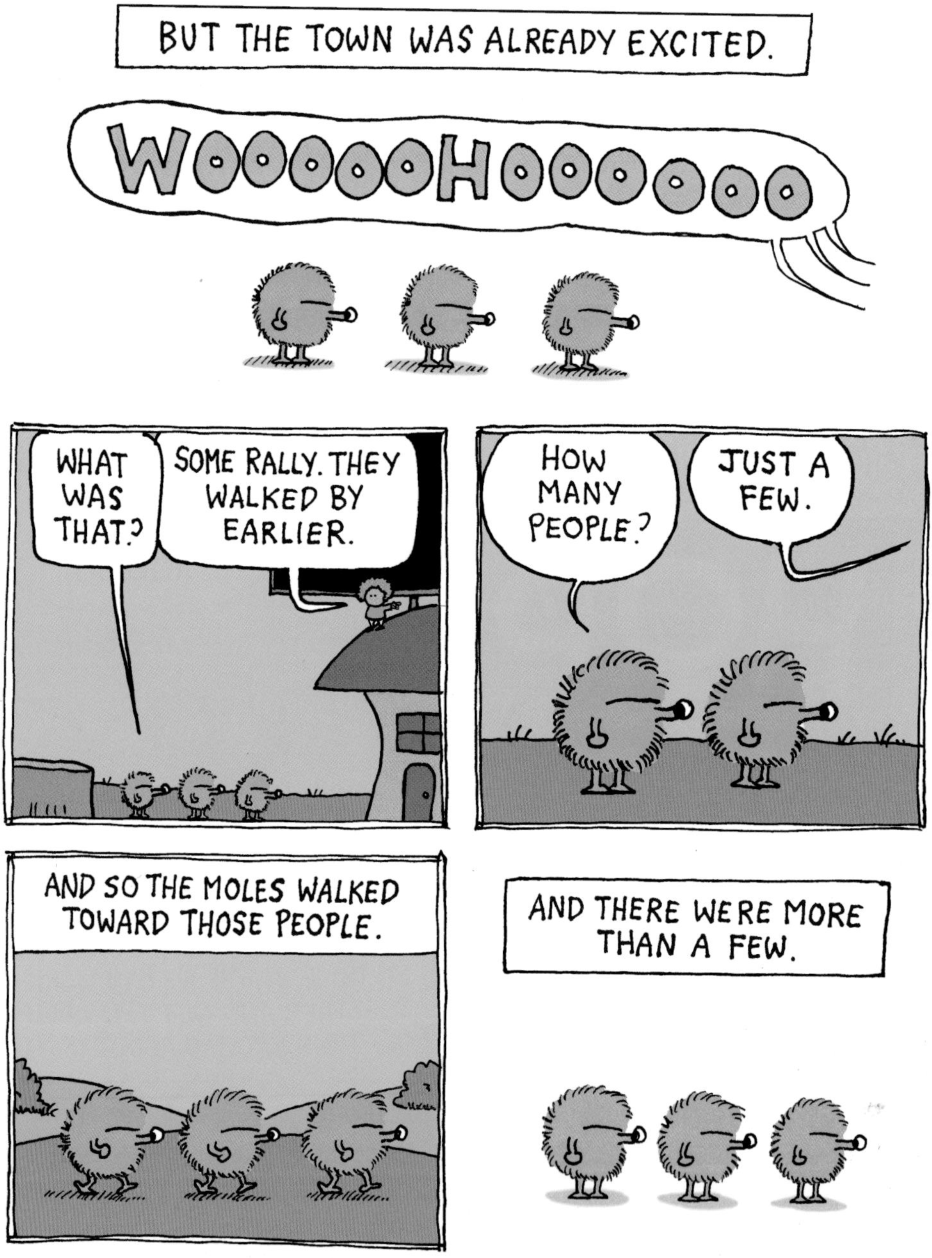
BUT THE TOWN WAS ALREADY EXCITED.
WOOOOOHOOOOOOO
WHAT WAS THAT?
SOME RALLY. THEY WALKED BY EARLIER.
HOW MANY PEOPLE?
JUST A FEW.
AND SO THE MOLES WALKED TOWARD THOSE PEOPLE.
AND THERE WERE MORE THAN A FEW.

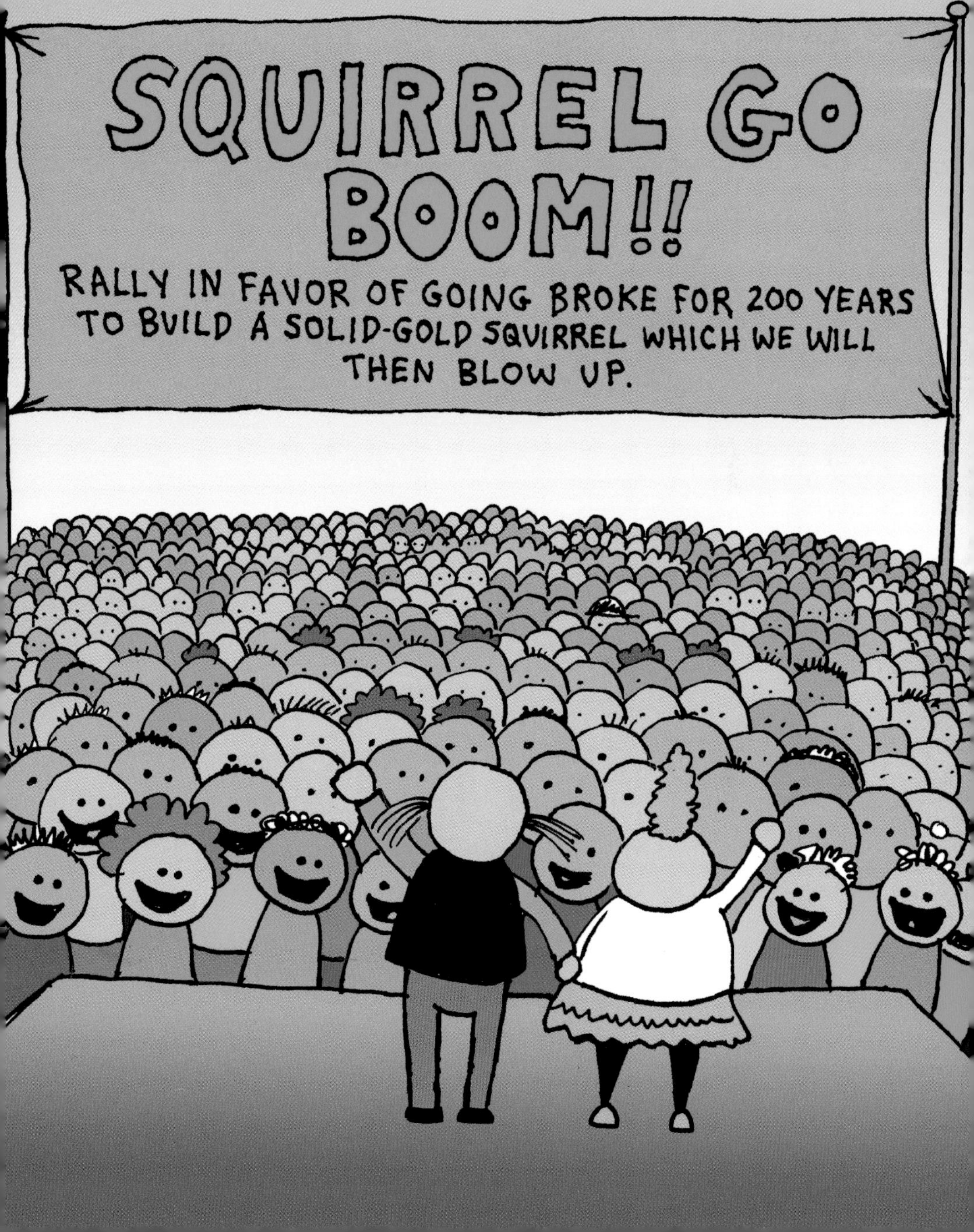
SQUIRREL GO BOOM!!
RALLY IN FAVOR OF GOING BROKE FOR 200 YEARS TO BUILD A SOLID-GOLD SQUIRREL WHICH WE WILL THEN BLOW UP.

CHAPTER
CHAPTER

IN WHICH...

WE GET
REPETITIVE

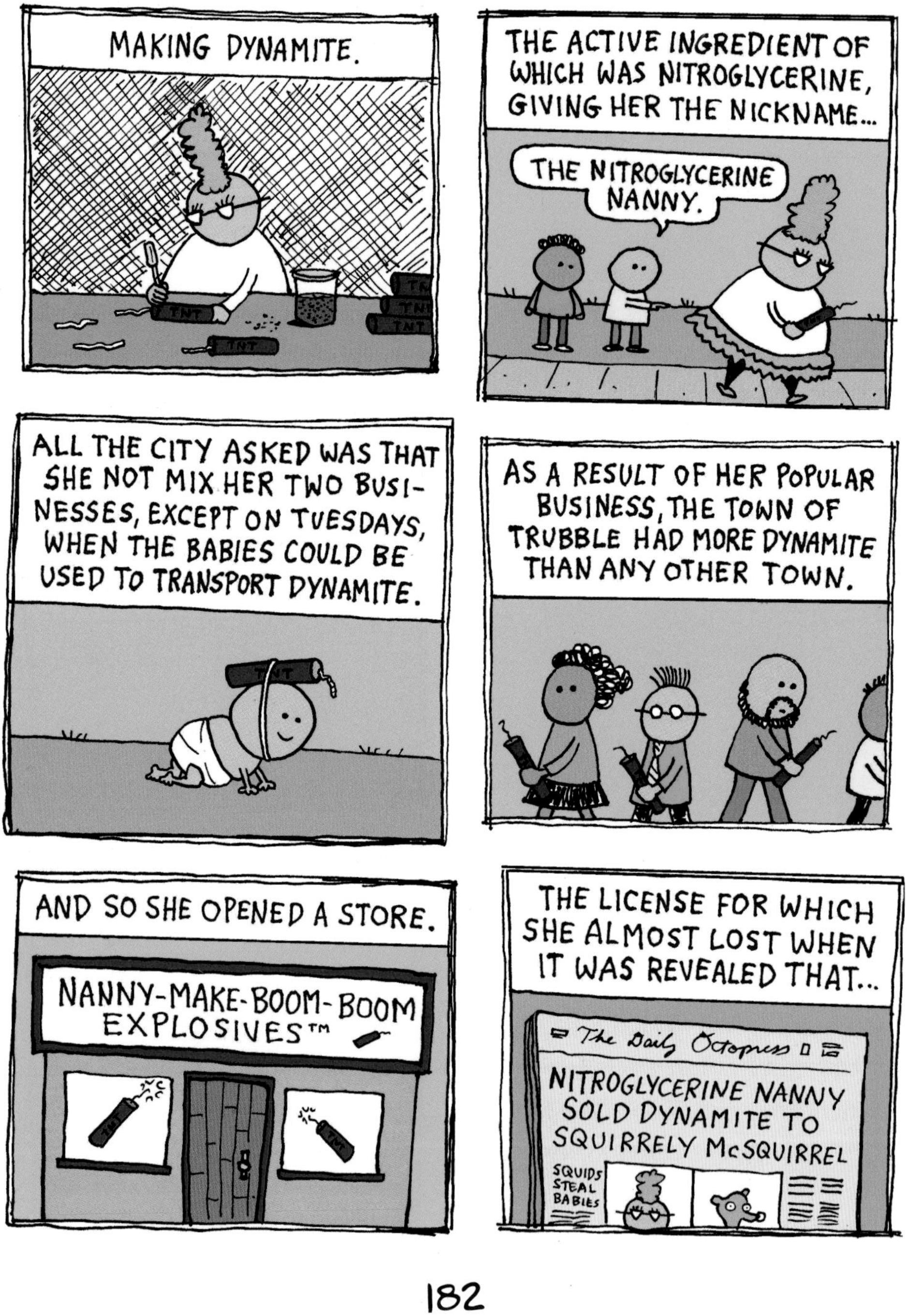
MAKING DYNAMITE.
THE ACTIVE INGREDIENT OF WHICH WAS NITROGLYCERINE, GIVING HER THE NICKNAME...
THE NITROGLYCERINE NANNY.
ALL THE CITY ASKED WAS THAT SHE NOT MIX HER TWO BUSI-NESSES, EXCEPT ON TUESDAYS, WHEN THE BABIES COULD BE USED TO TRANSPORT DYNAMITE.
AS A RESULT OF HER POPULAR BUSINESS, THE TOWN OF TRUBBLE HAD MORE DYNAMITE THAN ANY OTHER TOWN.
AND SO SHE OPENED A STORE.
NANNY-MAKE-BOOM-BOOM EXPLOSIVES™
THE LICENSE FOR WHICH SHE ALMOST LOST WHEN IT WAS REVEALED THAT...
The Daily Octopuss
NITROGLYCERINE NANNY SOLD DYNAMITE TO SQUIRRELY McSQUIRREL
SQUIDS STEAL BABIES

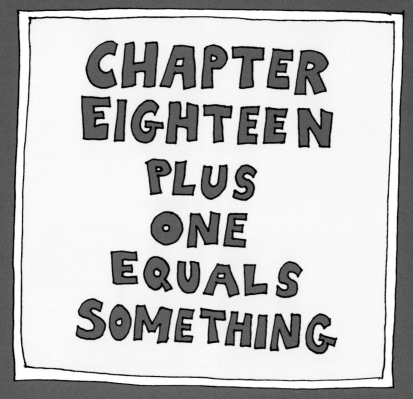

CHAPTER EIGHTEEN PLUS ONE EQUALS SOMETHING

IN WHICH...

WE SHOW WE CAN ALMOST COUNT

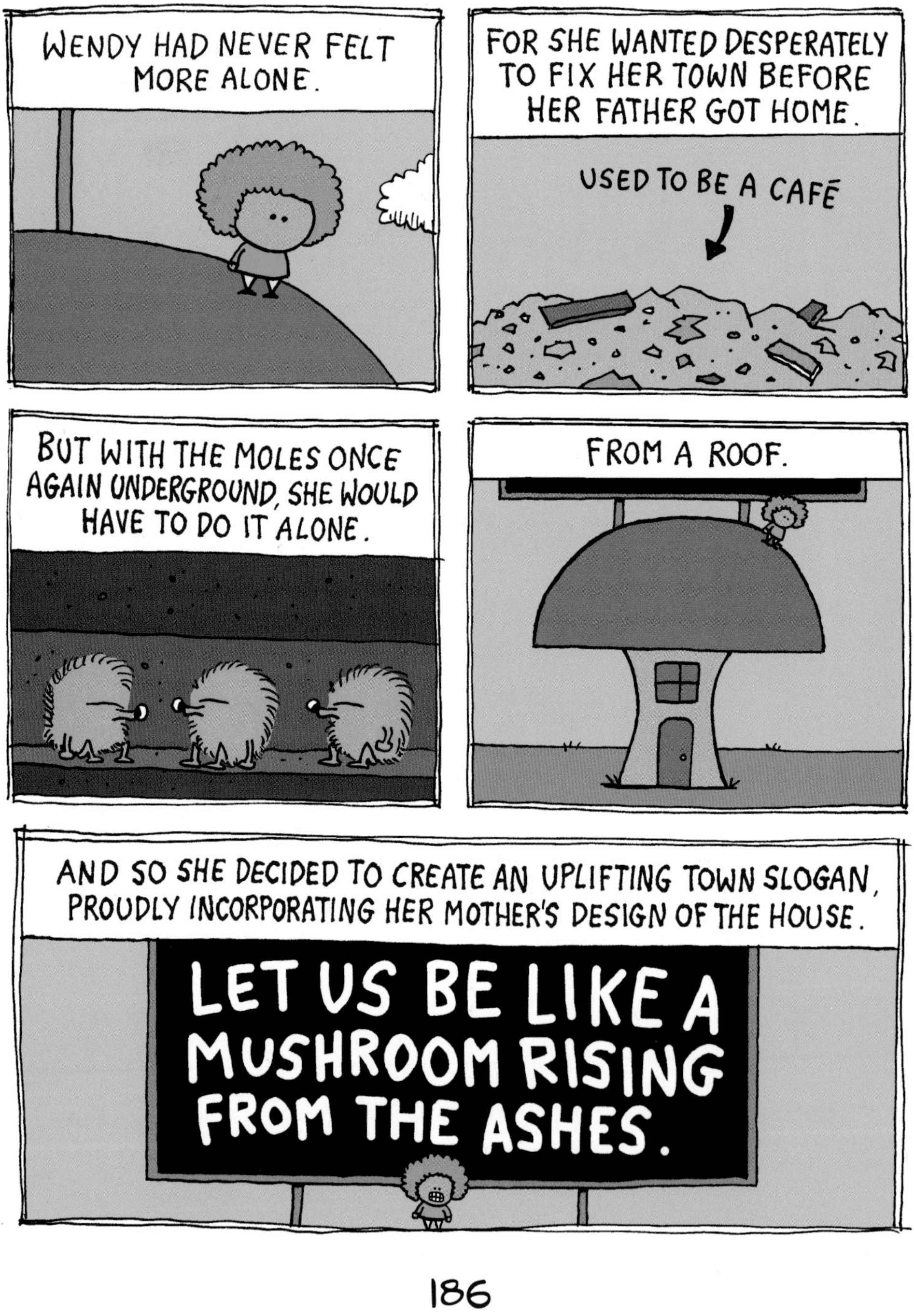
WENDY HAD NEVER FELT MORE ALONE.
FOR SHE WANTED DESPERATELY TO FIX HER TOWN BEFORE HER FATHER GOT HOME.
USED TO BE A CAFÉ
BUT WITH THE MOLES ONCE AGAIN UNDERGROUND, SHE WOULD HAVE TO DO IT ALONE.
FROM A ROOF.
AND SO SHE DECIDED TO CREATE AN UPLIFTING TOWN SLOGAN, PROUDLY INCORPORATING HER MOTHER'S DESIGN OF THE HOUSE.
LET US BE LIKE A MUSHROOM RISING FROM THE ASHES.

AND WAS PAINED TO SEE THEM MENTIONED IN THE TOWN'S SLOGAN.

BE THE MUSHROOM

GRRR

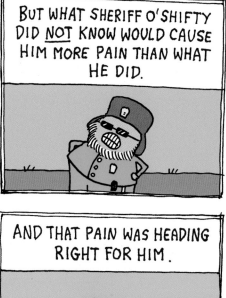

BUT WHAT SHERIFF O'SHIFTY DID <u>NOT</u> KNOW WOULD CAUSE HIM MORE PAIN THAN WHAT HE DID.

AND THAT PAIN WAS HEADING RIGHT FOR HIM.

CHAPTER
SNAPPED
HER

WHICH...

RHYMES NICELY
AND TELLS YOU
THAT A FEMALE
CHARACTER IS
ABOUT TO SNAP

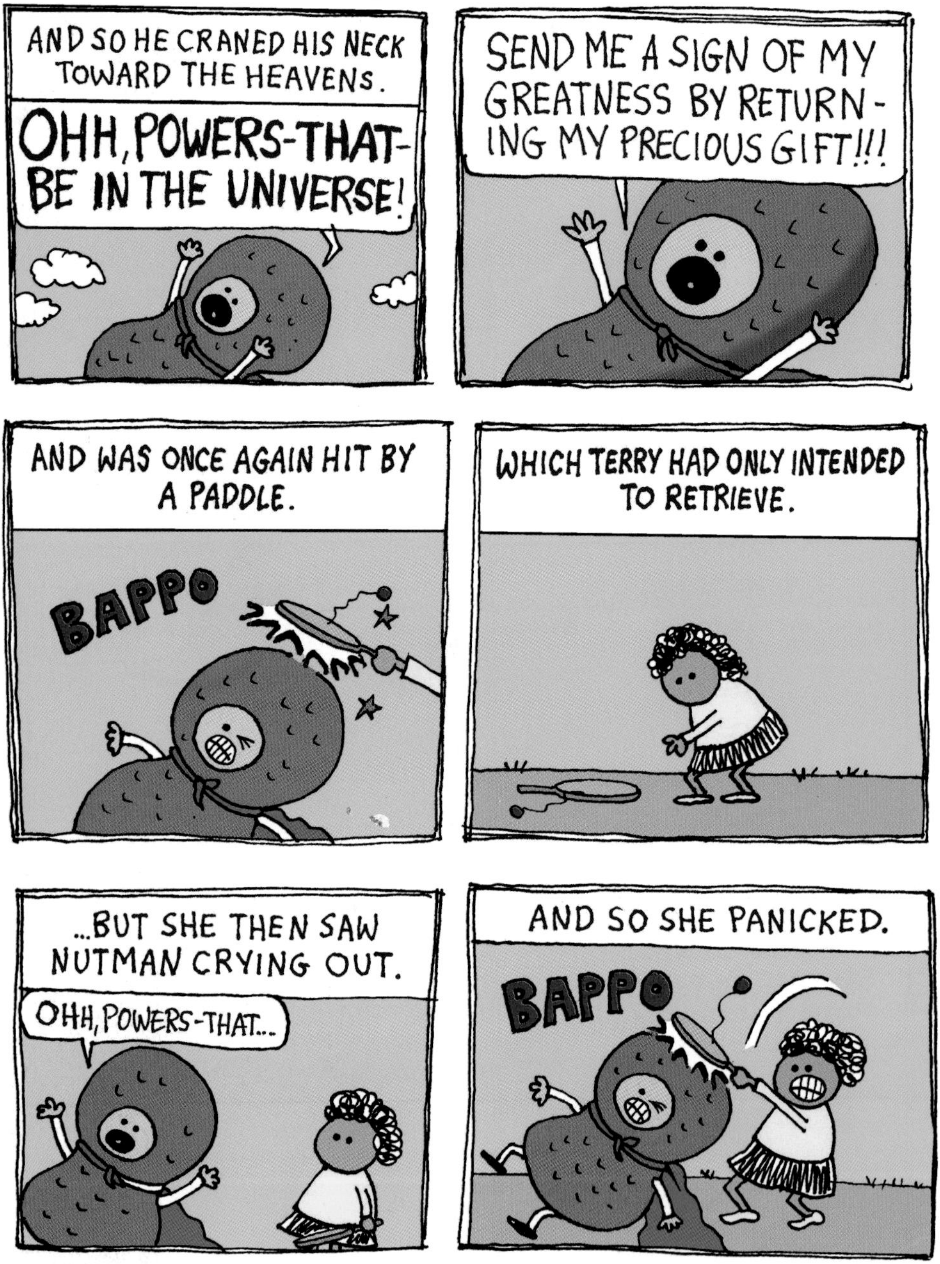
AND SO HE CRANED HIS NECK TOWARD THE HEAVENS.
OHH, POWERS-THAT-BE IN THE UNIVERSE!
SEND ME A SIGN OF MY GREATNESS BY RETURNING MY PRECIOUS GIFT!!!
AND WAS ONCE AGAIN HIT BY A PADDLE.
BAPPO
WHICH TERRY HAD ONLY INTENDED TO RETRIEVE.
...BUT SHE THEN SAW NUTMAN CRYING OUT.
OHH, POWERS-THAT...
AND SO SHE PANICKED.
BAPPO

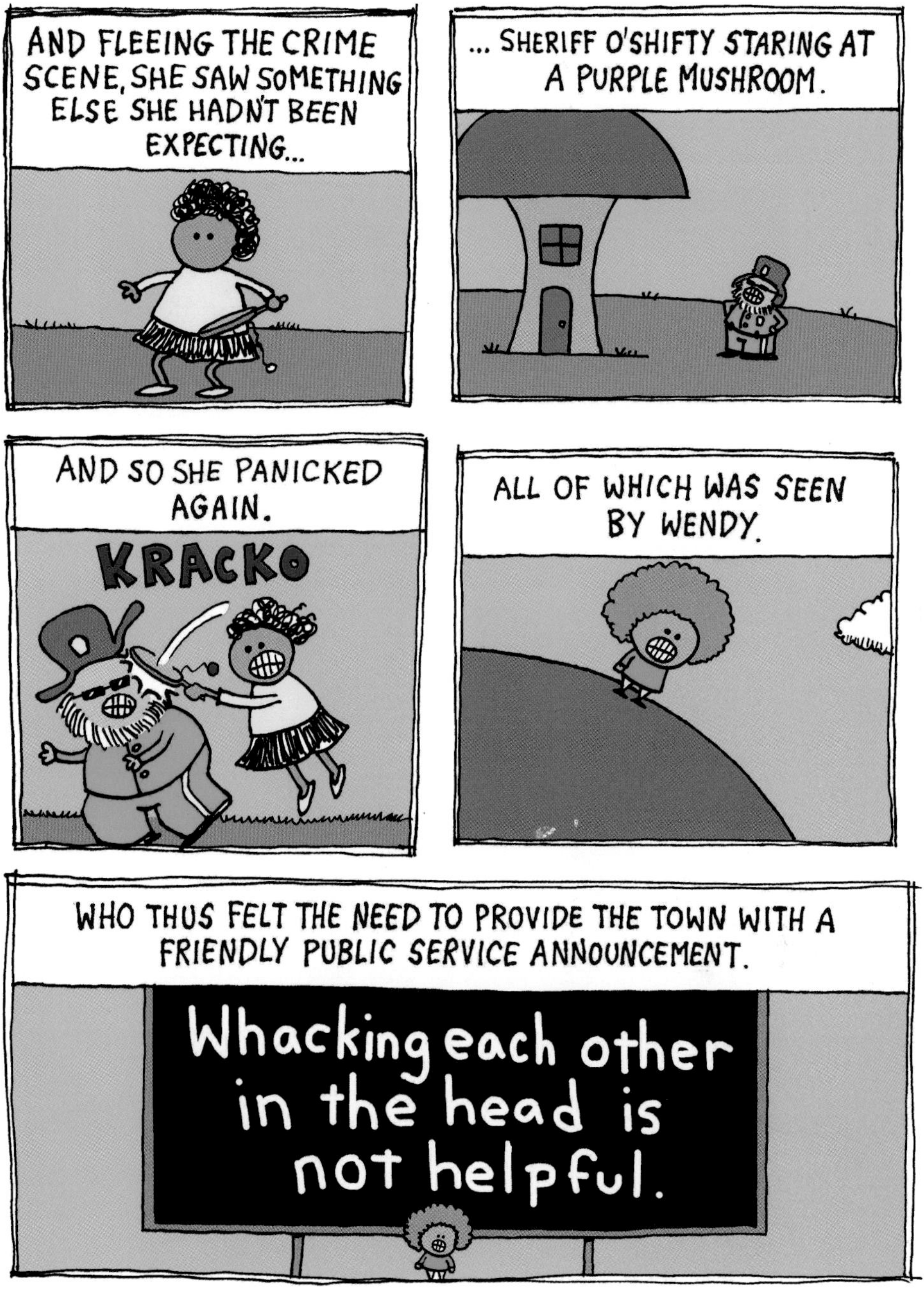
AND FLEEING THE CRIME SCENE, SHE SAW SOMETHING ELSE SHE HADN'T BEEN EXPECTING...
... SHERIFF O'SHIFTY STARING AT A PURPLE MUSHROOM.
AND SO SHE PANICKED AGAIN.
KRACKO
ALL OF WHICH WAS SEEN BY WENDY.
WHO THUS FELT THE NEED TO PROVIDE THE TOWN WITH A FRIENDLY PUBLIC SERVICE ANNOUNCEMENT.
Whacking each other in the head is not helpful.

CHAPTER SUPER BRIEF

IN WHICH...

WE ARE SUPER BRIEF

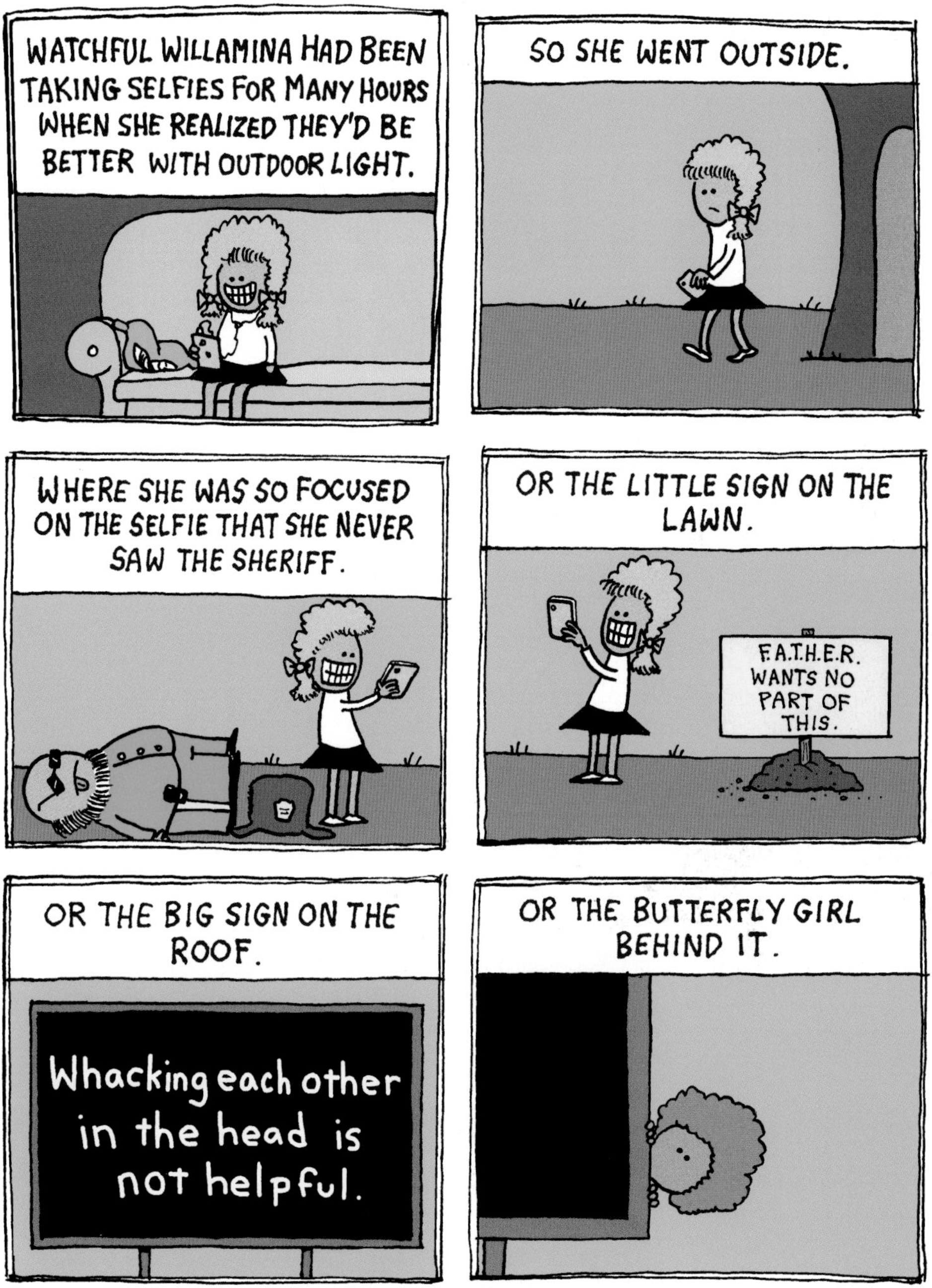
WATCHFUL WILLAMINA HAD BEEN TAKING SELFIES FOR MANY HOURS WHEN SHE REALIZED THEY'D BE BETTER WITH OUTDOOR LIGHT.
SO SHE WENT OUTSIDE.
WHERE SHE WAS SO FOCUSED ON THE SELFIE THAT SHE NEVER SAW THE SHERIFF.
OR THE LITTLE SIGN ON THE LAWN.
F.A.T.H.E.R. WANTS NO PART OF THIS.
OR THE BIG SIGN ON THE ROOF.
Whacking each other in the head is not helpful.
OR THE BUTTERFLY GIRL BEHIND IT.

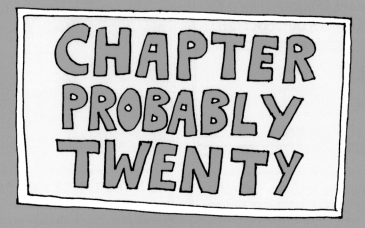

CHAPTER PROBABLY TWENTY

IN WHICH...

YOU WILL BE GLUED
TO THE EDGE OF
YOUR SEAT, BUT
HOPEFULLY NOT
WITH ACTUAL
GLUE

198

200

AND JUST THEN, THE SHERIFF SPOTTED A CLUSTER OF MUSHROOMS GROWING IN BARRY'S YARD.

AND IT REMINDED HIM OF THE LAST THING HE SAW BEFORE HE LOST CONSCIOUSNESS.

FLASHBACK

I MUST GO. BUT SAVE ME A DONUT. I LIKE THE ROUNDY ONES.

Donuts

AND AS SOON AS THE SHERIFF WAS GONE, BARRY TOOK OFF ONE OF HIS TOSS-A-BOSS SHOES AND SET THE BOX ATOP IT.

Donuts

OUT OF MY LIFE FOREVER, YOU CURSED LITTLE BOX!!

Donuts

AND PRESSING THE EJECT BUTTON, HE SENT SQUIRRELY HURLING PERILOUSLY THROUGH THE AIR.

Donut

INADVERTENTLY TOWARD A MAN WHO WAS NOW STANDING ON THE GROUND BELOW...

...TO WHOM SQUIRRELY MEANT MORE THAN ANYONE ELSE IN THE WORLD.

AND WHO HAD JUST ASKED THE HEAVENS FOR A SIGN.

PLOP

IN WHICH...

WE RUN OUT OF
CLEVER CHAPTER
TITLES

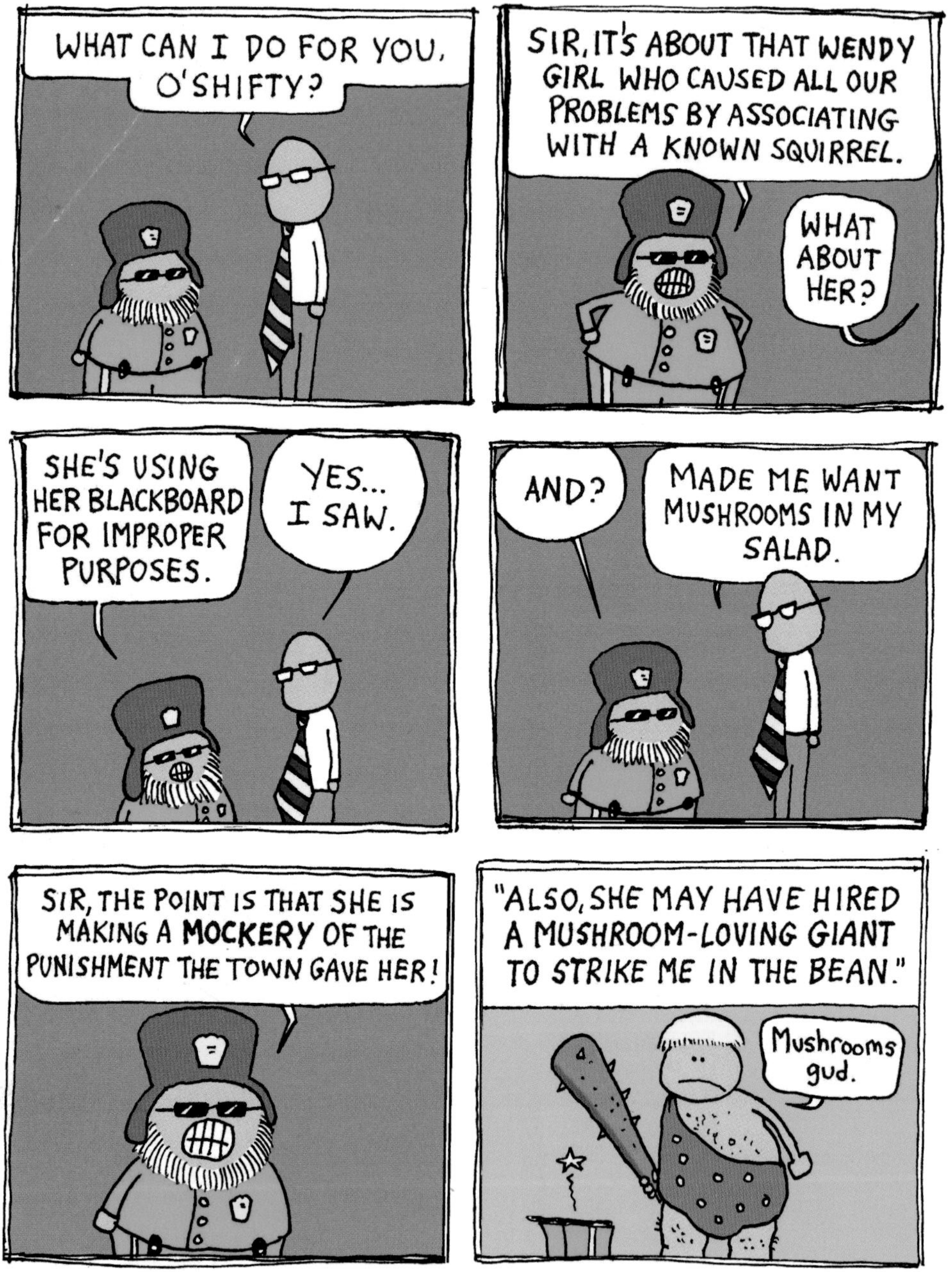
WHAT CAN I DO FOR YOU, O'SHIFTY?
SIR, IT'S ABOUT THAT WENDY GIRL WHO CAUSED ALL OUR PROBLEMS BY ASSOCIATING WITH A KNOWN SQUIRREL.
WHAT ABOUT HER?
SHE'S USING HER BLACKBOARD FOR IMPROPER PURPOSES.
YES... I SAW.
AND?
MADE ME WANT MUSHROOMS IN MY SALAD.
SIR, THE POINT IS THAT SHE IS MAKING A **MOCKERY** OF THE PUNISHMENT THE TOWN GAVE HER!
"ALSO, SHE MAY HAVE HIRED A MUSHROOM-LOVING GIANT TO STRIKE ME IN THE BEAN."
Mushrooms gud.

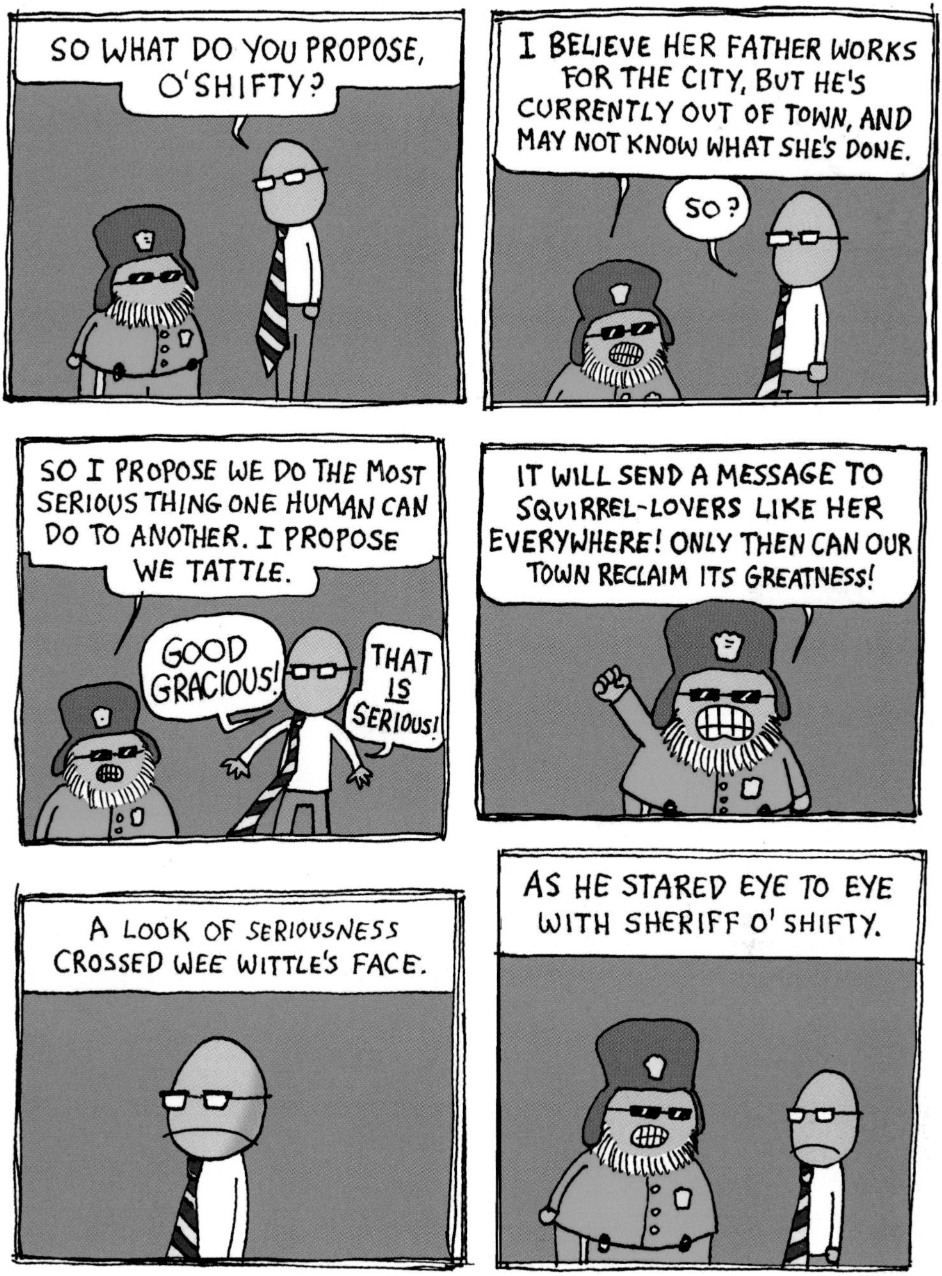
SO WHAT DO YOU PROPOSE, O'SHIFTY?
I BELIEVE HER FATHER WORKS FOR THE CITY, BUT HE'S CURRENTLY OUT OF TOWN, AND MAY NOT KNOW WHAT SHE'S DONE.
SO?
SO I PROPOSE WE DO THE MOST SERIOUS THING ONE HUMAN CAN DO TO ANOTHER. I PROPOSE WE TATTLE.
GOOD GRACIOUS!
THAT IS SERIOUS!
IT WILL SEND A MESSAGE TO SQUIRREL-LOVERS LIKE HER EVERYWHERE! ONLY THEN CAN OUR TOWN RECLAIM ITS GREATNESS!
A LOOK OF SERIOUSNESS CROSSED WEE WITTLE'S FACE.
AS HE STARED EYE TO EYE WITH SHERIFF O' SHIFTY.

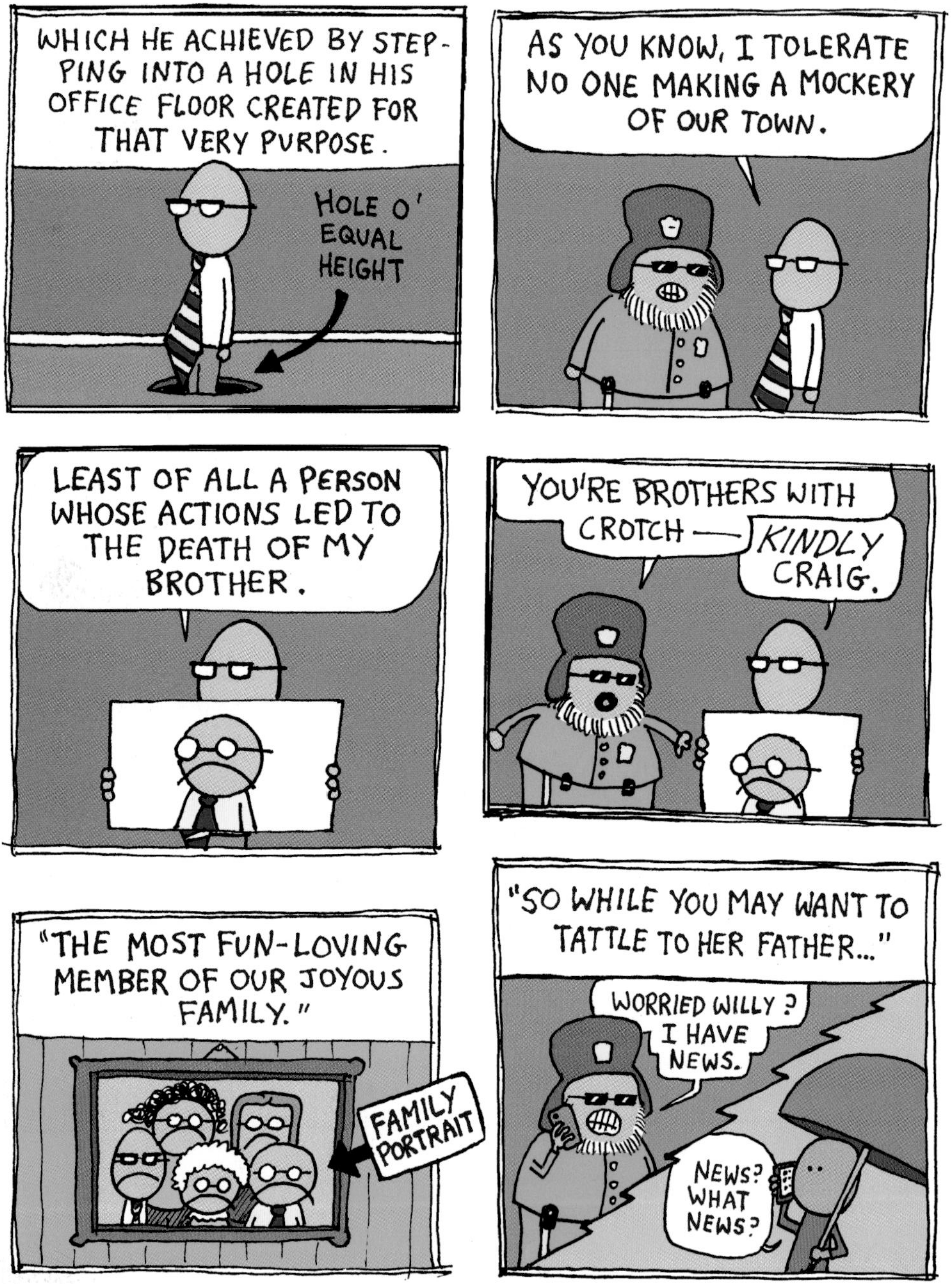

WHICH HE ACHIEVED BY STEPPING INTO A HOLE IN HIS OFFICE FLOOR CREATED FOR THAT VERY PURPOSE.
HOLE O' EQUAL HEIGHT
AS YOU KNOW, I TOLERATE NO ONE MAKING A MOCKERY OF OUR TOWN.
LEAST OF ALL A PERSON WHOSE ACTIONS LED TO THE DEATH OF MY BROTHER.
YOU'RE BROTHERS WITH CROTCH—
KINDLY CRAIG.
"THE MOST FUN-LOVING MEMBER OF OUR JOYOUS FAMILY."
FAMILY PORTRAIT
"SO WHILE YOU MAY WANT TO TATTLE TO HER FATHER..."
WORRIED WILLY? I HAVE NEWS.
NEWS? WHAT NEWS?

AND IN A BURST OF JOYOUS MERCY, THE TWO MEN THEN FREED EVERYONE FROM THE TRUBBLE TOWN JAIL AS WELL.

LET'S GO STEAL CARS!

ROB BANKS!

AND WHILE EVERYONE IN THE TOWN OF TRUBBLE HAD THEIR HOMES BURGLARIZED OVER THE NEXT TWENTY-FOUR HOURS, THAT WAS OF NO CONCERN TO SHERIFF O'SHIFTY AND WARDEN WEE WITTLE.

AWWW... THERE GOES MY DRYER.

YES, AREN'T PEOPLE WONDERFUL?

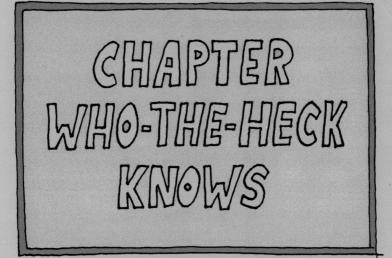

CHAPTER
WHO-THE-HECK
KNOWS

IN WHICH...

WE ARE
CONFUSED

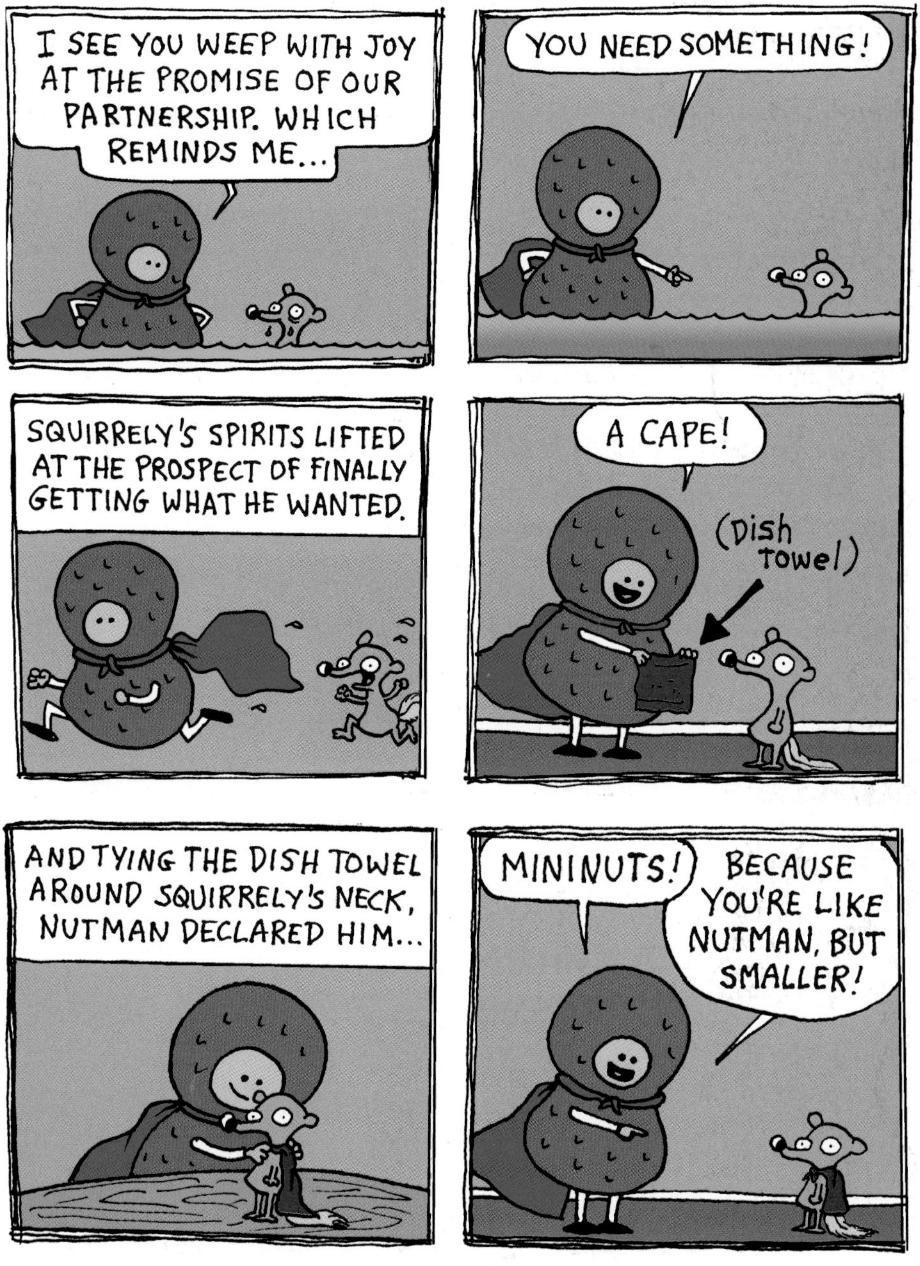

I SEE YOU WEEP WITH JOY AT THE PROMISE OF OUR PARTNERSHIP. WHICH REMINDS ME...
YOU NEED SOMETHING!
SQUIRRELY'S SPIRITS LIFTED AT THE PROSPECT OF FINALLY GETTING WHAT HE WANTED.
A CAPE!
(Dish towel)
AND TYING THE DISH TOWEL AROUND SQUIRRELY'S NECK, NUTMAN DECLARED HIM...
MININUTS!
BECAUSE YOU'RE LIKE NUTMAN, BUT SMALLER!

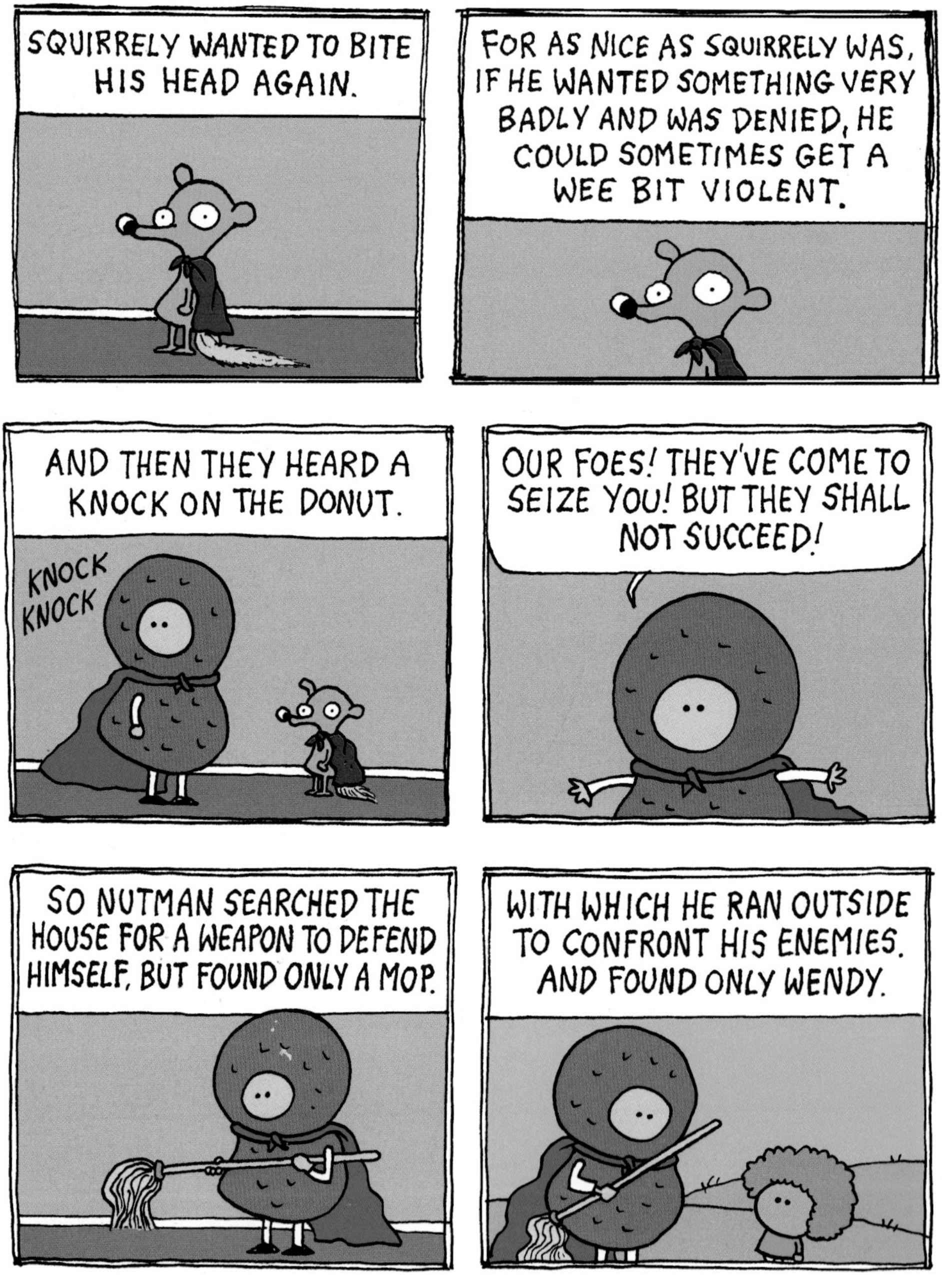
SQUIRRELY WANTED TO BITE HIS HEAD AGAIN.
FOR AS NICE AS SQUIRRELY WAS, IF HE WANTED SOMETHING VERY BADLY AND WAS DENIED, HE COULD SOMETIMES GET A WEE BIT VIOLENT.
AND THEN THEY HEARD A KNOCK ON THE DONUT.
KNOCK KNOCK
OUR FOES! THEY'VE COME TO SEIZE YOU! BUT THEY SHALL NOT SUCCEED!
SO NUTMAN SEARCHED THE HOUSE FOR A WEAPON TO DEFEND HIMSELF, BUT FOUND ONLY A MOP.
WITH WHICH HE RAN OUTSIDE TO CONFRONT HIS ENEMIES. AND FOUND ONLY WENDY.

217

218

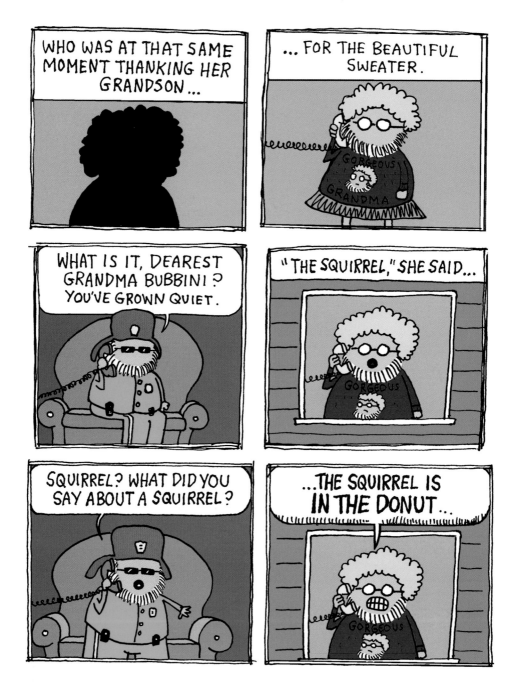

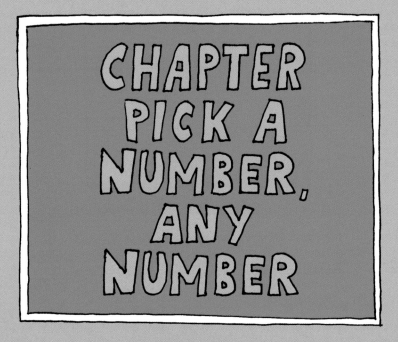

CHAPTER PICK A NUMBER, ANY NUMBER

IN WHICH...

YOU'RE MORE KNOWLEDGEABLE THAN THE AUTHOR

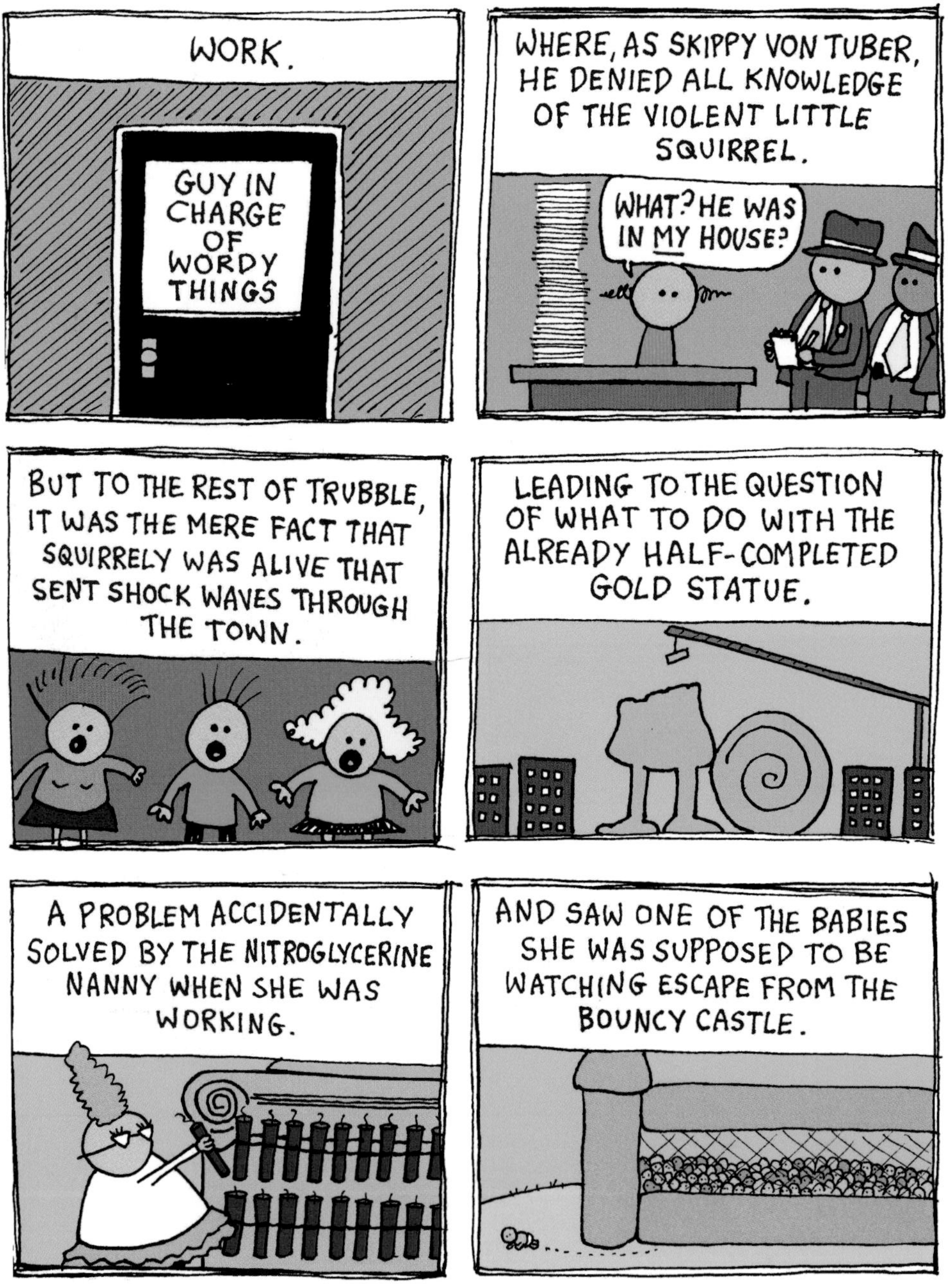
WORK.
GUY IN CHARGE OF WORDY THINGS
WHERE, AS SKIPPY VON TUBER, HE DENIED ALL KNOWLEDGE OF THE VIOLENT LITTLE SQUIRREL.
WHAT? HE WAS IN MY HOUSE?
BUT TO THE REST OF TRUBBLE, IT WAS THE MERE FACT THAT SQUIRRELY WAS ALIVE THAT SENT SHOCK WAVES THROUGH THE TOWN.
LEADING TO THE QUESTION OF WHAT TO DO WITH THE ALREADY HALF-COMPLETED GOLD STATUE.
A PROBLEM ACCIDENTALLY SOLVED BY THE NITROGLYCERINE NANNY WHEN SHE WAS WORKING.
AND SAW ONE OF THE BABIES SHE WAS SUPPOSED TO BE WATCHING ESCAPE FROM THE BOUNCY CASTLE.

CAUSING HER TO RUSH DOWN THE LADDER SHE WAS ON AND FALL.

RIGHT ON TOP OF THE DETONATOR.

BLOWING UP THE HALF-COMPLETED STATUE THAT THE TOWN HAD ALREADY SPENT $499,999,999,999.50 ON.

KABLOWEEEEE

SHOWERING THE TOWN OF TRUBBLE WITH GOLD.

WHICH MAYOR CHUCK CHOWDER-HEAD REMINDED THE TOWNSFOLK THEY WERE REQUIRED BY THE TOWN'S HONOR SYSTEM TO RETURN.

WE ♥ OUR HONOR SYSTEM.

... WITH THE EXCEPTION OF A SQUIRREL...

... WHO WAS AWAITING TRIAL IN A STEEL CAGE OVERHANGING AN ELECTRIFIED SHARK TANK.

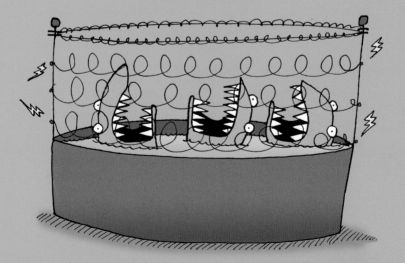

... AND A PURPLE- HAIRED GIRL...

... ABOUT TO TELL HER DAD EVERYTHING.

CHAPTER DOOM AND GLOOM

WHICH...

PRETTY MUCH TELLS YOU ALL YOU NEED TO KNOW

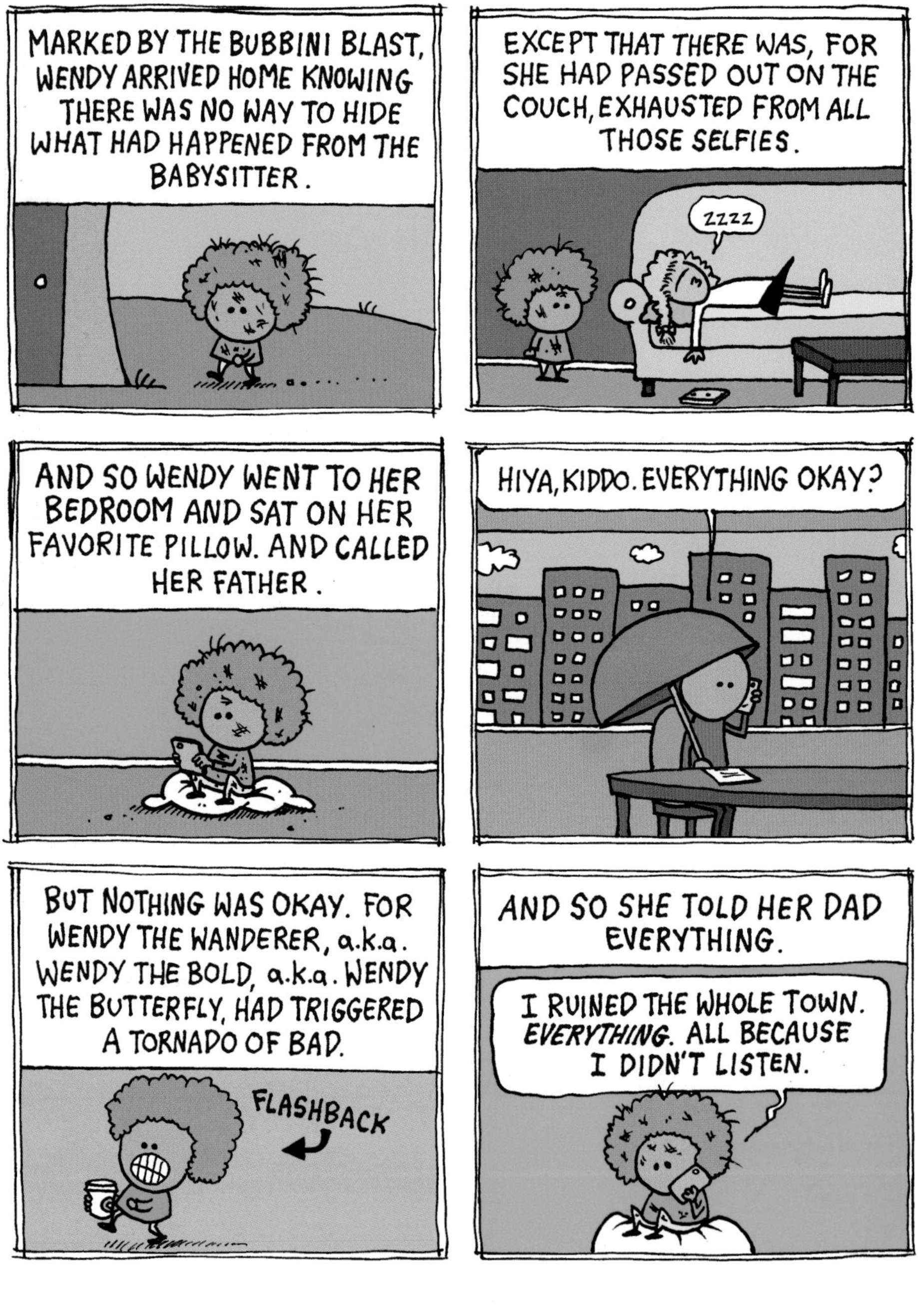
MARKED BY THE BUBBINI BLAST, WENDY ARRIVED HOME KNOWING THERE WAS NO WAY TO HIDE WHAT HAD HAPPENED FROM THE BABYSITTER.
EXCEPT THAT THERE WAS, FOR SHE HAD PASSED OUT ON THE COUCH, EXHAUSTED FROM ALL THOSE SELFIES.
ZZZZ
AND SO WENDY WENT TO HER BEDROOM AND SAT ON HER FAVORITE PILLOW. AND CALLED HER FATHER.
HIYA, KIDDO. EVERYTHING OKAY?
BUT NOTHING WAS OKAY. FOR WENDY THE WANDERER, a.k.a. WENDY THE BOLD, a.k.a. WENDY THE BUTTERFLY, HAD TRIGGERED A TORNADO OF BAD.
FLASHBACK
AND SO SHE TOLD HER DAD EVERYTHING.
I RUINED THE WHOLE TOWN. *EVERYTHING*. ALL BECAUSE I DIDN'T LISTEN.

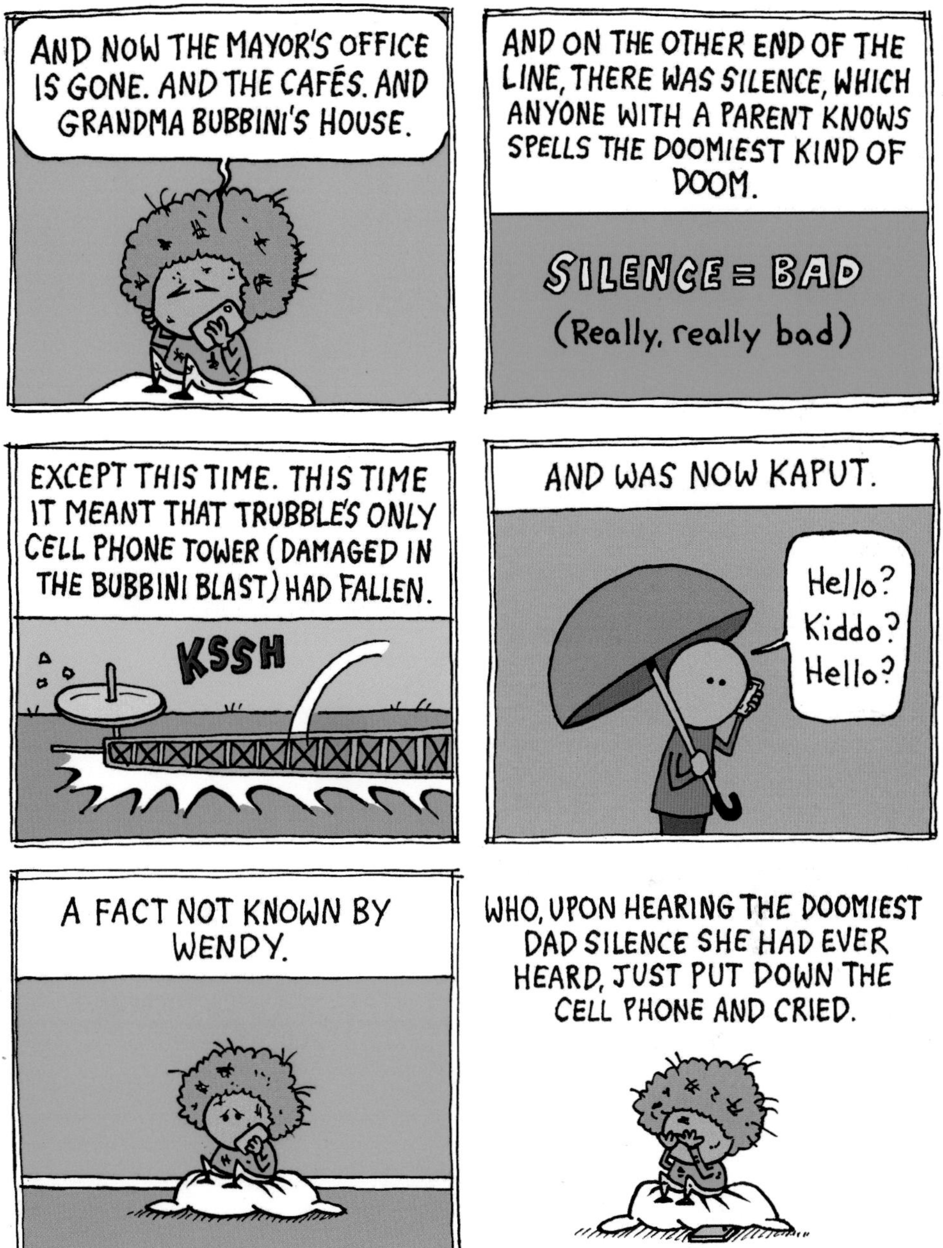
AND NOW THE MAYOR'S OFFICE IS GONE. AND THE CAFÉS. AND GRANDMA BUBBINI'S HOUSE.
AND ON THE OTHER END OF THE LINE, THERE WAS SILENCE, WHICH ANYONE WITH A PARENT KNOWS SPELLS THE DOOMIEST KIND OF DOOM.
SILENCE = BAD
(Really, really bad)
EXCEPT THIS TIME. THIS TIME IT MEANT THAT TRUBBLE'S ONLY CELL PHONE TOWER (DAMAGED IN THE BUBBINI BLAST) HAD FALLEN.
KSSH
AND WAS NOW KAPUT.
Hello? Kiddo? Hello?
A FACT NOT KNOWN BY WENDY.
WHO, UPON HEARING THE DOOMIEST DAD SILENCE SHE HAD EVER HEARD, JUST PUT DOWN THE CELL PHONE AND CRIED.

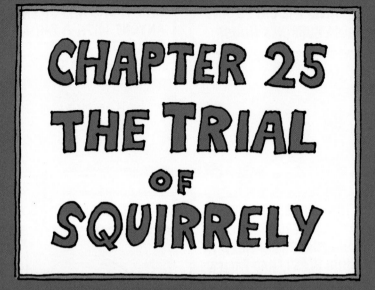

CHAPTER 25
THE TRIAL
OF
SQUIRRELY

IN WHICH...

WE PROVE WE CAN
NUMBER A CHAPTER LIKE
A NORMAL PERSON

236

ONLY IT TURNS OUT HE WASN'T BECAUSE THE SQUID WHO HAD SEIZED HIM WAS ACTUALLY...

...a really nice vegetarian.

AND THE COURTROOM DRAMA ONLY GREW WHEN MAYOR MO REVEALED HIS MOTIVE FOR SELLING THOSE BANNED MOOSHIES TO SQUIRRELY.

Money!

BUT BY FAR THE BIGGEST SURPRISE IN COURT WAS THE APPEARANCE OF THE GIRL WITH HOMEMADE BUTTERFLY WINGS.

IF YOU'RE GONNA BLAME ANYONE FOR THIS, BLAME ME. I'M THE GUILTY PARTY.

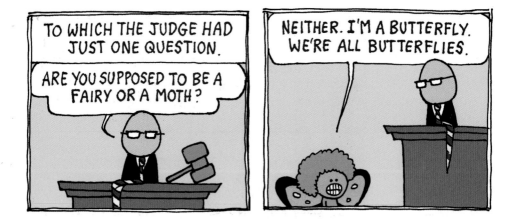

240

AND DECLARED THE LITTLE SQUIRREL...

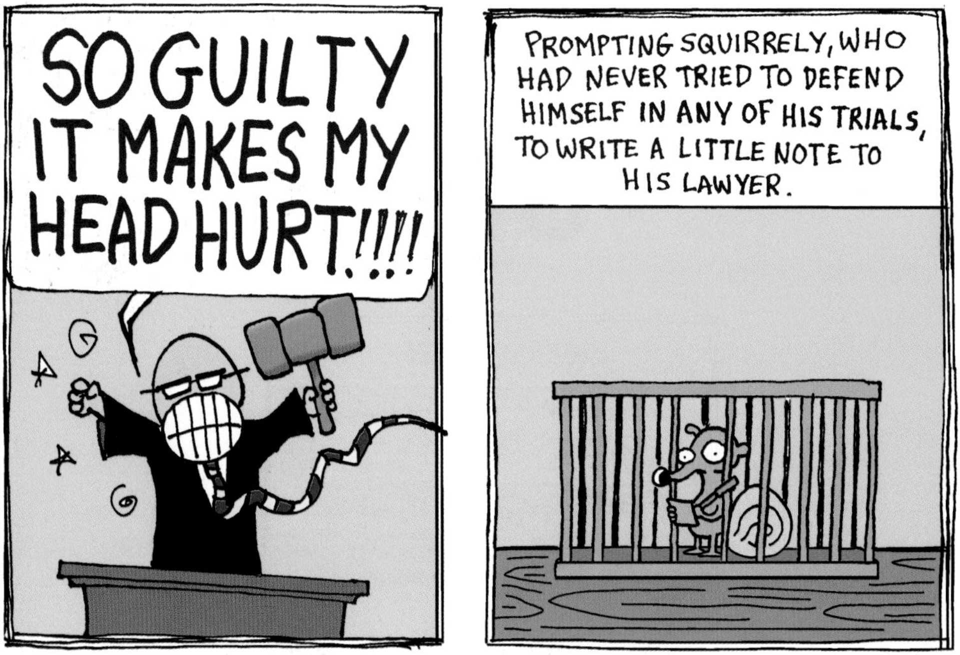
SO GUILTY IT MAKES MY HEAD HURT!!!!
PROMPTING SQUIRRELY, WHO HAD NEVER TRIED TO DEFEND HIMSELF IN ANY OF HIS TRIALS, TO WRITE A LITTLE NOTE TO HIS LAWYER.

SAYING ONLY...

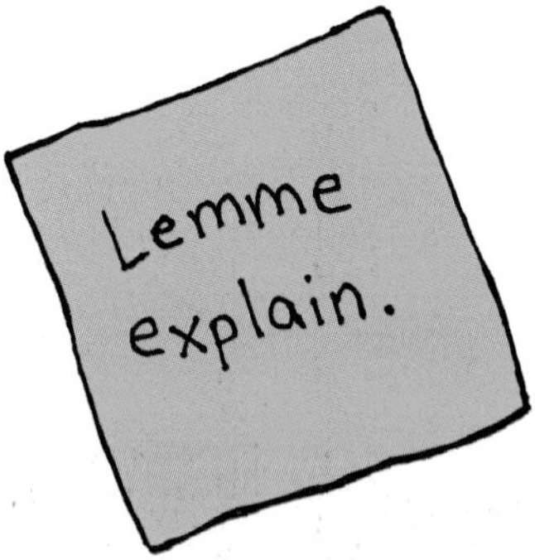
Lemme explain.

AND THAT LEFT ONLY THE PUNISHMENT.

CHAPTER MORE

IN WHICH...

OUR DEAR LITTLE FRIEND GOES BYE-BYE

245

Daily Octopress POLL:

THE VERY GUILTY SQUIRREL

SHOULD SQUIRRELY BE PUNISHED BY:
(A) BEING THROWN INTO GORGEOUS GORGE; OR
(B) 762 YEARS IN JAIL

THEN OLLIE THREW IN A THIRD OPTION JUST AS A JOKE.

OR (C) BEING FIRED IN A ROCKET TO THE SUN (HAHA ☺)

AND THE TOWNSFOLK CHOSE:

GORGEOUS GORGE: 0%
JAIL: 0%
ROCKET TO SUN: 99%

THE ONLY REASON IT WASN'T 100 PERCENT WAS BECAUSE ONE VOTER CHOSE...

BLAME ME INSTEAD.

AND EVERYONE KNEW WHO THAT WAS.

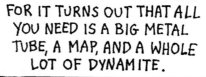

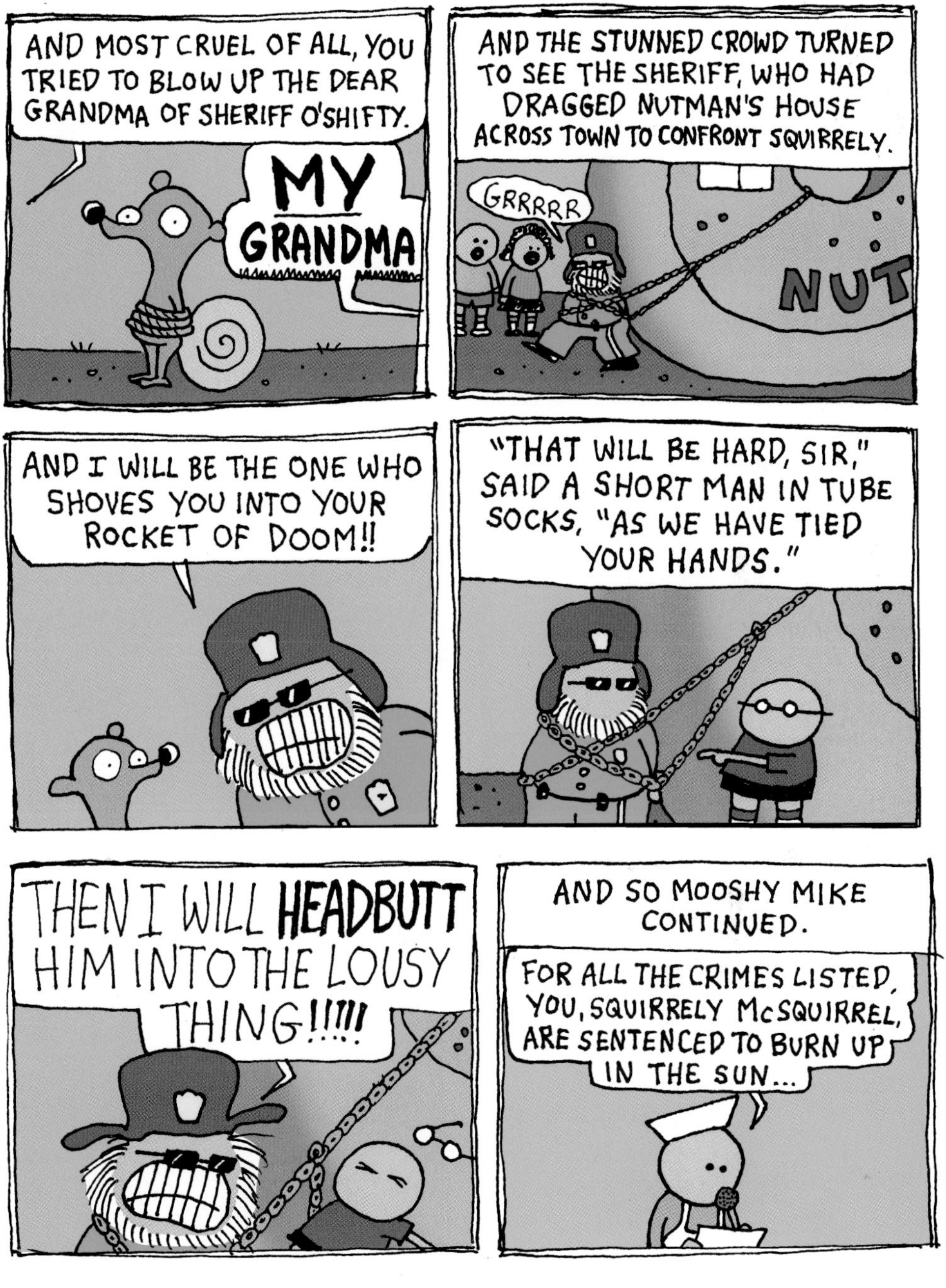
AND MOST CRUEL OF ALL, YOU TRIED TO BLOW UP THE DEAR GRANDMA OF SHERIFF O'SHIFTY.
MY GRANDMA
AND THE STUNNED CROWD TURNED TO SEE THE SHERIFF, WHO HAD DRAGGED NUTMAN'S HOUSE ACROSS TOWN TO CONFRONT SQUIRRELY.
GRRRRR
NUT
AND I WILL BE THE ONE WHO SHOVES YOU INTO YOUR ROCKET OF DOOM!!
"THAT WILL BE HARD, SIR," SAID A SHORT MAN IN TUBE SOCKS, "AS WE HAVE TIED YOUR HANDS."
THEN I WILL HEADBUTT HIM INTO THE LOUSY THING!!!!!
AND SO MOOSHY MIKE CONTINUED.
FOR ALL THE CRIMES LISTED, YOU, SQUIRRELY McSQUIRREL, ARE SENTENCED TO BURN UP IN THE SUN...

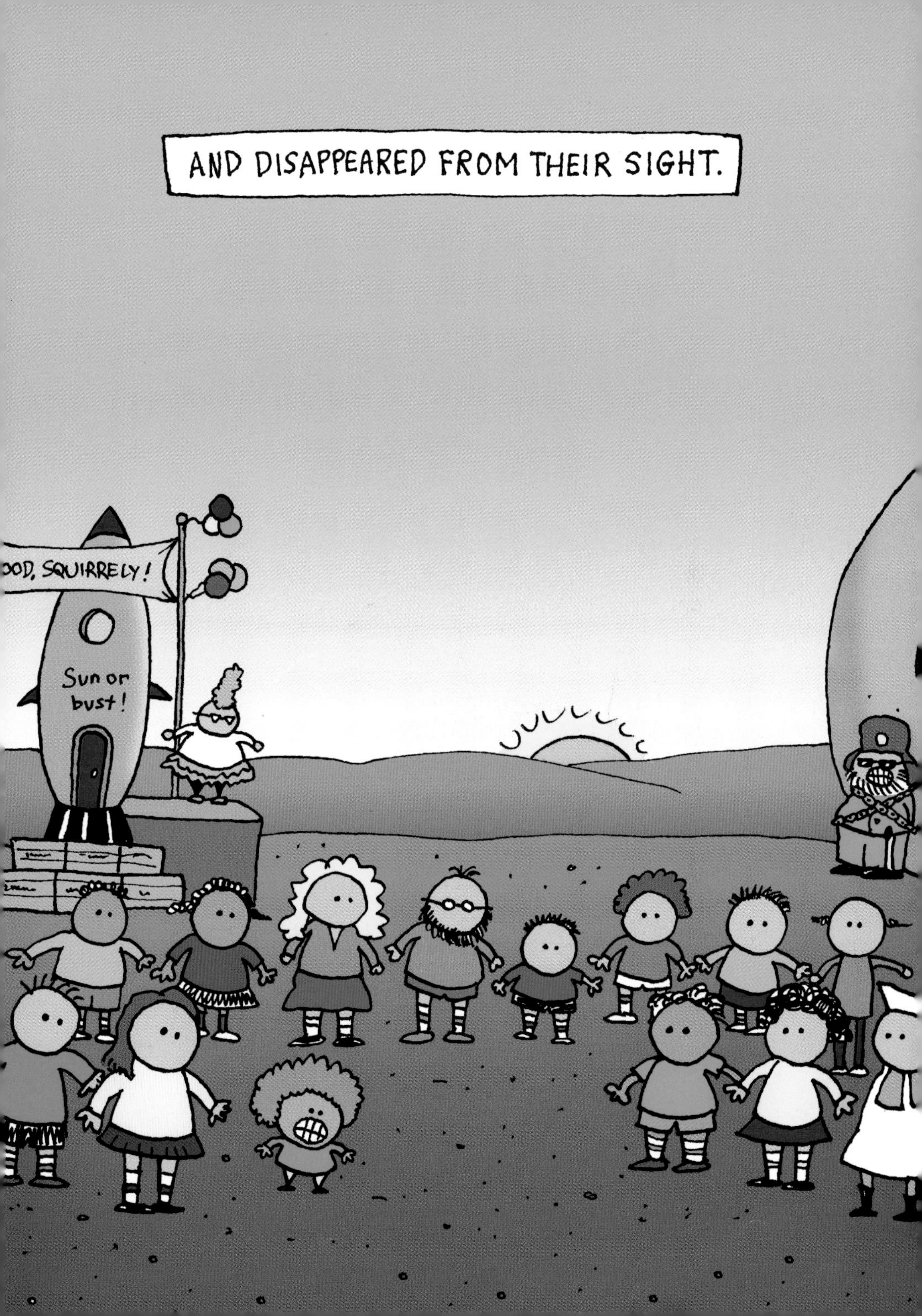
AND DISAPPEARED FROM THEIR SIGHT.
OOD, SQUIRRELY!
Sun or bust!

CHAPTER SOMEWHERE IN THE TWENTIES

IN WHICH...

THINGS GET SUPER DEEP

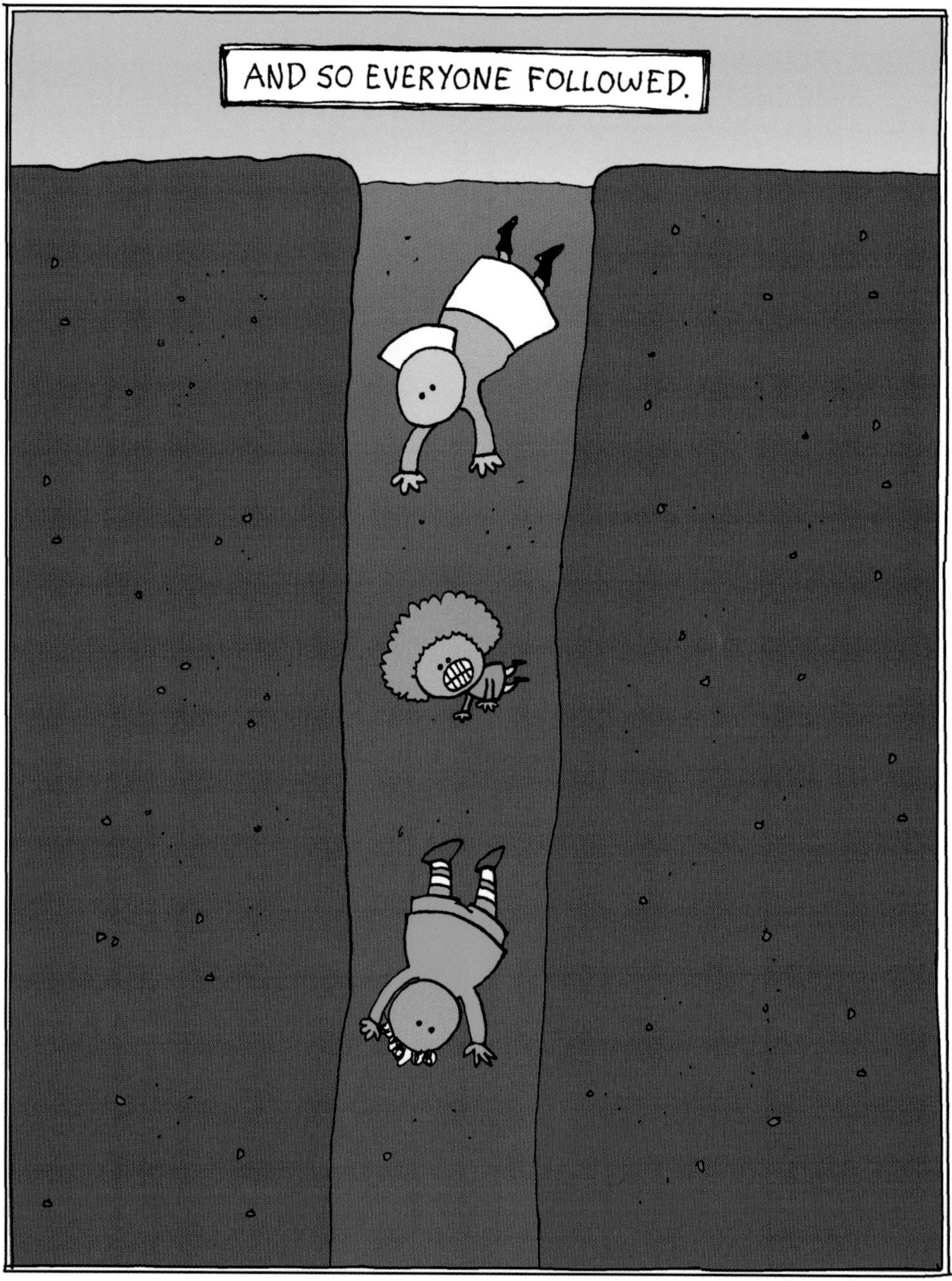
AND SO EVERYONE FOLLOWED.

WHERE THEY WERE SURPRISED BY THREE SMALL VISITORS.

AND ENOUGH DYNAMITE TO BLOW UP MOST OF THE TOWN.

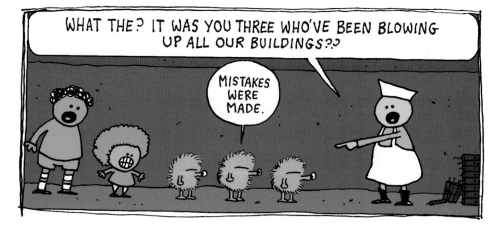

WHAT THE? IT WAS YOU THREE WHO'VE BEEN BLOWING UP ALL OUR BUILDINGS??

MISTAKES WERE MADE.

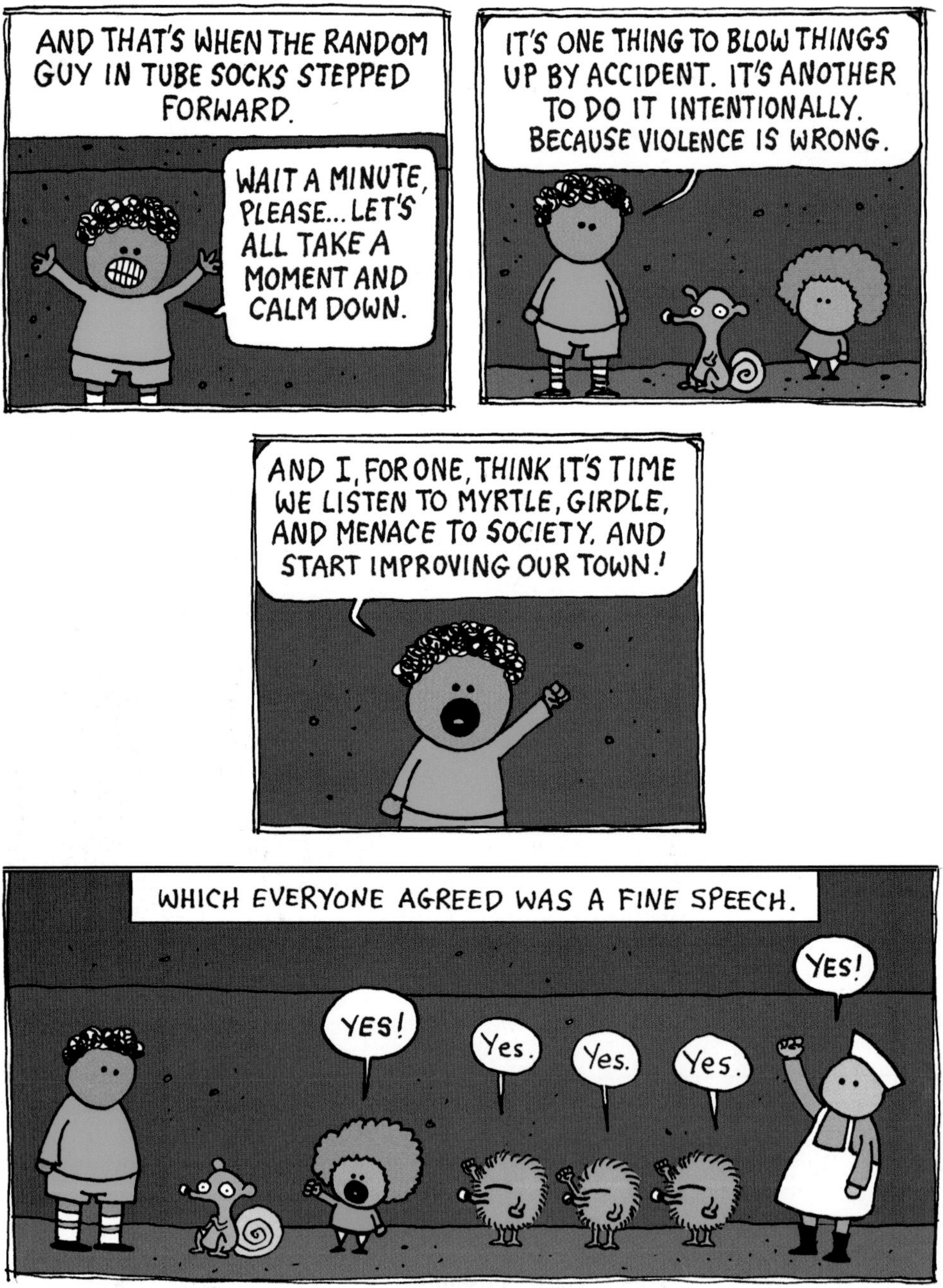
AND THAT'S WHEN THE RANDOM GUY IN TUBE SOCKS STEPPED FORWARD.
WAIT A MINUTE, PLEASE... LET'S ALL TAKE A MOMENT AND CALM DOWN.
IT'S ONE THING TO BLOW THINGS UP BY ACCIDENT. IT'S ANOTHER TO DO IT INTENTIONALLY. BECAUSE VIOLENCE IS WRONG.
AND I, FOR ONE, THINK IT'S TIME WE LISTEN TO MYRTLE, GIRDLE, AND MENACE TO SOCIETY, AND START IMPROVING OUR TOWN!
WHICH EVERYONE AGREED WAS A FINE SPEECH.
YES!
Yes.
Yes.
Yes.
YES!

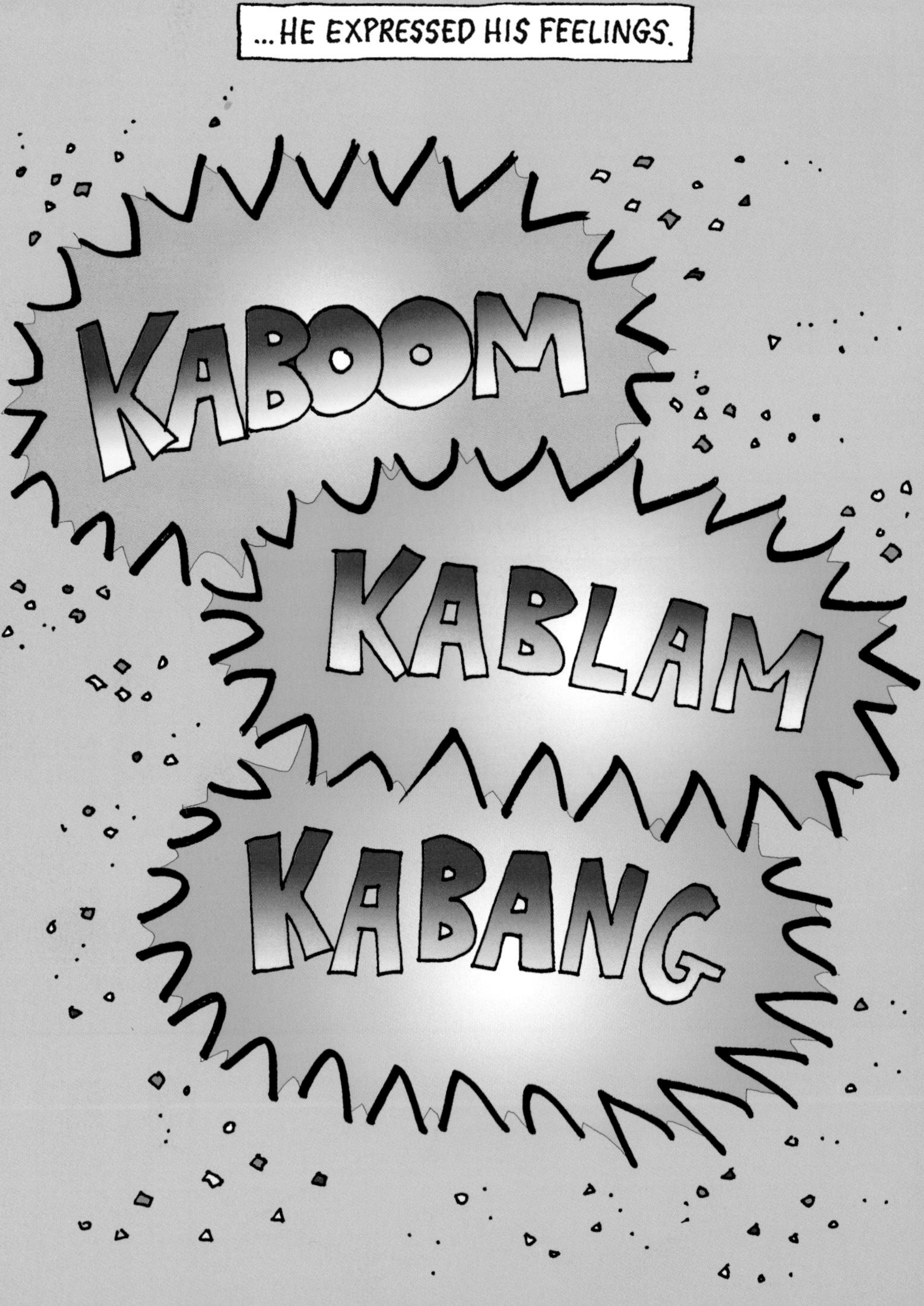
...HE EXPRESSED HIS FEELINGS.
KABOOM
KABLAM
KABANG

CHAPTER LAST

IN WHICH...

WE SAY, "IT'S ABOUT STINKING TIME."

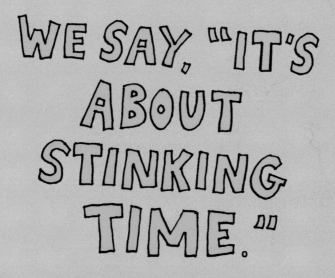

NO ONE WAS HURT IN THE EXPLOSIONS THAT REDUCED HALF OF TRUBBLE TO RUBBLE.

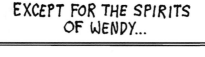

EXCEPT FOR THE SPIRITS OF WENDY...

...WHO KNEW SHE COULDN'T POSSIBLY SELL ENOUGH SWEATERS TO FIX THE TOWN BEFORE HER FATHER GOT HOME.

270

272

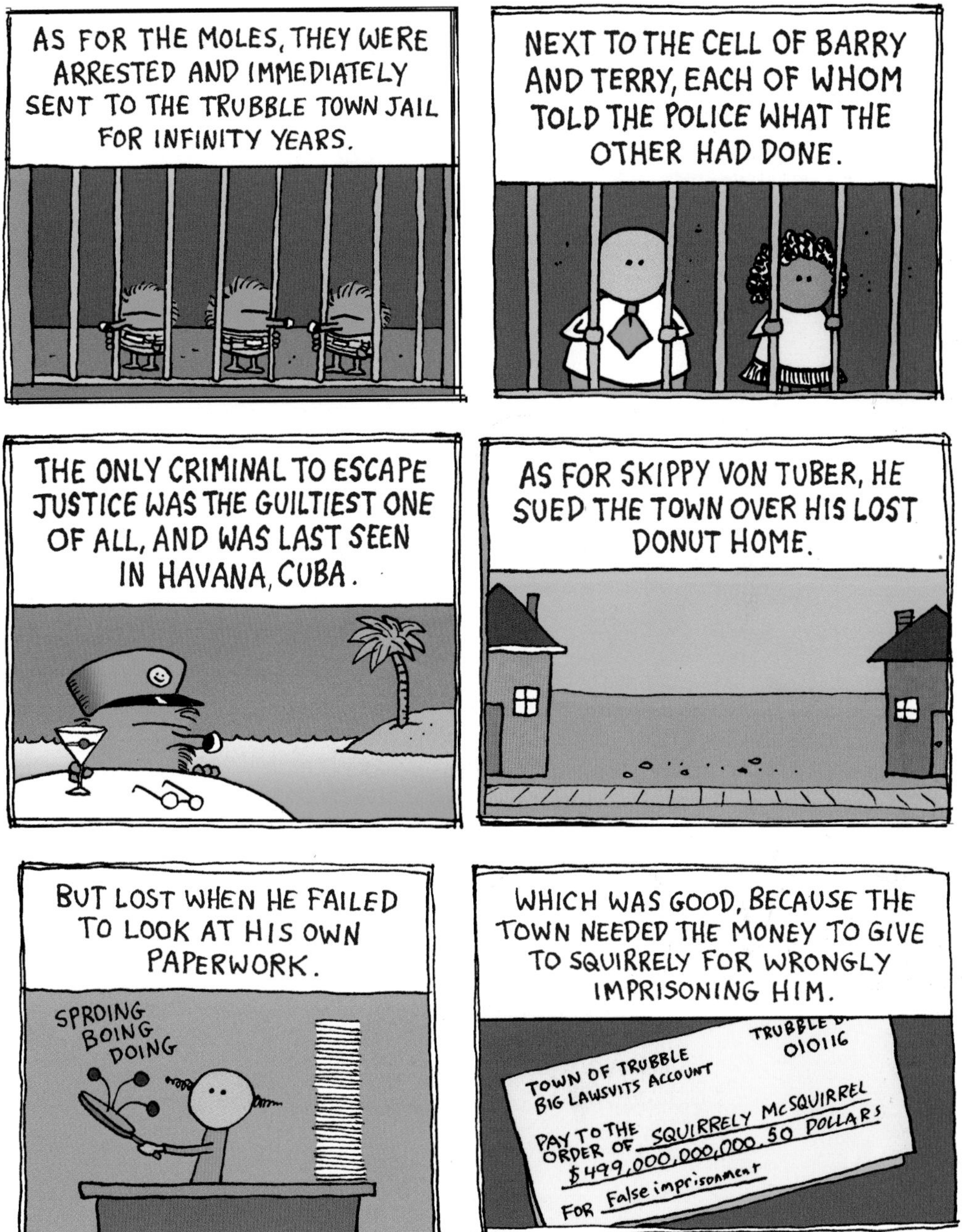
AS FOR THE MOLES, THEY WERE ARRESTED AND IMMEDIATELY SENT TO THE TRUBBLE TOWN JAIL FOR INFINITY YEARS.
NEXT TO THE CELL OF BARRY AND TERRY, EACH OF WHOM TOLD THE POLICE WHAT THE OTHER HAD DONE.
THE ONLY CRIMINAL TO ESCAPE JUSTICE WAS THE GUILTIEST ONE OF ALL, AND WAS LAST SEEN IN HAVANA, CUBA.
AS FOR SKIPPY VON TUBER, HE SUED THE TOWN OVER HIS LOST DONUT HOME.
BUT LOST WHEN HE FAILED TO LOOK AT HIS OWN PAPERWORK.
SPROING
BOING
DOING
WHICH WAS GOOD, BECAUSE THE TOWN NEEDED THE MONEY TO GIVE TO SQUIRRELY FOR WRONGLY IMPRISONING HIM.
TOWN OF TRUBBLE
BIG LAWSUITS ACCOUNT
010116
PAY TO THE ORDER OF SQUIRRELY McSQUIRREL
$499,000,000,000.50 DOLLARS
FOR False imprisonment

SO TWO LONELY SOULS COULD FINALLY MEET.

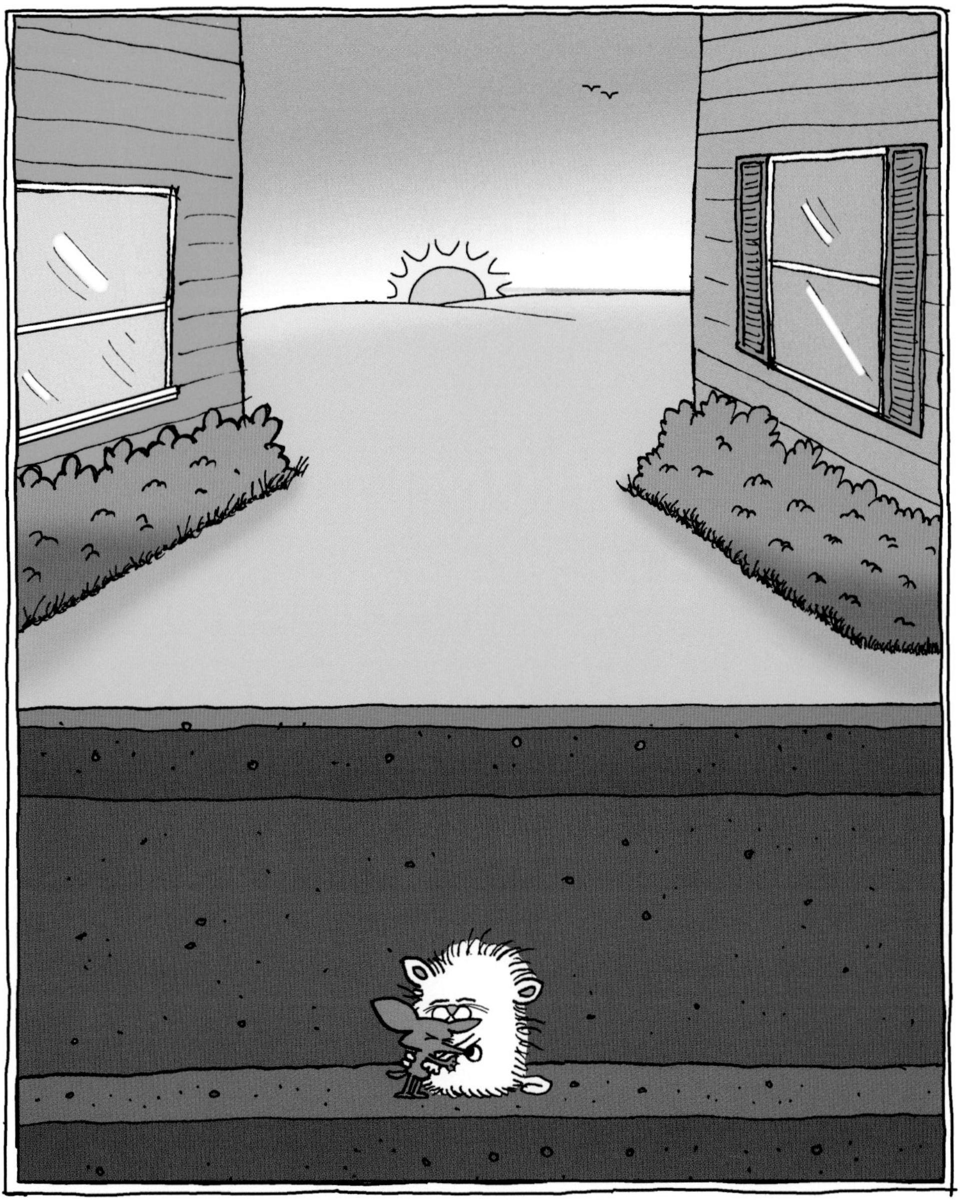

AFTERWORD

IN WHICH...

WE ADMIT WE DON'T REALLY KNOW WHAT AN AFTERWORD IS

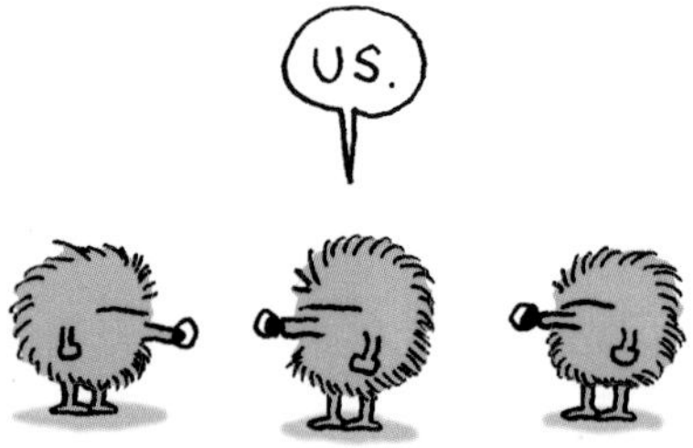
US.

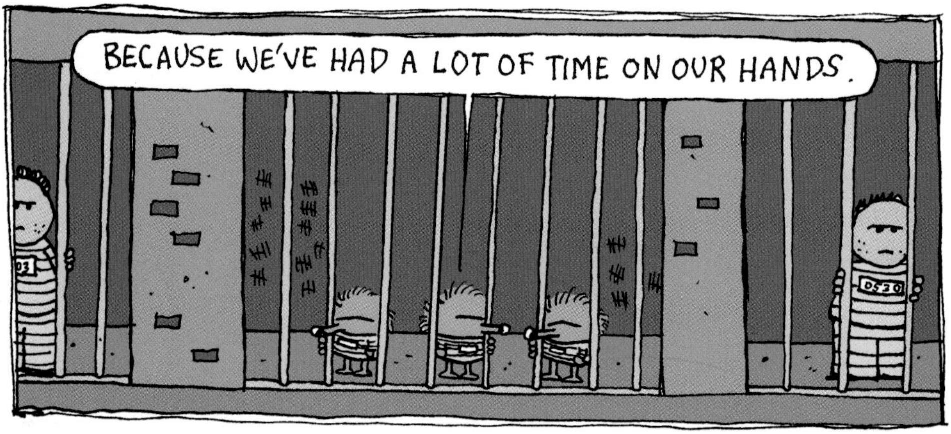
BECAUSE WE'VE HAD A LOT OF TIME ON OUR HANDS.

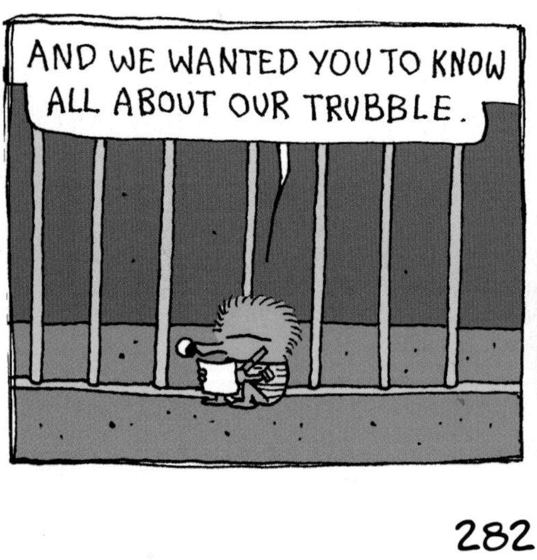
AND WE WANTED YOU TO KNOW ALL ABOUT OUR TRUBBLE.

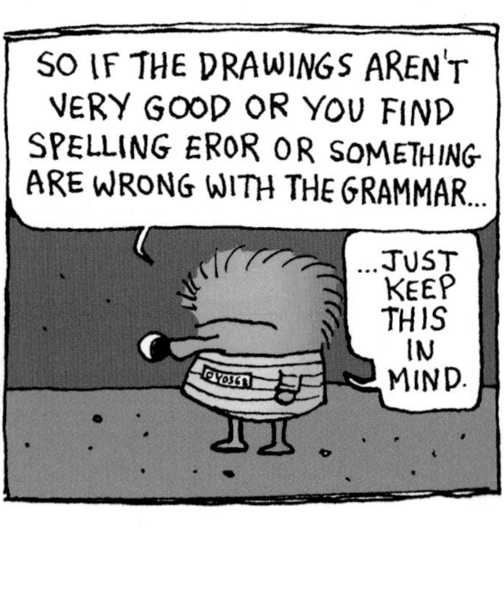
SO IF THE DRAWINGS AREN'T VERY GOOD OR YOU FIND SPELLING EROR OR SOMETHING ARE WRONG WITH THE GRAMMAR...
...JUST KEEP THIS IN MIND.

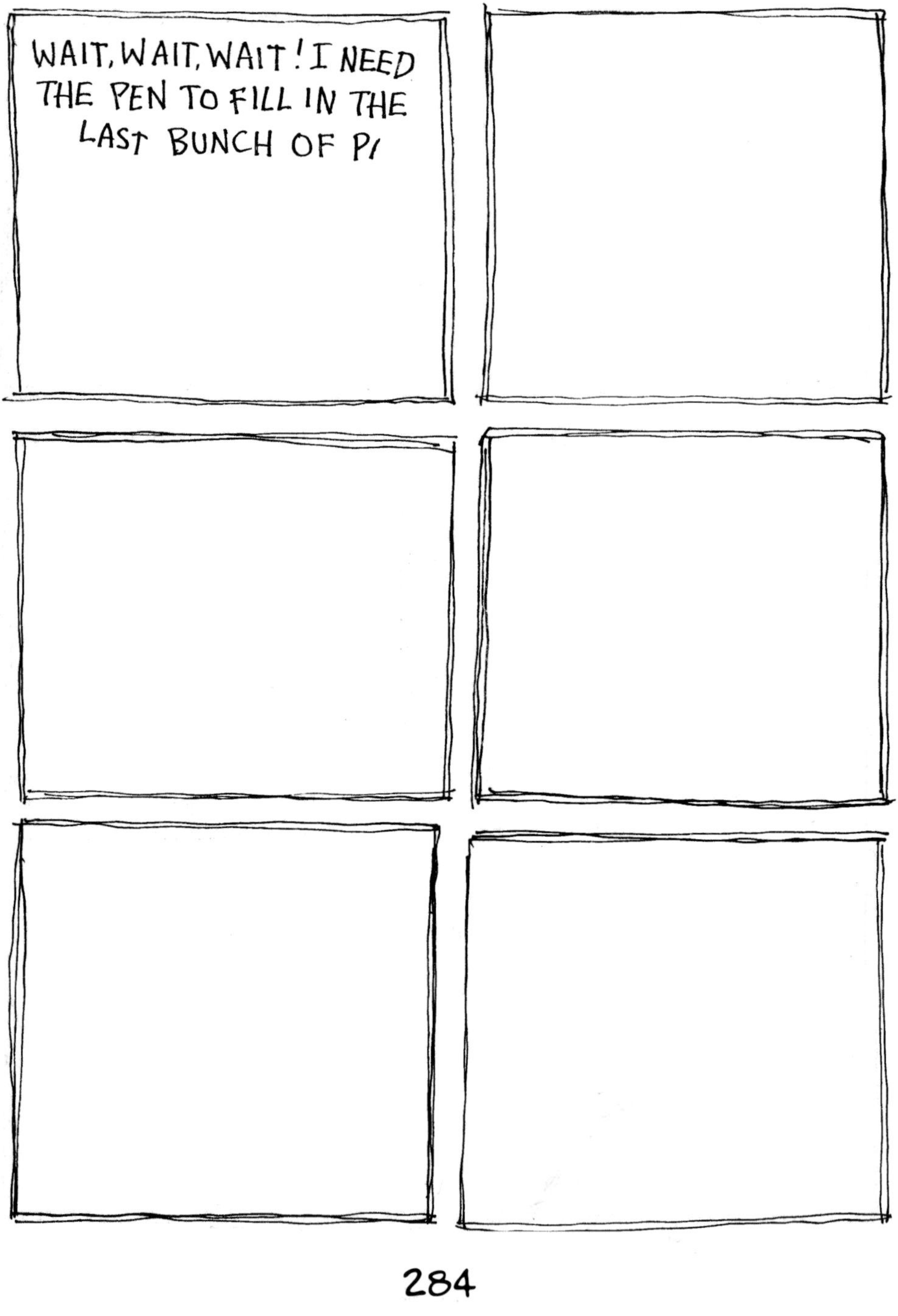
WAIT, WAIT, WAIT! I NEED THE PEN TO FILL IN THE LAST BUNCH OF PI

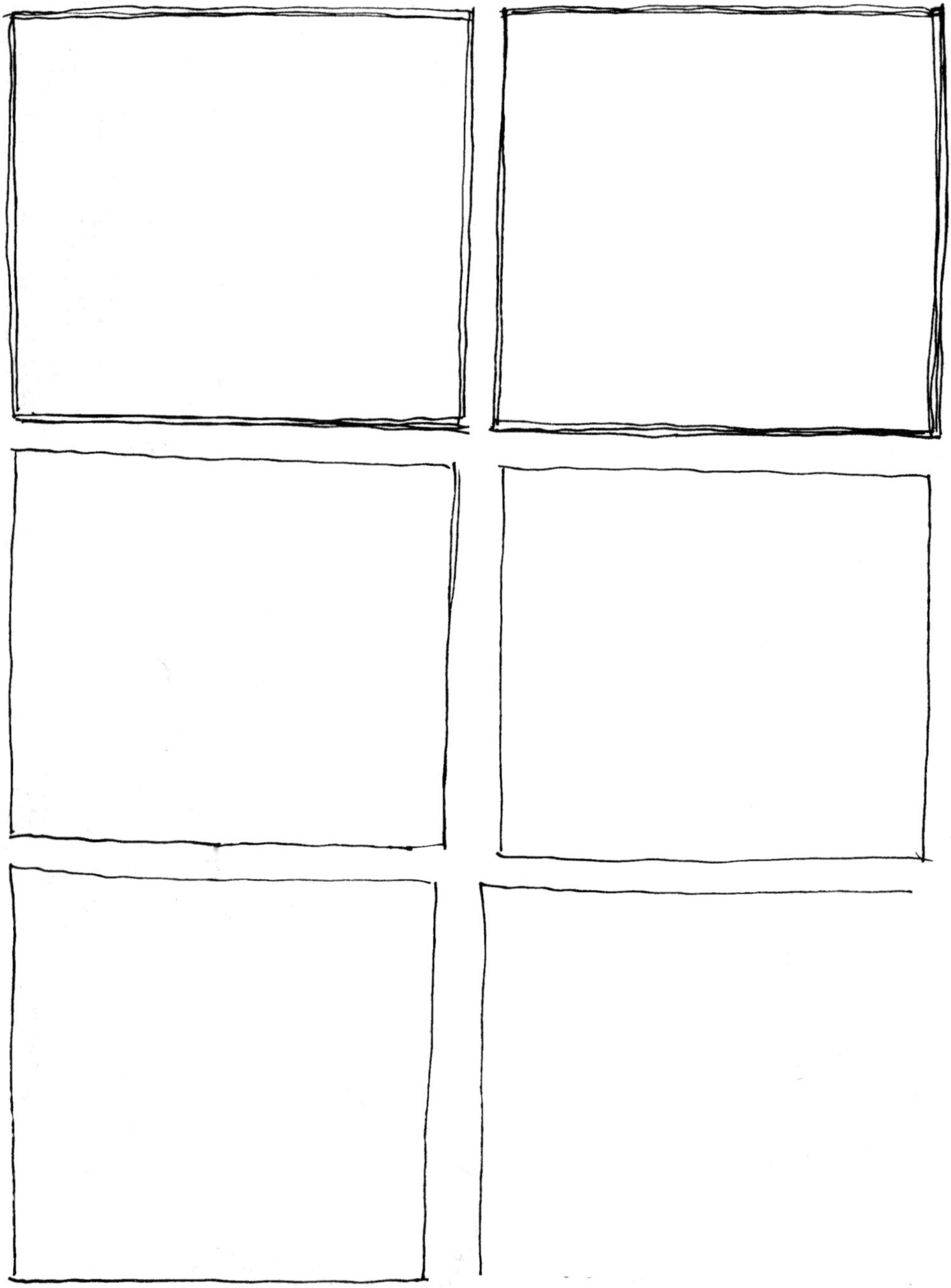

THE END
(Finally)

ABOUT THE AUTHORS

The moles are currently serving a prison sentence of infinity years in the Trubble town jail. This is their first published work.

If you would like them to speak at your school, they cannot.

They can be reached at: **trubbletownjail@gmail.com**

Please be aware that your message will be screened by jail personnel.